WITH ONE STONE

MARK JENKINS

This book is a work of fiction. Any reference to real events, people, or places are used fictitiously. Other names, characters, places and incidents are the products of the author's imagination. Any resemblance to actual events, locales, or persons; living or dead, is entirely coincidental.

Copyright number: TXu002342287 / 2022-10-22
Printed in the United States of America

Cover design by Tim Barber of Dissect Designs

Killing Two Birds With One Stone

- thought to have originated from the story of Daedalus and his son Icarus from Greek Mythology where Daedalus, an inventor, killed two birds with one stone to obtain the feathers used to build the wings for Icarus to fly

PROLOGUE

December 16, 2021

They say your first kill is the hardest. They were right.

But not for the reasons you may think. I had a hell of a time executing this. I remember it clearly as if it were yesterday. Hmm. Maybe that's because it was *yesterday.*

I had been stalking her for the past three and a half weeks. Ugh. I hate to admit I'm a stalker. Funny I don't mind admitting I'm a murderer, but a stalker just seems so creepy and I'm not a creepy person. When I was younger, I would stalk the kids in the neighborhood to see what new clothes they were wearing or which video games they were playing. Standing on my tip toes peeping into their bedroom windows, unseen, as they unbagged their new clothes and played dress up with friends who were sleeping over. Or maybe laying on my belly on the cold grass to look into the dark basement windows to see the remote controls in grubby little hands furiously pushing buttons to kill this zombie or steal that car. I was never invited to participate in any sleepovers or game nights so me being a Peeping Tom - yet another creepy title I wear uncomfortably - was my way of participating whether they liked it or not.

My mother, always the consoling one, would tell me not to fret over how other kids treated me because I was born special. Lucky, she would say. Lucky? Lucky my ass. When I came into this world, 3 weeks early mind you, I was born with arrhyth-

mia. An annoying heart condition which causes my heart to race and requires I take medication daily, but no one has to remind me because I never forget anything. Ever. Still, I was considered lucky by just about anyone but me. But when my mother said it, I felt I was special. She always had a way with words. I felt I was untouchable. And absolutely anything I set my mind to I would succeed at doing. Because I was the most spectacular child in the world! I was going to own the world! I couldn't wait for the day all my dreams would become realities.

But here I am. Still waiting.

And stalking.

Now, in broad daylight, I am in New York City and I am watching my target. Her name is Rachel Meadows and she's awfully pretty. Like one of the girls from my youth. The ones who would try on their pretty new clothes and parade around like they were supermodels. My heart was fluttering like I had a crush. Nah. She's not my type. I don't think I have a type, actually. My heart was probably twitching because it's just a bad fucking heart.

She's looking down at her phone, probably texting. Ruining another life, no doubt. Her heels clack along the sidewalk but are drown out by the cacophony of honking cars and people talking around her but the absent sound of her steps is familiar. She is oblivious to her surroundings, which is perfect for what I need to do.

The freezing wind on this December day has made her put on a chic merlot turtleneck, a black A-line skirt, end of season cognac boots and a mustard-colored woolen coat that goes perfectly with her pale skin and freckles. Her long strawberry hair sways softly as she walks down the gray pavement. If someone were looking for a Nicole Kidman-type to grace the cover of their magazine, she would be her. Smiling, she looks at her phone again, no doubt having received some sort of "sure! Drinks sound fine!" comment from one of her many girlfriends. She continues her pace, navigating against the throng of people coming her way, like a lone fish swimming against an upstreaming run of Salmon.

I watch Rachel stop on the sidewalk in the middle of the crowd. She raises her phone and aims it towards her, but her arm suddenly drops. She turns and says something to an elderly couple behind her and they leave with their mouths hanging open. The old lady shoots Rachel the bird and I can't help but chuckle. Rachel swiftly turns back, raises the phone, and starts talking. I inch closer to listen. She's making a video of her next appearance. Of course. It's her self-marketing schtick. Her little videos of self-promotion to her throngs of followers. And now I understand the shocked elderly couple, an obvious unwelcome photo-bomb in the background of her

shot. No doubt she said something insulting to shoo them out of her sh
manners whatsoever.

As huge as this city is, the hordes of people still give off a claustroph
bet half the people's feet aren't touching the ground, just lifted by th
other shoulders, levitating down the sidewalk. My shoulder gets jarred
suit not paying attention to where he's going. My left earbud rattle
"Hey!" I turn and yell. But my word seems to just rise and evapor
street noise. Vanishing into the air. Poof. It's gone. Like it was never sai
but find it rude that my stalking mission was interrupted and sudden
I've taken my eyes off the prize. I whip around and my eyes dart feverish
see her. That bright red hair and mustard coat standing out in a sea of
overcoats, like a flamingo amongst zebras. Relieved, I continue my hunt.

People dart across in front of others just to get to where they need t
immediately swallowed by another herd. The symphony of noise plays lou
ing. I almost expect canons to go off just to put an exclamation point
ruckus. It's VERY, VERY LOUD!!

Cars are whizzing by with such speedy disregard, her coat flares
People are packed on the sidewalks like a thousand wind-whipped Emper
huddled together during mating season. They are standing dangerously
curb and the vroom vroom vroom of the vehicles make it seem you're on th
of the Indy 500. Some of the piled-up snow along the curb splashes up on
walk. It may be madness but it's perfect for my task.

I keep my distance behind her, walking with a purpose, but blending
crowd. My ear buds are in but there is no music; my head bops a little but
rhythm; my mouth lip syncs a bit but there are no words. If she were to
she wouldn't see me. It's all in the presentation of how I am just another
the street, minding my own business, becoming one with the masses. Inv
when I was younger. My anger rises at the thought. But that's not what's
to do what I need to do. No. There is a much more important reason.
people understand but never do anything about. I represent many. They
know it yet.

She stops. She's at the intersection of the busiest street in the middle
hysteria, standing on the curb ready to continue her journey. Phone still
Mid-message. Taxis are honking and cars are still zipping by. My ear buds
the outside noise level still makes my eardrums throb. The red hand on t
blinking for us to STOP with a 30 second countdown. The sign will tell

t. She has no

bic feeling. I
energy and
y a dick in a
in my ear.
te above the
. I can't help
y I'm aware
ly but then I
ark, gloomy

be and are
dly, deafen-
n the daily

out a little.
r penguins
close to the
e front row
to the side-

in with the
there is no
ook at me,
person on
sible. Like
riving me
One many
just don't

of all this
in hand.
are in but
e sign is
s with a

walk. But I can't wait for the little green man. He
oday, time doesn't matter. It's all about to stop for

25 seconds left….

, not acknowledging the people around me so as not
die up on my sweatshirt helps me blend easily into
now only 4 feet in front of me.

20 seconds….

loser.

15 seconds….

h it if I wanted to. I outstretch my arm a bit and my
p against the back of her coat.

10 seconds….

felt something. I freeze. The crowd behind me presses
ring to walk as one big lumpy mass across the street.
urn yellow, signaling the oncoming speeding traffic to
e always, they do just the opposite and speed up, cars
to make it before the lights turn red. It's all a vehicular

r now. A bicyclist rushes by. Taxis. Moving vans. The
l on her back but harder now. My heart is racing but in a
ne on my face. This will be my first. A lump forms in my

5 seconds….

city bus is the last vehicle to race towards the light. Like a even drove a Prius, for God's sake. Nina said Kelly realized to get her trust fund, she had to marry someone at least presentable with a future. Owen fit the bill. Kelly dropped out of college after her sophomore year to be with Owen and help him with his career. She was a woman in love. That, or she hated college. The likelihood both situations were correct was pretty good.

Like Jack, Owen was a runner and had a couple of marathons under his belt. And like Jack, his reputation in the business world was one where he was a powerhouse and used his intelligence to pursue a secure life in the corporate environment. But unlike the six-two Jack, Owen was only five-five, a good two inches shorter than Kelly, even. "My little pocket husband," she once dubbed him. Owen's big job and big confidence were compensation, but Kelly obviously loved Owen and they were a good match. Owen made good money and Kelly spent good money, but she never spent Owen's. Her $10 million trust was turned over to her when she turned twenty-five and things for the newlyweds changed overnight. The Andrews apparently adored Owen as he was the mature son they never had. He seemed, Jack had decided, the perfect son-in-law.

But Owen had a dark side. Jack knew of this only too well. Owen's manipulative streak was one very few outside the courthouse got to witness. *I guess I'm one of the lucky few,* Jack thought, rolling his eyes. Like this last comment Owen made. About there always being another person involved in the deterioration of a marriage. Jack pursed his lips. *This has to end. Now.*

Too late, Jack heard a noise behind him and started to turn.

"Cowabunga!!" Addy screamed, came out of nowhere and smacked right into Jack nearly knocking him over.

"Oof," Jack puffed, clutching his daughter tight. "C'mere you." Noah attacked from the other side and Jack instantly went in for the tickle. Noah giggled uncontrollably.

"St-op!" Noah stammered in-between laughs. "Dad-dy stoppp!"

Jack relented. "So, how'd you do? Get good things?"

They reached into their pumpkins. Noah held up a Wonder Workshop Dash robot; Addy showed him a $100 Amazon gift card.

"We got these from grandmother! Cool, huh? I can get more episodes of my favorite TV show," she said, "C.S.I.! I love that procedural drama stuff. I'm going to marry Gil Grissom one day," she said matter-of-factly.

Owen's eyes got wide and Jack cocked his head. "Wow. You guys scored some great things." He checked his watch. They'd been gone for a little over an hour.

"Probably time we headed back, don't ya think," he asked the kids.

He was immediately met with whines of "noooo" and "it's too early" and "just a couple more houses" and "pleeeasssee?"

Owen spoke up. "C'mon Jack, another thirty minutes isn't going to hurt. Besides, the girls are probably just getting to the good stuff," he shoots a thumb towards the house.

Jack knew Owen was right, but he didn't look forward to spending much more time out here. Owen was extremely persuasive which made him a hell of a lawyer, he could argue his way out of anything. But it could also make him uncomfortable to be around. Jack was no pushover, but Owen made it easier to succumb to saying "fine" at the end of a conversation rather than trying to convince him otherwise.

"Fine," Jack said. "Two more houses or thirty more minutes - whichever comes first. Just make sure you're back by -" but the kids had already raced down the road and up to another house. "Meet us back right here!" Jack yelled to the darkness.

He and Owen walked a little bit down the road, the glass in the pentagon-shaped tops of the street lanterns rattled slightly from the wind gusts.

"Your kids are great," Owen said, putting his hands in his pockets. They stopped walking and Jack turned to face Owen. "They seem very happy. And Addy. Wow. What a trooper."

Jack felt his stomach drop. He knew what Owen was saying and the backhanded threat that came with it. It was always this way with Owen. This was the dark side Jack was wary of. Threat or no threat, Jack had to play along. For the sake of his family. For the sake of Nina's future.

For the sake of absolutely everything.

Jack's words were stern. "Yes, they're happy, Owen. And I intend to keep it that way."

Owen's hands came out of his pockets and he raised them in the air in defense. He looked up at Jack. "Of course, Jack. Of course! I don't want anything to jeopardize that either. It's the last thing I want. I hope you know that. Our wives are best friends and Nina is enjoying such wonderful success and, well, I would never want anything to come out that didn't need to."

And there it was. The veiled threat of exposure. Maybe not so veiled. But Owen knew how to drop subtle hints that got under Jack's skin. Jack decided not to correct Owen on his assessment about Nina's current success status.

"I'm not a jury, Owen," Jack said a little perturbed. "You don't need to try to convince me of anything. I know where things stand."

Jack turned and looked towards where the kids had run off to. He looked at his watch. They'd been gone only 5 minutes. *God, could this night get any longer?*

Behind him, Owen spoke, breaking the taut silence.

"Does Nina know?"

Jack knew what was coming. He knew what was next. He took and released a deep breath then turned to face Owen. He stood his full height and squared his shoulders.

"No," he seethed, "Nina doesn't know." He looked Owen dead in the eyes. "And she never will."

Owen looked at Jack and smiled. He turned and started walking towards shrubs at the end of a property. *This was too easy,* Owen thought. And his smile grew wider.

CHAPTER FOUR

October

After their talk, Nina led Kelly to the largest of all the guest suites and made sure she was tucked in the large fluffy bed safe and sound. Nina walked over and turned on the bedside lamp then dimmed it to a soft glow. The tequila had done its job and Kelly was sound asleep, her breathing a little heavy.

Nina went to the mini fridge she had put in each of the guest suites and grabbed a bottle of Fiji water. Then she went into the bathroom and grabbed some Tylenol, which she placed alongside the water on the nightstand. Nina kissed her gently on her forehead and Kelly rolled over to her side mumbling something. Nina smiled and walked toward the bedroom door. "Welcome home, sweetie," she murmured, turning the crystal knob, and quietly closed the door behind her.

She walked down the long hallway passing Addy's room on the left and Noah's room on the right. She headed down the curved staircase.

She wondered if Addy and Noah had any idea how unhappy she and Jack have been recently. She knew Noah was probably too young to pick up on the subtlety but Addy - Addy was a different story. That girl was so dang smart. Nina had never seen anything like it, nor had Addy's counselors.

Addy was speaking full-on sentences at 10 months, or so Nina was told. At five, she could hold a conversation with anyone about any topic and you'd think she taught at Fairfield University. Nina sighed.

Over the years, it was clear Addy was not only intellectually superior to kids her own age - hell, any age - but she was also more withdrawn and didn't have as many friends as Noah did but Addy was unfazed by the whole thing. Once when Nina asked Addy if she'd like to invite her classmates over for her eighth birthday party, Addy had responded "I find kids my age mundane and lacking acumen." Nina never asked again.

At the end of the day, she was still just a twelve-year-old little girl who liked the color pink, and magical unicorns and jigsaw puzzles. Albeit 1000-piece ones, but still. *Who just so happened to have a crush on a 60-year-old forensic entomologist on a fictional TV show set in a crime lab,* Nina thought sardonically.

Nina reached the foyer, walked a bit further and headed into the large library. She flipped a switch and six wall sconces illuminated a room with built-in bookshelves on opposite walls filled with books from all genres. She slid the dimmer down so the lights resembled the faint glow from candles. The books on the right belonged to Jack. Books like *Superintelligence* by Nick Bostrom, *Freakonomics* by Levitt and Dubner, and *The Wisdom of Crowds* by James Surowiecki. The shelves on the left were reserved for Nina. Novels like *The Eight* by Katherine Neville, *The Secret History* by Donna Tartt, and the entire collections by both James Patterson as well as her very own mother, Willa Greyson.

In the middle bay, second shelf down, there were five books side by side. And five books only. Nina's books.

A Dutiful Wife

Truth be Told

The *Shaken* trilogy

And next to those, an empty space, for the book that never saw the light of day - *A Dark History*. It was supposed to be Nina's sixth book. But Nina had lost her gumption and her drive. Having two kids under the age of eleven and a husband at home who needed her started to take its toll on her, and so she let it all go. Just...let it slip away. Much to Margo's bewilderment. Ahh, Margo. Agent extraordinaire. The Midas of the literary world.

Nina shook her head and snapped back to the here and now. She turned from her shelves and walked to the opposite wall and admired Jack's selections. She put her forefinger in the spine of a book and slid it out of place. She opened it up to one of the front pages. It was signed by the author and addressed to Jack. *"The smart ones are never the nerds. But in your case, you're both. Love you, man!" - Charles Stallings*

Nina smiled. Jack was definitely a nerd. *But a hot nerd.* She took the book and laid down in a chaise lounge. She began to wonder where it all went wrong…

NINA THOUGHT SHE HEARD A NOISE AND LIFTED HER HEAD FROM THE CHAISE lounge. She must've dozed off in her memories. She looked down and Wookie was curled up in a little ball by her feet, a little raspy snore came from his mouth. Nina's head was a little foggy from her rest, but she got up careful not to disturb Wookie, set the book down on the lounge then headed out to the hallway. Maybe Kelly was in the kitchen needing some food to absorb the liquor swimming in her stomach.

"Kelly?" Nina called out. No answer. She walked into the kitchen and flipped on the lights. The empty drink glasses were still on the island but there was no one there.

She moved from the kitchen to the den and felt a little creepy vibe from all the Halloween decorations still lying around. She made a mental note to call Norma tomorrow and see if she could come off her weekend to clean this up. She knew she would have to pay Norma extra. *It's going to cost me an arm and a leg,* she thought, smirking at her joke.

"Kelly? Are you down here?" Nina called out, her voice echoing up to the massive, vaulted ceiling. But she got no answer still. She could feel her heart beating. She heard the front door open, followed by footsteps and children laughing.

"Jack? Is that you?" She started walking towards the front door.

"Yeah, it's us," he responded.

"Mom! We got some really good stuff," Noah was saying turning his pumpkin over and dumping out his collection: humongous candy bars, some Matchbox cars and…. a robot.

"Let me guess. Grandmother?" Nina questioned.

"Yup," he said. "And Addy got a $100 gift card!" Nina looked at Addy who was holding up the card proudly, fanning herself with it as if it were a spread of hundred-dollar bills.

"Cool! That'll come in handy, huh?"

"Oh, yes! Gonna upload it tonight!" Come on, Noah, let's go look at our loot!" Noah started packing his pumpkin back up then raced up the stairs after Addy.

"Kids?" Nina called, as they were halfway up the curved staircase. "It's almost bedtime. One hour, okay? I'll come to tuck you in later."

"But mom, it's a holiday! Can't we stay up just a little later?" Noah whined. "Pleeeeease?

Hoping for his input, Nina looked at Jack, who cocked his head and raised his hands as if to say, "I've had my time with them, it's your turn now". Owen, who stood in front of the fire to warm up, said nothing and Nina didn't want to cause a scene in front of him.

Somewhat annoyed, Nina made her decision. "Fine," she said. "*Two* hours. But that's it. Deal?"

"Deal!" Addy said, grabbed Noah's hands and together they started down the upstairs hallway.

"And keep it down. Aunt Kelly's asleep."

"Ok. G'night," she whispered. "Love you."

"Love you more, sweetheart," Jack said. Nina blew Addy a kiss then turned to face Jack and for the first time she noticed his face was a bit flushed.

"Your cheeks look a little rosy. You feeling okay?" Instinctively she raised the back of her hand to his forehead. Jack moved her hand away and his head moved a little back.

"I'm good. It's pretty windy outside and we had a long walk home." He walked away. "I'm heading up to take a shower and then turn in," Jack said as he went into the kitchen.

She could still feel the tension in the air. Nina caught Owen's eyes. She was silent for a moment the forced a small smile. "Ok, honey. I'll be up soon to keep you warm." She knew she didn't sound too convincing, but she wasn't about to let on to Owen there was trouble brewing in their marriage. To her relief, Owen seemed to be oblivious to it all.

"Is, uh, Kelly okay?" Owen, asked, interrupting her thoughts.

"Um, yeah. She fell asleep. About an hour ago. I left some water and pain reliever on her nightstand just in case...." She trailed off.

"That bad, huh?" Owen said.

"That bad."

"Okay. Well, then on that note, I'm going to head on upstairs, see how she's doing. Thank you for watching out for her." He leaned in and kissed her gently on the cheek.

"My pleasure. Good night, Owen." She watched him head towards the stairs. "It's the last door on the left," she said.

He turned on his heel, saluted her, then turned back and headed up to his suite.

Nina was left alone downstairs. She watched the fire burning in the fireplace. She pushed a severed arm off the overstuffed chair and curled her legs underneath her. As she watched the flickering blaze, she wondered at which moment did her perfect life turn to shit.

Her husband and two children and her best friends were all under the same roof. Her mother lived not more than two miles from her. She had an agent who had bent over backwards for her. And she had millions of adoring fans all around the world.

All these people in her life.

And she'd never felt more alone.

CHAPTER FIVE

October

A couple hours later, Nina awoke to a smoldering fire. She covered it with ash and watched as the orange and white wood reduced the fire to a thin line of smoke. She replaced the fire shovel and headed upstairs to bed. Jack would be fast asleep now and Nina couldn't help but feel a bit happy she wouldn't have to deal with any more of her disintegrating marriage tonight. Once upon a time, their love life was a rampant blaze, all-consuming and hotter than lava, but over time, it, too, was reduced to nothing but cinders and a thin line of smoke, disappearing into the air. She sighed as she reached the upstairs landing. Instead of going left to her room, she headed in the opposite direction towards Kelly's room and the kids' rooms.

She peeked in on Noah. His Buzz Lightyear costume was strewn across a chair, and he was sound asleep under the covers, his Halloween candy laid next to him on his bed, protected. On his nightstand, a desktop planetarium projected over 6,000 stars and constellations onto his ceiling. Noah had always had a thing for outer space and right now, his room was an amazing array of galaxies and planets and the occasional shooting star. It was peaceful in here. Nina walked over to Noah, tugged the covers up to his chin and gave him a peck on his forehead. "Good night, sweet boy," she murmured.

She silently closed the door behind her and then opened Addy's door. She was sitting up in bed with her earphones in watching something on her iPad. *C.S.I., no doubt.* Addy looked up and saw her mother. Nina mouthed "go to bed". Addy held up five fingers and Nina nodded in agreement to five more minutes. "Love you," Nina mouthed.

"You, too," Addy said a bit loudly, because of the earphones clogging her ears.

Nina put her index finger to her pursed lips and breathed out a *shh*. She shook her head and smiled and shut the door behind her.

As she walked towards the end of the hall, the last room on the left had a faint light coming from under the door. Kelly and Owen's room. As she got closer, she could hear some muffled words. The voices were not raised so Nina couldn't really make out what was being said. As she got closer, the words became a bit clearer.

".... she deserves to know..." *Kelly.*
".... will break her heart..." *Owen.*
".... not keeping...secret...any longer..." *Kelly.*

Nina felt uncomfortable eavesdropping on a private conversation but the writer in her was a tad curious who they were talking about. Someone who had a secret about them. Someone Kelly and Owen both cared about. Someone they needed to talk to quickly.

And then it hit her: Mrs. Andrews. *Of course!* Kelly and Owen were in town to see Kelly's parents because of a possible divorce and now there's this secret Owen wants to expose. Something that is so terrible it would break her heart. It had to be about Kelly's mom. Poor Evelyn. *Was Charles cheating on her? Or was it something else? Owen was their lawyer so maybe they were having money trouble? Another shot or two of tequila and I probably would've gotten it out of her,* Nina thought, a little miffed.

Nina heard movement in the room and quietly hurried back down the hall towards her own room. She cast a glance back just in time to see the light under the door turn to blackness.

Whatever it was they were talking about, it was going to wait. Nina reached the door to her room, reached down for the knob, turned it silently then entered. Jack was gently snoring, indicating his day had come to a close. Nina's shoulders sagged a bit as she closed the door behind her.

She looked down at her sleeping husband. He looked so peaceful. But she knew the chaos that swirled beneath his skin. Nina remembered back to a time where she walked in on Jack once before when he was sleeping, and he never knew she was there. At first, her emotions wanted her to pick up his alarm clock and bash in his skull; to end his life then and there. But he was her fiancé, and she was writing her first book and, so, she let those emotions dissipate and be taken over by ones of understanding and love. She didn't want to wake him and confront him, either. *No. This can wait.* And it had.

Now, standing above him on Halloween night, she felt the same urges. She wanted to talk to him about what was going on. But things between them hung on a precipice and she was afraid if she so much as breathed in the wrong direction, everything would plummet over the edge, beyond recovery. She decided to wait, again.

It was *all* going to have to wait, she thought, then went to bed.

CHAPTER SIX

October

Kelly opened her eyes. Everything was a blur. She squinted to see better but nothing came into focus. She squinted more, bunching up her nose and saw something flat on the nightstand next to what appeared to be a bottle of water. *My phone.* She reached over and touched the screen which came to life, illuminating a time of 3:17am. As her head began to pound, she sat up in bed, scooching back until her back was against the pillows.

"Ugh," she moaned, rubbing her temple. She was still alcohol-groggy and felt a little shaky. She smacked her dry lips together a couple of times, still tasting the reposado on her palate. "Bleh." She noticed the Tylenol Nina must've left for her next to the Fiji water, took three of the red and blue pills then chased them down with half the bottle of water.

A grunt sounded beside her and she saw Owen on his back, snoring the world away. Kelly nudged him and he rolled over on his side and the snoring ceased. She foggily recalled the conversation she and Owen had before she zonked out to the world. She closed her eyes and tried to shake the memory loose. They both agreed to keep quiet for the moment. *It's for the best,* Kelly thought. She swung her legs over the side, planting her feet on the fluffy rug beneath the bed then stood up, a little sway to her stature.

The room was nearly pitch dark and but there was a slight illumination from the moon above the Long Island Sound just beyond the wall of windows on the other side of the room. The plush rug squished between her toes as she took her time finding her footing while she walked towards the window.

Kelly stood at one of the huge paned windows and peered out into the vast backyard of her best friend's house. She reached out and pushed the thick Valencia damask drape back fully, letting the full view be exposed,

Nina's house, the largest in Darien, had the perfect classic appeal of a Nantucket-style home and was perched directly on the Long Island Sound. As she looked out the window, Kelly could see the grotto-style pool and spa in front of the oversized pool house. In the dark of the moon, the maple and oak trees that peppered the rolling landscape looked ominous and something from a horror movie, but Kelly knew in the afternoon sun, the leaves danced in various shades of scarlet, gamboge, and carnelian, and reminded her of the vibrant sunrises you could see from the property. Beyond the Sound were panoramic views of the Sound, Noroton Harbor, and the Manhattan skyline. It really was the quintessential New England estate.

Kelly took in a big breath and smiled. She sipped her water as she stood, admiring her view from high above the grounds. Beyond the rolling landscape, the late Fall wind caused small waves to ripple across the expanse of the sound, whitecaps glistened every so often in the moonlight.

Kelly couldn't be prouder of her best friend for all she'd accomplished and earned and how far she'd come: the difficulties getting pregnant, the eventual adoption of Addy, the miracle birth of Noah, the literary success of her books that has afforded her a beautiful lifestyle, marrying the man of her dreams -

Out the window, her eye caught something else. Another, different type of glistening, almost silvery. And definitely longer than a whitecap.

She squinted to get a better look but couldn't quite make out what it was. She thought maybe the tequila was messing with her mind. *No.* There was certainly something out there. And whatever it was, it wasn't moving.

That's odd, she thought. *What* is *that?* She rubbed her eyes and shook her head slightly to focus better.

She moved closer to the windowpanes, sure something else was out there but then with horror, her eyes widened as she made out what was shining. It wasn't outside. It was inside! And it was reflecting in the window. *Oh God!*

She spun around. Noah was standing in the doorway to their bedroom.

And he was holding a knife.

CHAPTER SEVEN

October

Kelly froze. Her blood turned to ice, and she instinctively backed up against the window. The cold glass seared through her thin sleep shirt and chills ran from her head to her toes. All she could do was stare at the big knife Noah was holding down by his side. Noah was just standing there in his Toy Story pajamas looking like a normal six-year-old. Well, except for the knife.

Her hand was shaking, the water in the bottle sloshing. "No-ah…" her voice cracked. "Honey, are you okay? Are you looking for your mommy?"

No answer.

"Noah, sweet pea," Kelly half-whispered, "can…. can I get you something?" She took a couple of tentative steps forward.

Suddenly, as if triggered by her movement, Noah raised the knife above his shoulder, poised to stab her if she moved any closer.

Shit.

Kelly felt she could take him. He's just a child, after all. She could surprise him and rush up to him. Grab him by the shoulders and shake the knife out of his hand. *Or I could rush up to him, trip and he'd plunge the knife into my chest.* She thought better of catching Noah off-guard. Kelly could feel her heart pounding in her chest. Out of the corner of her eye she saw Owen in bed, still asleep and unaware of Noah's presence.

"Owen," she whispered loudly to him, not taking her eyes off Noah.

Nothing.

"Owen!" She tried again, this time a bit louder. Owen made some sort of sleepy groan, but he just pulled the sheets up and continued sleeping.

Shit shit shit!

Then she hurled the water bottle at him, hitting him squarely in the chest. He bolted upright. Kelly was standing a few feet in front of the window and standing like a mannequin.

"Kelly? What the fu…."

"Shhhhhhh," Kelly said, her head cocked towards Owen but her eyes averting him to look towards the bedroom door.

Still irritated, Owen looked and saw what Kelly was staring at. Noah was standing in the bedroom and brandishing a knife over his shoulder as if he were about to ram the blade into something.

"Oh crap," Owen said, then grabbed his phone.

"What are you doing?!" Kelly asked but Owen didn't answer. He fiddled with the phone before putting it in a pocket of his pajama pants. He slid out of bed and went to Kelly, putting his body in front of hers. Kelly felt safe, protected. If only for a moment.

Owen was talking to Noah, trying to get him to drop the knife. To kill time? To distract him? Kelly wasn't sure. Owen took a few steps towards Noah. Noah lifted his eyes and they seemed to be peering right through Owen and Kelly. Suddenly, Noah took a step forward. And then another. And now he was stepping quickly across the room. The knife raised high and aimed to drive deep into Owen's flesh. Noah was only three feet away. Kelly screamed.

Behind Noah, Jack suddenly appeared, quiet and stealthy. He rushed up behind his son and at once, grabbed the knife with one hand and scooped up Noah with the other, separating the two in an instant. Noah yelped, his legs kicked in the air.

Kelly rushed up to hug Owen. Nina appeared in the door frame, breathless.

"What…. happened?" she asked but surveyed the scene and figured it out quickly. "Is everyone okay? Kelly? Owen?"

Noah was now hugging Jack and seemed to be sniffling his way to falling asleep in Jack's arms. "Addy…." Noah whimpered.

"Shhh buddy," Jack comforted him, "you're okay." He put his hand on the back of Noah's head and pulled him closer to his chest. Seeing Nina behind him, Jack passed the knife to her.

Nina went up to Noah and kissed him on the forehead. "Sweet boy, it was just a bad dream. Let daddy take you back to bed, okay?"

"…mmm'k," Noah said.

"Hey, Owen," Jack said, "thanks for the text. Sorry about all this." He turned and left the room with a sleepy Noah.

"Text?" Kelly asked.

"Yeah," Owen sighed. "I sent him a text on my phone to let him know Noah was in here with a knife."

"Quick thinking," Kelly said. "Wow, Nina, what was that about? Is he okay?"

"I'm going downstairs to put on a pot of coffee. I don't think we'll be getting any sleep tonight," Owen said.

"I believe you're right," Nina said as Owen left the room. Nina sat on the edge of the bed, seemingly exhausted.

Nina told Kelly, "Noah's been a little prone to sleepwalking every now and then, but never like this. Never this startling. It started when he was about four. He's only sleepwalked a few times, so we've never really been too alarmed. Sometimes it's after he stays up too late past his routine, so….oh, gosh. He stayed up later to be with Addy. That must've been it. I'm just really sorry it escalated to this tonight. Maybe it was because of the Halloween decorations I did. Who knows?"

"But the knife?" Kelly asked. "I mean, this is pretty serious. Someone could've been hurt. Or worse."

Nina didn't have an explanation for the knife, either. Since Addy was the last to see Noah last night, maybe she knows something and could help figure this out. But Nina knew Kelly was right and that she and Jack would have to deal with this with the kids later. *This is all my fault,* Nina thought. *Life is so crazy I can't even manage my own kids.* She looked at Kelly defeated.

"Oh, it's okay," Kelly said, trying to make light of the situation. "I'm just glad no one was hurt. I'll just have to start locking my bedroom doors," she said smiling.

"Mommy, what's going on?" Addy asked, standing in the door, yawning and rubbing her eyes.

"Oh, honey, I'm sorry we woke you. Everything's fine. Why don't you go back to bed?" She stood up from the bed and pulled Addy into a hug.

"Then what's that for?" Addy asked, pointing to the large knife on the bed.

Nina knew Addy was too smart to try to bluff her way out of this one, so she told her what happened.

"Oh, mommy, it's my fault! When you gave us a couple more hours to stay awake, Noah wanted to watch the movie "Halloween" and I told him he was too young to watch it, but he insisted, and I didn't want him to be mad at me and…." Tears were flowing down her cheeks, and she was gasping for air, clearly feeling guilty for tonight's events.

"Shhh, honey, it's not your fault," Nina said, trying to console Addy. "You know your brother sleepwalks every now and then. This was just…. different. But not your fault at all, okay? Do you understand?"

Hiccupping for air, Addy nodded her understanding.

"Okay, love. You get back to bed and sleep tight, okay?" Nina kissed Addy on the top of her head and gently nudged her out the door.

Kelly walked up behind Nina and wrapped her arms around her shoulders, resting her chin on Nina's shoulder.

"Tomorrow's gonna be a blast," Kelly said playfully.

"No shit," Nina said and laughed.

CHAPTER EIGHT

Mid-November

Nina couldn't remember the last time the house had been this quiet. Jack left yesterday to go to Philadelphia for a meeting. Addy was at Valentina's and Noah was on a morning playdate with his best friend, Easton.

Her phone rang, jostling Nina out of her thoughts. She noted the caller I.D.

"Hi, mother," Nina said.

"Hello, my girl," Willa Greyson said. "How are you doing? Are you in need of anything for the gathering?"

The 'gathering' her mother was referring to was Thanksgiving dinner Nina was hosting this year. In the past, she simply would never have the time to organize such a large soup-to-nuts dinner. This was the first time Nina had hosted the family Thanksgiving because in the past, she had been busy with her writing. But as of late, not so much.

"Nina, darling?" Willa spoke to the silence.

"Mother, no, sorry, I've got it all covered, thanks. I've got a big meal planned."

"Who's doing the catering," Willa asked, Nina could hear the smirk through the phone.

Nina laughed. "You know me too well, mother." She frowned and hoped her mother could hear the pout in her voice. "But what makes you think I won't be slaving away in the kitchen myself, hmm?"

"Oh, my darling, because we're from the same cloth. Plus, Addy and Noah would want to help and that would just equal a disaster on such a monumental scale and all in your beautiful kitchen. I'm afraid you'd have to redecorate again."

Nina knew Willa was right.

"Now, if you had a hired nanny to help out with the kids and their activities and schooling and such...." Willa let the rest of the suggestion hang in the air.

This was a sore subject Nina and Willa and, well, almost everyone, disagreed on. Nina didn't want the children raised by a nanny because it sent out a message that the parents were too busy to handle the kids and to the rest of the world, it became "rich people problems" and Nina tried very hard to keep as much normality in the kids' lives as possible.

Jack supported the idea. He just wanted him and Nina to get back to normal, whatever that took. Things hadn't been normal for a while but once they decided to adopt, things would get better. Or so they thought.

The adoption process proved to be quite the challenge. Nina remembered Jack did everything he could to find a child to adopt and after a short time, Jack brought Addy into their lives. He surprised Nina one day by bringing a smiling, two-year old blonde-haired little girl into their home and introducing her as Aderyn Travers, their daughter. Nina's tears were instant, and her questions were many, but for the moment, she let them all go out the window for the sake of holding her little girl. Nina remembered that emotional meeting like it was yesterday.

"How..."

"An emergency...some tragedy or something, came up in Miami and Owen was in the right place at the right time.....a client of his knew of a child needing a home and..."

"But what about her parents..." Nina's breaths were heavy through her tears.

"I believe they were killed. Died in an accident. Car, maybe? I'm not sure of the details..." Jack was trying to keep up with her questions.

"But…how can we be sure…."

"Owen is an excellent lawyer, you know that. There's nothing to worry about." He walked up to Nina holding Addy tightly in her arms and stroked Addy's blonde curls. Nina was gently touching the thistle-shaped birthmark under her chin.

"Her name is Aderyn. But we can call her Addy. Addy's parents are no longer alive and now she belongs to us…."

Nina shook her head. Not believing the miracle. She smiled through her tears.

"This is what you've always wanted. What we've *always wanted."*

Nina looked at her little girl and couldn't believe Addy was here. Just minutes ago, she was a wife. Now, amazingly, she was a wife and *a mother.*

"Are you happy?" Jack asked Nina, looking into her navy eyes. He looked so hopeful.

Nina found her voice again.

"Oh yes, my darling," she laughed until she cried. "I'm happier than ever!"

That was ten years ago, and Nina still couldn't believe how quickly Addy had made her a mother. Like a pesky fly, Nina couldn't shake from her mind the swiftness of the adoption, that it didn't take months, or even years for it to happen. She had heard horror stories of how long they could take, and Addy's own adoption just blew that theory out of the water. But Nina decided it best not to look a gift horse in the mouth. No matter how Addy got here, she was here.

Five years later, Noah was born. The pregnancy was a massive surprise to both Nina and Jack because neither had really come to expect any positive pregnancy news in their lives. But once Addy had come into their lives, all worry and wonder, and excruciating disappointments and trial and errors and heartbreaks were no longer.

"It's like all the stress went away and *poof* - Noah arrived," Nina had told Jack then. "We released all the sadness, and happiness was its replacement."

Jack and Nina had told Addy she was adopted a few years ago when they felt she was old enough to handle it and she didn't even blink an eye. "You're the only family I've ever known and the only family I could ever want," she had responded after receiving the news. *And I'm not about to introduce a nanny into the situation and take that comfort away from her,* Nina thought.

"Mother. You know how I feel about the kids being raised by a nanny. I simply don't want Addy and Noah to rely on a total stranger on learning the ways of the world."

Willa sighed. "Nina, my dear, Addy is so smart she could teach *us* the ways of the world."

Nina laughed loudly. Willa was right, again. When she was five, Addy came to Nina and Jack and said she'd like to learn Portuguese.

"Because of Valentina," she had said. "She just moved here from Brazil and no one in class wants to play with her because she's *different*. She doesn't speak our language. And just because someone is different doesn't mean they should feel excluded," Addy had said, rubbing the thistle birthmark beneath her chin.

For years, Addy had felt self-conscious about her birthmark and had been relentlessly teased about it from schoolmates. Nina and Jack felt horrible every day when Addy would come home from school upset and defeated.

Nina would explain that not everyone was blessed to have something so unique and beautiful about them and she should wear her birthmark proudly.

So, it came as no surprise Nina and Jack were in agreement to let Addy learn Portuguese from a top tutor in the city. Addy was helping a fellow classmate who was being ostracized like Addy used to be. Addy may have been twelve but was far more advanced than people twice her age. So, whenever Jack would visit the Manhattan GenTech location, Addy would tag along and he'd drop her off with her tutor.

"So…have you written any more of your book?" Willa asked, somewhat hesitantly. If the nanny conversation was touchy, talking about Nina's lack of writing was seriously off-limits. Willa braced herself for Nina's retort.

But instead of words, Willa heard a snort, like the chuff of a bull before it charged.

"Mother, please. You know I am at a standstill and just…just don't want…. I don't know where to go with it from here and….," Nina paused. Another chuff.

Nina knew she should take some responsibility, but she was tired. Life had thrown her too many curveballs and she was exhausted from dodging them all. And then all those other writers took over. For Nina, it was easier to offer excuses and to blame others.

"If only none of them existed!" Nina had said one day when she was in a mood. "I mean, why can't they just…. go away!?"

Willa was well aware of Nina's excuses and quite honestly, she was sick and tired of her daughter's insolence. She had prepared for this conversation.

"Nina. You listen to me. For years you've been giving everyone who will listen excuses for why you haven't written or why you won't finish "A Dark History", and quite frankly, it's getting tiresome."

"Mother, I…."

"No. Now, we've been very supportive of you all your life. When you were in college and wanted to follow in my footsteps, we were skeptical at first, but you showed us your talent and we were behind you 110%. And you soared. My darling, you rose above everyone. Even me. And, if I'm being honest, I was a tad jealous of you."

"Oh. Mother, I had no…."

"Now, I have not admitted that to anyone and I swore myself to secrecy I would never, ever mention that to you, yet here we are. I've been writing for years, I'm about to launch my 20th book, and you've written 5 and suddenly everyone else - including your dear ol' mom – was a nobody."

"You know that's not true! You're loved around the world and have more fans than you can count."

"But not as many that can compare to you. You were at the top and my dear, like they say, the brightest star has the furthest to fall."

Willa paused, then continued.

"I'm no longer jealous of you, my darling. I love you. And I'm so very, very proud of you. You are in a world I will never be a part of. Margo made sure of that. She made sure we were successful no matter what. And you can - you *will* - be successful once again. There is no doubt in my mind. I know it. Jack knows it. *You* know it. You just need to dust off your knickers and get back to work."

Nina laughed. She knew what she was about to say would sound like an excuse, but she couldn't help herself.

"I've got a family to raise now," she said. "It's not easy being a full-time mother to two young kids and pump out books to satisfy the masses. I don't have any help as you know and…." She saw the trap too late.

Willa sighed. "Exactly, my darling. You need help. And look, hiring a nanny to help isn't the worst thing in the world and it could just be temporary. Let them help take the kids out of your hair for a couple hours a day and do busy things around the house and next thing you know, you'll be typing "The End" to your next book."

"I know, but…."

Willa played her ace.

"Besides, aren't you still under contract and don't you have to deliver your book to Margo in four months?"

The mere mention of Margo's name sent a cold ripple down Nina's spine. Nina always delivered her books on time - usually earlier than expected - but right now she was just going through a slump. But Margo was not having the excuses. Although they loved each other like family, they could also argue like family. Currently, Nina had no room to argue, and she knew it. And Margo knew it. And then there was the matter of the contract. Margo had already extended Nina's deadline several times. But Nina knew her mother was right. Again! She was getting tired of this game of her mother always being right. But she couldn't help but smile.

"Fine. I'll think about it."

"Nina….?" Willa lulled.

"What? I said I'd think about it. That's progress."

Willa accepted that. For now.

"So, when are you going to bring my beautiful grandchildren out to see me?"

"How about late this afternoon? Jack is out of town for business, and it'll just be me and the kids when they get back from their activities. I can bring them over and we can plan Thanksgiving more."

"Perfect. I'll get Imelda to make them their favorite cookies."

"That'll be nice. I'm sure they'll…."

But Nina was interrupted when her phone beeped, and she saw she had an incoming call. As she looked at the phone screen and saw who it was, her heart stopped.

CHAPTER NINE

November

Nina saw Margo Flagg's name pop up and knew this wouldn't be a pleasant call.

Margo was Nina and Willa's agent and to be honest, she was the best in the biz. Everyone wanted to work under Margo because every manuscript she represented was a huge success. She was the Warren Buffet of the literati and was revered in her world.

She was short in stature, only 5 foot tall, but her mannerisms and character made her seem much taller. She would walk into a crowded room and you could feel her presence before you even saw her. Her thick hair was just above the ears and was more grey than brown. She wore rectangular tortoise shell glasses that sat on her high cheekbones. When she smiled, her lips never parted so no one could tell if she was happy or pissed off.

Right now, Nina could feel the pissed off smile coming through the phone, and she began to sweat. She said a quick goodbye to Willa then clicked over to answer Margo's incoming call.

"Margo! Hi!" She tried to sound cheerful. She knew what was coming and so she had to quickly develop a plan of attack.

"Nina, hello. I haven't heard from you in a week, so I take it that means good news for me?"

This bluntness was out of the norm for Margo, so Nina knew by her tone she was on edge. She could sense Margo's smile fading. A drop of sweat dripped down Nina's back. She pushed her blond hair behind her ear and switched the phone to the other side.

"As a matter of fact, I have some news, yes…."

"Great. Tell me."

Nina's conversation with Willa was playing in her head. She knew she only had a few short weeks to present Margo with a fantastic manuscript, one she should have been working on for *months* already. One that was nearly halfway done but still had so much longer till completion. And then there would be the editing and reading groups and…

"I'm waiting, Nina."

Margo's words bit down hard. Margo had been waiting a long time. The world had been waiting. Nina felt she had let everyone down. Nina decided to go for broke and just be honest with Margo. Surely, she would understand where she was coming from especially knowing what all she had been through to get her happy family.

"Yeah, so…I've got some grand ideas of how I want this book to end! I've really thought about it and Chloe Barrington's story is going to be one the readers will never forget. "A Dark History" will once again put me on the top of the…."

"Cut the bullshit, Nina."

Nina felt as if she were slapped. She let out a small audible gasp.

"I know you, have you forgotten that? I know you better than you know yourself. Hell, I even dropped every one of my authors just to focus on you and Willa, so of course, I know every in and out of you. You've given thought to this book about as long as I've thought about eating a non-kosher dinner. Zilch!"

It was rarely seen but when Margo let her "Angry Jewish Woman" out, it was not to be taken lightly.

"Margo, truly…I…. I've had some…." but Nina thought better of provoking the AJW in Margo. She sighed. She closed her eyes and caved in. "Margo, I'm sorry. You're right. I haven't even thought about "A Dark History" for months."

"Hmmm mmm."

Why was it every woman in Nina's life was right all of a sudden? She didn't like the feeling.

"Truth is, Jack's work has taken him out of town a couple of times, the kids are out of school for winter break, Kelly and Owen came to visit, I'm hosting Thanksgiving at my house this year, I've got mother's book launch in a few months...." A noise in the background distracted Nina's thoughts. She turned and Wookie was yapping and trying to jump up into her lap, his little legs just short enough so he'd bump his head into her shin. She reached down and put him on her lap. There was stint of silence on the phone.

"Nina?"

"Yeah, sorry. Bit hectic around here."

"I can tell. Look, thank you for being honest with me - finally. But that doesn't negate the fact you are contractually bound to have a book on the shelves by summer. I need something to look at. I know I've extended your deadline – *yet again* – and you have, what, sixteen weeks left, but I need something on my desk soon. End of December at the latest. I know it's the holidays, but you've had ample time to come up with something. We need "A Dark History" on the shelves by June." She paused. "No pressure."

Nina had never *felt* such pressure: from her mother, from Margo, even from Jack. Jack just wanted things back to the way they were. When things were simpler. But the pressure to reignite her flame kept building and spreading until it became a wildfire beyond her control. The pressure was consuming her, and she was suffocating from the....

"Nina? Are you there?" Margo asked a little bothered.

"Yes, Margo. Sorry, again. Look, I'll have something for you soon, I promise."

"Good. And, before I go, and I know you've heard this *spiel* before - have you given any thought to hiring some help? A nanny, perhaps. I will handle all the interviews on my end, of course, because quite frankly, I need you to be too busy to even sit and interview someone. Just submit to me what you're looking for and I'll use my industry connections to post the advertisement in all of the biggest papers and websites."

Here we go, again. Nina was so tired of everyone suggesting she hire a nanny. No doubt, Willa or Margo had suggested this to the other and decided to join forces to make Nina feel guilt-ridden into hiring someone.

But if Nina were to be honest with herself, she didn't have much of a choice. With Jack out of town more and more and the young kids demanding a lot of attention lately, there was no way Nina would be able to devote time and concentrate on finishing her novel.

She sighed. She shook her head then stopped. Would it really be that bad? Maybe the help would do her some good, both physically and mentally. She would still have time at nights to spend with the children. And who was it that said this situation could possibly be just temporary? Her mother, she thinks. And aren't mothers always right? *Ugh. And here we are again,* Nina thought, but smiled despite herself. Fine. She surrendered.

Nina closed her eyes and through a gritted-teeth smile, she spoke. "As a matter of fact, I have." She opened her eyes. "I've decided to go ahead and," she took a deep breath, "hire a nanny to help out with the kids' schedules."

At hearing the news, Nina pictured Margo on the other end of the phone, sitting upright with wide-open eyes.

"Mazel tov!" Margo said. "Congratulations! Send me the advertisement tonight by 7:00pm and let's get a book written."

Tonight? Oy vey.

"Oh, and Nina?"

"Yes?"

"Don't you dare go back on your word. We'll get this nanny hired and you'll finish your book. I hate to say it, but I don't want to instigate a dispute over a broken contract. Don't force my hand. Understand?"

Nina found herself shaking. She knew Margo was tough and actually, that's what Nina liked about her. She got the job done no matter what and Nina wouldn't be a hundredth of successful as she was if she didn't have Margo. She knew this was her last chance.

"I understand, Margo. I won't let you down."

"See to it that you don't," Margo said, and the line went dead.

CHAPTER TEN

November

Margo found herself shaking. *Oh my god, what have I done?*

She had never spoken to anyone like that before in her life, let alone Nina freaking Travers! Nina was the biggest female writer out there and Margo felt like she just pushed Nina off a cliff.

I had to be stern! I had no choice! She put her phone down on her desk and ran her fingers through her short, graying hair.

Margo opened her bottom right drawer and pulled out a small glass and a bottle of Four Roses bourbon. She poured herself two fingers of the amber liquid and gulped it down. The alcohol burned clear down her esophagus into her stomach. She winced. She repeated the pour-and-gulp routine two more times. By the third time, the sensation of fire was gone and replaced by a welcoming, calming feeling.

She stood up and walked to the window of her office. She overlooked 9th Avenue on the Upper West Side. Her first place was a small, roach-infested one room office in Hell's Kitchen, right above a Thai restaurant. It took Margo, a transplant from Iowa, ten tough years to get to where she is now. She was a conundrum. She could be a bully in front of people, always getting what she wanted and yet her humble upbringing never left her mind, and she would sit alone and contemplate her actions. The badass side of her made her a success; the vulnerable side of her kept her human.

As she peered out the window of her $8,000 a month office, Margo couldn't help but think of Nina and what all she meant to her.

Margo knew nothing could jeopardize this relationship. She was completely dependent on Nina and Willa as clients. After Margo whittled her client list down to two, her name became mud in the literary world. Sure, people knew she still held amazing power in their circles, but she now had no one banging down her doors to become clients. Nina and Willa were it. Margo wasn't even sure what she would do if either one of her two clients' popularity waned. Her future depended squarely upon the shoulders of Nina Travers and Willa Greyson.

And now, Nina Travers' shoulders have collapsed. And Margo's world had slowly begun to crumble along with them. She eyed the stack of unpaid bills on her desk. Pretty soon she wouldn't be able to afford this office. And with that thought, Margo poured herself another drink.

After a rough start, Margo had situated herself in Manhattan as the premier agent to have in your corner. Anything Margo touched turned to literary gold and authors were clamoring to jump ship from their current agents to her. Because of her power and connections, popular authors like Gregory Wynn and Leslie Fontaine relocated their lives to be close to Margo. And there was Rachel Meadows. And Harris Markham. And so many others. But within a few years, she dropped them all.

All were miffed, but some were more gracious than others. Rachel was a huge Instagram influencer already and knew she could be successful with or without her books; Leslie was too drunk to care about anything half the time but she had a following of ladies who also had liquid lunches such as herself so she would pretty much be okay.

But Gregory Wynn and Harris Markham took the drop the hardest. Gregory had two book lines going - his psychological thrillers (under the pseudonym Rebecca Sanchez) and his more successful children's line - so he wasn't hit as hard in the wallet as he was in the ego. But Margo gave him a recommendation to Angela Vine, a young, hungry up-and-coming agent who could give Gregory the attention he required. And so far, he was doing fine. *Whew!*

But then there was Harris Markham. Harris Markham became bitter and resentful. Four years ago, after depleting his accounts and retirement plans, he picked up and relocated his family from Utah to New York, and banking on Margo's "Midas" reputation, had just purchased a huge second home in the trendy Hamptons. Two years into the astronomical mortgage payments, his contract was not renewed, and he was out on his own. Margo tried to give him a recommendation to Angela Vine, but Harris was too bitter to accept anything from Margo, let alone her pity. Harris did not take any of this well and made it his own personal mission to make Margo's life as miserable as possible.

He spray-painted "TRAITOR BITCH" on the side of her car and spread vicious rumors of her being an "incompetent alcoholic" on popular literary sites. One night, he burst into her office and tossed a huge stack of unpaid medical bill on her desk and demanded she pay for them. "How do you expect me to pay these doctor's bills? *HUH?!* Now they are refusing to see me until these are paid and I can no longer afford my heart medicine. I could die without it. But do you care? NO! You have ruined everything about me!"

Harris Markham was definitely a threat. Everyone else, it seemed, had moved on. But she still couldn't help but feel a little trepidatious about what she had sacrificed for the sake of Nina and Willa.

The bourbon in her glass was gone. She walked back to her desk and sat down with a heaviness. She tried to stack her own unpaid bills neatly, but the stack was too high, and it kept slipping apart. She tried again to no avail then gave up. She couldn't tell if the envelopes were lopsided or if she was. *Who cares?* She poured herself more of the Four Roses amber liquid and sipped slowly this time.

She spun her chair and looked at the bookshelf behind her. The spin made her woozy. There were books from all the authors she had handled in her career. Sally Young. Thomas DeBarre. P.J. Green. Rachel Meadows. Rebecca Sanchez. And so many more. *Ghosts. All of them,* she thought, waving her arm, the bourbon sloshing out of her glass. *All gone.*

And then there were books by Nina Travers. "Ahhhh. My savior," she said. "And also, my downfall. Cheers!" She raised her glass and more bourbon sloshed out. She chuckled.

Next to the books was a photograph of Margo flanked by Nina and Willa at the release party for *Truth Be Told,* Nina's second book. The smile faded from Margo's lips.

She was worried about how her future would play out now that Nina was not producing any more blockbusters - Margo would be completely ruined. She couldn't make it on Willa's success alone. And if Nina's little slump continued...Margo didn't even want to think about it. But she really didn't blame Nina. Nina was like *mishpocha* to her. *Family.* Margo really blamed all the other authors. The ones who kept pushing their mediocre books out for the world to read. The bourbon made her brain shift. *They* were the real culprits in all this. *They* were the ones who caused Nina's problems. And ironically, they were also the ones who Margo had kicked to the curb.

Margo sighed. Had she caused this herself? *Did I set all of this in motion? Was Nina not writing because of something I did? Oh god, what have I done?* She put her head in her hands. *No. I will not blame myself. Those writers, they're the ones who are in the way of it all. If only....*

Traitor.

Ass kisser.

Bitch.

Margo had no idea *what* she was. Everything she had done had been for the sake of Nina and Willa's success. *Or was it for my own success? Who am I?* What *am I?* Everything was becoming a blur.

But one thing was clear to Margo: she needed to find Nina help or else Nina's downfall would become her own.

CHAPTER ELEVEN

November

Scribbler's Cove was the largest and oldest estate in Darien. The house was a modest five bedroom, seven bath colonial home, white with sea-green shutters and multiple glass doors leading to an outdoor patio with heavy iron furniture. The yard around the house was surrounded by mountain laurel and mature trees. But it was the rest of the estate that was truly the showstopper.

Along the front of the estate by the road stood enormous Leyland Cypress trees that stretched the entire length of the property, and the house itself sat so far back, it was unseen from the road. Peppered throughout the manicured lawns were flowers of all varieties and colors, which in the spring made the place seem like a kaleidoscope. In the back of the estate, just before the edge of the Sound's water, were the fruit trees: plum, pear, fig, and cherry. The land was magical and held a very special place in Nina's heart. After senior year, Nina's parents, Willa and Roy, moved to this estate and Willa, wasting no time, renamed the place Scribbler's Cove as an homage to her vocation. At least half of Willa's books came from her time spent here, including her 20th, *Lust Kills*. It was at this estate Nina got the itch to write before heading to college and turning that itch into a full-fledged scratch, finishing her first book, *A Dutiful Wife*.

Nina, Addy, and Noah pulled into the gravel driveway and made the two-minute drive to the house, winding along a perfectly manicured lawn which was now covered in a light dusting of snow from the night before. It wasn't freezing outside, but it was just chilly enough that the cool winds from the Sound blew in a feathery coating of snow. Now covered in a thin veil of white, Scribbler's Cove looked like something out of a Lewis Carroll book.

She parked her Range Rover at the wide-berthed stairs leading up to the front porch. Noah was the first to the door and he opened it and ran inside. "Grandmother! It's Noah!" He called then disappeared down the long hallway that led directly to the comfy kitchen. Willa greeted him with a big hug.

"How's my big man?"

"I'm not a man. Not yet." He said almost sadly. "Not till I'm 7!" He grinned.

Willa laughed as Nina and Addy joined them in the kitchen.

"Hello, Addy, sweetheart. My, don't you look pretty?"

Addy set down her backpack. "This old thing?" Addy said, twirling in a circle, her new cream wool coat flaring at the bottom like a whirling dervish.

"Well, I think it's divine. Come, Imelda has made you your favorite cookies."

Addy and Noah each grabbed two and a napkin and headed into the den.

"*Avó! Esses biscoitos são deliciosos!*" Addy exclaimed.

"Huh?" Willa said.

"I *think* she said your cookies are delicious," Nina said, chuckling. "She's learning Portuguese, remember."

"Oh. Sounds like she's already fluent. Well, thank you, my darling," Willa responded to Addy.

"*De nada*!"

Willa looked wide-eyed from Nina to Addy and just closed her eyes and shook her head. "Addy, dear, I think there are some American Dolls in the cupboard to play with."

"I don't play with those anymore," Addy said. "I did when I was younger."

"Younger?" Willa blinked. "But my dear, you're still very young. You're a little girl. Little girls play with dolls." *Don't they?* Willa mouthed to Nina. Nina shrugged.

"I meant when I was like eight or nine. *That* kind of younger."

"Oh, okay," Willa nodded knowingly.

"Once Addy turned ten and hit the double digits, that's when she said she stopped being a 'little girl'. She was now a 'young woman'", Nina lifted her shoulder as if to imply "what can I say?"

"Well, you'll always be my little girl," Willa stated. "Double digits or not."

"You're funny, grandmother," Addy replied, giggling.

With that, Addy picked out a 750-piece jigsaw puzzle and Noah opened a cabinet and pulled out a basket containing some of his toys. Addy dumped out the puzzle onto the coffee table and began putting it together. Noah grabbed some handheld electronic game and Nina heard beeps and boops emitting from it. She and Willa sat at the marble-topped kitchen island. Noah came back up and grabbed another cookie.

"I love peanut butter!" he said before bounding off back to the den.

"Mother! You can't eat those. You're allergic to nuts."

"Oh, I know that, dear, these aren't for me, and I was very careful not to be near anything even resembling a nut." She paused. "Speaking of nuts, have you spoken to Margo?"

Nina laughed. "Yes, I have. And I told her I would send her my write-up tonight advertising for"- she whispered so as not for Addy or Noah to hear - *"a nanny."*

"Why are you whispering," Willa whispered. "Don't you think they'll know they have a nanny the moment she shows up?"

"Why ruin the surprise?" Nina shrugged, smiling. "Speaking of surprises, I have something for you."

While Nina was searching in her bag, Willa asked "So how does my handsome son-in-law feel about getting a nanny for the children?"

"He's for it. He's all for making my life easier, you know that. He's in Philly tonight but I called him and he's in 100 percent."

Nina reached into her Birkin and pulled out a glossy envelope and handed it to Willa. "Here. For you."

Willa opened the envelope and pulled out the thick card inside. Two corners of the card were festooned in embossed flowers in amethyst and lavender. Eighteen karat gold flakes were furrowed within the cardstock as minty eucalyptus branches reached towards the words:

Please join us in the honoring of the
always fascinating

Willa Greyson

as we celebrate the incredible release of
her twentieth book "Lust Kills"

SAVE THE DATE

Saturday January 14, 2022
7:30pm

at the home of Jack & Nina Travers
450 Long Neck Point Road
Darien, CT 06820

PLEASE RSVP BY DECEMBER 12
(203) 555-2665

Willa clasped her hand to her mouth. Her eyes moistened.

"Oh, Nina. This is.... just beautiful. Just...it's simply beautiful. Thank you, so, so much."

Nina was happy Willa was pleased. Ever since she was a little girl, she had always tried to make Willa proud of her. It's one of the reasons she took up writing in college and was determined to be a successful author like her mother.

"I'm so glad you like it, mother. They were just delivered this morning and I'm quite pleased at their outcome. I ordered 100 but..."

"A hundred?!"

"Well, yes, because I want everyone who's anyone to be there to celebrate you and I'm sure some won't show up. You know how these things go. I'm sure Margo's former writers won't show up. Well, Leslie probably will, as long as there's an open bar. And Rachel might. Anything for publicity," Nina rolled her eyes.

"Exactly. Those scoundrels are killing your vibe, my dear. They have all come in and just taken advantage of you while you were down and out and encroached on your hard-earned spot at the top! It's disgusting. I hope they don't show up. I hope Leslie's wheelchair wheels rust and she can't go anywhere."

"Mother! You're horrible!" But despite herself, Nina laughed. "I have another surprise for you."

Willa put down the invitation. "What is it now? You've invited your father to the book launch, too? You know how I hate having him around when everything is about *me*. He's such a drip."

"Mom, hush. No, I haven't invited him, but keep it up and I will."

"Hmmph," Willa pursed her lips.

"What I was going to say is that I'm inviting Margo to spend Thanksgiving with us. Kelly and Owen planned a long time ago to come back home for Thanksgiving but now they're not going to spend the holiday with her parents - "

Willa's eyes grew inquisitively large.

"Don't ask!"

Willa shrugged.

"Anyway, they'll be in town, and I know Margo has no one in her family so I thought it would be a good time to have Margo over to spend time with the family and - "

"And smooth things over, perhaps?" Willa chimed in.

Nina couldn't help but agree that after Margo's harsh phone call this morning, part of the reason she wanted Margo there was to show her she meant well and there were no hard feelings between them. And maybe she could even dangle a literary carrot in front of Margo about what she's been writing. She just needed to hunker down to her computer and come up with said carrot. She looked at Willa's waiting expression.

"Yes, that, too. We talked this morning and -"

"It didn't go so well, did it?"

"No. She was a little harsh, but she had every right to be. I've been slacking a little and - "

Willa cocked her head and raised her left brow.

"Fine. A lot. I've been slacking a lot. But" - and she emphasized the 'but' – "*but* I'm taking your advice and hiring a nanny. That should help. And if it doesn't - "

"It will. It has to," Willa said, placing her hand on Nina's. "I have faith. Trust me. Mothers always know best, right?"

Nina couldn't help but realize she herself was a mother and had no clue if she was right or not. She hadn't been making the right decisions lately. She had made a mess of her life and her marriage, and she really needed to fix it. Pronto.

Willa pushed a strand of her silver hair behind her ear. "So, you're going to submit the advertisement to Margo this evening. Do you know what you're going to put in the ad?"

"I have no idea! I've never done this before."

"Darling, you're a *writer*. Write what you want. Put down exactly what you're looking for. Honestly, this should be a piece of low-carb cake for you. Do you need me to do the interviewing? I know exactly what my lovelies need," she smiled a sweet smile, but Nina sensed a bit of mischief behind the smile.

"Nah, but thanks. Margo is handling that end. She knows me better than I know myself and I trust her. Always have. She's been with the family a long time and made huge sacrifices for us so yeah, I trust she'll find exactly what I need. Besides, that's just one more thing off my plate I don't need to worry about. The kids will be fine."

She looked over in the den and Noah had already discarded his game and was now on his iPad and Addy was only a few pieces away from completing her puzzle. Nina was shocked but not really. Addy was an amazing child and putting together a 750-piece puzzle in 30 minutes was par for the course. Still, Addy's intelligence took Nina's breath away.

Willa shook her head. "Maybe *she* should do the nanny interviewing," and they both began laughing.

"A nanny?" A small voice spoke.

Nina and Willa stopped laughing and they looked up. Addy was standing at the end of the island looking at them.

"Did I hear you say you're getting us a nanny? What for? Don't you want to take care of us anymore?"

Nina's heart sank. She looked at Willa who gave her a steely look as if to say, "Don't back down now".

"Of course, I still want to take care of you, honey. I love you. And Noah. You guys are my life." And she meant it.

"So why do you need to get us a nanny? A stranger to watch us?" Addy's voice was quivering, and she seemed unsure if she wanted to know the answer to her question.

Nina felt Willa's hand on her forearm. A light squeeze.

Nina smiled cheerfully, hoping Addy would fall for the nonchalance. "Oh, Addy. Mommy just needs to get some work done and...well, I feel like I just need a little help around the house. You guys will have school and projects and playdates, and I must finish writing my book. You know the one I started a couple years ago? It's all very exciting!"

"Plus," Willa added, "this will be a new friend in the house for you. Someone to hang out with and do things with like shop or go out to eat occasionally. Wouldn't that be fun?"

"I guess," Addy said. She looked at Nina closely. Nina hoped she couldn't see how she felt. She kept the big smile on her face.

"Grandmother's right. It'll be fun!"

"Will this make you happy?" Addy's words cut Nina like a knife. But Nina knew Addy was no fool and if anyone could sense a discord in the house, it would be her. She wasn't going to lie to her daughter.

"Yes, Addy. This will make mommy – and daddy – very happy."

Addy seemed to take it all in. Her eyebrows furrowed and her lips curled like her brain was thinking through the Pythagorean theorem. She looked over at an oblivious Noah.

"Okay," she said. "We accept." Addy grabbed a couple extra cookies. "For Wookie. He loves peanut butter."

And just like that, Nina felt she had nothing in life more to worry about.

CHAPTER TWELVE

November

Philadelphia this time of year could be a nightmare. The weather was as unpredictable as a drunk: you had no idea what it was going to do or how it was going to behave.

Jack Travers found himself braving the colder side of Philly as he walked the three blocks back to his hotel from GenTech, the parent company of his employer. He and his team had had a productive and very cerebral conference. His mind was ready to explode.

Jack needed to run. A run always did him good. He headed back to the hotel and quickly changed clothes.

He grabbed his AirPods and decided for tonight's run, the jukebox from the '80's was on the menu: Quarterflash. Kajagoogoo. Thomas Dolby. Toni Basil. Dressed in his warmup suit and Brooks jogging shoes, Jack came out of The Four Seasons and turned onto 19th Street and headed toward Aviator Park. The air was chilly and brisk, but he loved this time of year. The clear air meant for a clear head. The sidewalks were empty, and he had a clean shot to the park.

But instead of work, his mind was elsewhere: *Nina.*

After graduating from Andrews Prep, Jack and Nina both attended the same college. They didn't see each other much during the first year but really reconnected at a drink social after mid-terms Sophomore year. Nina's best friend Kelly was there with some guy named Owen Ford, an up-and-coming young hotshot who was going to law school and had met Kelly through her father's business where Owen was interning. He was a short dude but what he lacked in height, he overcompensated in charisma and confidence. Owen was not Kelly's normal cup of tea - he was clean cut and wore gold-rimmed glasses and Kelly preferred motorcycle-riding chain-smokers. *Opposites attract.* But Jack figured Kelly needed the stability and reputable influence Owen brought to the table to secure her trust fund. Jack just wasn't sure how long Kelly was going to be able to resist visiting the forbidden side of the tracks from time to time.

He didn't have to wait long.

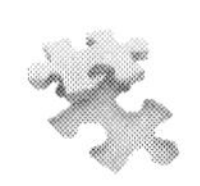

Five months after the drink social, Jack and Nina found themselves as a solid couple whereas Kelly and Owen were already engaged. The four friends were at dinner.

"Omigod I'm so happy for you!" Nina exclaimed. "Owen is such a.... nice guy." She almost choked on the words.

"Hey! I'm right here!" Owen protested.

Kelly looked at Nina and they both burst out laughing.

"Yeah, I know, he's not my usual order but he is a sweetheart and he's really into me and honestly, what more could a girl ask for?" Kelly reasoned, sounding more like she was trying to convince herself than Nina.

"Well, we're happy for you both," Jack said, sounding genuinely happy.

"Most definitely," Nina said, linking her arm with Jack's. "Maybe this'll light a fire under Jack's cute butt."

"Hey! I'm right here!" Jack teased.

"He does have a cute butt," Kelly winked at Nina, and the girls doubled over in laughter.

JACK'S BODY TEMPERATURE WAS RISING. AS HE APPROACHED THE CIRCLE, HE TOOK a right onto Logan Square and decided to run the circumference of the park before heading back towards Cherry Street. He saw a couple walking in the park, gloved hands intertwined, her head was resting gently on his shoulder and Jack wondered about them. Had they known each other a while? Or were they just starting the courtship process? Maybe they were married? And if so, were they married to each other? Or to other people and their meeting was more clandestine than appearances led one to believe? Jack's mind shifted gears.

If only Nina hadn't left that night so early. If only he hadn't gone out to the bar. If only....

He remembered the night it happened.

IT WAS IN SUMMER OF THEIR SOPHOMORE YEAR AND JACK WAS PLANNING A SPECIAL night with Nina. Maybe it was because Owen and Kelly were already engaged and love was in the air, or maybe it was because Kelly kept egging Jack to pop the question to Nina, or maybe it was because he had already bought the ring, but whatever the reason, Jack was determined to make Nina his wife.

Nina and Jack were at his apartment and had just finished dinner then Jack got up and went into the kitchen.

"Jack? I need to ask you something..." Nina's faint voice came down the hallway and around the wall into the kitchen.

"Be right there, hon," Jack replied. He had waited for this night for longer than he thought. He was going to ask Nina to be his wife. He leaned both hands on the kitchen counter to steady himself. What if she says 'no', he worried. What if she thinks they're too young and he's crazy? He started to feel sweat bead on his forehead. He took his palms off the countertop and found they were sweaty, too. He wiped them on his jeans. "Screw it," he said. "I'm doing this."

"Jack, I hate to cut this lovely night short but"- she saw his hands behind his back. "What...what do you have there?" she asked, leery.

He sat next to her on the couch. "Oh, nothing. What is it you needed to ask me?"

"Please don't think bad of me, but, and I'm sorry, honey, but I'm really on a roll

here with this book and I don't want to stop. I'm at such a good part! Can you ever forgive me?" she pleaded.

Nina had taken up writing and was more serious about this than anything else she had put her mind to. He knew she had been diligently writing her first novel and he wanted to support her in her endeavor. He also knew she had a lot to prove with her mother and to herself.

He scrunched his nose and had a worried look on his face. Her eyes pleaded forgiveness.

"Well," he moved his hand to his front. "I was going to ask you to marry me but if you'd rather…" He faced the ring box towards her and opened the lid. He could see Nina's eyes widen. Her hands slowly rose to her mouth.

"Wait. Whaaaat?" Nina cried out behind her palms. "Oh, Jack…. I…."

"But if you really need to leave right this minute…" he started to close the lid.

"Oh my god! Yes! Yes! Yes! I'll marry you!" she exclaimed. "Give me that ring!" She held out her hand and he slid the ring on her finger. She held it up and examined the setting. "It's beautiful! Really. It's just…I love it so much. And I love you." She kissed him softly. "And it's emerald cut. My favorite!"

Jack gave a side-mouth grin and shrugged. "What can I say? I know you. Well, I better after all this time."

"You sure do," she paused. "Speaking of time…. oh god, I hate to do this right now…." She gave him a look of "forgive me?"

Then he remembered. He was a tad disappointed she needed to leave, but in the end, tonight he had accomplished what he set out to do, they were engaged, so it was only fair he not get mad that she needed to accomplish her goals, too. Besides, he did spring this engagement on her in the middle of her task, so the least he could do was be supportive. He grinned. Of course, he understood. Of course, he would forgive her.

Ironically, he could never imagine the question later would be if she could forgive him?

"Absolutely, Neen. I'm so proud of you." And he meant it.

"You're the best!" she squealed. "I'll make it up to you, I promise!"

"Oh, I know you will," he said with a smirk.

"Mmm hmm," she purred. "Just you wait."

"Think I'll just go out to M&M's and grab a beer," he said. Mermaids & Minotaurs, or as the locals called it, M&M's, was their local hangout a couple of blocks away, within walking distance of his college apartment. "Do you need a ride home?

Not too tired?" They both stood up. She grabbed her purse and slung it over her shoulder.

"Are you kidding? I'm on top of the world! I am wide awake and now I am just so motivated to finish up these next couple of chapters!"

He pulled her into a hug and kissed her on the lips. "I'm proud of you, Neen. I really am. And I love you so much." They kissed again. "Call me when you're done?"

"I will, and if I'm done at a reasonable hour I might come back over. But don't forget you're picking me up at 8:00 tomorrow morning to go to my folks'."

"I haven't forgotten. I'll be there. Alright, you go. Get back to your masterpiece. Don't put anything in your book I wouldn't do," Jack teased. They walked to the door. She looked at the ring on her finger again.

Nina sighed. "I love it. And I love you. G'night, babe."

"Love you more. 'Night." He shut the door behind her.

JACK KEPT RUNNING. HE TURNED RIGHT ONTO CHERRY STREET AND PICKED UP the pace. His heart was racing faster than he was running and he noticed his pace had quickened to a sprint. He came to a bench and stopped. He dared not sit down because he could cramp up, but he walked around the bench a couple times to catch his breath. He had run like this before, but his heart never beat this fast before. He checked his pulse. It, too, was faster than normal. Was his heart pounding because of the running or because of his memories? He shook his head and once again, pictured himself sitting at the bar at M&M's.

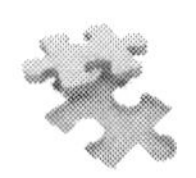

THREE LARGE MUGS OF BEER IN AND FEELING A TAD TIPSY, HE FELT A PRESENCE next to him before he actually saw anyone. He turned and saw long, thin brunette hair cascading over bare shoulders, the straps to a thin mint-colored tank top slightly digging into the skin. He looked down and noticed cut-off jean short shorts and long tan legs. She turned to face him, and it looked as if she'd been crying.

"Kelly? Wha.... what are you doing here? Is everything okay?"

Kelly wrapped her arm through Jack's and pulled herself closer to him, resting her head on his shoulder, her long hair brushed against his forearm.

"Oh, Jack. Tha Owen is sush a prick..." She was slurring her words. Tequila was Kelly's drink of choice and it sounded like she had already downed a few too many shots. "I hate him tho much..."

Jack really didn't want to get in the middle of Kelly and Owen's drama, that was more Nina's thing since she and Kel were BFF's. Great. This was not gonna be fun. The bartender looked understandingly with a raised eyebrow at Jack and put another beer in front of him which he gulped down. Another beer replaced it quickly and it went down just as quick. Kelly put her head in her hands and sobbed. A new beer appeared, and Jack found it hard to focus, his eyes blurred, and his fingers numbed. Kelly grabbed the beer before Jack could say anything and she chugged it like a champ.

"Look, Kel, I'm really sorry tha Owen upset you.... but I gotta go." His words seemed crooked. He stood to go but wobbled a bit. "I need to get some rest be... because Nina and I are going to her parent's tomorrow for breakfast an' I gotta get up early and...." Kelly had gotten quiet. "Kelly? Are you okay? Do I need to call you a taxi?"

He put his hand on her bare shoulder and she slowly turned to look at him. "No....no taxi. I... can't go back there tonight...." She put her head back in her hands

Jack knew his place was only a couple blocks away and there was no way he was going to send a drunk Kelly back to a mad Owen, so he made a decision.

"Fine. You can sleep it off...on my couch. We'll walk back to my place. Can you.... walk?"

"Yeah, think so."

Jack threw four 20's on the bar then helped Kelly off the bar stool. They staggered out into the warm air and walked the two blocks back to Jack's place. Once inside, Jack gently laid Kelly down on his couch and she started lightly snoring immediately.

He stumbled back into his room, stripped off all his clothes and fell on his bare stomach onto his bed. As quickly as the room began to spin, he saw his bedside clock read 1:14am, his eyelids got heavier, and he blacked out.

He dreamed of the ocean, swimming with a beautiful mermaid in the warmest water. She smiled at him and sang the sweetest song he had ever heard. The song beckoned him to hold her, to touch her, to feel her. His hands moved over her lithe body, the curve of her shimmery hips swaying side to side as if she were dancing underwater just for him. He felt himself getting aroused and wasn't sure how it was going to happen, but he knew it had to.

She swam closer to him, and her smile was radiating in the ripples her fantail caused. She was surrounded by light and song. Her long dark hair floated in slow motion around her face, her features unlike anything Jack had ever seen before. Her breasts were suspended in the water's gravity and her mint-green scales glistened as if encrusted with diamonds. He swam towards her and grabbed her waist and she kept swaying back and forth. Suddenly, inexplicably, he was deep inside her. Her eyes grew wide, and she tossed her head back and gasped, bubbles emitted from her O-shaped lips. Between the motion of her hips and the water and his thrusting, the climax was unlike anything he had experienced before. It was, simply put, the most hypnotic, beautiful, mesmerizing experience of Jack's life and before he knew it, she was swimming away. Farther away.... deeper into the depths of the ocean...the darkness enveloping her until she was no more.... gone...and sleep came to Jack once more.

The next morning, Jack lay on his back in his bed and opened his eyes. He smacked his dry mouth a couple of times and blinked his eyes. His head hurt as if it'd been run over by a truck. He swung his legs over the side of the bed, feet on the floor. He stood and stretched and glanced at the clock. 7:24am. Shit! He had to pick up Nina at 8:00! He ran into the bathroom for a quick shower. He brushed his teeth and ran his fingers through his dark hair. He couldn't really see that well because his glasses were fogging up but as he emerged from the bathroom, he could see perfectly, and he stopped dead in his tracks.

There on the other side of his bed, on her stomach, her gentle smiling face turned towards him, her dark hair strewn across the pillow lay the woman of his dreams. The mermaid. The one he had slept with. Nina's best friend.

Kelly.

A HORN HONKED AND STARTLED JACK. HE REALIZED HE WAS STANDING IN THE middle of Market Street and wasn't even sure how he had gotten there. He waved to the car who swerved around him, the driver gave him the finger and muttered something under his breath. Jack found himself shaking and jogged to the sidewalk. He was almost back to The Four Seasons where he would take a hot shower and crash in the king size bed.

His mind had taken him to a place he had recollected many times before and each time, he was unnerved and knew he had to tell Nina. Each time, though, he chickened out and found the reasons why he hadn't told Nina were really just excuses:

- she was writing a new book
- she had a miscarriage
- she was worried about the kids
- she *wasn't* writing a new book

There never seemed to be a right time to tell his wife he had slept with her best friend - on the night they became engaged to be husband and wife, no less. He had to tell her what happened, even though it happened a long time ago. He didn't like keeping secrets from Nina. Even though keeping secrets from Nina seemed to be what Jack was best at.

CHAPTER THIRTEEN

November

Nina was ecstatic Addy, and by association, Noah, had accepted the idea of a nanny. That was a hurdle Nina wasn't sure she would be able to jump over but she had been pleasantly surprised by the reaction.

On the ride home, Addy had even asked when they would get to meet the new nanny? Where were they from? How old were they? What do we call them? Where would they live?

She remembered Kelly's philosophy on nannies: "You definitely don't want a hot nanny because look at that actor who literally got caught with his pants down, and Jack is quite a catch. No, you need someone who is top notch at what they do. And who cares if they have a wart or two?"

Nina imagined Kelly's 'skills-before-looks' ideal would result in childcare experts who were even remotely attractive being sent packing, and the only ones that remained would be the witchy crones who really don't like children at all. *Except in casseroles like the Hansel and Gretel witch in the woods,* Nina thought.

As long as she doesn't look like Gisele Bündchen, I'm good. Nina didn't have an answer to any of their questions, but she tried to curb their curiosity a bit.

"Not really sure of all that yet, but I promise you they will be professional and of the utmost caliber."

Noah cocked his head. "What's calamer?"

"Caliber," Addy corrected. "It means 'boring'."

"It does not," Nina smiled. She looked in the rearview mirror at her son in the backseat. "It just means they'll be wonderful."

Addy looked at Noah and whispered. "*Boring.*"

But Nina couldn't stop smiling. She was glad she had made this decision and felt a giant weight had been lifted off her shoulders. She finally could see that a caregiver for the children would free up so many hours of the day for her to dive into her work and for her and Jack to reconnect.

Later that evening, Nina sat at her computer at the kitchen table and typed out the nanny advertisement. She switched her phone to silent so she could concentrate. Two hours later, she felt comfortable with what she had written. Before sending the email, she added an invite to Margo to spend Thanksgiving with the family.

Hesitating for only a second more, Nina hit "send" and the email disappeared from her screen.

There. No turning back now.

"Mommmmmmy!!" Addy screamed, breaking Nina's thoughts. "MOMMMMMMY!! Tell Noah to STOP barging in my room without knocking! AAAAHHHHH". In the background, Wookie was barking his head off.

"DID NOT!!!" Noah yelled back in retaliation.

"DID TOO!!"

Nina rubbed her temples. *Maybe that witch in the woods was on to something.*

KELLY AND OWEN STOPPED BY THE HOUSE SO THE GIRLS COULD GO SHOPPING FOR new Thanksgiving outfits ("I want to *eat* turkey, not *look* like one," Kelly had said.).

At 8:30pm, Nina and Kelly got home and dropped their many garment bags on the cashmere sofa. They plopped their weary bodies in chairs. There was a fire in the fireplace that had warmed the entire den. The house smelled of cooked spices and warm cedar. The scent immediately enveloped the women.

"Ughhhh. I've forgotten how tiring shopping can be," Nina says.

Kelly shot upright. "Are you high? Shopping is therapeutic. Shopping is everything. Shopping is…. omigod I'm exhausted! What is wrong with me?"

Nina laughed. "We've just, um, matured, I guess. It's more of a chore than it is fun anymore."

"For sure. But we can never admit that. We're from Darien, for Pete's sake! We have an image to uphold!"

Nina flipped the bird towards the front door. "They can uphold *this*!" She put her feet up on the matching ottoman. "I need a drink."

"I'll get us something," Kelly pushed herself up with an "oof" and went into the kitchen. She came back with two empty glasses and an open bottle of Marcassin Estate Chardonnay.

"The good stuff," Nina said, smiling.

"We deserve it," Kelly reasoned, pointing the bottle towards the many shopping bags on the sofa.

"Pour," Nina agreed.

Owen walked into the den wearing jogging shorts and a robe, water droplets glistened on his chest and stomach.

"Oh, hi, girls," he says. "You're back. I was just going to get another beer." He eyed their wine glasses. "I see you're all set."

"You sure are sweaty," Kelly said. "You okay?"

"Yeah, fine. Just got out of the shower and didn't dry off all the way. Now I'm just thirsty."

"Jack around?" Nina asked hopefully.

"Uh, yeah. He's upstairs showering…. I believe. Had a good run and just cleaning up for the night. I think Carmen has fixed some sort of casserole and left it in the oven."

"Yeah, we knew we smelled something. I'm starving all of a sudden," Kelly said standing. "Let's *mangia*!"

As Kelly and Owen went into the kitchen, Nina couldn't help but think about Jack upstairs and why he hadn't said more than two words to her since he got home from Philadelphia. She remembered she never got a chance to tell him the good news that she was moving forward with hiring a nanny.

She picked up her phone and sent him a text, then added "xoxo" at the bottom before hitting the send arrow.

Setting the phone down on the end table, she found herself kind of amazed at how quickly she herself had come around to the nanny thing but when she weighed the pros and cons, the pros won out. And Jack was at the top of the pros list. Their relationship meant too much to her to let it fail. Her not writing and remaining in her slump was a selfish move on her part and she refused to put herself over her family any longer. Writing the book was *for* her family.

Yes. Hiring a nanny will be the best thing for us. I mean, what's the worst that could happen?

CHAPTER FOURTEEN

November

Margo's phone dinged alerting her to an incoming email. She opened it up and saw Nina had kept her word and sent the advertisement for the nanny position. She then saw the invitation to spend Thanksgiving with Nina and her family. *That's sweet,* Margo thought. But she wasn't sure if going was the right thing to do. *If I don't go, it'll look like I'm snubbing Nina and Willa, which could have a horrible adverse effect. And if I* do *go, we could get into an argument about the due date for "A Dark History", which could have a horrible adverse effect. Great.* She'd decide later. Right now, she wanted to read the advertisement.

She read the ad thoroughly and then read it again. "Wow, this is detailed. *Too* detailed" she said to no one. "Oh, Nina. We'll never find anyone this qualified. At least not quickly." And Margo was aware time was running out. She looked at the stack of unpaid bills on her desk, the overwhelming expenses screaming at her, reminding her she was stupid to drop all but two clients.

She looked at the nanny advertisement again and pursed her lips. Her eyes darted to the expenses pile and back again to the ad. She made her decision then.

She began to tweak the ad. Margo knew to find someone this qualified in the short time she expected would take forever. *And I don't have forever.*

She knew she should probably show Nina the changes first, but Margo took the initiative and decided against that route. Taking out most of the things Nina was requiring would help increase the volume of applications. She made the changes, looked them over and was very satisfied she just cut down the hiring time by 75%. The changes were necessary.

With that, Margo placed the ad on ten different nanny hiring websites and all the major local online newspapers. With the touch of a button, the ad was strewn in a wide web across the nanny-verse.

With that part done, Margo revisited the Thanksgiving invitation. Thanksgiving with the Travers. Margo knew she was a very lucky person to have Nina and Willa as her clients and *of course,* she was going to say 'yes' to the invitation. It was the right thing to do. She needed to keep Nina happy, and Willa, too, for that matter. Willa had a launch party for *Lust Kills* coming up in January at Nina's, and hopefully, coinciding at the same time, Margo would be able to announce to the guests a teaser about Nina's new release date. *Two birds, one stone,* Margo thought. And Thanksgiving could be the perfect casual setting to make amends.

Margo organized her email to Nina: 1) the ad had been placed and she will let her know as soon as a candidate has been hired. *Hopefully sooner rather than later,* Margo thought. She also 2) accepted Nina's invitation to Thanksgiving and said she'd bring some wine. She hit 'send' then closed her laptop.

Even though the nanny thing was a go, Margo still had this tingle in her spine that nagged at her, warning her that Nina may not finish her book and Willa will retire one day and then Margo would be left with nothing. She made herself feel guilty for even contemplating this possibility. *Jewish guilt is real,* she thought caustically.

So not for the first time, Margo wondered if she should - or even *could* - visit her old clients about rejoining her firm. But how would it be received? Would they be accepting? Last time Margo tried to talk to Rachel and congratulate her on her latest release, she was shut down with "Yeah, no thanks to you, you ol' crone. Dry up and die, why don't you? Have a nice day!" Margo shook her head and mentally crossed her off her "get in touch with" list.

And then there was Harris Markham. He was a definite "no". Margo cringed.

So, what about Leslie Fontaine? Margo was always close to Leslie. Perhaps it was an age thing. Or that Leslie's 4th husband was Jewish. Maybe enough time had passed where Leslie would be more inclined to come back to Margo. *It's not an improbability,* Margo thought. Unless she was too far marinated in French Martinis to even remember who Margo was.

Margo hated this. She hated she may have to resort to groveling and begging them to come back. She hoped it wouldn't come to this. Margo had worked hard to get to where she was today and had sacrificed a lot and she was a proud woman. This was beneath her.

"Why can't they all just go away?" Margo yelled to the office walls. She thought the easiest thing would be for them to just disappear off the face of the earth. *Maybe some sinkhole will open and swallow them all in. Or maybe just me. At this point, I don't care,* Margo thought. She sighed a heavy breath, took off her glasses and rubbed the bridge of her nose. She looked at her watch and saw it was nearly 10:30pm. Thanksgiving was in three days and Margo was putting a lot of eggs into her basket to get a lot resolved by then. Her choices were thinning out and she was losing faith in her hopes, but she had no choice but to suck it up and make this work. For her, for Nina, for everyone.

Her phone dinged again to alert an incoming email. She opened the file and there was an application for the nanny position as well as a resume. In two short hours, someone was already responding! Her spirits started lifting and her email dinged again. It was another applicant! Margo checked her voicemail and there were two accommodating messages. A big smile erupted on her face. She would respond tomorrow morning first thing.

Her day was looking to end positively!

CHAPTER FIFTEEN

November

Jack knew Nina, Owen and Kelly were downstairs eating a late dinner but the last thing he wanted was to join them. And really the last person he wanted to see right now was Kelly. They had successfully kept their affair a secret for all these years but there was something that just wasn't comfortable about being in the same room as Kelly.

His phone chirped and he saw a text from Nina.

"Hey, hon. Wanted to let you know I sent the nanny advertisement to Margo so we can proceed with hiring someone! And believe it or not, the kids are on board. Glad that's off my plate! Speaking of plates, Kelly, Owen, and I are grabbing some of Carmen's casserole. Come join us if you're not too tired. xoxo"

Jack was relieved. Nina had finally taken a step to turn her life around and Jack could already feel the weight coming off his shoulders. But he knew he was still carrying a lot around. There was the Kelly thing. And now Owen kept bringing up the past. *Shit.* None of this was good and Jack, for the first time in a long time, felt like he had zero control of his life. Jack liked control: in his life, at his job. And right now, his job was the only place that seemed to have any sort of semblance of firm direction.

Here, now, all he wanted was to go to bed. But first he had his ritual.

Jack walked out into the hallway and down to Noah's room. He opened the bedroom door and saw the constellation lamp dazzling the universe onto the ceiling and Noah was in bed, clasping his Buzz Lightyear doll to his chest. His covers were all over the place, his pajama pants scrunched up past his calves and his little legs were sticking out. Jack smiled and walked over to the bed. He had to maneuver the covers a bit because Noah was sleeping on top of most of them. The covers moved, Noah moaned and after a bit of tug-of-war, Jack successfully covered his son up. "Good night, bud," Jack whispered, kissing Noah gently on the top of his head. "Sweet dreams." He left the room and closed the door quietly.

He walked the 20 steps to Addy's door, and he saw a light coming from underneath. He gently rapped on the door but there was no answer. "Addy?" he asked, knocking quietly again. "Addy, it's dad." Quiet. He opened the door and peered in. Addy was sitting up in bed with her AirPods in staring intently at her iPad. Wookie was curled up in her lap and lifted his fluffy head and looked at Jack.

"Addy," Jack said again but she didn't see or hear him. He walked closer to the bed, and she turned her head and took out her ear buds.

"Daddy! I didn't see you there." She turned her iPad facedown.

"I knocked but you didn't answer. Sorry to barge in." He scratched Wookie on the head who wagged his tail happily.

"It's okay. I was just watching a little bit of PLL."

"PLL?" Jack asked, sitting on the edge of the bed.

"Duh. Pretty Little Liars! Geez, daddy. Get with it." She rolled her eyes.

"Oh, sorry," he said placing his hand on his chest in forgive-me mode. "Is that an approved show for you?"

"Yes, daddy. You and mommy approved it last summer. These are repeats anyway. I was just getting ready to go to bed."

"Me, too, hon. Just wanted to come in and say 'good night' and 'sweet dreams'."

Addy reached up both arms to hug his neck. "Good night, daddy. Sweet dreams, too!" She pecked him on the cheek.

Jack stood up and headed towards the door. But before he left, he turned around. "Addy?"

"Yes, daddy?"

"Are you excited about getting a nanny to help out?"

Addy scrunched her eyebrows and curled up one side of her mouth. "I wasn't at first, but then mommy said it would make both of you very happy and that's all I've ever wanted. I'm so happy you picked me to be your daughter." She paused. "Are you happy? That I'm your daughter?"

Jack walked back over to the bed. "Oh, Addy. More than happy. Both your mommy and I couldn't be happier you are our daughter. Yes. A million times, yes." *She had no idea just how significant the word 'million' was with regards to her adoption.* He shook the thought out of his head.

He bent down to kiss Addy on the top of her head. "I love you, my girl. And yes, having a nanny around to help you and Noah should make mommy and me very happy. We'll have to wait and see but I'm hopeful. Now go to sleep. iPad off."

"Yes, daddy. 'Night," she said, smiling, as the door closed behind him.

Jack stood in the hall and leaned against the bedroom door, breathing heavy. He hated talking about Addy's adoption. To anyone. He found that he was rubbing his hands together. He just needed to get to bed and sleep it all off. In due time he would tell Nina everything. But not now. Not until she got things back on track with her own life. Addy's adoption, for now, would remain between him and Owen. Jack sighed.

It was a Pandora's Box that was best left closed.

CHAPTER SIXTEEN

November

I had to get moving. I had things to do. So many things to do. On the outside, it looked all peachy-keen, but I knew better. I know what's happening here. It's all for show. People cannot change their feelings that quickly. I have been toying with this idea for months and wasn't sure what my next step should be. But there was too much riding on this not to go ahead with my plans.

But first, I needed a drink. I went to the kitchen and opened the fridge. Apple juice, water, OJ, milk - where the hell was the good stuff? I see the beer in the back, next to a bottle of Manischewitz. No. I grab a bottled water and head back to my room.

With my plans, I wasn't sure which direction I should go in first, but then I saw the answer right in my lap. I was perusing the most recent list of bestsellers and then saw the top thriller authors and the names made me sick to my stomach.

Rachel Meadows (Really? Her books are dreck! Plus, she's annoying as hell)
Rebecca Sanchez (boooooring. The end.)
Willa Greyson (a sweet old lady that needed to retire)
Leslie Fontaine (probably uses a ghostwriter because she's too inebriated to type the first word)

Carly Kaufman (I hear she gets someone on the inside to send her the rejected manuscripts so she can fluff and put her name on them. Cheater!)
Henry Corbyn (English. Enough said.)

And so, my mind was made up. I would start at the top and work my way through the list.

On my device, I pulled up Rachel Meadows' Instagram. 673k followers? What the heck?! I get she's an influencer first but good god, that's a lot of sheep. No wonder her books are always pushed to the top. She could write 350 pages about grass growing and it'd be a bestseller tomorrow. All because of her followers. Well, I can't get rid of all of them, but I can do something about their leader.

I scrolled through the multitude pages of her pictures and videos. After a while, I figure something out: the girl definitely had a routine. Hundreds of photos and videos explaining where she is at all times of every day: what store will host her next book signing (the Bookworm next Saturday at 1:00-3:00), what restaurant she'll eat her next salad (a Cobb at Lettuce Entertain You), who and where she'll be meeting friends for pre-club drinks (Zondra, Samir, and Andi at V-Bar). Her whole life is detailed on her IG page, and she is not ashamed to promote herself. She is everywhere! And thanks to Rachel Meadows herself, I know just where to find her anytime I need her.

Rachel Meadows? Come on down!

Let the games begin!

CHAPTER SEVENTEEN

November

"Happy Thanksgiving everyone!" Addy bounded into the den where Nina and Jack were seated on the sofa. Kelly and Owen were standing near the fireplace keeping warm, each with some sort of pumpkin drink in their hand. Noah came running in right behind Addy.

The four adults were all decked in dresses and vests and pants and tops in various shades of mahoganies, coppers, and mochas. Candles from Nest burned on every table and shelf in the room. A 6-foot-wide autumnal wreath filled with berries, pinecones, willow branches and maple leaves in all colors hung over the fireplace. If a stranger would walk into the room, they'd immediately think *Architectural Digest* and *Harper's Bazaar* were collaborating to do a Fall photo shoot.

"Happy Thanksgiving, Addy," Nina said. "Don't you look pretty?"

"This ol' thing," she said, twirling, her cinnamon-colored dress flaring.

"If that's an ol' thing, then I need it in my size!" Kelly said. Nina moved beside Addy, and they hugged. Noah leaped into Jack's lap. Noah was wearing a crisp, white Brooks Brothers woven shirt and khaki pants by Catimini held up by Burberry suspenders. His golden blonde hair was gelled up into a fashionable point. He looked like a perfect little model from a children's clothing magazine.

"And Noah, how dapper you look," Owen said.

"What's 'dapper' mean?" Noah asked, scrunching his face.

"It means fancy-looking, but for boys," Addy said.

"Word," Noah said, while everyone gave a little chuckle.

"Addy, why don't you play us something," Owen suggested, pointing to the Fazioli Grand piano in the middle of the room. The large cream-colored piano was a gift from Willa and Addy was the only one who knew how to make it sing.

"Okay," she said. "Any request? Chopin? Vivaldi? Tchaikovsky?" She sat down on the thick, tufted bench.

"Well, it is Thanksgiving," Kelly said. "How about 'Bye Bye Birdie'," she giggled.

"Kelly! You're awful," Nina said, shaking her head.

"I don't get it," Addy said.

"Never mind, sweetie," Nina urged. "You pick."

Addy shrugged, bent over slightly, and placed her hands on the keyboard. In a slow motion, her fingers glided gently over the keys, as if she were barely touching them, delicately, feathery, like she was handling a newborn chick for the first time. But what came out of her motions was nothing less than spectacular. The music soared then lowered, rose then fell again. Addy was in a world of her own and she never opened her eyes. It was as if her fingers were possessed by those of a great composer. No one spoke. No one *could* speak. The room was mesmerized by her gift. When she was finished, she lifted her hands as if they had been dipped in liquid gold. She opened her eyes and sat up straight. The silence was deafening and then everyone began to clap.

My god, I'd forgotten how gifted she was, Nina thought. *No formal training and she's able to play by ear like that. Unbelievable.* She rose from the sofa and hugged her daughter. "Thank you, sweetie, that was magnificent. Truly. Happy Thanksgiving," and she kissed her on her cheek.

Addy got down from the bench, curtseyed, then ran into the kitchen. Noah saw her leave, jumped down and joined her.

"She really is amazing, that girl," Kelly said to Nina, walking over to her and grabbing her hand with a squeeze. "You're very lucky. Most adopted kids don't come with such qualities. I'm so happy for you." She hesitated before continuing. "Her adoption was a very fortunate circumstance. You all are the perfect *family*!" The emphasis on 'family' was unmistakable. She walked to the bar and refilled her drink. She drank half of it even before leaving the bar then topped it off once again. Nina felt maybe Kelly was hiding another meaning behind that. She didn't see the look Jack and Kelly gave each other.

"Yes, you're right," Nina said. "We're very blessed. We have been for 10 years now." She raised her glass to Owen in a silent 'thank you'. She also didn't see the look Jack and *Owen* gave each other.

"My husband, the brilliant lawyer," Kelly said, wrapping her arm inside Owen's. "He's really a miracle worker, isn't that right, honey?" Kelly was steadying herself in Owen's arms.

Jack tensed, thinking Kelly was on the brink of maybe taking this conversation too far. He stood and started to say something.

"He's always there to make sure other people get exactly what they want," Kelly continued. "*Other people*," she reiterated.

"Honey, I just do my job and make the best of everything, okay? Maybe you should have some coffee next?" Owen said. Clearly, he didn't want this conversation to go any further either.

"Carmen," Jack called out, "could you please bring us all some coffee? Thank you."

"I don't need coffee. I'm fine," Kelly spat. "What is everyone so afraid of? It's time we talked about it, don't you think? I don't want to keep this anymore."

Nina had a flashback to the night she heard Owen and Kelly in their guest suite.

"*.... she deserves to know...*" Kelly
"*.... will break her heart...*" Owen
"*.... not keeping...secret...any longer...*" Kelly

But that was *Kelly* wanting to tell someone something, not Owen. At the time, Nina was certain the person they were talking about was Kelly's mother, Evelyn. Was this about someone different? Nina looked at Jack to help fill in the blanks, but he avoided her gaze.

"Kelly, let's not do this tonight, okay? You've had a little too much to drink and besides, this is a nice gathering in your best friend's house. We don't want anything to spoil our fun, do we?" Owen said, eyebrows raised, coaxing Kelly by the arm. He tried to reach to take her drink from her, but she jerked her arm away too fast and some of the orange-colored liquid sloshed out on the creamy rug. "Shit, Kelly," Owen said, setting his drink on the mantle. He pulled out a handkerchief and started dabbing the stain.

Nina and Jack stood up as if electrically shocked. "Carmen! Please bring a wet towel and some baking soda," Nina called out. The doorbell chimed throughout the house and Jack went to open the door.

"Oh, Nina, I'm so sorry," Kelly said, regretfully. "I…didn't mean…"

"Shhh. It's okay. Remember, I have two kids under thirteen. Messes are a daily thing in this house. Trust me. It's fine."

But things weren't fine. Nina couldn't suppress the thought in her head that there were a couple of things that needed to be said and she was the only one in the dark. Was Jack aware of whatever it was that was going on? Kelly's conversation tip-toed around the adoption and Jack and Owen never really divulged anything from that time. From Jack's mouth, Nina knew the birth parents had died in some accident but was there another family member who wanted Addy back or something? Was that even possible after all these years? Nina shivered. *Over my dead body,* she thought.

"Darling! How are you? Happy Thanksgiving and all that!"

Willa stood in the foyer overlooking the sunken den. She was dressed in silver from head to toe. She wore shiny-silvery palazzo pants that fell all the way to the marbled floor. Her metallic sequined top peeked from beneath a gleaming jacket with a raised collar, her tinsel-white hair immaculately styled fell over the collar onto her shoulders. She looked like an expensive candlestick. Jack closed the door behind her and made his way back to the den.

"Mother, hi!" Nina said, turning her attention from Carmen working on the now-peach colored stain to her mother. She stepped up onto the foyer to give Willa a hug.

"Look who I found outside lurking around like the Great Pumpkin." She stepped aside and there was Margo, dressed head to toe in orange and brown and looking every bit like a, well, pumpkin.

Nina's eyes grew wide at the sight. She left her mother's arms and went to hug Margo.

"Nina! Thank you so much for inviting me." She handed her a bottle of Screaming Eagle Cabernet.

"Thank you, Margo. Of course, you're welcome here anytime. Come everyone, I believe dinner's ready." She swooped her arm and waved her hand as if to shoo everyone to the dining room. Owen was still on his hands and knees with Carmen trying to erase his wife's spill. Kelly was standing far away on the other side of the fireplace looking mortified. "Owen, leave that. Carmen can finish up. Let's eat."

Owen got up and gathered Kelly, joining their arms, and guided her out of the den. Jack let them go ahead and took up the rear as everyone made their way to the dining room.

"Nina, a word?" Margo said.

"Certainly," she said. She waved Jack on. "We'll join everyone in a second."

"Do we need to sit," Nina asked, a little hesitant.

"No, not at all. I just wanted to update you on what has transpired with the nanny search."

Nina's heart leapt. "Oh? Good news, I hope."

"Most definitely," Margo assured her. "In fact, I feel it's very good news. I already have sixteen resumes and out of those I've selected eight for interviews."

Nina was shocked. "Sixteen? Really? Already! Wow. I can't believe it. That's…that's wonderful. And eight interviews? Margo…. this is terrific news. Honestly."

Margo smiled, pleased. "Yes, I think so, too. Those eight candidates have remarkable credentials so I'm feeling very confident your nanny is somewhere in that group."

"Wow," Nina said again. "So, when are the interviews starting? Sometime next week, I suppose."

"Oh, no. Tomorrow. My first one is at 11:30 in the morning. And then the rest are spread out over the next couple of weeks. And we'll probably have a few more during that time, as well."

Nina was taken aback. This was happening so much quicker than she could've imagined. Was she ready for this? She'd have to be. She committed to doing this. To Margo, to Jack, to her kids, to her career. To herself. Yes. She was ready. *Ready as I'll ever be.*

"Margo, that's fantastic. I'm impressed, really. Great work. I was kind of nervous with all the accomplishments and qualifications I was looking for, it would be tough to find someone with everything."

Margo's heart skipped a beat. "What *we* are looking for," Margo corrected. "This is for both of us, remember."

"You're right. You're absolutely right." Nina's smile was big and genuine. "Come on, let's go join the others and tell them the great news. They are going to be just as excited as *we* are. And Kelly is going to just love this wine," she held up the Cabernet. They started heading towards the dining room.

Margo breathed a sigh of relief. So far, she had gotten away with editing the nanny advertisement. It absolutely had to happen, and Margo wasn't proud of what she had done but what she did was for the greater good. Sad, but necessary.

LONG AFTER WILLA AND MARGO HAD LEFT, KELLY AND OWEN DECIDED TO crash at Nina's, mainly because the drinks flowed at dinner, and no one was in any shape to drive.

"Oh, just stay," Nina said to a protesting Kelly. "Neither one of you are in any condition to get behind a wheel tonight."

"THAT is probably more dangerous," Kelly said, pointing to the tall, curved staircase.

"We accept, thank you," Owen said, taking Kelly's arm. "We know the way."

"Have a good night," Nina said. Everyone retired for the evening.

Jack couldn't sleep. His mind was still full of thoughts from Kelly's near-disaster conversation before dinner.

"What is everyone so afraid of? It's time we talked about it, don't you think? I don't want to keep this anymore."

Damn. She had come *thisclose* to ruining everything. Jack rubbed his eyes. He rolled over and touched his phone. It lit up 3:20am. He swung his legs over and got out of bed. Nina was on her side facing away from him. He needed something to help him sleep so he headed downstairs. Maybe some warm milk. *Does that really work? We're about to find out.*

Once in the kitchen, he started heating up his milk when he heard a little noise behind him. He turned.

Kelly.

"Can't sleep either?" she asked.

He turned back to his milk. "No."

She came up next to him and looked in the pot. "Enough for two?"

Jack closed his eyes and took a deep breath. She was wearing Owen's dress shirt and she smelled like him. Jack wasn't in the mood to sit up and talk to Kelly right now. But he couldn't help himself.

"Dammit, Kelly. What was that about tonight? You almost ruined everything."

"Jack.... I...."

"Are you trying to get Nina to hate me or divorce me?"

Kelly was taken aback. "Jack, no! I'm sorry. I had too much to drink and quite honestly, I'm tired of keeping this from my best friend. Do you know how difficult that is?"

Jack pulled a face and looked at her.

"Okay. That was a dumb question. Of course, you do. I'm sure it's just as tough on you, probably tougher."

Jack turned back to his milk and stirred.

Kelly came up and hugged Jack from behind. "I'm sorry, Jack. I really am. I'd never do anything to hurt you guys on purpose." She leaned her cheek on his back. "Can you forgive me?" She squeezed his waist tighter.

Jack slowly turned around, her hands still around his waist. Kelly looked up into Jack's eyes. His long eyelashes fluttered. She could feel his hardness between them. Jack took a deep breath and swallowed.

"I love her, you know."

"I know you do." Her breasts raised and lowered with short, quick breaths.

Like a flash fire, he cupped her ass with his hands and lifted her off the floor. He carried her over to the island and sat her down on the cold marble. He pushed down his boxer shorts and entered her immediately. Her hands were clasped behind his neck as he thrust into her over and over, the white-hot searing pain pierced though her every nerve. They rode the wave over and over until it crashed on them, thrashing them into a velvety, wet ecstasy.

Jack lowered his head, sweat slowly dripped off his brow.

It was over. He looked at Kelly, shook his head and left.

Kelly got down from the island and slowly walked over to the stove. She turned off the eye and looked into the pot.

It's ruined, she thought. And she started to cry.

CHAPTER EIGHTEEN

December

Robin Kemble was excited. And fidgety. And anxious. And literally about to throw up. But she didn't come all this way from the U.K. to throw up.

I'll go with excited, she decided.

She had only been living in New York for a short time, but she already hated it. From the get-go, she never adjusted to the hustle and bustle and freneticism of the city. It was a far cry from her hometown of Grimsby in Lincolnshire, England.

Robin shivered at the memory.

Grimsby lived up to its name. It was the grimmest place on earth as far as she was concerned. Thick with grit and grime. Her mum was the town slag, charging most of the local men a day's wages to experience her vast talents. "A pound for a pound", she would explain to Robin, and she would laugh at her bawdy joke. Robin never found it as funny. Sometimes, the situations in her mother's bedroom seeped out into other rooms and Robin found herself smack in the middle of it all. In fact, the whole situation was despicable and horrific, and Robin did all she could to protect herself and her sister, Caryn.

Caryn was younger than Robin but more mature by years. They were opposites in almost every way: where Caryn was grounded, Robin was a dreamer; where Caryn was homely and awkward, Robin's ethereal beauty and grace were outward; and while Caryn was content being silent and still and alone, Robin needed to be active and rambunctious and couldn't sit still for long. She had to keep moving.

Robin's reasons for wanting to leave Grimsby were beyond anything she could've fathomed but she knew she had to. She convinced herself God wanted her to leave so she got it in her mind it was the right thing to do.

So, one day, Robin planned her escape, but sadly, that did not include Caryn.

"Why is this so important to you?" Caryn asked.

Robin was not ready to tell Caryn everything, so she treaded lightly and relied on her experience with reading so much fiction. "Because there's so much more out there for me. For us. There's love and light and bliss." She paused. "And glamour," she smiled. "Please?" Robin looked hopeful,

"I need to stay with our mum," Caryn said, not really knowing why she needed to stay except that something in her bones told her it's what she must do.

"Caryn, no! You must come with me! You'll decay here with the lot of them! There's so much more of a world out there than what you know of here. Look!" Robin would show Caryn her books by Nina Travers, Willa Greyson, and Barbara Cartland.

"Don't be daft, Robin. They write fiction and of worlds and lives that don't exist."

"Maybe so," Robin said, straightening up. "But there's still some truth in their words. They can't make up everything. They have to ground their books on some familiarity. Something in their lives is the basis to their stories. And I believe there is such beauty and grandness out there. Hell, even a traipse to Blackpool would be better than lagging in Grimsby," Robin said with a smirk.

Caryn laughed. "You are a funny girl, Robin. And a dreamer." Her laughter faded. "But I cannot go with you. I'm sorry, but our mum needs…"

"Our mum needs to stop shagging around and remember she has a family to take care of!" Robin exploded.

Caryn cowered back. "Robin, I…"

"No!" Robin interrupted. "I'm going. With or without you but I really hope it's with. You will not survive here. Our mum will see to that."

"Maybe," Caryn whispered. "But I cannot leave her. You go. You need to go. And I need to stay. It is God's will. Deep down, you know this is how it's to be."

Robin could not argue with God. As opposite as they were, the one thing they agreed on was that God was the one who made all the decisions, whether they agreed with them or not.

And so, she left. Robin's journey to the United States began and it was long and arduous and nearly broke her, but she survived and made the most of things. Florida was a good place to land, and so Robin decided to settle down.

But God had other plans.

THAT WAS WELL OVER A DECADE AGO AND NOW ROBIN FOUND HERSELF IN THE largest city in the world, surrounded by grit and grime once again. Only this time, it was backlit by invigorating reds, whites, and yellows: flashing lights and billowing subway steam and zooming taxis, all erupting before her very eyes.

She was on a mission. A mission she never imagined would come. She had an interview in a couple weeks for a job she had to get. She sat on a park bench and looked at the fiction in her hands: *A Dutiful Wife* by Nina Travers. *Full circle,* she smiled. She put the book down. *All my careful planning over the past few years has come to this,* she thought. *I have created a new look, a new history, and a new truth.*

And truth, as they say, is stranger than fiction.

CHAPTER NINETEEN

December 13, 2021

The next two weeks flew by. Margo couldn't believe how fast things were coming together. Since Thanksgiving, she had received another fourteen resumes and had narrowed those down to five. She had already interviewed almost a dozen candidates and was quite disappointed in the majority. She was sure that by now she would have found the perfect nanny for the Travers. Her nerves were starting to fray and her heart began to race. She reached into her purse and pulled out an orange medicine bottle, opened it and popped a little pink pill. She grabbed a bottled water from her fridge and swallowed the pill down. She sat down in her chair and closed her eyes, willing the medicine to take quick effect.

Did I cut out too much of the requirements that all I'm getting now is dreck? What if I've screwed this up? She couldn't think about that right now. She had two candidates coming in today for interviews and she really needed to focus.

She turned on her computer and her Google News homepage popped up. She scrolled down till she found what she was looking for and clicked on the link. One more click and she was in. And there it was. The list. The most recent top 25 bestselling books and their authors. And at the top of that list sat three names that made her catch her breath: Rachel Meadows. Leslie Fontaine. Rebecca Sanchez. The last two names in the top ten were Willa Greyson and Carly Kaufman.

Margo felt sick. These names used to never be ranked that high, until Nina forfeited her spot, then these vulturous writers pounced on her like a panther to prey. *This can't be happening. We have come too far to let these mediocre wordsmiths have all the glory!* Margo slammed her computer shut. She put her elbows on her desk and clasped her hands above her bowed head.

What am I to do? What if I can't find a nanny in time? Nina's downfall will continue, and I'll be ruined.

The names of authors flooded Margo's mind over and over and over, blending and echoing in her brain, bouncing from one side of her skull to the other and back again, ricocheting and getting louder and louder until she could take it no more! She put her fingers on her temples. It was too much.

She clinched her jaws and took three deep, controlled breaths. She was calming down now.

And she knew what needed to be done.

CHAPTER TWENTY

December 13, 2021

It was December and the kids were driving Nina crazy. With the weather being so cold with the occasional snow, Addy and Noah had spent an abnormal amount of time indoors.

There was some reprieve, though. On days like today, Jack would go into the city and take Addy for her Portuguese lessons. *"Adeus mãe. Eu vou te ver esta tarde"*, she would say, which Nina found out was Addy telling her bye and she'd see her this afternoon. "Don't forget to text me when you get there," Nina yelled to Addy, who gave a thumbs up before closing the door. Then Noah would run around the house like a little headless chicken with no direction and no goal in sight. Except to drive Nina crazier. Once he did all that, he would tire himself out then go take a nap.

Nina found the sudden quiet calming. And yet, there was so much to do. Willa's book launch was soon and taking up 80% of her time. It had to be perfect because this was the first time Nina had put herself in the view of the public since she crashed on the charts. This party made her more nervous for herself than it did for her mother.

There were the gift bags to prepare, the band and caterers to coordinate, the cleaners to schedule, the decorating and wait staff to hire, the RSVPs to tally.

And she only had a month to finalized it all. And this was just for the *party*. None of this included normal day-to-day chores around the house or getting the children ready for all their various activities. For someone who never wanted a nanny, suddenly hiring one moved to the top of her list. *Oh, the irony,* she thought.

In addition, the RSVPs for Willa's launch party were coming in fast and furious. Anyone who was someone in the literary world knew an invitation to the home of Nina Travers, was an invite not to be ignored.

There were only a couple of regrets but there was one in particular that made Nina's skin crawl. It was from Rachel Meadows, the one sitting at the top of the charts at Nina's expense. Nina looked at Rachel's RSVP card in her hand.

Dear Nina.

It's sweet of you to invite me to a party you think I would even bother to attend. Why on earth would I come to a lame-o gathering of blue-haired crones celebrating a close-to-death writer who has no business writing about sexual escapades? That turns my stomach. I appreciate you thinking of me, but I will be having my own party that evening celebrating my newest release in two months. If you get bored, you should come over and see a real party! Hope to see you on the bestseller list soon.

But probably not! lmao

Love, Rachel

Nina crushed the RSVP in her hands and threw it in the trash can with a huff. "What a *bitch*!" Nina said. "Ughhh!" Rachel Meadows had no business being on the top of the bestseller list - or any list for that matter. Unless it was a list of people that needed to.... Nina couldn't finish the thought.

Nina huffed her annoyance. She knew Rachel was number one simply because Nina had stopped writing and left the door wide open for others to come in and steal her crown. *But that won't last much longer,* Nina vowed. She knew she should be cool about it, but what she really wanted to do was to rip Rachel's eyes out, nerve by nerve.

I will *be back on top. No matter what it takes!*

CHAPTER TWENTY-ONE

December 13, 2021

Jack heard the back door slam shut. *Nina must've left.*

He couldn't help but overhear Nina's frustration and it broke his heart. She was such a dedicated and passionate writer, and nothing could've prepared her for when she took a slide backwards in her career. She didn't deserve what came her way. No one did, but then again, Jack was completely biased when it came to his wife.

He was relieved nothing more came of the conversation Kelly had drunkenly started on Thanksgiving but that didn't mean he could hold the secret much longer. *But which secret?* Jack thought, heavily. *There are so many I can't keep them straight nor what person knows which one.* He sighed. For now, he had to settle on one. Since Kelly - and her mouth - had gone to stay with her parents for the Christmas holidays, Jack felt safe. For the moment, at least. But knowing Kelly, one more visit with her friend *José Cuervo* and all bets were off. No, he had to get to Nina before that happened. He had planned on telling her tonight but something she read upset her and she stormed out of the house, got in her car, and sped off.

Jack moved into the kitchen where Nina had been sitting at the table. He opened the cabinet hiding the trash can and pulled out a balled up crumpled piece of card stock. It was an RSVP to Willa's book launch party. He unfolded the ball and read the response written on the card. He couldn't believe what he was reading. How could Rachel be so cold? So insensitive? Jack felt his blood pressure rise. He could feel his heart beating faster and he touched his hand to his chest. He closed his eyes. *Breathe, Jack. Breathe.* He let his inner voice try to calm him down. *Don't let her get to you. Just keep breathing. You need to protect your family.*

He loved his family and would do anything for them. *It's just better they don't know everything I've had to do.*

But Rachel Meadows was a different story. And Jack knew one thing was certain. *Something had to be done.* He pulled out his phone and called Owen.

Owen answered. "Hey, Jack, what's up?"

Jack was quiet for a minute. When he spoke, Owen's blood ran cold.

"There's this girl. Rachel Meadows...."

CHAPTER TWENTY-TWO

December 15, 2021

Margo put her drink down on her desk. The gin this morning was going down easier than normal and that wasn't a good thing. She emptied her glass, screwed the top back on the bottle and put the bottle and the glass in her bottom drawer.

She looked down at her fingers and they were raw from where she had been biting the nails to the quick. She squeezed some lotion on her hands and rubbed furiously. Her nerves were starting to get the best of her, but today was going to be a good day. *I hope.* She had an errand to run, and she had an interview with Robin Kemble, a candidate whose resume was stellar. Robin had moved from the U.K. not too long ago and came with amazing credentials and references. Margo had a good feeling about this one.

Both items on Margo's list today could be game changers. At least that's what she was counting on. She looked at her watch. 9:10am. She had exactly thirty minutes. And then Robin's interview was at noon. To her calculations, Margo figured her life would either be better or much, much worse by 1:00pm this afternoon.

She grabbed her purse and locked her office door. She headed down the flight of steps and into the freezing December winds. Crowds on the sidewalks were already swarming with tourists and shoppers doing their holiday shopping. Margo didn't celebrate Christmas, but she appreciated how the city transformed into one of the most magical, enchanting places on earth during this time of year. She paused and sucked in a deep breath, the coldness filling her nostrils and head. Margo looked to her left and saw the traffic was heavy. She pulled up the hood on her outfit and started walking. At the corner, she hailed a cab, told the cabbie her destination and she was on her way. Oddly, her heart wasn't pounding like it should be. Maybe the gin helped but, in her mind, Margo also knew what she was doing was for the greater good. It was a necessary act. *I just hope it works,* she thought.

Ten minutes later, she was at her destination. She paid the cabbie, got out and walked the rest of the way. In front of her, she saw who she was looking for. She stopped and took a deep breath and drew herself fully erect. *This is it.*

Then she kept walking towards her target.

CHAPTER TWENTY-THREE

December 15, 2021

Everything was gone. His wife. His children. His homes. His career. *My life,* Harris Markham thought, his bowed head being held in his hands. *Gone.* As freezing as it was outside in December in Manhattan, Harris Markham felt nothing. He was detached to everything around him. And numb to everything inside him.

He sat on a bench under a bus stop clutching a paper bag, the world whizzed by him, oblivious to his loss, his pain. *Margo.* It had started with her eliminating him as a client.

But then he discovered later Margo had dropped all her clients except for Nina Travers and Willa Greyson. Even cash cows Rachel Meadows and Gregory Wynn. But they seemed to be flourishing, taking over spots on the bestseller lists where Harris Markham's name should've been, but he couldn't compete. Not with them. They had fallback careers unlike Harris. And they didn't have families like Harris either. No one to suck their lives dry. Harris felt like he could be doing much better but wasn't, no thanks to them.

He decided then they were now the enemy.

That was more than three years ago. It took that long for everything to fall apart. He tried writing again but nothing came close to the success of his *Poison Pen* series. He did some side work as a journalist for *The City Ledger* newspaper but during the pandemic he was one of the first to be laid off.

His bank account was empty, his cars were repossessed and his two homes, including the Hamptons house, went into foreclosure. After the divorce, Brenda remarried, and she took the kids and moved to Greenwich.

And now, Harris Markham sat on a cold, metal bench, trying to keep warm under a bus stop shelter. Besides the clothes on his back, the paper bag and what was in it were his only possessions. He was dirty and his clothes were ragged. He hadn't had a proper shower in nine days, and he was sure he smelled like rotted eggs. People were looking at him like he was a threat to their appearance, like if they got within a foot of him, his stink and filth would rub off on their Chanel coats and Gucci shoes. They stepped outside the shelter risking cold over contamination.

He held the paper bag tighter to his stomach and he could feel its contents. Hard. Cold. Stiff. He looked around but no one was paying him any mind. He opened the bag and what he saw wasn't alcohol. Oh, how he wished it was a bottle of Blanton's. But instead, he was staring into the steel grey barrel of a pistol. A car honked its horn and he jumped. He looked up and around and figured if he did it here, the mess would be contained within the bus shelter. He didn't want anyone else to have to suffer around him if they were caught up and covered in the crossfire of the devastation.

He had one last thought. He pulled out his wallet and opened it to the pictures. There was a picture of Brenda and him and their two children, Charlie and Lilly. They were at the beach outside their Hampton home and the sun was shining and the waves were crashing behind them. It was taken in late Spring four years ago when everything was right. When everything was perfect. But then, like the waves behind them, everything came crashing down. His heart broke all over again looking at the picture, but he wouldn't cry. He was done crying for the family that no longer wanted anything to do with him. Brenda had brainwashed the children into thinking he had left them, and they were too young to realize daddy loved them beyond measure, so they believed what they heard and began a new life with a new father and moved on with their lives. *Everyone has moved on with their lives except me,* he thought wearily. *But now, I'm done. And I can move on. I can stop the pain and move on - to whatever awaits.*

He put his wallet away and reached into the bag. Just to make sure he was still going unnoticed, he glanced around the shelter. No one inside. No one near the -

But then something caught the corner of his eye when he glanced outside the shelter. There! Walking fast. *It was her!* Where was she going? He needed a closer look. Harris closed the paper bag and stood up, exiting the shelter as people parted to let him pass. He put the paper bag and gun in his coat pocket.

He followed behind her as close as he could without being seen but it was hard because his raggedy appearance stood out in the crowd of designer outfits on the busy sidewalk. The chilly wind blew hard against him as he walked, and he was thankful he was downwind. *That bitch could probably smell me a mile away.* He saw her stop and look around. He ducked behind a light post.

He peered around and she continued to walk. Faster. She was in a hurry for something. She had her phone out. What was she doing? And then she stopped again. Harris froze in his tracks, and someone bumped into him. But the bustling, noisy crowd kept moving around them. They exchanged heated words never heard and middle fingers never seen.

He saw her ahead near the intersection and the closer he got, the clearer his head got. *Is this for real? Is this opportunity really in front of me?* He couldn't believe his good fortune or timing. "Holy shit," he whispered to himself. He was now standing right behind her. Realizing he has nothing left to lose, he closed his eyes and prayed for a miracle.

He reached out his hands to touch her.

CHAPTER TWENTY-FOUR

December 15, 2021

When Margo got back to her office, she was shaking like a leaf. She ran up the stairs, slammed the door behind her and went right to her bottom drawer. She filled the glass halfway with the clear liquid and swallowed without taking a breath. It was difficult to get the shaking glass to her mouth without the liquid sloshing out too much, but she managed. Then she repeated the process.

She dropped down into her chair and threw her hands on her head.

What have I done? Have I just made things worse than they are already? The events of the morning replayed in her head until she felt dizzy. Too quickly, she could feel the bile rising in her throat and she bent over the trashcan and threw up, the alcohol burning her nostrils. She wiped her mouth with a tissue and ran into the bathroom. One of the perks of paying $8,000 a month for this office, it came with a bathroom. She opened the medicine chest, grabbed some mouthwash, and rinsed her mouth out and spit in the sink. Her hands rested on either side of the sink, and she looked in the mirror.

A stranger was staring back at her.

"Who *are* you?" she asked herself. She yanked her glasses off and rinsed her face off with cold water. She put the mouthwash back in the cabinet and took out an orange medication bottle and threw two pink pills in her mouth.

"Hello?" a voice called out.

Margo turned her head. *Who was that?*

'Hello? Margo Flagg?" the voice said in a British accent

Margo looked at her watch. 11:58am. *Shit. My interview.* She closed her eyes to try to remember who it was with. Rhonda. Roselyn. *Robin.* Robin Kemble. The girl from the U.K.

"Be right out," she called. She checked herself in the mirror. Reaching back into the cabinet, she took out a lipstick and applied a light covering. She wet her fingers and styled her hair quickly then placed her glasses on her face and stood up straight. Good enough.

"Coming, Robin," Margo said, and she stepped out into the office.

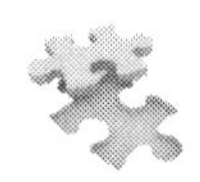

The interview was going exceptionally well. At first, Margo was worried she wouldn't be steady enough to have a professional conversation, but Margo was an expert at dealing with problems and unusual situations and this one, after the morning she had, was certainly no exception. At first glance, Margo noticed Robin was a bit uneasy. Or was it something else? Margo would try to break it down. She crossed her legs behind her desk, opened her file, looked over Robin's resume and began.

Robin's British accent was light and musical. If anyone asked Margo to describe it, she would use words like "lovely", "cheery" and "makes you want to drink tea from real china". It lilted through the office like a dragon-fly, raising and lowering gently. At once, Margo liked Robin although the beautiful, full-figured woman who sat across from her resembled more Melissa McCarthy than Mary Poppins.

One thing Margo found out the gate was that Robin Kemble was very passionate about her profession. She even *looked* happy. She was overweight with ruddy cheeks. *Chubby and jolly,* Margo thought. *Like a female Santa Claus.* She wore a sweater that was a size too small and a scarf that was a size too big. Her black dress pants were too short, but her rubber boots covered that slight flaw.

An hour later, Margo was offering the job to a stunned Robin.

"I can't...I simply cannot believe it! Oh, this is wonderful! I can't thank you enough, Ms. Flagg!"

"Margo. Call me Margo. You're going to be working for my number one client. You're now considered *mishpacha*."

"I'm sorry. Mish what?" Robin asked, bewildered.

Margo laughed. "I'm sorry, hon. Old Yiddish term. *Mishpacha*. It means 'family'"

Robin's mouth grew into a wide grin, her dimples were deep and rosy. "Mishpacha," Robin said, trying the word on for size. "I like it." The grin stayed on her face.

"So, I assume you accept the offer," Margo asked tentatively.

"Oh, yes!" Robin replied. "Most definitely. I accept and I can start immediately!" Robin's happiness was genuine, and Margo was pleased. *Nina will be thrilled*, Margo thought.

"Obviously you'll be living with the family in Connecticut - " Margo heard an audible gasp from Robin "- so if you have an apartment here, we're prepared to buy you out of your lease, if that's okay. We just feel staying with the family you're working for, being closer to them, will benefit everyone involved and -"

"That's absolutely fine," Robin interrupted, shaking her head in agreement. "I'm prepared to go wherever needed. For the family, of course," Robin said.

"Perfect!" Margo replied. "Now, I need to go over a few details about the family you'll be working for so - " she looked at her watch. 1:17pm. "- how about we have a working lunch? Does that sound okay to you? We can cover what I need to go over with you and I can answer any questions you may have. Are you hungry?" Margo got up from her desk and collected her files. As she headed to get her coat, she noticed Robin smiling but her eyes were wet with tears.

"Robin, dear, are you okay?"

"Yes.... I'm fine, thank you. It's just..." she shook her head.

"It's just what?" Margo coaxed.

"I just.... I can't believe this is happening. In a good way, I mean. Things have been different since I left the Walker's - that's the family I worked for in London. The kids grew up and I was no longer needed. I felt aimless, like I had no purpose in life anymore. Being a caregiver for children was all I knew and all I wanted to do with my life." She paused and took a breath.

"Do you know what it's like to have no one to validate your life? No one to say, "you're doing a great job!" she paused. "It's lonely and a bit sad. But today…today was the validation I was looking for." Robin looked at Margo. "Do you know the book *The Hero with a Thousand Faces* by Joseph Campbell?"

Margo knew it well. It was one of her favorite books of all time. "Of course! It's magnificent. In fact…" she moved to behind her desk to the bookshelves. On a shelf sat a hardbound copy of *The Hero with a Thousand Faces*.

"Extraordinary! Well, it was my mother's favorite, too. And that author said something once. He said, "We must let go of the life we planned, so as to accept the one that is waiting for us." I believe, in my heart of hearts that this job was waiting for me. And I, for it."

Margo could feel her heart swell. "You're right. That *is* extraordinary. And I'm so glad we met, Robin. Which reminds me, I need to cancel all of my other interviews!" She made a note in her phone.

Robin smiled. Dimples. "And Connecticut! Oh, my goodness, I can't believe I'll be getting out of this city! People here are bloody mad!"

Margo chuckled. "They can be a little aggressive, that's for sure."

"It's not just the people out and about, it's the drivers. Goodness! I just don't feel safe here anymore. Today, just before this interview, there was a huge accident involving a coach and I think someone was killed. It was a mess." Robin closed her eyes and shook her head in sorrow. She raised her right hand and made the sign of the cross across her chest.

Margo froze. An accident. And Robin was a witness. Margo thought back to the beginning of the interview and remembered Robin was a bit shaky but maybe that was Margo not seeing quite clearly herself after swigging the gin. Margo blinked. She was happy the interview had gone as well as it had, accident or not. It only proved that Robin was excellent at composing herself in a crisis. Robin spoke of validation, well, this certainly validated Margo's decision to hire Robin.

"Wow, I am sorry you had to be a part of all that. And I feel bad for the person involved. I really do." Margo paused.

"The city can be a bit unpredictable," Robin nodded in agreement. "Not that children can be predicted."

Margo laughed, trying to lighten the mood. "But Connecticut should be a little more peaceful. So, what do you say? Shall we go grab a bite?"

Those dimples again. "Let's go," Robin said.

"I think this is the beginning of a beautiful friendship," Margo said. "I have a really good feeling about this."

The City Li

Friday, December 16, 2021

Author dies in bus accident

Local author, Rachel Meadows, was killed Thursday when she fell from a curb at a crosswalk at the intersection of Grand and 42nd Streets and was struck by an oncoming bus. She was 24 years old. The independent author, once a client of the formidable agent Margo Flagg, was writer of such bestselling thrillers including "The Girls in the Mirror", "Mother, May I?" and "Shock Value". Meadows was in the finishing stages of her 9th book when she died. Her fans, known as "Meadowfiles", have laid flowers, photos and other mementos at the site. "She was a smart and talented author with a huge following and we will miss her terribly", said her sister Kiersten Meadows Anderson. "We will make sure her next book will be published in her memory." A spokesperson for the the NYPD said "this was a gruesome accident" and yet "another casualty of the busyness of the city." Police do not suspect foul play.

Rer
foll
imp

The
that
rela
the
beh
of a
exp
in l
its
beh
con
or v

It m
tota

CHAPTER TWENTY-FIVE

December 16, 2021

Even though she was an author, Nina had rarely been at a loss for words but after Jack showed her the online news article about Rachel Meadows' death, all she could say was "what a shame such a bright, young author's life and future was cut short". But she said it through her teeth. But she had said it in case anyone else was listening. Or was it to convince herself she wasn't a bad person?

But Nina had another reason to not say anything else: selfishly she had wanted Rachel Meadows out of her life and now, ironically, she was. And in such a horrific way. Nina sighed. Part of Nina, the motherly, nurturing side, felt horrible for Rachel and her friends and family and how much she would be missed by her fans. But the other side of Nina, the one that was jarred by the hateful RSVP and the constant reminders by her husband, mother, and agent that Rachel was always on top of the bestsellers list, no thanks to her - *that* Nina wanted Rachel dead. So, Nina was torn. She was sad Rachel was dead, but she also couldn't help but feel a little relief knowing that her pathway back to the top of the charts just got a little easier.

"Nina!" She scolded herself. "Stop it! You cannot think this way." Her phone rang. She snapped to attention. It was Margo.

"Margo, hi. I just heard the news. So horrible. Poor Rachel." *Did that sound sincere?*

"Yes, I know. Poor dear," Margo replied. *Did that sound sincere?* "How are you doing?"

"I'm good. We're all good. I'm all done with my Christmas shopping and - oh, that reminds me! I'm having a little gathering on Christmas morning after the kids open their gifts. I know Christmas isn't that big of a deal to you, but we'd love to have you come over. Just for a light breakfast and mimosas."

"I'd be glad to, thank you," Margo said. "But I have some news and I'd like to stop by this afternoon if that's okay with you. Say noon?"

"Uh, sure. Noon is fine. See you then."

They hung up and Nina pursed her lips. "Hmmm. Wonder what that's about?" She walked to the kitchen island and put her palms on the countertop.

"What's what about?" Jack asked, coming up behind Nina and wrapping his arms around her. Nina was surprised at his impromptu show of affection but didn't flinch as she leaned into his arms in familiarity.

"Oh, Margo wants to stop by this afternoon with some news. Probably about the nanny position. She's probably hit another dead-end with the candidates," Nina sighed.

"Have faith, my dear. Things will work out." He spun her around and embraced her tight. "Trust me. She'll find you someone soon and then all things will be right again."

Nina was a little taken aback by Jack's sudden closeness since it had been such unaccustomed territory for a few months now, but she wasn't going to deny it felt good. Really good. But she couldn't help but think how odd today was shaping up to be: first Rachel's death and now Jack acting...*different*.

"I wish I had your confidence," she said.

"Hey. Didn't I hear you in your office last night on your computer? Were you doing some preliminary writing or were you just typing out recipes?" he grinned. When he smiled and looked at her with those brown eyes and long eyelashes, Nina melted. She always loved Jack's long eyelashes. Every time he ran and would perspire, the tiniest droplets of sweat from his forehead would glide down and get caught on his lashes, like dew on blades of grass.

His lashes were so long she wondered if they fluttered against the lenses of his glasses.

She laughed. "I don't cook. No, no, not recipes. God forbid. I was actually typing up a new outline for the book." She closed her eyes and shrugged. "Just some thoughts I had, that's all." She looked into his eyes. "But it felt *good,* you know? It was like I never stopped writing. I don't know what it was, but it felt really, really nice." She rested her head on his chest and could feel his heart beating. It seemed to be beating faster. She hugged Jack closer, the warmth of his body melding into her. She felt his hardness between them and looked up. He was smiling back at her.

"God, this is so cheesy," he said, laughing. "I feel like I'm on a first date with you."

"I sure hope not!" Nina said. "I remember our first date vividly. M&M bar, you lost a hundred bucks to me at pool, I stabbed my finger with a dart, we had to go to the ER for me to get a tetanus shot and *then* we had a flat tire on the way home. It wasn't romantic in the least! Oh god, how did we survive past that?" She was laughing.

Jack looked up at the ceiling amazed. "Thing is, we *did* survive it. And we've survived worse." His voice dropped to a more serious tone. He lifted her chin and face upward. "And we'll get past this. I promise." He bent down and kissed her gently. Then harder, and she pushed herself into him.

This is it. This was what I've been waiting for. All this time and now it's here, Nina thought. She was with her husband, the man she loved with every fiber in her body. It had been so long…

Jack swooped her up in his arms and carried her towards the sofa. He laid her down gently onto the creamy cashmere. He pulled his head back suddenly remembering. "The kids?"

"Out. It's Saturday so the staff's off. We have the house to ourselves," she whispered into his ear.

He looked at his watch. 11:10am. "And Margo's not due until noon?"

"Yup."

And there, in their empty home, for the first time in what seemed like an eternity, they made love. Nina wasn't sure what put a spring in Jack's step since yesterday but whatever it was, she wasn't about to look a gift horse in the mouth.

CHAPTER TWENTY-SIX

December

At exactly 12:00pm on the dot, the doorbell rang.

Then it rang again.

Finally, Nina opened the door a little flushed, tucking in her blouse behind her. Margo stood there wide-eyed, not a greying hair out of place. Next to her stood a young woman, a couple inches taller than Margo.

"Margo, hi! Come on in....and who is this?"

"Nina. Hi." Margo acknowledged. "And hi to you, too, Jack," Margo waved over Nina's shoulder, spying Jack in the den. Margo grinned and Jack smiled, all teeth.

"Hello, Margo. Good to see you," he bounded over to the front door and pecked her on the cheek. "You're looking rather beautiful today."

Not used to this flirty side of Jack, Margo's chin dropped, her mouth still closed. "Let me take your coats." He noticed Margo's smelled like mothballs and cedar.

"Nina. Jack. I'd like you to meet Robin Kemble. Your new nanny."

Nina's mouth opened. "Our new.... really?" Margo had come through. And so quickly. And at least Robin didn't *look* like a serial killer. *Or Gisele Bündchen.*

"Hello," Robin said in her sweet British accent. "I'm thrilled to meet you both." Jack and Nina shook her hand over introductions. Nina noticed Robin's hand was a bit sweaty. She casually dried her hand on her slacks.

"Oh, sorry," Robin said, noticing. "I'm a bit nervous. Not the being a nanny part, oh no, I'm all good there. But it's getting to work for *the* Nina Travers. I'm a huge fan of your books. Truly."

Margo looked at Robin. "You didn't tell me you were a fan of Nina's."

"Well, when you told me over lunch the other day, I about choked on my sandwich, but I didn't want you to think I was a massive dingbat who was just here to work for *her*," she said excitedly, gesturing to Nina.

"Well, then, Nina, my dear, you get two for one today. A most excellent nanny *and* a big fan. Shall we sit?" Margo asked, gesturing towards the den.

"That's...awesome," Nina said slowly. "I'm sorry, but I'm still in a little bit of shock. I had no idea you were hired nor that you were coming over," she said still smiling, but glaring at Margo who just smiled back. "I would've kept the housekeeper around today to straighten up a bit." Nina liked Margo, but let's face it: she was a bit of a prude. Nina didn't need Margo to discover her and Jack's afternoon tryst.

As they neared the sofa, Nina noticed her bra on one of the cushions where she and Jack had been. She feared Margo would spy the lingerie, but Robin found the sofa and plopped herself down. She moved her hand slightly and Jack noticed she had shoved the bra behind the cushion. Margo hadn't noticed a thing. Jack grinned and Nina let her shoulders drop in relief. Nina smiled appreciatively at Robin.

"You have a lovely home, Mr. and Mrs. Travers. Blimey, but it's massive! I can't wait to explore it. Are the children here? I'd love to meet them if that's possible. Margo has told me nothing but wonderful things about the wee ones."

"I'll get us some drinks," Jack said and excused himself to the kitchen.

"Not at the moment, I'm afraid," Nina said. "They're both visiting friends."

"Well, I'm certainly looking forward to meeting with them and getting to know them. I'm sure we'll all get along famously."

Margo's phone rang. Her face went white. "Excuse me a minute," Margo said. She left the room to take the call. Nina heard the door to the library close.

"Robin, I wanted to thank you for…." Nina pulled out the bra Robin had hidden from Margo's sight. "Margo is very conservative and well, I just don't want her to get the wrong idea…."

"Say no more," Robin replied. "I learned all about Margo at lunch. I'm a quick learner and an excellent judge of character. I knew something like this would shock her and probably embarrass you so I just did what any good person would do."

"Well, I wouldn't be embarrassed, really. I just wouldn't want Margo to feel uncomfortable. You understand."

"Of course, Mrs. Travers. Of course."

"Nina, please. Call us Nina and Jack. If you're going to be staying with us taking care of our children, there should be no formalities, okay?"

"Okay…. Nina," Robin smiled, and Nina noticed her deep dimples.

Jack came back with four glasses of hot chocolate on a tray. He handed them out. "Where's Margo?" He set the tray down on the credenza.

"She had to take a call…. there she is."

Margo's face was no longer white. Instead, it was beet red, like she was angry.

"Everything okay?" Jack asked.

"Uhm…yeah. Everything is fine. Thanks. But I think we should get going. Robin?"

Robin and Nina stood up and started walking to the door. Jack got their coats.

"Robin will be staying here with you as discussed. She has agreed to the salary, and I have the signed NDA at the office. Her apartment lease has been paid off so she will be moving in here on Sunday. I have arranged transportation for her to be here by two o'clock. Is that satisfactory?"

"Yes, Margo. That is more than satisfactory," Nina was wondering what all the formality was about.

"Fine. Robin, we should go." Margo opened the door and headed outside.

Robin turned towards Jack and Nina. "It was a pleasure meeting you both and I look forward to being here on Sunday."

"Same here, Robin. We'll see you on Sunday. And we'll make sure the children are here for your arrival."

"Take my card with my number and please don't hesitate to call if you need anything between now and Sunday, okay?" Jack said, handing Robin his business card.

"Thank you. I will."

"Robin." Margo called impatiently from beside her car.

"Okay, then. Bye for now," and she scurried off behind Margo down the steps and towards Margo's car which was already started and put into drive.

Jack and Nina waved from the porch as Margo sped off, the gravel kicking up.

"Well, Robin seemed really great. But Margo? What the hell was *that* all about?" Jack asked.

"No idea," Nina replied. "But that phone call really messed her up." *Maybe that call was about Rachel's death. But why would Margo be so upset about that? There was certainly no love lost there.* She shook her head in confusion.

"Nooo idea," Nina repeated.

CHAPTER TWENTY-SEVEN

December

On Sunday, Robin showed up at the Travers' estate right at 2:00pm.

The limo pulled up to the house and parked under the porte-cochere. The driver unloaded Robin's two cases from the trunk and brought them up to the porch and rang the bell with his white gloved finger. Robin had to admit, she was impressed. *This was a far cry from squalid Grimsby,* she thought.

Robin joined the driver on the porch. The door flung open and there stood the most charming little boy she had ever seen. Robin bent down so they were eye to eye.

"You must be Noah," Robin said extending her hand. "I'm Robin and it's a pleasure to meet you, young lad."

"You talk funny," Noah said. He scrunched his face, then ran off into the house somewhere.

Robin heard heeled footsteps. "Robin?" Nina spoke, coming around the corner towards the door.

"Hi," Robin said.

"Come in, come in. It's freezing out there!" The driver carried the suitcases into the house.

"Where to, ma'am?" He was a huge man who held the two overstuffed suitcases as if they were from Barbie's Malibu collection.

"Upstairs, to the left, first door on the left. Thank you." She shut the door behind them. "Come on, let's go by the fire and warm you up. Jack is out running so we can get started getting to know one another."

"Thank you," Robin said.

Nina moved to the bar and mixed them both a hot toddy. "I wanted to have something special and warm for your arrival. Do you drink?"

"Not while I'm on the job."

Nina smiled, pleased. "Well, you can start tomorrow," she said, handing Robin a steaming mug of hot water and honey-infused whisky. Robin stirred the drink with the cinnamon stick then took a sip and let the warm liquid take over her shivers. She warmed up immediately. The lemon was just the right amount.

"This is perfect," Robin said. "Really delightful."

The limo driver came back down the stairs. "Is there anything else, ma'am?"

"No, thank you. I appreciate it," Nina said. They headed towards the door. Nina opened her purse and handed him a $50 bill. "Thanks, again. Stay warm!" She closed the door.

"So, I see you already met Noah."

Robin laughed. "Very briefly. He's a cute one."

"Mommy's heart," Nina said. "And Mommy's reason to drink," she said as she lifted her toddy towards Robin then took a sip.

They heard footsteps coming down the stairs. Robin looked up and sucked in a breath. *Oh my god, she's beautiful. Just like her mother.* Robin couldn't believe how lucky she was to be here. In this house. With these people.

"Addy! Come here, honey. I'd like you to meet someone."

Addy came and stood next to her mother.

"Robin, this is Addy, my oldest. Addy, this is Robin. She's going to be your nanny."

"Addy." Robin said. "Is that short for something?"

"Aderyn," Addy replied. "But I prefer Addy."

"Aderyn is a beautiful name. It means 'bird' where I'm from."

"Oh," Addy said. "That's interesting."

Addy looked Robin up and down. She was heavier than Addy had expected but not un-pretty. Her skin was a little blotchy, and she had deep dimples. Her eyes were a kind, gentle blue, and her hair.... Addy squinted her eyes. *Her hair had seen better days, probably*. She saw Robin's arm extended.

"Nice to meet you," Addy said, shaking Robin's hand.

"Likewise. My goodness, but you're beautiful. I can't get over it. Have you done any commercials or ad prints?"

Addy loved her immediately. She beamed ear to ear. Her parents had called her beautiful before but they're her parents. They had to. But here was a total stranger and at first look, saw past the birthmark and too-curly hair and thought she was beautiful.

"Thank you," Addy replied. "No, I haven't done anything like that. I'm more of a science shows and cerebral kind of girl than I am a beauty queen."

"Well, I think you're a beauty queen, for sure. And I like science, too. I used to love an American TV show from a long time ago called C.S.I. but it's not on anymore, so you probably don't...."

"*C.S.I.?!* That's my favorite show! *Ever!* And it did come back on for a new rebooted season! I've seen every episode at least three times! I know almost every word by heart! I'm going to marry William Petersen one day," she said matter of factly. Addy was almost out of breath with excitement.

"Addy, you know that's not possible," Nina corrected.

"Says you," Addy said.

"Oh, I find William Petersen simply divine!" Robin replied. "I had a bit of a crush on him myself. In my younger days," she winked, shrugging.

"You'll have to come to my room later and I'll show you my collection of stuff I have about the show!"

"Addy, Robin will be here a long time so let's give her some time to unpack and unwind. She's had a whirlwind of a couple of days. I'm sure she'd like to take a bath and just relax before she gets into...everything."

"It's fine, really," Robin said. "But I must say, this drink is getting to me a bit. I was so busy packing and traveling I skipped lunch, so the alcohol is..."

"Oh my gosh, I'm so sorry. I'm such a bad hostess," Nina exclaimed. "You must be starving. Let's go into the kitchen and I'll get Carmen to make you something. She makes a terrific chicken and peppers quesadilla."

"Sounds wonderful. Addy, will you join us?" Robin asked.

"Nah, I ate already. But I'll be upstairs if you wanna come up later." She scurried up the stairs.

"Duly noted," Robin replied. "And what about Noah," Robin asked Nina. "Should we get him a bite to eat as well?"

"He eats all day so he's probably already in the kitchen. Let's go find out." They headed to the kitchen.

While Nina was ahead of her, Robin looked back at Addy going up the stairs. She feels she's made a good impression already on the girl.

So far, so good.

CHAPTER TWENTY-EIGHT

December

Robin knocked lightly on the library door. "Nina?" she whispered. She swung the door open slightly. "Do you have a moment?"

"Sure. Come on in." Nina closed her computer. "What's up? Has Noah been putting fake roaches in your bed again?"

Robin laughed. "No, not since I put a fake snake in his."

Nina threw her head back and laughed heartily. "Oh my God, that's brilliant! Good for you."

"I think we're squared away now," Robin assured her.

Nina was still laughing. "Good, good. So, what can I do for you?"

Robin consulted her clipboard. "All of the vendors for your mother's party are confirmed except for Saint Laurent. Claude is on holiday, but his assistant Elodie will call me back by this afternoon." She flipped a page. "I've put together 150 gift bags for the guests, and they are set up in the gift-wrapping room for now. I know we have 92 confirmed guests but just in case someone brings an unannounced date, I took the liberty to make more bags so we should be covered. If we have any gifts left over, I've already contacted two shelters in the area we can donate them to." She flipped another page. "I just met with the string quartet, and we've got them to be set up in the west corner of the den, away from the bar so there's something on each side of the room. I've also confirmed with Gloria's Catering for tomorrow's appointment at 11:30 in the morning. I just wanted to keep you updated. I hope that's alright." She paused. "Oh. And the kids have had their snacks and are napping."

Nina's mouth was open. "Uhh, who are you and where did you come from? Robin that's incredible. Thank you so much. I'm not sure what I'd do without you."

Robin had only been here a couple of days, but she had already proven she is a quick study. Nina had gone over the party pre-planning lists just once, handed her the names of all the vendors, catering, musicians, cleaners and decorating companies, as well as Margo's informative guest list, and hoped she'd be able to at least read everything over the next few days. But to have accomplished what she had, literally overnight, was beyond a miracle.

"Oh, you'd be fine without me," Robin said humbly. "You're quite the organized person yourself. I mean, just look at this library. One side is for Jack, and this side," she walked over to the left side of the library, "is for you. "Wow. Look at all these books." She ran her fingers lightly over the spines. "It even smells organized, you know? The whole room is just...I mean, I know they say the kitchen is the heart of the home, but something about this room...the sconce lighting, the lounges, the windows to the outside, the warmth - it just...I just feel like this is the heart of this home."

Nina was moved. "You're exactly right." She stood up and walked over next to Robin. "I spent a lot of time designing this room. The thought behind it was 'opposites attract', like Jack and me. Our families travel in different societal circles, our tastes are different - I'm more high heels, he's more running shoes; I'm more "sleep on a yacht, he's more "sleep on a cot". His books over there are very scientific, very cerebral. Mine, on the other hand, are thrillers, fiction, pop culture. Opposites." She walked a bit further down the shelves. "This house is so big and our tastes are widespread throughout. But when you come into this room, it all comes together. A stranger could walk in here and know everything they'd need to know about us."

"A stranger just did. And does. And I love it. I absolutely am mad about this room." She saw Nina's own books on the shelf. "Oh my god, your books! I've read them all. I love them so much. But these!" She pointed to the

Shaken trilogy. "These are my favorite. In my humble opinion, of course." She sighed contentedly.

"I'm flattered," Nina said sincerely. "I'll give you signed copies, if you'd like."

"Oh, my goodness, you've made my day. Thank you so much. I'm honored." Robin's voice dropped a little. "My life back home was not the best. It was dark. And your books were my light. They helped me escape. When I read one of your books, I was transported to a different place and for that, I will be forever grateful."

Nina was touched. She knew she had fans around the world but to meet one, face to face, who had been so moved by her words, it was inspiring.

"What's this space here?" Robin asked, pointing to the empty slot next to the trilogy.

"Oh, that. Well, that is reserved."

"For...?"

"For something extremely special. Hopefully, for that," Nina pointed to her computer. "For the new manuscript I have been working on. And, thanks to you, I'll be able to focus and get much more done. Keep this up and I'll have a new book on the shelves in just a few months."

"Oh, that's wonderful to hear," Robin exclaimed. "It really is. And that's why I'm here. To help in any way I can."

"Thank you, Robin. That means a lot." Nina hesitated. She wanted so much to ask the next question, to get to know Robin better but wondered if it was too soon. Earlier, Robin had mentioned her dark life back home, so technically, she opened the door for the conversation to be had. Nina decided she had nothing to lose.

"Robin, may I ask you something?"

"Anything. I'm an open.... book," she said, smiling and gesturing around her.

Nina smiled. "I'd like to get to know you better. Can you tell me about your home and your family? I'd love to hear your story."

Robin paused. "Nina? May I go on a break now?"

Nina was disappointed. She had really hoped Robin would open up to her. "Of course. And Robin, you never need to ask me about going on break. You work here and I want you to do whatever you want to do, you understand?"

"Yes. But I told you I never drink while working." Robin put down her clipboard and went over to the bar cart. She put ice into two glasses and poured them both a bourbon. "And now that I'm on a break, I'm not working. And if I'm to tell you about me, then we'll both need this."

Nina smiled. "Are you sure?"

Robin hesitated. "I am. But my story is harsh. It's not for the good hearted. I will tell you because I owe you that, as I attend to your children. I don't mind being open because my past never allowed me to keep things hidden. Just know I have forgiven my past." Robin looked pensive, then she said, "Your family's never in your past. You carry it around with you everywhere."

Nina's eyes crinkled. "M.L. Stedman. *The Light Between Oceans.* I know it well."

Robin smiled. "So, if you're ready..."

Jesus, forgive me, Robin thought.

She handed Nina the glass and began her story.

CHAPTER TWENTY-NINE

February 2009

I was a beautiful child. I really was. I know people say that but this time, it was true. Skin, porcelain as a doll; hair, long and shiny, golden as a sunrise; petal soft lips and cerulean eyes. My body was deficit of any pudges and crinkles. I knew I outshone all the girls in Grimsby, and yet, I was surrounded by ugliness. Even at home. Dark shadows within even darker halls in our house, men came in and out at all hours, trampling mud and shedding fish scales on the threadbare runners.

It was during these visits my mum would keep me hidden. At first, I could not say why, but soon, through the lewd looks and lip-licking, I came to the horrible filthy truth: I was desired by the undesirable. The men in the town would whistle and say foul things to me whenever I passed on my way to the market. "Bugger off!" I would yell back, and for some, that seemed like an invitation to cackle and continue with their boorishness. I acted brave but couldn't wait to hurry home to the safety of our ramshackle home. At least, I thought it was safe. And that safety – and my sanity – were about to be put to the ultimate test.

I was twelve, on the brink of becoming a teenager. A time when I should be playing with schoolmates and dolls; dreaming what the local boys would be like in an innocent kiss; and maybe getting a puppy I could call Buddy and enjoy him jumping into my arms upon returning from school. But none of that happened. Instead, every night, my own mum would ignore my piercing screams for help. Sometimes my mouth was too full to scream, usually by the member of the foul brute my mum was calling her boyfriend.

I wasn't sure why God was abandoning me but no matter the reason, I would never leave His side. I needed Him. But if He abandoned me, no one would have me as their daughter, their child. I would only be had by that grotesque man who did whatever he wanted to me. I would wail with pain and disgrace, my own mum in the other room doing nothing to save her child from this monster. I blamed myself. I knew I was prettier than my mum and I believed all of this to be my fault. I lived with this guilt every day.

NINA'S SNIFFLING JOLTED ROBIN FROM HER TALE.

"Oh, Robin. I am so sorry about all this. I cannot imagine you going through this alone."

Robin paused. "I wasn't alone. I had my sister, Caryn. She was safe. I made a cot for her in the outside shed where she would hide every night after her chores. She was never subjected to any of the horrors in that house. I made sure of that."

And Nina then understood that Robin had selflessly taken the place of her sister on many occasions in that home. "I'm sorry, hon. Continue if you'd like. Tell me about your hometown," Nina hoped it would lighten the subject matter a bit.

She was wrong.

MY MUM, CARYN AND I LIVED IN GRIMSBY, A ONCE THRIVING FISHING PORT IN Lincolnshire, England. Thrust upon the south bank of the Humber Estuary near the North Sea, where the townsmen were overworked, underpaid, and always smelled of rotted fish. The muddy banks of the river were home to insects and slimy underground creatures that brought forth disease and disgust. The town's once booming fishing business fell sharply after the Cod Wars. It is said the town is named after

Grim, a Danish fisherman from the 9th century, but to the locals, it's Grimsby because it's just a grim, declining village, a fact to which I can attest.

Everyone knew everyone in Grimsby proper and my mum was known by at least half of the entire male population (and it wasn't because of her cooking). My mum was an expert in the bedroom and had men lined up outside on our front porch all hours of the day. It also didn't help that the sickening smell of rotting fish-flesh didn't matter to my mum. But the men were generous. My mum had a shag-jar by her bed where they would give her tips. "Really, it's hush money," she once told me. "So's I won't spill their shite secrets to their little shite wives," she smiled. So, she kept their secrets, their adultery. And the money in her shag-jar grew and grew. Every now and then she would put the money in paper sacks in the back of her closet and put the empty jar back out on the bedside table. Ready for the next tips. "And we need the money to survive, the three of us. This is all for you, sweetheart."

Eventually, I could leave the house and stay in the shed with my sister. I had filled it with things like blankets, pillows and sandpapery rucksacks filled with old sheets. I surrounded us with comforts like sugary bread, marionberry jam and wheat crackers and yogurt I would bury in the cold ground to keep it cool. And books. Lots of books by Agatha Christie, Gillian Flynn, Willa Greyson and of course, you, Nina. We would read to each other by a small lantern I had confiscated from the house. Our shed wasn't a fine hotel, but it was a comfortable dwelling that kept us safe. But one day, I decided I had to leave. For good. My sister refused to leave my mum's side. So sadly, I made plans to make my solo escape.

Unbeknownst to my mum, I would pilfer money from her paper sacks bit by bit until I had enough to buy voyage on a cargo ship bound for the eastern coast of America. Florida, to be exact. It was from reading your book, A Dutiful Wife, that encouraged me to dream of sunning myself with the elite crowds of South Beach, staying at the best hotels, drinking Mimosa's for brekky as I lounged around an azure pool with the gorgeous models who frequented the hotel. It was the life I wanted. The life I needed. So, with my one small bag in hand, I boarded the voyage with other people fleeing from dying U.K. ports. Refugees from Immingham, Spilsby and Hunstanton shivered in masses, unsure of what exactly waited ahead. It was a different time, and it was all we knew. Poor souls paying for voyage on a rusty ship.

After three weeks of dealing with the filth and stench of the cargo ship, the scorching sun turning the metal hull into branding irons straight from the fire, and a rumbling belly from scarcely having eaten in 21 days, I stepped foot on glorious south Florida soil. But the beauty was an illusion. And like God, the beauty had abandoned me. I was in a vast shipyard where we all vomited ourselves off the ship, still in a huddled mass unsure of where to go. Everyone just stood there, like they were quite literally frozen in time. I had no time for their indecision, so I hoisted my tiny bag over my shoulder and started walking. Fifty steps later, I turned to see the ball of immigrants still huddled. Lost. And suddenly, I, too, felt lost. I was in a strange land, alone. It was sickly hot, and I was feeling like I was about to faint. The cargo journey was painful, and I truly felt like I could die where I stood.

I cupped my face in my hands and started to sob. Oh God! What have I gotten myself in to?

"My God," Nina said, dabbing her eyes. "What horrors you've been through. I cannot imagine the pain and sorrow you've experienced." She took a sip of her bourbon and blinked hard. "So, what happened next?"

"Well, I decided to walk. And walk and walk and walk some more. Until I simply could not take another step. I was looking for a sign. And, well, I found it. It read 'vacancy'."

"Excuse me?" Nina said disbelievingly.

Robin laughed. "Vacancy. As in I was standing in front of a motel. And come to find out, they were looking to hire a night clerk and I got the job and a free place to live. It all kind of worked out, I guess."

"That's a stroke of luck, for sure," Nina said.

"Yes. I was gobsmacked that within five hours of landing in Florida, I had managed to find a job and a room and board. I really felt like my life was on the mend."

"But it wasn't." Nina guessed.

"Not really. But it was starting and that's all I needed. I'm a "silver-linings" kind of lass so I knew in my heart that moving to the states was the best thing for me. I missed Caryn, but we reconnected after a few years and we're all good now. A few months after I left, she relocated to Hertfordshire near London and met a man and they got married. Her three young ones came soon after. We talk at least twice a month," she smiled at her thoughts.

"And your mother?"

Robin got quiet. "She died shortly after I left. My sister said she got sick, and she just never got over it. Some sort of cancer, I believe." Robin shrugged slowly. "I want to accept she's better off now. It wasn't a good life for her in Grimsby. For any of us. And at the end of the day, we all escaped that life and are better for it."

"Silver lining," Nina replied softly.

"Silver lining," Robin nodded.

Nina asked, "So after you found the motel, what happened next? How did you get from Florida to New York?"

Robin's cell phone rang. "Ahh. Right now, I need to postpone the story. It's Elodie from Saint Laurent. I need to take this." She got up from her chair and walked to the door. "Hello, Elodie? Yes, this is Robin Kemble. Thank you for getting back with me so quickly. I wanted to…." her voice drifted off as she left the library.

Nina just sat there, dumbfounded.

"Amazing," she said, shaking her head. "What a story." *Such a dark history,* she thought. Her words reverberated in her head and her eyes widened. In an instant, she knew exactly what needed to happen. It was fate and the stars and every circumstance and ordinance coming together in the clearest rush she'd ever experienced. Nina felt an inspiration like never before.

She stood up, went to her computer and began to type.

CHAPTER THIRTY

January 14, 2022

The next month flew by and Willa Greyson's launch party for *Lust Kills* was in three hours.

Nina had to admit, Robin had done a stellar job and the place looked stunning. The den had been transported back in time to the Regency Era in Britain. It was Robin's idea. When Robin told Nina the era was ruled by elegance and etiquette, full of balls, duels, debutantes, and Corinthians, she knew it was the right aura she wanted for the night. Robin sealed the deal when she mentioned the era was a time of the Romantic Movement, when the country was thriving in literature, and prose and poetic works by Byron, Shelley, and Coleridge. For a book launch event, this was the most superb theme.

The food tables were laden with boards of meats and cheeses from around the world, fruits from every vine, shrimp, iced caviar and huge Coffin Bay king oysters. Desserts ranged from tiramisu to tiny red velvet cupcakes topped with edible 24K gold flakes. Nina stepped down into the den. The decorations were elaborate and exquisite and represented the Regency Era perfectly.

Nina smiled. This room was perfect. Was it overkill for a book launch?

Nina didn't think so. This was a historic time in Willa's life. Her twentieth book! A special occasion was in order to mark such a momentous time. This night would be perfect. Willa deserved every minute of it. Nina looked at the grandfather clock and saw she had two and half hours before the guests would be arriving. Jack, the girls and Robin were all in their rooms getting ready. Robin should be down soon to meet with the staff and the band. Nina turned and went upstairs to meet with her team to get ready for the gala.

THE STRING QUARTET PLAYED PIECES BY HAYDN, MOZART, AND PLEYEL AND THE music soared through the house, rose the full height of the mansion, and wafted down every hallway. It was like something out of *The Great Gatsby*, only grander.

Nina and Jack came down the stairs together, arm in arm. Nina's floor length lavender, sequined Alexander McQueen dress reflected light into every nook and cranny. Jack, more handsome than ever, wore black tails with a black vest, topped with a deep, aubergine ascot. His black-framed glasses reflected the era perfectly as did his slicked back hair. By appearance, they were royalty.

Robin, standing by the front door with her trusty clipboard, looked up as they descended. "Holy *shite*," she said, too loudly. Her face flushed. "Oh my god, I'm so, so sorry. It's just…you two…. you look…wow."

Jack laughed. "You're forgiven," he said as he pecked her on her cheek, which flushed scarlet immediately. Robin had become family in the short time she'd been there. Nina was a completely different person since Robin arrived and truth be told, Jack was, too. He kissed Nina on her cheek, then headed down to the bar.

"You look lovely, as well," Nina said, grasping Robin's hand. And she meant it. She let Robin use her Black AMEX to find the right gown for her and she chose well. A strapped deep blue chiffon Empire-waist gown with a lighter cerulean blue velvet belt just below her bosom. It fit her perfectly. Nina had set aside a private time for Robin to sit with her private hair and makeup team and the result was stunning. To complete her look, Robin chose to wear opera length gloves for the occasion, and she looked right out of the pages of a 19th century novel.

"Looks like you're all set for the night?" Nina asked.

"More than ready." She consulted her clipboard. "The bar staff is already here, the wait staff is in the kitchen awaiting my direction and the children are upstairs finishing getting ready. I'll check on them before I talk to the staff."

"Marvelous. Thank you, Robin. This night would've never happened if it weren't for you."

"Thank you, Nina, but you started all the hard work. I just took the next steps."

Nina smiled. "I'll go chat with the staff and let you finish what you need to do and then you can go see the children," Nina said.

"Absolutely not!" Robin said. "Jack is bringing you some bubbly, so you just enjoy yourselves." Right on cue, Jack handed Nina a glass of champagne. "See? I'll speak with the staff. Now scoot! I've got this all under control." She left for the kitchen as Nina shook her head in wonder and joined her husband in the den.

Jack hugged his wife tight. "Wooof. Did I tell you how beautiful you look tonight, madam?"

"Why, no, sir, you have not. In the past twenty minutes, rather."

"Well, my apologies, m'lady." He lifted her forearm and gently kissed the top of her hand, bejeweled with an antique 18k amethyst ring. "That ring is exquisite," he said.

"It's mother's," Nina replied, admiring the bauble. "Daddy gave it to her for her 15th book and I found it only fitting to borrow for this evening."

"It's perfect. Just like you," he kissed her on her lips, then deeper, and he felt her go nearly limp in his arms.

"Jack...stop. The guests will be here any minute," but her protests were weak.

He pulled her tighter and kissed her again, his hand cupping her bottom and pulling her into him.

"Ahem. Sorry," came Robin's voice from behind them. "The children are here."

"Oh," said Nina. Jack only smiled.

"Hey, kiddos!" Jack said. "My goodness, don't you look pretty!"

"I'm not pretty," Noah said disgusted.

"Of course, not, darling," Nina went to him. "You are simply the most handsome young man in this room!" She pulled him into a hug.

"Mommmm, I'm the *only* young man in the room!"

"No, you're not. There's the band. There's daddy. And none of them compare to you, honey." She looked at him and she raised her hand to her heart. She couldn't help but be proud of the young man Noah was becoming. She smiled. He was dressed identical to his daddy, in a miniature tux with tails and purple ascot. His blond hair, thick and pulled up into a stylish mohawk. *He's going to be a heartbreaker one day,* she thought. *Just like his daddy.*

"Whatever!" He said, marching up to the dessert table.

"Don't touch anything," Nina reminded him. "We've got special plates ready for you guys to take to your rooms later, okay?" Noah grunted his disapproval.

"My goodness, Addy, would you look at you! You look like a princess!" Jack said.

"Why, thank you, kind sir. Robin helped me pick it out at Petite Oiseau Boutique," she said with a French accent.

"Well, it certainly is a lovely shade of.... what color is that?" Jack asked.

"Pomegranate. It's velvet and you can't see the shoes because it's so long but look," she raised up her dress a little to show him her sparkly Stuart Weitzman shoes. "They match mommy's."

"Well, I think you look lovely," he kissed her on the top of her head.

"Don't mess up my chignon!"

"Oops. I won't. I swear," his hands raised in the air. "You're still divine. Promise."

"Oh, I know." She joined Noah walking around the den looking at all the decorations and food.

The doorbell rang and a doorman stepped up to open the door for the first guests.

Jack and Nina raised their champagne-filled glasses to each other. "Let the festivities begin," he said.

And with one final sweep of her eyes, Nina scanned the room. *Everything was beautiful. It was going to be a perfect evening.*

She proved to be a poor prophet.

CHAPTER THIRTY-ONE

January 14, 2022

Within forty minutes, 116 guests had arrived and were scattered throughout the house. Some braved the outdoor cold as they puffed on their cigars and cigarettes. Others had taken it upon themselves to wander the downstairs square footage while most were gathered in the huge den. Kelly and Owen had made it and they looked like some sensational couple right off the pages of *Regals & Royals Magazine*. Kelly's long, dark hair was lightly curled, and she wore a small tiara ("*My mother said it belonged to a Spanish Princess. A little too gauche for my taste, but what the hell?!*") Her floor-length cream dress accented her Miami tan. Owen was in a cream tux that matched perfectly to his wife's dress. They were, simply put, stunning.

She looked up towards the second-floor banister. Addy and Noah were grasping balusters and peering through down to the beautiful scene below them. Nina smiled. Vivian and Norma, the maids, were standing close to the kids to monitor their every move. Nina smiled and waved up to the kids, blowing them kisses. Addy grabbed her air kiss and Noah turned his head away in disgust. Nina laughed. *That little monster*, she thought, smiling.

The string music could barely be heard over the din of the crowd, but it played softly and wasn't too intrusive. Nina surveyed her guests.

The mix of people were the best of the best of the literary ilk, all here to celebrate Willa. *Or to gawk at the elusive Nina Travers,* Nina thought sardonically.

She turned and looked around. She saw Margo by the band, looking rather dour. She knew inviting some of Margo's ex-clients to the party would put Margo in an uncomfortable position, but this party was for Willa, and if Willa wanted them there, there was nothing Margo could say. Nina could see Leslie Fontaine by the bar, confined to her wheelchair from a horse-riding accident years ago. And of course, she had a cocktail in her hand. Leslie Fontaine was never without a drink. But the night was early, and her head was already bobbing downwards. A sign she'd probably had a couple of drinks on her way over to the party. It seemed everyone except Leslie knew that Leslie was an alcoholic, but she was Willa's longtime friend, so Nina felt obligated to invite her. Leslie lifted her head and her eyes found Nina's. They raised their glass to each other in acknowledgment. In the movement, Leslie spilled her vodka-cranberry. She yelped as the pinkish liquid started spreading on the white carpet. *Lush,* Nina said through her smile.

Gregory Wynn was here as was Carly Kaufman, who flew in just for the occasion. Henry Corbyn looked dapper in his three-piece suit as he was sidled up to his date, another dapper-looking gentleman. Was that Kevin Flanders? He was a well-known COO of Macmillan Press. Nina's chin dropped and her eyebrows raised in surprise. *Looks like Henry's moved up in the world. Nice.*

And in the middle of this intimidating crowd stood the star herself, Willa Greyson. Kelly and Owen flanked her as they chatted. But even among the partygoer's glamour, Willa stood out. Her flowy voile and chiffon gown had been custom-made for Willa. The pale green set off her eyes and her silvery locks. She wore a King's ransom worth of emeralds around her neck and wrists, another lavish gift from her husband, Roy, for their 25th Anniversary. She looked, for all intents and purposes, like a Queen surrounded by her court. And she was living it up. She was like a glamorous magnet and everyone around her was weak metal, drawn to her whether they wanted to be or not. They were helpless to her pull. Everyone hoped that just by being in her orbit, their own sad universe would change for the better.

Nina couldn't see Robin anywhere in the crowd, but she knew she was there somewhere. Pulling off some sort of unseen miracle.

Nina walked into the den. "Hi, Kel and Owen. Wow, you two look… amazing." They hugged.

"Back atcha, Neen. You've outdone yourself with this party." Kelly turned to Willa. "But Ms. Greyson, where is Mr. Greyson? Not out cavorting, I hope."

Willa laughed. "Hardly, my dear. Roy and I made a pact years ago. I wouldn't go and be bored out of my gourd by any of his gigs and he wouldn't raise the mundane quotient by attending one of mine."

Owen chuckled. "Are you serious?"

"My dear, I had it written into our vows."

Nina nodded in confirmation. She turned to Willa. "Mother! You look stunning," Nina said, wandering up to Willa. They air kissed cheeks.

"As do you, my darling. And must I say, this," she waved her arms around her, "is simply phenomenal. I am honored you went to so much trouble. Thank you, my love." They hugged.

"You're worth it." Nina looked around. "So many people here. Did you see Leslie and Gregory? They don't seem to be even acknowledging Margo's presence."

"Can you blame them, darling? It is kind of awkward, I mean you and I are the reasons she dropped them as clients. It has to be a little embarrassing, don't you think?"

"And yet, they're here. To celebrate you."

"Oh, darling, don't be delusional, it's not your style. They're here to see *you* and to see what has become of *you*." She laughed. "To celebrate me," she mocked. "That's a laugh. Leslie and Gregory would soon rather come to my funeral than to miss out on what's going on in your life."

Nina knew Willa had a point. Willa wasn't the only star at this party, unfortunately. Only, one happened to be a shining star and the other a fallen one.

"In fact," Willa whispered, "I wouldn't be the least bit surprised if Rachel Meadows rose from the dead and tromped her muddy, grave-ridden self in here just to satisfy her cravings of not knowing what you've been up to!"

"Mother! You're awful! Don't say that," Nina said, putting her hand to her chest. "She'd ruin the carpet."

They both burst out laughing. "Come on," Nina said. "If I know you, you haven't eaten all day. Let's get you some food. I paid a bloody fortune for it, might as well eat it."

"Bloody? I see Robin's been wearing off on you a little, darling, what with your British slang."

Nina smiled. Robin was good for Nina. And for the family. "I sure hope so," Nina responded, leading Willa to the food table where they loaded up.

CHAPTER THIRTY-TWO

January 14, 2022

D*ing! Ding! Ding! Ding! Ding!*

Nina put her knife down. She was standing on the foyer overlooking the den, holding her glass of champagne.

"Ladies and gentlemen, friends and esteemed colleagues. Thank you so much for coming tonight. This is a very special evening, and we are very fortunate to be spending it with you. Tonight marks a momentous milestone a very few of us - me included - have achieved (*light laughter*): the remarkable launch of book number twenty! (*applause*) Every person in this room has had a generous hand in helping make this happen and that is why you are here tonight. And on Tuesday, the rest of the world will be able to enjoy this novel, so in that vein, I wanted to say, in reality, this celebration is for all of you! (*hearty applause*) However! (*light laughter*) I would be remiss if I didn't acknowledge the real reason you are here, to recognize and celebrate the true force of nature, the 8th wonder of the literary world (*laughter*), my mother - and my friend - Willa Greyson!" Champagne and cocktail glasses raised high. (*loud applause; whistles; cheers*)

Willa set her near-empty plate on a table then stepped up to the foyer alongside Nina, they hugged and pecked cheeks. The applause continued and Willa turned to face the crowd.

"Friends…and foes," she began (*laughter*), "thank you so much for coming to this lovely, lovely party. I am so honored you would give up your Saturday night to be here. Then again, I know some of you are just here for the food (*laughter*). But that's okay, you're here and that's what matters. *Lust Kills* is my twentieth book, can you believe it? (*applause*) It seems like yesterday I wrote my first book, *Haven's Revenge*. But that manuscript is best left not talked about (*laughter*)."

Someone in the crowd yelled "You've come a long way, baby!"

"You better believe it!" she replied. (*applause*) "Thank you, thank you! Now, I won't hold you up any…. any…." Willa stopped talking. "Long…. long…" Her lips started quivering but nothing was coming out. Her hand grasped Nina's.

"Mother? Are you alright?" Willa's grasp got tighter.

Willa looked straight ahead. She could feel her knees growing weak. "I…. I…. uhhhhh…." Then suddenly, her hand released from Nina's, and she collapsed to the ground on her knees with a crack and fell over on her side.

The crowd gasped.

"Oh my god!" someone yelled.

"Mother! Are you okay? *Mother!?*" But Nina got no response. Willa lay on the floor and began to convulse. Her eyes rolled back in their sockets. Nina dropped to her mother's side. Kelly ran to Nina.

Someone yelled "Call 911!" Kelly pulled out her phone and dialed.

But Nina had seen this before. She looked around quickly and her eyes landed on Willa's dinner plate. What remained was caviar, a shrimp, some fruit and crackers and…. *omg!*

"I need her purse! It's green with a silver buckle! I need her EpiPen! She's going into anaphylactic shock. Hurry, please! Hang in there, mother! Please, hang in there!"

People started scrambling looking for Willa's purse. The din of the room rose tenfold as the guests started to panic right along with Nina.

Margo stood on the sidelines looking in horror.

Nina saw Margo close by. "Margo! Help her! Do something!!" Foam started coming out of Willa's mouth.

Margo couldn't move. Her eyes widened. *If Willa dies, my career is ruined.*

I'll have no one! Nina's in a slump – what would I do? Margo's selfish thoughts caused her to freeze in place. She just stood there. Staring.

"Margo!! *Please!* Don't just stand there, help her! I don't know what to do!"

Help her! Margo heard in her head. *Help her!* Then something snapped in Margo. In an instant she realized one of her only two clients was dying. No, one of her only two *friends* was dying. She needed to do something and quick! Margo looked around quickly and spied Willa's purse on a chair sticking out under a fur coat. She darted for the purse and grabbed it then ran to the foyer. She opened the purse and yanked out the EpiPen. Taking off the cap, she held the orange tip against Willa's outer thigh. She swung and pushed the auto-injector firmly until she heard the click. She counted 1….2….3….

"My god, Nina. Are you okay?" Jack ran up next to her. Owen wasn't too far behind. "Is Willa…??

Nina's breathing was staccato.

Kelly spoke. "She's going to be fine. She had an allergic reaction to something, I don't know what.

Nina said, "she…I think…." she looked at Margo for an answer. The sound of an ambulance was faint.

"She should be fine but let's get her to the hospital just in case," Margo said. Robin appeared from the hallway next to Margo.

"Jesus, forgive me," she whispered, covering her mouth.

"No…no…hospital," Willa whispered.

"Mother! Thank God you're okay. Look, no arguing. The ambulance is here and they're going to take you just to check you out. You should be fine, but we want to make sure." She bent down and kissed her mother's forehead. "You gave us quite the scare."

The kids had rushed down the stairs and were standing next to Jack. "Grandmother….?" Addy said, her voice quivering. "Are you going to be okay?"

"Grandmother's going to be just…. fine," Willa said. "Don't you worry your pretty little head, okay?"

Addy nodded.

Robin spoke. "Children, why don't you go ahead and go back upstairs.

Your grandmother is going to be just fine but let's not crowd her. Say goodnight and I'll be up shortly to make sure you're tucked in, ok?"

"We'll take them up," Kelly said. "Come on, kiddos." The kids said their goodnights to Jack, Nina, and Willa.

"C'mon sport," Owen said to Noah, lifting him up in his arms.

The doorbell rang and Jack went to let in the paramedics. After 20 minutes, Willa was strapped to the stretcher and wheeled out. "Mother, I'm right behind you," Nina called out. As the door closed behind her, Nina spun around.

"Robin. How the *hell* did this happen? You know my mother has a severe nut allergy!" She grabbed Willa's plate. There among the caviar, fruit, crackers, and shrimp was a half-eaten round of Italian Mortadella ham studded with pistachios. "Here." She shoved the plate towards Robin.

"Nuts? No...that's.... oh my god, I thought I was ordering olive loaf. I would've never...I didn't mean to...I just pointed to a picture in the caterer's book...I thought it was olive loaf...my god, I am so, so sorry. I didn't mean to...." Robin's voice trembled.

"Of course, you didn't," Jack consoled. "It was an accident. Look, Willa is going to be fine. It could've happened to anybody, isn't that right, Nina?"

"I gave Robin the list." She turned to Robin. "I gave you the list. Of allergies and everything. You should've been more careful."

"I know. I'm sorry. Really, I am," she said sorrowfully. She looked around and noticed the crowd just standing there not knowing what to do. She made a decision. She stepped down into the den to be with the guests and answer any questions they may have.

"And you," Nina turned her anger towards Margo. "Why did you just stand there and stare? You just.... *stood* there and stared waiting for my mother to die!" Her hands were flying around angrily.

"No...I.... Nina, I found the purse and got the pen. I *saved* her."

"Not at first!" Nina's anger was burning. "You sure took your sweet time! My mother could've died!"

Jack sidled up to Nina. "Honey, it's okay. Margo did what she could. She found the purse in time and it all worked out." Nina walked away, her arms across her chest. He looked at Margo. "Thank you, Margo. You did great."

"It's okay. You're welcome. I understand it's a scary situation." She stepped back down in the den.

The front door flew open. "*Margo Flagg!!*" came the deep male voice. "I need to see Margo Flagg. *Right now!*"

"Whoa there, pal. Who are you and why are you barging into my house," Jack said stepping up to the man.

"I need to see Margo Flagg!"

He was dressed like a beggar and Jack could smell alcohol on his breath.

"Harris?" Nina asked. "Harris Markham? What on earth are you doing here?" She walked up next to Jack.

"Well, if it isn't little miss perfect. Little miss 'I'm gonna be her client so there's no room for you now'." Harris was getting belligerent.

"Harris, you're drunk. You need to go home. Jack, call him a cab."

"I'm not going anywhere until I speak to Margo. *Margo!!!*" He yelled.

The crowd started to get riled up again. "Come for the drinks, stay for the show," one whispered to another. Some pulled out their cellphones to capture the moment.

"Harris! What the hell?" Margo said, stomping up to the foyer. "You don't need to be here!" Margo's voice was steel, but her insides were jelly. This was, after all, the man who blamed her for his complete ruin.

"Margo?" Jack asked.

"I've got this, thanks. You go be with Willa." Jack nodded, took Nina's arm and they got their coats and left.

Margo looked over her shoulder. The whole room was staring at her and what she would do next. In the back, phones were raised high above the crowd.

"Harris, come with me. *Now.*" She knew what this conversation was about. She could feel the sweat running down her sides. *Let's get this over with,* she thought. She walked down the hallway, turning only once to make sure Harris was following her. They went into the library, and she slammed the door, leaving the guests with their mouths hanging open.

CHAPTER THIRTY-THREE

February

It came as no surprise to anyone *Lust Kills* landed at number two on the New York Times best seller list in its first week and after its second week in circulation, it jumped to the number one spot and had remained there since.

"I guess I should be more upset my ruining your party was what got me to the top, but I'm not. The book is fabulous, and I know it," Willa said. "It would be at the top, tragedy or not."

"Oh, for sure," Margo said. "It's your best book yet. And I know I'm a little biased - "

"Just a little?" Willa egged.

"Okay, a lot," Margo laughed. "But I've been doing this a long time and I have to say, it's right up there with *Weathering the Storm* and *Dark Lake*. Honestly."

"Hmmm," Willa paused.

"She's right, mother," Nina said, taking a bite of her seafood salad. The three had gathered at Delano's for lunch.

"That's sweet of you two to say, but I'm no fool. Yes, *Lust Kills* is a very good book but because of what happened, I'm sure there was a little boost to sales." She sipped her wine. "By the way, how is Robin? Has she forgiven herself? Have *you* forgiven her?" She eyed her daughter.

"Yes," Nina said. "I have forgiven her. And more importantly, she has forgiven herself. She's fine now. But I think she's now vegan."

Margo laughed. "Poor thing. She's going to be fine. She's weathered worse storms than this."

"I agree," Nina said. "She really is a wonder."

Willa turned her head in Margo's direction. She lifted her wine glass, pushed a silver strand of her hair behind her ear and spoke clandestinely. "Now, Margo. Do tell about Harris Markham. What do you have going on with him?"

Margo bolted upright. "What do you mean?"

Nina joined in. "Oh, don't act so innocent. I was there, remember?"

Margo looked at Willa.

"She told me," Willa said pointing to Nina with her thumb and nudging her head in her direction.

"Oh, it was nothing, really."

"Bullshit," Willa said. The people at the next table looked at them. "*Bull-shit*," Willa whispered. "Harris Markham is a loose cannon! He barged into a party he wasn't invited to - "

"- in the middle of winter!" Nina added.

"- in the middle of winter," Willa continued, "demanding to speak to you and you alone."

Margo's eyes were wide. "How did you...." She looked at Nina. "Oh, never mind. I know the videos are out there, too." She sighed. "Drunk ex-client threatens agent!" Margo said, her hand swiping across the sky as if what she said was a headline. "Fine, I'll tell you."

Nina and Willa put their elbows on the table and rested their chins in the heels of their palms. They leaned in. "We're all ears," Nina said.

Margo shrugged. "He wants me to take him back as a client."

Nina and Willa looked at each other. Then back to Margo. "That's it?" Willa asked incredulously, her arms dropped to the table in disappointment.

'That's it," Margo replied.

"What?!" Nina said.

"No, really, that's it." Margo could see they didn't believe her. *Oy vey.* "Well..."

"I knew it!" Willa said. "There *is* more!"

"Well, he sort of blames me for ruining his life. Ever since I dropped him as a client his life has gone to crap and apparently, I'm to blame. For all of it."

Nina said, "I think he holds us a little responsible, too, which is really idiotic. We had nothing to do with this."

Willa looked at Nina. "Technically."

"But you're right," Margo said. "He is a loose cannon. I don't trust him. Ever since he vandalized my car I haven't…."

"He *what*?!" Nina yelled. "He vandalized your *car*? Oh my gosh, Margo, I had no idea. Did you go to the police?"

"No, no. It was just after I dropped him. I knew he was hurt so I just chalked it up to him feeling broken and having a bruised ego."

"A bruised ego does not vandalize a car, darling," Willa said. "A scary, unstable man does."

"Mother's right. And now with him coming to the house last month in such a rage - do you feel safe around him at all anymore? I can hire someone to watch -"

"No, no. I'm fine. I can handle Harris Markham. Don't forget about the AJW."

Willa crinkled her eyebrows. "AJW?"

"'Angry Jewish Woman'," Nina said. "It's the side of Margo no one wants to see."

"Exactly. Harris Markham now knows about the AJW. And after the incident at your house, I don't think he'll be bothering me anymore. Trust me." She could see skepticism in Nina's eyes. "Really. I'm not taking this lightly. Okay?"

Nina sighed. "If you're sure. But I can still hire someone to protect you. Even if it's for a short while. Just until Harris calms down a bit? I know I'd feel safer if…."

"Absolutely not. Now look, I've told you more than I really intended but…" Margo sat up straight. "…I consider you two my friends. And Willa, I'm very sorry I hesitated even a second before coming to your aid that night. I just…I was just scared that…" her voice started to break.

"Shut up, Margo," Willa said sweetly. "Darling, look. It's going to take a lot more than some Italian ham to take me down. And that was my fault. I should've known the difference between Mortadella and Olive loaf, for heaven's sake. I mean, the price alone...."

Margo smiled.

Willa glanced at Nina. She rested her hand on top of her daughters' then looked at Margo. "Margo, darling...I forgive you. You did nothing wrong."

"What?" Margo asked.

"You're not deaf. In fact," Willa continued, "I should be thanking you. For saving my life. I wouldn't be here today if it weren't for you. What you did was very brave. So, thank you, my dear. From the bottom of my heart."

Margo sniffled. "But..."

Nina spoke. "Margo, don't you see? You're her 'Robin'. You needed forgiveness from mother in order to forgive yourself, just like Robin needed mine."

Margo adjusted her glasses. She didn't want the girls to see her tearing up. She thought she heard Nina and Willa sniffling, too.

"On that note, I think we should go," Willa said, standing up, taking a deep breath. "Besides, this conversation has gotten a little too sappy for my taste."

Nina walked over to Margo and kissed her cheek. "We'll chat soon, okay?"

"Yes, yes. Okay. Now you ladies go. I'll get the bill," Margo said.

Willa walked over to Margo and pecked her other cheek. And as she walked away, she smiled and said "It's the least you could do. After all, you nearly killed me."

"Mother!" Nina's voice was faint as she grabbed Willa's arm and they headed out. Margo could hear Nina laughing.

Margo grinned ear to ear. Yes, they were her friends. And for that, she was ecstatic. She was sorry she had to dampen the mood with all the Harris Markham talk. Her grin faded.

She was even more sorry that what she told Nina and Willa was a complete lie.

CHAPTER THIRTY-FOUR

March

"Are you sure you made it okay?" Nina asked Addy over the phone. Addy had gone over to Valentina's to study. Nina was thrilled her daughter had found a friend she could spend some time with.

"Yessssss mommy, I'm fine!" she whined dramatically. "Stop worrying! I can ride a bike, you know!"

Nina chuckled. "I know you can, honey. Okay. Well, if you - "

"Nina! Did you tell Kelly and Owen we'd have dinner with them tonight?" Jack yelled.

"Is daddy mad?" Addy asked. She heard him in the background.

"Uh oh. I guess I forgot to tell him we had dinner plans tonight."

"Nina! I have a huge project due tomorrow first thing! I can't possibly go out tonight!" Jack's voice was deeper than usual. Irritated.

Nina cupped the phone so Addy couldn't hear everything. "Jack, honey, it's their anniversary. I told you about this three weeks ago."

The muffled voices reverberated dully. They sounded like Charlie Brown's teacher. But Addy could hear some words.

"...too busy.... dammit..."

"...friends......important......we promised...."

"...remind me...."

"...not my fault.... we're going..."

"Mommy? Is daddy upset?" Addy asked again.

"Hold on, Addy...*best friends....be out long...*"

"Mommy?"

"Yes, Addy, I'm here."

"Is daddy upset? I don't like it when you guys are unhappy."

"Honey, we're fine. Your daddy just forgot something important, and I had to remind him. He's fine. Or will be."

"If you're sure you're okay. Do I need to come back?"

"Not at all, honey. Besides, we won't be here. Your daddy and I are going out with Kelly and Owen for their anniversary. Robin will be here with Noah when you get home. Carmen is planning a special dinner just for the three of you. Lasagna, your favorite!" Nina made a mental note to tell Carmen to fix lasagna for the kids tonight.

"Okay, well, I'm here. Have fun and tell Kelly and Owen I said congratulations."

"I sure will, honey."

"Oh, and mommy? *Eu te amo.*"

Nina knew that phrase. "I love you, too, sweetheart."

JACK WAS FURIOUS. HE CHARGED INTO THE LIBRARY AND SLAMMED THE DOOR. HE did not look forward to this dinner with Kelly and Owen, considering their pasts. *And present,* Jack thought. *How could Nina not remind me again. She knows my mind is on this project at work. At least that's my reasoning to her.*

But it was more than that. So much more. Jack went to the bar and poured himself a bourbon over ice. He threw it back then poured another. He sat in his desk chair and spun it around. As he looked out the massive paned window, he could see the snow on the ground, making the estate look like a shimmering spread of marshmallow fluff, all the way down to the boat house. The waves on the Long Island Sound were choppier than usual today but the weatherman did say a small front was coming inland but nothing to worry about. *I wish a blizzard would come and cover the state. Then I wouldn't have to go to this damn dinner.*

Jack looked at a framed picture on his desk. It was of the family. Everyone looked so happy, but Jack knew the lies behind the smiles. At least his own. He swallowed a gulp of bourbon and felt the sting of the alcohol in his throat.

Ever since Thanksgiving, Jack had avoided Kelly, or at least tried to. He was on edge that at any given moment she would continue that drunken conversation and blurt out something that shouldn't be blurted out.

Like the wedding.

KELLY AND OWEN'S WEDDING WAS THE BIGGEST SOCIAL EVENT DARIEN, Connecticut had seen since Kelly's own parents got married. A lavish event where costs were rumored in the seven figures. Everyone from the King of Sweden to Queen Latifah were there. Nina was the maid of honor and Jack, by default, was Owen's best man. Jack couldn't stop looking at Nina.

"Smile!" A photographer quickly snapped their photo.

Jack kissed Nina. She was, without a doubt, the most beautiful woman at that wedding, including the bride herself. Jack had never felt prouder of Nina. She was now a successful author and was riding a high wave of popularity. She was at the top of her game and with only one book under her belt. Jack knew she was just beginning. As he watched her catch the bouquet, he never felt luckier.

"May I break in?" Owen asked Jack on the dance floor. "It's my turn to dance with the maid of honor."

"Of course," Jack said. "But I warn you, she has two left feet."

"Oh hush," Nina replied. "I have the bruises on my toes to prove otherwise."

"Just sayin'," Jack said, and made his way over to a waiting Kelly.

"Finally!" she said. "I've been waiting to dump him all night," she laughed.

"It was a beautiful wedding," Jack said sincerely. "I know ours won't be as lavish but - "

"Stop it. It'll be magnificent. Nina won't have it any other way. You know that."

Jack laughed. "Yeah, you're right. I better start saving now."

"Her parents will pay for the wedding, don't you worry."

"No way. This is on me. She's going to be my wife and I'm going to pay for the whole thing out of my own pocket."

Kelly pursed her lips. "So, you're going to elope?"

"Hey! I can afford something nicer than that," Jack laughed. "It'll be perfect."

"I know it will," Kelly whispered. "Just like you."

Jack stopped dancing and pulled back. "Kelly…. I…"

"Oh, Jack, I'm sorry. I shouldn't have said anything. I know. I'm being stupid. It's my wedding day! And I love Owen, I do. It's just…. we…"

"It's just nothing, Kelly," Jack urged. "And there is no "we". Not anymore." He looked over at Nina and Owen, wondering if they heard anything. They were dancing and smiling, oblivious. Jack and Kelly continued dancing.

"I know…but I can't look at Owen and not feel a pang of guilt every single time."

"Same with Nina," Jack replied. "She's the love of my life. I'd do anything to take it back."

Kelly looked hurt. "I wouldn't. Those times were very special to me. We didn't end up together, but we still made some memories I will always cherish." Kelly started to tear up.

"Don't cry. This is a happy day," Jack said hopefully.

Kelly looked up at Jack with her big brown eyes. He blinked. She closed her eyes, turned her head, and ran off the dance floor.

"Hey. Where'd Kelly go?" Owen asked.

"I think her stomach was hurting a little?" Jack replied.

"I should go after her," Owen said.

"I'll go," Nina said. "It's probably a woman thing. I'll be right back." Jack watched Nina head off the floor.

"Hope she's okay," Owen said.

"Yeah," Jack said, uneasy.

"By the way, thanks again for being my best man. It meant a lot to me. And to Kelly. You're a good guy, Jack Travers." Owen patted Jack gently on the arm.

If he only knew, Jack thought. "No sweat, bud. Happy to do it."

"Drink?"

"You bet," Jack said, relieved this conversation was coming to a close.

Over the next few minutes, Owen talked about their honeymoon destination (the Maldives) and where they would live (Miami).

"Miami just makes sense because that's where I'm going to start my business.

Interning for Kelly's father at his company gave me the itch to set up my own practice and that's what I'm going to do. I've already got the blueprints for the office drawn up."

He seemed so sure of himself, Jack thought. Owen was not quite five and a half feet tall and yet he had the confidence of a bull in a ring. It was that confidence Jack would come to later regret knowing. Owen was a runner, also, and they would often hit the streets for a run, so they had that in common.

Jack looked up and saw Nina walking back towards them with Kelly. Something else we have in common, Jack thought, looking at the bride. He felt his stomach churn.

"Feeling better, sweets?" Owen said, wrapping his arms around Kelly's waist.

"Much. I guess we need to say 'hi' to the other guests. Shall we mingle?"

"As you wish, Mrs. Ford." He linked his arm in hers and they made their way towards a group of people.

"Uh, was Kelly okay," Jack asked Nina.

"Yeah. But it was weird. It wasn't her stomach at all. Or a woman thing. She was just in there sitting in the lounge with her head in her hands. She said she felt fine, but I could tell something was up."

Jack pushed his glasses up. "Um, did she say what it was?"

"No. Not a word. Well, she said two words actually. She said, 'I'm sorry.'" Nina looked puzzled. "That's it. Just 'I'm sorry'".

"Huh," Jack muttered, his breathing became heavier. "Wonder what that was about?"

"No clue," Nina said softly. "Absolutely no clue."

Before leaving for the Maldives, Kelly and Owen, as well as Jack and Nina, had planned to stay the night at Kelly's parents' large estate in a final farewell to the Bride and Groom. Jack did his best to get out of the overnight stay, but Nina insisted, pulling the "she's my best friend and I won't see her for a while" card, so in the end, Jack gave in.

The couples joined up in the den. Owen was pouring vodka cranberries for the girls and whisky over ice for him and Jack.

"It was a beautiful day," Nina said. "Kelly, you looked gorgeous. And did you even get to eat anything?"

"No. And I'm starving. But I have the teeniest bikini for the honeymoon and I'm not about to put carbs in me before I put that thing on. This alcohol is fattening enough."

"Don't remind me," Nina sighed. "I ate like a pig today. I'm surprised I haven't floated away like I was in the Macy's Thanksgiving Day parade."

"Stop it," Kelly laughed. "You're stunning. Isn't she stunning, Jack?" Kelly prodded.

"The most stunning person here," Jack said too quickly before realizing his mistake.

Kelly looked crushed.

"Other than my wife, of course," Owen said, smiling.

"Of course," Jack said. "I didn't mean anything.... of course, she's...."

Owen laughed aloud. "Jack, it's okay! They're both amazing looking. We are two very lucky men, indeed."

"Yes, you are," Nina said, cozying up to Jack. "Kelly, don't stay in the Maldives too long! You know my own wedding is in two months!"

"Wouldn't dream of it. I'll be by your side always. Except for now. I'm going to bed," Kelly said. "I'm really tired and we have a long day ahead of us tomorrow. G'night everyone."

"But it's only 11:30!" Nina scoffed. "It's early still!"

Kelly went over and hugged Nina. "I'm whipped. But thank you for today. It meant the world to me."

"You're very welcome, honey. I love you!"

She looked at Nina in the eyes. "I love you, too." She looked over at Jack. "G'night, Jack."

"'Night, Kelly. You guys have a safe trip."

Kelly smiled and nodded. Owen came up behind her and hugged her waist. "We'll talk with you guys when we get back."

"We won't see you in the morning?" Nina asked.

"Nah. Charles's driver is taking us to the jet at 5:00am. It's a long ass flight and we need to get an early start. But hang out and let Esther fix you one of her famous breakfasts. It won't disappoint."

"Alright then. You guys sleep well and we'll see you in a couple weeks. Text me pictures!"

"I will," Kelly said. She and Owen made their way up the stairs to their room at the end of the hall. Jack and Nina heard the door close. She raised her glass to him and asked "Wanna stay up a bit?"

"Maybe we should hit the hay, too. I'm a little beat." He stifled a yawn.

"Yeah, okay. Party pooper." She walked over to him and hugged him, resting her head on his chest. "Promise me something," she said.

"What's that?"

"That we never get so old where 11:30pm is time for bed," she yawned.

Jack laughed. "Whatever you say, sleepyhead. Let's go."

"Mmm hmm," she mumbled sleepily. With his arm behind her back, he led her to their room - right next door to Kelly and Owen.

Within 20 minutes, Nina was sound asleep, a light snoring sound coming from her mouth. But Jack's eyes were wide open. He was sitting up, his back and head against the wall. And just on the other side of that wall was.... he closed his eyes and shook the thought from his head.

It was going to be a long night.

An hour later, he heard a tapping on the bedroom door before he saw it swing open slowly. He looked towards the door and saw Kelly pop her head in.

Jack got out of bed and went into the hall, closing the bedroom door behind him.

"What are you doing? Nina is sleeping!"

"I had to see you! I'm sorry, I really am but I couldn't go to sleep without talking to you first and apologizing for everything."

He knew he should send her back to her room and then he could get back into his own bed and go to sleep.

But instead, he said "Fine. Where can we go talk?" He looked at her. "Just talk."

She looked relieved. "Come with me."

She took his hand and lead Jack to a bedroom at the other end of the hallway. When they entered, she turned on the light then dimmed it down. Jack could see this room was twice as big as his and Nina's and there was a seating area in front of a fireplace. Kelly closed the door behind them, and they sat on the sofa.

"Kelly, we can't keep doing this. You're married now. And even if you weren't married, I'm engaged to Nina. This isn't right!"

Kelly leaned into Jack and kissed him. "Owen knows about us," she said.

He nudged Kelly away from him. "He what?" Jack asked, shocked.

"He knows about us.... about that time in college. I had to tell him. We'd had that fight and I went back to him, and I was crying, and he was consoling me, I got caught up in the moment and just told him. He wasn't happy at first, but he said he was glad I told him. That we needed to start our relationship with 100% honesty."

"We can't do this anymore. I am in love with Nina."

"And I'm in love with Owen, but I can't stop thinking about you. There's just

something between us. I know you feel it, too."

"Kelly, I…yes, there used to be…but things are different now. You're married, I'm engaged - things are completely different"

"Are they? Are they really?" She leaned into him and removed his glasses. She grabbed his crotch as she kissed him and buried her tongue in his mouth. The fire was back, and Jack felt a burning in him. His hands found Kelly's breasts and he raised her nightgown. She was not wearing any underwear and he grabbed her and pulled her on top of him. She had released him through his pajama bottoms and as she straddled him, he entered her deep, filling her. She tossed her head back and moaned. She rode him hard and soft, hard and soft, oscillating between the two until he groaned and erupted into her. She orgasmed at the same time and the feeling was hot and velvety, sweet, and vigorous. Her long hair was wet and sticking to her forehead. He brushed her hair from her face and kissed her. He fell back onto the sofa, and she fell on top of his chest, he was still inside her. They lay there for a moment, and he felt another stirring. Within minutes, the ride began again.

The next morning, Jack and Nina went downstairs for breakfast and there was a note on the kitchen island.

To my two dearest friends in the world. Our wedding was possible only because of you standing up for us. Here's to new beginnings! No matter what the future holds, we are bonded for life!

- Love,

Kelly

Jack no longer had an appetite.

Now, mad at Nina for not reminding him about tonight's dinner, he jumped up from his desk chair and threw his glass of bourbon across the room. Amber liquid and shards of Baccarat crystal exploded everywhere. *How the hell am I going to get through this dinner?*

CHAPTER THIRTY-FIVE

March

Kelly and Owen were already seated in the back of *Basil's on Main* when Nina and Jack walked in. Kelly raised her hand and waved them over.

"Be nice," Nina whispered through her smile.

"I always am," Jack replied. Nina gave him a side eye.

"Hi, you two! Happy Anniversary!" Nina squealed. Kelly stood up and the two hugged.

"Owen, happy anniversary," Jack said, shaking Owen's hand.

"Thanks, man. Appreciate that. Sit, sit."

The waiter come to the table and introduced himself. He asked for drink orders.

"I'll take a Carlsberg and she'll have a glass of Riesling," Jack said.

'With a glass of ice on the side, please," Nina added.

"You and your ice with wine," Kelly said. 'Crazy."

"I'll have the same as him," Owen said, "and - "

"Just a sparkling water, please," Kelly said.

"*What?!*" Nina acted surprised. "No Champagne? No tequila shot? Talk about crazy! What's wrong with you? Pregnant?" Nina laughed.

Kelly looked at Nina and just smiled. Nina's eyes widened.

"*What?!*" Nina said, genuinely surprised this time. "You're...you're pregnant?!"

"I am! We are!" Kelly responded. "We wanted to wait and tell everyone until the first trimester was over, just to be safe."

"Twelve weeks? You went *twelve weeks* without telling me? Your best friend? What the hell?!" Nina said playfully, sort of.

"Sixteen, actually. But we just wanted to be sure, you know? I mean, especially with you, we wanted to be - "

"Sensitive," Owen interjected. "We didn't want to stir up any old emotions, that's all."

Nina knew exactly what they were talking about. It was such a difficult time in her and Jack's lives when they were trying to conceive. So many failed attempts and miscarriages and disappointments after elations. It was horrible. But they had Addy in their lives now *and* they were blessed with a full-term pregnancy with Noah. So, everything worked itself out in the end.

"We understand," Jack said. "And congrats. You two are going to be terrific parents." He looked at Kelly and she did not return his stare.

"Awww, thanks, pal," Owen said. "If we're half the parents you guys are then I'll call that a success."

The waiter came and took their dinner orders. Jack went first and then Owen. The girls were being indecisive, per usual. Jack's phone beeped. A text. He read it and his face flushed with heat. He looked at Owen. Jack looked down at his phone and read the text again.

O: *Meet me in the bathroom. We need to talk.*

What the hell Owen? Now's not the time, Jack thought. He looked at Owen covertly and shook his head imperceptibly 'no'.

Owen's look back was one of disappointment. But he could wait.

"Well," Nina said, "you guys are going to make wonderful first-time parents." She caught Kelly and Owen quickly glancing at each other. "Ohhh-kay. What was that about?"

"What was what about?" Kelly asked Nina.

"That look you two just gave each other," she wagged her finger back and forth in front of them. "Very secretive. What did I miss?"

"Yeah, I saw that, too," Jack said, his brow furrowed. "What gives?"

Kelly put her hands in her lap and grew silent.

Owen reached under the table and grabbed Kelly's hands. "Wow. Well, we really didn't want to tell you guys this. Or tell you ever. We know the pain you guys went through trying to conceive - "

"Yes," Nina interjected. "You guys were with us every step of the way. We would've never gotten through any of that without you, you know that. We are so grateful." Her eyes started to moisten. "But then you got the adoption process expedited for us and then we were blessed with Addy. But what does our pain have to do with" - then Nina looked at Kelly, her head looking down in her lap, and she knew. She just knew.

Kelly looked up, a tear fell from her eye, and she placed her clasped hands under her chin.

"Oh my god, Kelly! *No!* You had a mis-" Nina couldn't finish the sentence. "What? *When?*" Her hands flew across the table to grasp Kelly's. "Why didn't you ever tell-" But the pain in Kelly's eyes resonated her own pain she felt all those years ago and at that moment, she couldn't have loved her best friend more. Kelly held in her own pain as to not let Nina's suffering resurface.

"Oh, man," Jack said. "I am so sorry. We both are. We know what you went through." He looked at Owen and although he didn't care for the man too much, he did feel a pang of sympathy towards him.

"When? When did this happen?" Nina asked quietly.

"In college. Before we were engaged," Kelly whispered. "It was around the time you just started writing your first book." She looked at Jack. "Sometime around then."

Jack felt a lump in his throat. *Sometime around then. Oh my god. Could the baby have been - no! NO!* Jack wanted to scream. *That can't be possible!* He didn't want his mind to go there. He felt sick.

"There's more," Owen said.

Jack couldn't look at him. He swallowed.

Owen continued. "Kelly had carried the baby full term. She…the baby…. was stillborn. Pre-eclampsia."

Kelly's eyes locked with Jack's then she looked away and stifled a sob. She placed her hand on her belly. "It was for the best," Kelly said shakily. "There's no way we were ready for a baby. Owen was focused on his career and my trust had a codicil in it that was pretty clear -"

"A…a codicil?" Nina asked baffled.

Owen said "When Kelly turned twenty-five, she received her trust but ol' man Andrews had put in a codicil forbidding children a) out of wedlock, and b) for the first five years of us being married. It was his way of having a say so in the security of our relationship."

"Wait," Jack started. "So, Charles put in your trust you had to *prove* your marriage was a good one before you could have children?"

The waiter brought another round of drinks.

"Basically, yeah," Kelly said. "If the marriage wasn't good then why bring children into it?"

Jack asked, "What would've happened if you - "

"Had the baby?" Kelly finished.

"Yeah."

"I would've had to give the trust back."

"All of it?" Jack asked, wide-eyed.

"Yup. One hundred percent."

"That's unbelievable!" Nina said incredulously, shaking her head. "Wow!"

"Right? Turns out my father is a complete asshole."

"Explains their divorce a little better, huh?" Owen said.

"No kidding," Nina said, still shaking her head.

"So," Kelly said, taking a deep breath, "that's why having a baby so soon wouldn't have been good. I know that sounds selfish but -"

"No, no," Nina said. "Honey, your choice was.... *impossible*. Besides, it wasn't your fault the baby...*died*." She didn't know what else to say. "It's just a sad situation all around, I suppose." Then she remembered. "Wait. You left college after your sophomore year. Was that because -"

"Yes," Kelly said. "I went away to have the baby. Told my parents we were going to travel the world before settling down. They thought that would be healthy for our relationship, so they didn't protest." She shrugged. "Sure showed them, huh?" She looked defeated and Nina noticed.

Nina's eyes widened. "But now! Now you've got reason to celebrate! This one will definitely be the one for you. This baby will make all your dreams come true!" She winked at Kelly.

"And so far, so good. My doctor said things have come a long way since then and they can detect things much quicker so there's a 99.9% chance this one will be healthy. And at least with this baby," Kelly said, "I'll get to see it."

"See it? What do you mean?" Nina asked.

Kelly spoke softly. "Well, when Owen told me she was stillborn, he took her away so I wouldn't have to look at her and suffer any more." Owen wrapped his arm around Kelly's shoulders. "I'm glad, too, because I just think seeing what she looked like would just have broken my heart even more."

The lump in Jack's throat reappeared. He didn't like where his mind was taking him, but he couldn't stop it. *What if.... what if the baby* wasn't *stillborn? What if Owen took the baby somewhere?* Jack was only half listening now to Kelly, his thoughts going crazy. *But that can't be. It's not possible. For almost two years, Jack?* He asked himself. *Come on.* Then he remembered that Owen's sister ran a daycare. Did he let her raise the baby for a couple years until a couple looking to adopt came along? A couple with money like Jack and Nina? Jack paled. He had to know. But he was also scared as hell to ask.

The waiter came and placed their food in front of them. Suddenly, none of it looked appetizing.

"I don't know if I can eat now," Kelly stated. "Some anniversary."

"Honey, you have to. You're eating for two now!" Nina said smiling.

"She's right, babe. You need to eat something."

Jack let out a little groan.

"Jack? You don't look so good," Nina said.

Everyone looked at Jack, who had paled considerably.

"You pregnant, too?" Kelly tried to lighten the mood.

Jack realized he had been silent while everyone stared at him. "Yeah," he chuckled. "That would explain the weight gain."

"Like you could gain weight," Kelly rolled her eyes.

Nina placed her hand on Jack's arm. "Are you feeling okay, hon?"

"Actually, no. Do you mind if we head out?" He looked at Kelly. Then he shifted his eyes pointedly towards Owen. "I feel sick, suddenly."

"That's too bad, brother," Owen said. "Sure hope you feel better."

Nina gathered her handbag and shawl. She stood and walked over to Kelly and kissed her on the cheek. "Congratulations, my friend. I'm so happy for you. For you both." She nodded towards Owen

"Thank you, sweetie," Kelly said. "Call me tomorrow?"

"Of course. Goodnight, you two." Nina stood next to Jack, who nodded his goodbyes.

As they were leaving, Jack turned back to look at the couple. Kelly was looking in a compact putting on lipstick and Owen was smirking.

Owen stuck out his thumb and pinky, forming a fake phone and put it to his ear. *Call me,* he mouthed.

Jack just stared, turned on his heels and left the restaurant.

CHAPTER THIRTY-SIX

March

Margo was getting nervous. Today she was meeting with Harris Markham. After their conversation at the launch party, Margo needed to nip his anger in the bud and have a come-to-Jesus meeting and get this explosive situation under control. She would meet with him but there was no way in hell she was going to take him back as a client. His behavior at the book launch party sealed his fate with Margo. She thought back…

Nina's house was full of guests still staring at Harris Markham and Margo Flagg on the foyer. She forced him into the library to shut down the gawkers. Whatever Harris had to say, Margo didn't want everyone to hear, let alone video their confrontation. "Margo, I'm sorry for barging in like this, I really am. But I have nowhere else to go."

"Harris, we have nothing further to discuss. I'm sorry you felt hurt when I dissolved your contract with me, but it was for the best. I was inundated with deci-

sions and projects when Nina's popularity skyrocketed like it did, and there was no way I could've possibly given you the fair time and attention you deserved."

"But I don't take up much space," Harris tried to make light of the situation. "I just need one more bestseller to get me through...and...and I need your help with that. Your name...it goes a long way.... you're powerful, Margo. Please. Help me." He was hoping his flattery would help his cause.

Margo didn't like who Harris had become. Did I do this to him? Did I make him the pathetic man before me? No. He's an adult with a family and he makes his own choices. No Jewish guilt here.

"Harris, the answer is 'no'. I gave your credentials to Angela Vine at Word-Master and - "

"Screw Angela Vine! She's a nobody in this business!" he boomed. He saw Margo take a step back. He softened but took a step closer. "Look, I'm sorry. I shouldn't have.... but please, Margo! I'm begging you and I don't like to beg but..." he dropped to his knees. "I'm begging here! I'm nothing without you and your guidance. I'm broke and my wife took the kids and left me, and I lost the house...." he trailed off and started sobbing.

"Harris, for god's sake, get up! This is pathetic, really. There are over a hundred people out there who saw you barge in here, uninvited I might add, just after Willa Greyson almost died! Do you think any of them are going to have sympathy for you? Let alone me? Willa is a client of mine and I need to be out there."

"Oh, I get it," Harris said, standing. "I'm not good enough for you now, huh? You know, I've been to tons of these launch parties before, and I fit in perfectly. Those were the good times, Margo," he urged her to remember. "We were a team. A good team. Please don't throw that away."

Margo was at a loss. This man in front of her was a loose cannon and she hadn't forgotten the last time he barged into her office threatening her. But something about him had changed. Something about the way he let his tears flow freely. He seemed.... vulnerable. She wasn't ready to take him back as a client, but she was ready to talk further. Just not tonight.

"Fine. Listen, Harris. I'll talk with you but not here, too much is going on but," she checked her phone calendar, "I can see you in two months. Monday March 14th, 9:00am at the office. Does that work for you?"

"Two months?" he asked. "That's so far...." He saw Margo raise her eyebrows and cock her head. "Sure, sure, no problem. March 14th. I'll be there."

Margo put her phone away. "Look, Harris, there are a lot of authors out there doing their jobs and doing them very well, and quite honestly, they will always stand in your way. If I take you back, and I'm not promising anything, you've got a long road ahead of you to get on the bestseller list. Or any list for that matter. You would have to have a killer of a book. Do you know what I mean? One that has never been done before. Something special and unique that would blow people's minds. Then and only then will I even consider pushing it to get published. Do you understand?" Harris's eyes became glassy and distant. She shook her head. Was he even listening? She walked over to the desk, set her purse down and reached inside to get a pen and paper to write the meeting information down for him.

"Yes," Harris responded. "Completely." And he did. His mission was clear. He looked at her and smiled. "I know what I have to do now. Thanks for the inspiration, Margo," he said.

She rummaged through her purse. "And what inspiration is that, Harris?" she asked. But when she looked up, he was gone.

THAT WAS TWO MONTHS AGO AND NOW, MARGO WAITED FOR HARRIS TO SHOW up. She looked at the clock. 9:14am. She didn't have all day. At 9:15am, she decided Harris Markham was out of luck and she locked her office door behind her and left.

CHAPTER THIRTY-SEVEN

March

Since the day I killed Rachel Meadows, I was one step closer to my goal. I liked reaching my goals, of which I had many in my life. One was to blend in, and I did that gloriously. Not just on the street with Rachel, but with the family. No one had any clue as to what I was doing, and I intended to keep it that way.

Another goal was to eliminate the writers standing in my way. Go ahead and laugh. I mean, who kills writers? What a stupid plot for any book, someone might say. But do they know me? I mean the real *me? No. Apparently not. Because I, what? I blend!*

So much is at stake, but it seems I've gotten away with Rachel's 'accident' and that has only boosted my confidence that I should continue with my plan. I feel inspired like never before!

But this next one. Whew! This one took a while. I've been plotting this one for two months and now is the time to strike. I'm like a cobra ready to.... no. Ugh. I hate snakes. How about a leopard? I'm more of a dog person than a cat person, but yeah! A leopard. I am a leopard, stealthy, staying out of sight, even while in plain sight, planning and determined to make my next move, pouncing just when the time is right. And now, the time is right. Two months in the making. I hope it was worth it.

My heart is racing. My breathing is fast.
I hope I can do this. I hope it works.
I hope Gregory Wynn suffers.

CHAPTER THIRTY-EIGHT

March

"Good morning, lovelies," Robin said, coming into the large kitchen. Nina was seated at the table with Addy and Noah, flipping through screens on her tablet. "It is such a beautiful winter day outside. What shall we do today?"

"Brekky," Noah said. "See? You're not the only one who knows another language," he said to Addy.

"Speaking British slang is not another language, Noah," Addy said rolling her eyes.

"Is so!" He said defiantly.

"Is not. It's just English with an accent."

"Oh. Well, bloody hell," he said.

"Noah!" Nina exclaimed, trying to hide a chuckle. "You don't say that. That's not proper for a young man to say," she said with a stern tone, but her smile said otherwise. She shook her head and continued looking on her iPad.

"I'm so sorry, Nina," Robin said. "He must've heard me say that a time or two. Or three." She blushed. She decided to change the subject quickly. "So, Addy! You have a big birthday coming up next month! You're going to be a teenager! That's an important one. What are your plans? Do you want a big party with gifts and friends? A bouncy house or pony? We need to start planning now!"

"Nah. I don't have many friends and besides, the ones I do have are a bit boring for me. I'd rather just hang out here with you guys and open presents, if that's okay."

"What about Valentina," Nina asked. "Maybe we could invite her. Or Charlotte Hanover?" Nina was hoping Addy would like to invite at least one friend over.

"*Charlotte Hanover?!*" Addy said with a disgusted look on her face. "Mommy, she is utterly puerile! I mean, she's okay for a little bit but there is no way I could spend a whole day with her. Ugh! So childish! I cannot believe you suggested her!"

"Sorry," Nina said raising her hands in defense. "I don't know what I was thinking."

"It's okay, lovey, we'll have a grand time with just us, yeah?" Robin said.

"Yup! We sure will - "

"Simone, relax. It's no big deal. Happens all the time. You of all people know how easy it is to spoof a phone number," Jack walked into the kitchen on his phone. He covered the mouthpiece. "Simone from work," he whispered, pointing to the phone. Jack took a seat at the island. "Look, I'm sure it's a harmless prank. You shouldn't have gone out with him in the first place. He's married! No. I know. Look, send me his phone number and I'll, I don't know, I'll add it to some porn site or something. I'm sure his wife would love that. Fine. I'll talk with you next week. Bye."

"What was it this time," Nina asked, but then something on her tablet caught her attention. She furrowed her brows as she read.

"Someone spoofed her phone and was playing a trick on her, that's all."

"What's spoof?" Noah asked.

"Well," Jack thought, "It's when if someone wants to play a trick with you and wants you to think you're receiving a text or a call from someone else, they "spoof", or clone, that person's phone number and make it look like the call is from that person. Understand?"

"Nope," he said.

"That sounds complicated. I mean, for a tech wizard like yourself it's probably very easy but…" Robin inquired.

"It's really not that complicated. There are apps out there like *ClonePhone* or *DupeMe* that shows anyone how to spoof a phone."

"Daddy! What's spoof?" Noah asked again.

"So, pretend your best bud, Easton, forgot to get you a present for your birthday -"

"I'd kick him!" Noah said.

"Don't do that," Jack said. "Anyway, say he forgets, but he wants you to think he got you something. So, at the party, he writes his name on a card and puts it on someone else's gift to you. He basically 'spoofed' the gift and now you think he got you something, but he really didn't. Now do you understand?

"Bloody hell," Noah said.

"Oh my god!" Nina said.

"I'm sorry, mommy," Noah said.

"No, honey. Not that." She handed Jack her tablet. "This!"

The City Li

March 19, 2022

2nd Author to Die in 3 mont

Gregory Wynn, 43, popular local author has died, according to NYPD spokesperson, Lt. Sylvia Harmon. "Mr. Wynn was discovered unresponsive in his apartment on Thursday, March 17th. A neighbor said she smelled something odd coming from down the hall and called the police department who made the discovery. It appears Mr. Wynn succumbed to carbon monoxide poisoning probably from a faulty leak in his fireplace. According to the Medical Examiner, Mr. Wynn died sometime between 4:30pm and 10:30pm on Friday March 11th. The apartment building was evacuated and is now clear for all tenants to return to their homes. This tragic accident could've been prevented if he had only checked the valving system of the fireplace. We urge all people with electric fireplaces to perform maintenance on their in-home fireplaces regularly." Gregory Wynn was the author of the bestselling children's book series "The Many Misadventures of Magnolia Muckitymuck". Under the pseudonym, Rebecca Sanchez, Wynn wrote thrillers such as

Rei
foll
imp

The
that
rela
the
beh
of a
exp
in l
its
beh
con
or v

It m
tota
thir
dec
mo
retu

Nina's voice went up an octave. "Jack! *Gregory Wynn?!* He's dead!"

Jack looked at Robin who got the hint.

"Come on, children. Let's go get dressed for a fabulous day!" She scooped up the children and shooed them out of the kitchen. Jack nodded his appreciation. The kids bounded up the stairs. Robin turned to Nina. "I've been meaning to ask, where are the children's sweaters? This New England weather is begging for additional warmer clothing."

"Umm," Nina tried to think, her mind elsewhere.

"We keep them in containers under their beds," Jack intercepted.

"Thank you," Robin said.

Jack sat down at the table next to Nina. "Yeah, this Gregory thing is crazy. Wasn't he a client of Margo's at one point, too?"

"Yeah, but this doesn't make any sense. I mean, he was just here! For mother's book launch. This is unbelievable."

"I wonder if Margo knows. I mean, I'm sure she'd like to know." He looked at Nina. "Hon, that's two of her clients who are now dead. Isn't that a bit…"

"Odd?"

"I was gonna say 'suspicious', but yeah, 'odd' works, too."

"Surely this is just a coincidence, right? I mean, what are the chances? And look," she grabbed the iPad back. "Right here. It says it was a 'tragic accident'. Rachel Meadows' death was an accident, too, right? So…"

"So?" Jack asked, confused.

Nina was just as confused. She didn't have an answer, but she felt something was wrong. She thought of Margo and how she will react once she hears about this. If she hadn't already. Nina shook her head. She couldn't put her finger on it but she was sure of one thing: this was no coincidence. "Bloody hell."

CHAPTER THIRTY-NINE

March

Margo was beside herself. First Rachel and now Gregory? She had just spoken with him a couple months ago. Once in December and then again at the launch party.

In December, he had agreed to meet with her "but somewhere public like a sidewalk," Gregory had said. "If you cause a scene, I want it to be known." Margo hadn't planned on making a scene, she just wanted to ask Gregory if he had any interest in coming back as a client. She hated she had to swallow her pride, but she still wasn't 100 percent sure Nina was going to make her deadline, so Margo decided she needed a backup plan. And what better backup than an author who successfully wrote for not one but *two* classifications: children's books and psychological thrillers. Margo imagined Gregory Wynn as a cash cow but unfortunately, he saw right through Margo.

He laughed out loud right there on Grand Street, in front of hundreds of spectators. He was laughing at Margo, and she felt the fire rush into her cheeks.

"Never mind," she said. "Forget I even said anything."

"Margo! You are rich! Not in the monetary sense, lord knows, but in the mental sense. Do you really think I'd come back after you ceremoniously dumped my ass with no remorse? You humiliated me but I, like the phoenix, rose again. My books are more popular than ever. Ever! 'Magnolia' is about to be translated into 35 more languages. Do you know what that means to the bottom line?"

Unfortunately, Margo knew only too well.

"It means I will be earning millions on that series alone. And once that happens, I'm sure my other books will follow suit. I'll be an international bestseller! You dropping me was actually the best thing that's ever happened to me. So, thank you for asking," he laughed, "but you can go to hell. And I, in the meanwhile, will laugh all the way to the bank! You really are pathetic." He turned on his heels and walked away, still laughing, leaving Margo alone on the sidewalk with her face red as blood.

She turned to leave quickly and could still hear his laughter ringing over the crowd.

BUT NOW, GREGORY WAS DEAD. AND FOR SOME REASON, MARGO FELT A TWINGE of satisfaction. She called Nina. She answered on the first ring.

"Margo! My god. Gregory!"

"I know. I can't believe it. Carbon monoxide. I heard he was found on the floor near his windows."

"Oh, I know, it's horrible. Poor Gregory," Nina said. "I'm in the kitchen looking at my tablet and I have you on speaker phone."

"Oh, so how is everyone this morning," Margo asked, trying to sound chipper.

"We're as good as can be expected," Nina replied. "The kids are here eating pancakes and Robin is trying to keep everyone in line. Tough job." Jack had come up behind her and wrapped his arms around her, his way of comforting her. He nuzzled her neck. Addy looked at them and smiled. Noah was destroying his pancakes with his toy dinosaurs. Nina excused herself to the den.

"I just wanted to tell you I scrapped my original plans for *A Dark History*," Nina said. She could hear Margo gasp.

"*What?* Why?" Margo asked shocked.

"Simple. It wasn't working for me. In fact, I found it rather boring. It also held a little bit of bad memories for me, and nothing seemed fresh, you know? I mean, I was writing that book when everything, well, fell apart. It didn't feel *right* to continue down that same path when my *own* path in life has completely changed. Does that make sense?"

Margo couldn't argue with that reasoning but it did not lessen the fear that percolated in her soul at this very minute. "Yes, of course, it makes sense. But, Nina, will you be able to get something out in time? There's now less than 3 months until your contracted deadline."

"Oh yes! In fact, I'm very excited of my new direction with this. I'm not going to give you any spoilers, you'll just have to wait and see. But trust me. It'll be a bestseller overnight."

It'd better be, Margo thought. "Well, even as good as you are, and…even with -" Margo cringed when she said it "- two huge competitors now dead, you have big mountains to climb. There are still other writers out there eating up the literary real estate and, quite honestly, I'm a bit nervous you think a book written in 3 months is going to be big enough to take everyone else down."

"Oh, Margo. You're so dramatic. Everything is going to be fine. Trust me."

"My dear, Rachel and Gregory might be gone but top authors like Henry Corbyn, Leslie Fontaine, Carly Kaufman and yes, even your mother Willa, are not going to go peaceful into the night. They see the opportunities out there now just like you do and if you don't think they're going to amp up their book releases this Spring, you're delusional."

Nina knew Margo was right, but she had more confidence in this new idea that she was willing to bet everything she had on it. It was too good to not write. The damn book was writing itself, it seemed.

"You're right, Margo, as always. But I have confidence in this new idea. Look. If it'll make you feel better, I'll send you a snippet for you to read. But just a snippet! And then you tell me what you think. Deal?"

"Deal."

"And I'm not worried about Carly, or…Corbyn or Leslie or even dear ol' mom. I've got this. Have faith, old girl." Nina was confident but she was not naive to the fact this next book would be the dealbreaker if she had any career at all in the future. Her voice spoke 'confidence'; her heart spoke 'anxiousness'.

"Mommy?"

Nina looked up and saw Addy standing there. "Margo, I've got to go. If you hear anything more about Gregory, please let me know. I'll get you that bit of manuscript shortly. Talk with you later." She hung up her phone.

"Mommy, are you okay?"

"Why, yes, honey. Why would you ask that?"

"Well, when I walked in you looked unhappy. Are you unhappy?"

"Not at all, sweetheart. Come here." Addy trotted over and sat next to Nina on the sofa. Addy was wearing her favorite sweater: cream color with a 3D multi-colored unicorn on the front. *I see Robin found their sweaters,* Nina thought automatically. She leaned in and pulled Addy into her. "Mommy is not unhappy. I'm just a little sad. Well, now, *that* sounded like a contradiction, didn't it?" She laughed.

"Yeah. But I think I understand. You're sad about your friend. Mr. Wynn, right?"

"That's right, honey. In fact, you know of him. He wrote "*The Many Mis-* "

"*The Many Misadventures of Magnolia Muckitymuck*?" Addy asked wide-eyed.

"That's the one."

"Oh, man! I love that series. So, this means he won't be able to write those anymore?"

"Unfortunately, no." Nina saw Addy's sad expression. "But look, why don't we get Noah and Robin and go to the museum? I know they're open today and are having a very special Van Gogh exhibit. I know you love Van Gogh."

"Noah won't like it. So maybe he can stay here and just us girls can go?" Addy asked hopefully.

"That sounds like a plan! I'll go let your daddy know the boys have the run of the house and the girls are going out. We'll have fun!"

"Oh, mommy! I'm glad you're not unhappy. We'll have so much fun today."

After the morning she'd had, Nina was counting on it.

CHAPTER FORTY

May

April had been a busy month for the Travers household. Addy turned thirteen (and grew an inch taller), Noah lost 4 teeth (and gained $20), Jack went back to Philadelphia and finalized details on a new project, and Nina - well, Nina was at a standstill with her book.

But in her defense, she had a lot going on in April. And, as expected, that didn't go over well with Margo.

"Seriously, Nina? Are you *trying* to give me a heart attack?"

"Don't try to push your Jewish guilt on me, Margo," Nina chuckled. "It doesn't work on gentiles."

"When you sent me that little - and it was *very* little - piece of your new manuscript, I saw the magic once again. It was brilliant and I wanted more. That's exactly how your readers are going to react, too. They won't be able to put it down. You have a winner on your hands, Nina, I'll give you that. But you must give me more. You can't stop. You have two more months to get this done, do you understand?"

"I do, and if you keep talking to me, I'll never get it done." Nina abruptly hung up the phone and pictured Margo on the other end, mouth agape. Nina smiled.

Nina sent Robin a text then sat back in her chair. She looked around the library and saw the empty spot next to all her books, the spot waiting for this new book. *Soon*, she thought.

"Hi, Nina, you needed to see me?" Robin stepped into the library.

"I did. Come on in. Sit down."

"Uh oh. What did I do?" Robin asked nervously.

"Absolutely nothing, hon. I just wanted to chat.

"Okay. About…?"

"Well, if you're up to it, and *only* if you're up to it, I'd like to continue our conversation we started a couple months ago about your home. Ever since our first conversation, I couldn't get your past out of my head and, to be fair, a lot has happened since then and we never got to finish the journey."

Robin looked pensive. "It's not an easy subject to talk about, my past."

"Oh, I understand." Nina hesitated. "Should I pour us some bourbon like last time?"

"It's 9:30 in the morning, luv!"

Nina laughed. "We gotta start sometime."

"Nah. I'm good without it. I've already told you the hardest part, I suppose. The rest I think I can talk about alcohol-free."

"Good. I think we left off with you working at the motel and how you came about ending up in New York."

For the next two hours, Robin told Nina her story. And for the next two hours, Nina absorbed every word. Robin's life was like a real-life fairy tale but instead of a castle in a faraway kingdom, there was the ramshackle shed in the rot of Grimsby; and instead of dragons to slay, there was a horrible man who did reprehensible things to a young girl. The only resemblance was the wicked mother figure. She knew life had to get better. Somehow, somewhere. So, Robin had to save herself and that meant finding the courage and grit to leave her home and her family behind to create a new life for herself.

While in Miami, she was in a car accident that totaled her vehicle. Her lawyer got her a large settlement which enabled her to leave Miami for New York. Once she arrived, Robin hunted for work and did odd jobs here and there but always kept up her childhood education credentials online. It was in one of the nanny sites Robin found the ad for this position. Life had worked out for the better for Robin, after all.

"I gotta tell you," Nina said, "your story is quite remarkable. I feel like you've been through so much in your life and yet look at you! You're a beautiful, happy, spirited young lady. We could all learn from you and how to turn our lives around. Thank you for sharing."

"Of course," Robin said.

Nina could tell Robin was drained from sharing her life story. She needed to do something nice for Robin. Something she probably has never had done before. She had an idea and texted Kelly. Kelly's response was immediate. Then she texted Willa.

"Robin, grab your bag. We have someplace to go."

"Now?"

"Right now! Kelly's at her parent's home for the week and she's going to meet us there. So is mother. I just need to make one phone call really quick." She pulled up a number. "Hello, Gunnar?" She covered the mouthpiece and whispered to Robin *"shoo! Get ready!"* and Robin hastily left the room having no idea what she was getting ready for.

An hour later, Nina, Kelly, Willa, and Robin were face down on firm white tables getting massaged by four big Swedish men, their wine glasses on the table in front of them. Nina and Kelly just moaned, Willa lightly snored, and Robin couldn't stop giggling. Nina couldn't tell if Robin was happy or ticklish. Either way, it was the best $2000 she had ever spent.

CHAPTER FORTY-ONE

May

"Delivery for Margo Flagg," the courier said at the office door.

"That's me," she said as she signed for the large manila envelope. It was addressed to her but there was no return address. "Thank you," Margo said, handing the young man a twenty.

She went back to her desk and opened the envelope and peeked inside. It looked like a manuscript. *Another one,* Margo thought.

Ever since the deaths of Rachel Meadows and Gregory Wynn, manuscripts started pouring in from everywhere. Margo was inundated with wannabe-authors who wanted one thing and one thing only: fame. And even though she was famously known in the literary world to have whittled down her client list to two, for some reason, authors thought she would come to realize her blunder and would need more protégés. And now that two of her ex-clients were dead, there was no agent in America more famous than Margo Flagg. "Agent Doom", one critic dubbed her. *They can go to hell,* Margo thought. *They don't know what I've been through to get to where I am.*

She tossed the envelope on the ever-growing pile of other incoming compositions but as she did, the manuscript slipped out and crashed to the floor. Margo bent down to pick it up and as she did, she saw the title staring back at her: *A Killer Among Us.* But that wasn't what made her heart stop. It was the author.

Harris Markham.

"Harris Markham?! What the - " but she stopped when she noticed a note stapled to the cover page.

Margo,

Thank you so much for the inspiration to write something unique and unlike anything that has ever been done before; in your own words, a 'killer book'. This is my masterpiece. It is a personal journey. It is my experience. My truth. I'm sorry it had to come to this, but something had to be done. I truly hope you enjoy it.

- Harris

"What does he mean it's his 'experience'? His 'truth'? And he's sorry? Sorry for what?"

Margo hesitated because she didn't want to read it, but she knew curiosity would get the best of her later, so she decided to dig in. She got up and locked the door to her office then took the phone off the hook. She sat on her office sofa and started to read…

By the time she was finished reading Harris's manuscript, 5 hours had passed, and it was dark outside. Shaking, she set the composition down on her desk. Then she picked up the phone and called the police.

CHAPTER FORTY-TWO

May

Robin enjoyed the massage. Not like the ones in Miami, that's for sure, where most tried to give you a happy ending. No, the ones here in Darien were much classier. She hoped Caryn had experienced something so indulgent at least once. She missed Caryn and her kids. But Robin had found a new family in Nina, Jack, Noah, and Addy. Oh, how Addy reminded her of herself when she was younger. Smart and caring, always putting other people's happiness before her own. Robin got the sense that if Nina and Jack were happy, then Addy was walking on sunshine. That was Addy's lot in life: to ensure her family's joy.

Robin admired that in Addy because she also felt that way. When her own mother ignored her pleas of help while being raped, Robin still only thought of Caryn and her safety. She made Caryn move out into the shed with her where she was safe. And Robin would sacrifice herself, going back into the main house, and leave Caryn behind, who would be oblivious to the horrors inside the bedroom. Robin shed a tear. Not for her memories of Grimsby and her mother, no, but for her new life here, in the states. Here, with the Travers. Moving to Connecticut was a long time coming.

In fact, it was part of Robin's plan all along.

Miami was just the starting point. Meeting her lawyer was a stroke of luck because what followed changed Robin's life forever. The car accident was devastating but the settlement set things in motion for Robin she could only imagine. She now had enough money to travel to where she needed to be: New York. It was closer to her goal.

She was already a huge fan of Nina Travers before moving to the states so getting this job was the cherry on top of her ever-evolving sundae. *I've worked damn hard to get to where I am today*. The irony of working for an author was that Robin realized her plan was coming to fruition and she couldn't have written the scenarios better if she tried.

She went into the ensuite in her bedroom and stood over the sink. She looked in the mirror. Her face was a little ruddy from the facial but then she noticed the puffiness of her once soft, perfect cheeks. Her double chin lapped over her turtleneck shirt, and she felt like she was choking. She yanked off her shirt and stood in her undergarments. Her breasts, large and heavy, overflowed over her bra like an exploded can of biscuits. Even her ears were fleshier than they used to be. As hard as she looked, she could not see the old Robin behind the corpulent reflection. In her mind, she saw her reflection move differently than she did.

"You're a fat cow," she told the reflection.

"Here we go again! Don't make me laugh," the reflection spoke back. *"You did this shite to yourself!'*

"Don't laugh at me," Robin said. "I had no choice."

"You're sad, you know that, right? Have you no friends? No respect for yourself. You're pathetic, really."

"Stop it! Everything I've done has been for the betterment of the situation. And now that I've discovered how bad things have really gotten, I know I'm here for a reason."

The mirror yelled *"The* betterment? *Are you mad?! This is all your fault, you know! You let yourself get raped by that giant, flaunting your goods in front of him every night in short dresses. You knew what you were doing, didn't you?"*

"NO! Stop it! It wasn't on purpose. It wasn't!" Robin was sobbing now.

"Oh, poor, pitiful me! You make me sick! I can't believe you think this is going to end well for you."

"It will! It must. I have to save these people."

The mirror laughed. *"And how's that working out for you? How many are dead because of you? I'd say you're doing a bang-up job. Bravo."* The reflection began to clap. *"Wow. You really are a crazy sot, aren't you now?"*

Robin found her steel. "I am not crazy. I'm *not*. You'll see. I'll make it all better." She wiped her eyes.

In a deeper, almost hypnotizing voice, the mirror said, *"To make it all better, why don't you just kill yourself?"*

Robin stood up straight. She looked at herself, the reflection smirked back as if it just laid down a gauntlet. Robin leaned in and put her hands on the granite sink. A stare-down began. "Jesus, forgive me," she whispered.

Screaming, she threw her head full force into the mirror, her forehead shattering the glass. She felt the warm blood trickling down her face before she saw it in the splintered shards. The reflection, now multiplied in the fractured mirror, laughed maniacally until Robin's heavy breathing drowned it out.

CHAPTER FORTY-THREE

May

"Are you Margo Flagg," the policeman asked.

Margo felt sick. She knew what was coming and she wasn't sure she could speak. Her mouth was dry as sand.

"Y-yes," she stammered. "Thank you for coming, I suppose. Please tell me I was wrong."

"May I come in," the officer asked. Margo ushered him into her office. She sat on the sofa and the officer pulled up a chair.

"Ms. Flagg, I'm sorry to tell you, but you were not wrong."

Margo sunk into the sofa. Her hands went to her stomach. "Oh dear, God. W-what happened?"

The officer spoke quietly. "I'm not at liberty to say too much about the investigation but may I ask you a few questions first?"

"Of-of course. Go right ahead."

The officer pulled out a pad and pen. Flipping to an empty page, he asked his first question.

"How well did you know Brenda Markham?"

'Did'. Past tense. *Oh god.* "N-not well at all, I'm afraid. I only knew her

husband, Harris Markham." *I guess I really didn't know him at all.* "I met her twice: once at a book launch for her husband's book series, *Poison Pen*, and once more at an awards banquet at the Met." Margo sighed. "She's a lovely - " she caught herself. "She *was* - a lovely person. Oh, I just can't believe this is happening."

"I know it's hard, Ms. Flagg. Were you aware Brenda Markham and her ex-husband, Harris Markham, were seeing each other?"

This took Margo by surprise. "No. Not at all. Once Brenda got remarried, I assumed she wanted nothing more to do with Harris."

"In a way, that's true. Apparently, Harris was trying to get joint custody of the children," he considered his notes, "Charlie and Lilly."

Margo had forgotten about the children! If the manuscript was true, then… she couldn't bear to think about it.

"I know he loved his children," Margo said. "He...he had a rough time when his wife…left and took the children with her. He suffered a great deal. And then he lost his home…" her voice grew silent.

"Yes, ma'am. We're aware of the timeline."

"Sorry," Margo swallowed. "I'm just nervous."

"I understand," the officer said sympathetically.

"So…so Brenda…and the children…are they…" Margo let the sentence hang in the air.

"Yes, ma'am. We found three bodies at their home in Greenwich. Her husband was out of town on business at the time of their deaths."

"And he shot them." Margo filled in the blanks.

"Ms. Flagg, I never said how they died. That has not been released yet. Why would you think they were shot?"

"It's why I called you," she said, standing. She walked to her desk and presented the manuscript to the officer. "It's all in here. He sent me this. It was to be his next big book. I read it and it all sounded so familiar, with the divorce of an author and his wife, house in the Hamptons, two children, the wife remarries and moves to Greenwich, an ex-agent who - " Margo stopped talking. She took a breath and then continued carefully. "And then the murders. In the manuscript, he shoots his ex-wife and children while the husband is out of town. And then - " Margo's voice caught.

"Ms. Flagg?"

"Yes?"

"There's a note stapled here." The officer read it. "He's thanking you for inspiring him to write this. What exactly does that mean?"

Margo blinked. "I-I'm not sure exactly what he meant by that. He was trying - well, he wanted to come back as a client and I told him he needed to write something that's never been done before and- oh god, did I make him do this? Did I make him kill his family?" Margo sat heavily on the sofa.

"Ma'am, I don't think it's possible to make someone else do something like that. If Mr. Markham is behind this then it will be on him. Not you or anyone else." He asked her a question. "And then what?" the officer asked.

"Huh?" Margo said, still shaken.

"You were telling me something about the manuscript. After this person in the book shoots his family, there was something next."

"Oh, yes. After he kills his family, he shoots himself. He kills *himself.* But you said you only found three bodies? Not four? You didn't find Harris?"

"No, ma'am. But that's kind of why I'm here."

"Oh?"

"Yes," the officer said. "Harris Markham is nowhere to be found."

CHAPTER FORTY-FOUR

May

"Goodness, what happened to your forehead?" Nina exclaimed.

"Oh, just a little burn accident with the curling iron," Robin said, pointing to the large bandage.

"That looks bad," Nina grimaced. "Did you see a doctor?" She looked at her watch.

"No, but I've put some salve on it and it's healing up nicely. Just me being clumsy. No need for a doctor," Robin said. "So, what's on your agenda today? Going to write some more? I'm very excited to read your next book! What's it about, can you share?"

"Top secret," Nina said coyly. "But it's a doozy. I think you'll like it. It's a special book."

"Oh, I'm sure I will love it. I love all your books. My favorite is the *Shaken* trilogy. Wow! That was amazing. So epic."

"Thank you, so much," Nina said appreciatively. Nina glanced at her watch again. "You're sweet. I feel good about this one. And at least it'll get Margo off my back for another year."

Robin laughed. She looked around. "I know where the kiddos are, but where's Jack?"

"Oh, Owen came over and they went for a run around the neighborhood." Nina looked at Robin's forehead again. "Are you sure you don't want to see a doctor? I can call Dr. Sims and he'll come over - "

"Not at all. It's feeling better already but thank you."

Nina looked at her watch.

"Nina? You keep looking at your watch. Everything okay?"

"What? Oh, yeah. It's fine. It's just…well, it's Jack. He's been out running for over a couple of hours already and that's a long time for him. Plus, we're going over to mother's tonight for dinner. By the way, could you make sure the kids are ready to leave by 6:00?"

"Of course, not a problem."

Nina heard the front door open and shut. Jack and Owen walked into the kitchen.

"There you are," Nina said. Jack and Owen's faces were both rosy. "Looks like you two had a hard run."

"Nah, wasn't too bad," Owen said, as he walked to the refrigerator and pulled out a cold water. "Want?" he asked Jack.

Jack didn't answer. "I'm going to shower," Jack said curtly. "What time do we need to leave?"

"No later than 6:00," Nina said.

Jack bounded up the stairs out of sight.

"Everything okay?" Nina asked Owen.

"Oh, yeah. Everything's good." He walked towards Robin. "You must be the famous Robin. I've heard a lot of things about you."

"I'm intrigued," Robin said, turning and walking around the other side of the kitchen island, her back to Owen.

"What? You two have never met?" Nina exclaimed. "I can't believe that. Robin has been here since…" she looked at Robin.

"Since December. But I've been busy with the kids and keeping them occupied so you can write. We were all at the launch party but never spoke," Robin said. She began to wash her hands in the sink.

"Maybe. But now I feel like a terrible employer. You should at least know our best friends! I am so sorry. My manners suck. Yikes!"

Robin laughed. "Don't worry about it. We're meeting now. I've heard a great deal about you, too, Mr. Ford."

"Please, call me Owen…." He let his sentence hang. He cocked his head.

"Hmmm, you look a little familiar. Are you sure we've never met each other before?"

Robin never fully turned around. "Mr. Ford...Owen, I never forget a face and I don't recall yours anywhere in my memory." She turned to Nina, "I'll go round up the children to get them started." She headed towards the stairs then stopped. She turned around and looked him in the eyes. "Nice to finally meet you, Owen." She slowly lugged herself up the stairs.

Owen walked to the stairs and rested his arm on the volute of the banister and watched Robin disappear from sight. "So that's Robin," Owen said. "Where did you find her again?"

"Actually, Margo did. She placed an ad for a nanny and interviewed her and loved her. And thank goodness she did because Robin has been a godsend."

"Where did she come from? How well do you know her? Does she have any family? What did she do before this?"

"Owen, reel in the lawyer bit. She's not on trial here. Robin is a good egg and we're lucky to have her. She's been an enormous help to me, and the children love her. That's all you need to know. So, take a chill pill."

"Hmmm. Okay. But I am a bit curious about -"

Nina's phone rang. It was Kelly.

"Yes, he's right here! Please take him away. He's driving me crazy and I need to start getting ready to go to mother's." She laughed. "Yes, I'll tell him. Love you, too. Mwah!"

"I'm going, I'm going," Owen raised his hands.

"She said if you don't come home and massage her tired-ass pregnant feet right now, she's leaving you for the gardener."

"Julio? But his hands are huge and rough like sandpaper and.... oh, I get it now. Later!"

Nina laughed and then headed up the stairs.

At the front door, Owen turned around and looked back up towards the second floor. For some reason, he thought he had seen Robin before, of course the large bandage on her forehead was covering quite a bit. Her body was a little pudgy and that wasn't anything he recognized, but her face.... Owen couldn't place it. And he hated not being able to remember things.

CHAPTER FORTY-FIVE

May

"Hi grandmother!" Noah exclaimed, bounding through the front door of Scribbler's Cove and into the wide stretch of Willa's arms.

"Oh, my goodness," Willa said, almost toppling over.

"Careful there, sport," Jack said. Noah released Willa and ran into the house.

"I could use some of that energy," Willa scoffed.

Nina, Jack, and Addy stepped into the kitchen, taking turns embracing Willa.

"Mother, please. You're the healthiest woman I know," Nina said.

"Perhaps. But lately - "

"Lately what?" Nina asked, setting her purse down on a chair. They all started walking towards the kitchen.

"Nothing. Really. I just need to make an appointment to see Dr. Sims. I've just been feeling a bit rundown."

"Maybe you need to up your vitamins."

"I need to up my wine intake," Willa replied. "White or Rosé?"

"Rosé, please."

"You guys sit, I'll pour," Jack said. The ladies went into the den to join the kids. "Besides, it smells incredible in this kitchen! What amazing concoction has Imelda made tonight?"

"Some of her fabulous Filipino dishes: *Chicken adobo, sinigang* and for dessert, *biko*."

"What's - " Nina started.

"Don't ask. I have no idea. But if it tastes anything like it smells, we could all die happy."

Nina laughed. "So have you been feeling okay, besides a little tired?"

"Yes, darling. Perfect. I thought we'd eat outside on the lanai. It's such a lovely night. Jack, any day now with that wine."

"At your service," he said bringing over three glasses. They walked out onto the back patio and sat in the heavy iron chairs around the table.

"I've always loved your property, mother. The landscaping, the pool. The fruit trees should almost be perfect, huh?"

"Oh, yes. The pears and plums should be ready next week. I'll get some and do some projects to take to the farmer's market like I do every year."

"Maybe take it easy this year?" Nina asked.

"Stop worrying, darling. I'm perfectly fine. Fit as a fiddle."

Nina smiled and looked at the table. The place settings were bone china with spring flowers and green vines around the edges. The silverware was actually gold plated and gleamed in the setting sun hitting the table.

"These plates were a gift from the Earl of Kent," Willa said. "A past love," she whispered to Jack.

"Mother! Stop telling stories."

"Darling, if I did, I'd be broke." She sipped her wine. *Lust Kills* is still on the top, can you believe it?"

"Actually, I can. It's a fabulous book. I'm sure Margo is beside herself with glee," Nina said.

"Oh, my darling, speaking of Margo, have you heard the latest news?"

Nina shook her head.

"It appears Harris Markham sent her a manuscript for his new book and then he-"

"Wait. His new book? Is she representing him again?"

"No. Now hush. Let me finish."

Nina lifted a hand to signal Willa to continue.

"Apparently, she said she would consider representing him if he wrote something unique and unlike anything else on the market. Something epic and grand. So, he did just that and had the book delivered to her office for her to read."

"And?"

"Well!" she said dramatically. "Turns out, the book is about a young author who has been dumped by his agent and he loses everything: wife, house, kids, money - everything. Sound familiar so far?"

"Harris Markham?" Jack asked, unsure.

"The very one," Willa replied. She sipped her wine. "Now this is where it gets interesting. In the *book* - " Willa does air quotes "- the young man goes to his ex-wife's new house and shoots her and their two children to death, all while the new husband is out of town."

"Sounds like a thriller trope I've read a hundred times," Nina said.

"Yes! Except in *this* thriller, Harris's family was shot to death while the new husband was out of town." She sat back as if finished. Then popped back up. "Oh! And Harris is missing."

"*Whaaaat??!*" Nina gasped. "He killed his family and wrote a book about it?"

"*Allegedly* killed his family," Willa said. "But Harris is a person of interest and cannot be located. Poor Margo. She's shaking in her sensible shoes thinking Harris is coming for her next." She clicked her tongue.

"That's just…unbelievable," Nina said. "And scary."

"I can't believe you haven't heard about it. It's all over the news," Willa chided.

"I've been busy. Writing. No time for television."

"Wait." Jack said. "Is this the same guy who broke into Margo's office that time? And he came to our house during your book launch. Him?"

"That would be him," Willa confirmed. "An unstable lad, unfortunately. Never was the same after Margo dropped him."

Nina sighed. Margo dumping all her clients except for her and her mother set in motion a lot of actions, most of them not good. In some ways, Nina felt guilty. But in other ways, she felt grateful. Having someone like Margo Flagg in your corner was a chance in a lifetime and she and Willa were reaping the benefits of her talents. And others like Rachel Meadows, Gregory Wynn, and Harris Markham.... Nina shivered.

"Mrs. Greyson, dinner is ready," Imelda said, stepping out onto the lanai.

"Can you please call the children, Imelda? Thank you, darling."

The kids came out and grabbed their seats. Addy sat in the chair next to Willa, much to Noah's chagrin. Willa looked at the sulking Noah. "Next dinner I'm all yours," Willa said to him. He smiled and sat up straighter.

Imelda brought out heaping plates and bowls of delicious smelling Filipino foods and they all ate until they were stuffed. Dessert came and Addy and Noah were the only ones with appetites left.

After dinner, Jack and Nina walked the grounds. The sun had set but hundreds of little lights in overhead branches illuminated the trees and grounds, creating a magical, almost otherworldly ambiance. Noah was busy playing in the den with his dinosaurs.

Addy sat with Willa in loungers watching her parents walk the property.

"Are you ready for next week?" Willa asked. "The plums and pears will be perfect."

"Oh, yes! It's my most favorite thing to do ever!"

"Mine, too," Willa leaned in and whispered to Addy. "And I'm so glad it's just you and me. Us girls need to stick together, don't we?"

"But mommy's a girl."

"Yes, dear, but you know this has just been our little secret for the past five years. I've never done something like this with your mother and I don't want her to feel left out. You haven't told her, have you?"

Addy smiled. Every year, Willa and Addy picked the ripened fruits from Willa's orchards. In June, it was pears and plums. Shortly after, it was cherries and figs. And after the fruits were picked, Imelda would turn the fruits into jams and jellies and sauces and pies and give them to the local farmer's market to sell and let them keep all the profits.

Addy liked that she had a secret with her grandmother. It made her feel more grown up.

"Nope. Cross my heart," she said as she used her finger to do the motion across her chest.

"Good girl," Willa said. "Now. What do you say we go join your parents?"

Addy grabbed Willa's hand and began to walk. Addy looked up at Willa. She hugged her tight. "I love you, grandmother."

"I love you, too, sweetheart. Let's go!" As Willa stepped, she caught her breath. She touched her chest on impulse. *Maybe I should increase my vitamins,* she thought, as she continued her walk with her granddaughter.

CHAPTER FORTY-SIX

May

"Dear god, what have I done?"

He was sitting in the back booth of an all-night diner. He'd never been to this part of town before so he was pretty sure he would go unrecognized. With over four hundred diners in the city, it was easy to blend into the red-leather benches and white Formica tables. And he needed to blend. It seemed his picture as "a person of interest" was all over the news. But here, the TV was on an entertainment channel. Some young female singer exposed herself getting out of her limo again. The waitress, a craggy too-thin woman with fire-red hair, smacking gum to hide her smoker's breath, brought him a cup of coffee. He sipped the hot liquid, his hands shaking profusely.

Harris had to speak to Margo. He had to clear up this mess. Yes, he had killed his family, but it was for the greater good. Margo told him to write something the world had never seen before, and what could be better than a firsthand account of a despondent man, with nothing to lose, doing the most despicable act he could think of, and gaining everything in the end? *Am I trying to justify what I've done,* Harris thought? *Who does that?* "You're sick!" he yelled.

"Excuse me?"

Harris looked up. The craggy red-haired waitress was standing over him with a pot of coffee. She smacked her gum as she held up the pot as if to ask, "need a refill?".

"I'm...I'm sorry," he stammered. "I...no, thank you. I'm good." He had to get out of there. He stood to leave and bumped the waitress.

"Hey!"

"I'm terribly sorry. So sorry...."

"Aren't you forgetting something?" She asked.

Harris turned to face her. She was holding out her hand with her painted-on eyebrows raised. "For the coffee?" she smacked, cocking her head.

"Oh, sorry," he said again. He patted his jacket and felt the outline of the hard revolver. He paused and looked at the waitress. *Did she notice?* She cocked her head to the other side, her patience growing thinner. *No.* He was safe. He reached down and dug into his pockets. His hand found a couple of singles and he handed them to her. "Keep it," he said. As he turned to leave, something on the television screen caught his eye.

There was a picture of Willa Greyson on half the screen and a copy of *Lust Kills* on the other side. The closed caption was mentioning how Willa Greyson's latest book was still at the top of the charts and showed no sign of slowing down. The screen now showed a picture of Willa in her house, in her glamorous kitchen. Harris read the captions between the show's co-hosts.

"Sixty-three-year-old Willa Greyson, author of twenty bestselling books, continues to top the charts, despite her books having a more, saucy tone. But maybe that's why they're so popular!"

"You're probably right, Gabe. I mean, that's why I *like them!"*

"I always thought you had a secret side, SueAnn."

"Not anymore, apparently," SueAnn stared at the camera and winked.

The lame banter continued, gushing over Willa Greyson and her latest novel. It was enough to make Harris nauseous. Especially after all he sacrificed.

Harris had had enough. He left the diner. *Soon they'll be gushing over me,* Harris thought. But first, there's something he knew he had to do.

CHAPTER FORTY-SEVEN

May

"Kelly! Get your big ass in here!" Nina said. She noticed Kelly's stomach was showing major growth. She was at least six months pregnant now and Kelly was absolutely glowing.

"Love you, too," Kelly said to Nina, air pecking her best friends' cheeks. She walked into Nina's house and handed Nina a box wrapped in silver-brocade paper with an expertly crafted velvet bow.

"What's this?" Nina asked.

"It's just a little something I had made for you. Go ahead, open it." Kelly moved down into the den and sat in one of the Chesterfield chairs.

Nina walked in and sat in a chair opposite Kelly. She had a suspicious grin on her face as she unwrapped the gift. Inside was a clear, acrylic rectangle box. It was about the size of a sheet of paper and no more than three inches thick.

"What is this?" Nina asked.

"It's for your new book. Well, the first printed copy, that is. I know it's been a long time coming and I know how much this new novel means to you so I wanted to get you something where you can display the first copy, on *your* shelf, for everyone to see."

Nina was touched.

"And see here, it also comes with some sealant so you can secure the box forever and no one can get their hands on it and get their grubby little fingerprints on it."

"Oh, Kelly. This is so special. I love it!" She stood up and hugged Kelly.

Kelly looked at Nina. "It was nothing," she waved her hand in the air. "Umm," Kelly started, her hand rested on her swollen belly. "Nina, can we talk?"

Nina pulled her head back. Kelly has never been one to shy away from a conversation let alone *ask* if a conversation can be had. Something was up.

"Of course, hon," Nina said. "What is it?"

Kelly shifted in her seat. Her arms went to the armrests. One arm came back down. She clasped her hands together. She was fidgety. Finally, she stood up and walked a little way away from the chair.

"I don't know how to tell you this, but I've been wanting to say something for such a long time and…" her voice started to break.

"Just take it slow, honey," Nina coaxed. "I'm listening. Whenever you're ready."

Kelly looked at Nina, her best friend sitting there. They'd been through so much together, more than most family members, but this…this was something that had been bothering Kelly for years and she wasn't sure Nina was ready to hear it. *Hell, I'm not even sure I'm ready to say it,* Kelly thought. She felt the sting of tears in the corners of her eyes. But her best friend deserved to know the truth. No matter what. No matter how many lives would be changed. She fought the urge to just grab her purse and leave.

"I…I wanted to tell you so many times. Owen fought me every step of the way. He didn't want me to say anything but…and maybe he's right, I don't know. I don't know anything right now. I'm just an emotional mess. These pregnancy hormones are making me feel all shitty," she grunted a laugh.

"I know those shitty feelings well," Nina said, pointing to the kids' rooms upstairs.

"Yeah, I guess you do," Kelly tried to stall. She closed her eyes and continued. "When we came for Halloween, Owen and I fought over whether I should tell you this or not."

Nina recalled what she had overheard standing outside their bedroom that night.

".... she deserves to know..." Kelly
".... will break her heart..." Owen
".... not keeping...secret...any longer..." Kelly

At the time, Nina thought this had something to do with Kelly's mom, Evelyn, and the impending divorce. But now, Nina felt the narrative was taking a different direction.

"Okay," Nina said, not giving any indication she was somewhat familiar with this conversation.

"I wanted to tell you," Kelly said, "but Owen was insistent it would only cause damage."

"Kelly," Nina said, standing up and walking towards her friend. She took Kelly's hands in hers. "You have to just tell me. We've been friends for far too long for either of us to pussyfoot around."

Kelly steeled herself and took a deep breath.

"Back in college. The night Jack proposed to you..."

Nina cocked her head.

".... we.... Jack and I.... we.... slept together." She looked at Nina for the anger that might erupt. "But I was drunk, and he was drunk, and Owen and I had just had a fight and, oh, Nina, I am so sorry. Truly, I am so sorry!" She put her hands on her cheeks and sobbed. "I'm trash and I shouldn't have let it go that far and.... oh my god, Nina, I'm sorry! Please! Please say something!"

Kelly expected Nina to grip her hands tighter and wring them until her wrists snapped in two, but that didn't happen. Instead, Nina pulled Kelly into her and wrapped her arms around her, hugging her tightly. In Kelly's ear, she whispered, "I know. I've always known."

Kelly jerked out of the hug. "What?! You know? H-how??"

Nina smiled. "I was there. I saw you two. Well, I didn't *see* the act, but I saw you in his bed, in his arms. You were both naked and well, I've always been good with math. Two plus two equals four and all that." Nina walked back over and sat down. Kelly followed suit. "Don't get me wrong. As I stood over you, I wanted to kill Jack. I was ready to bash him in his head with his alarm clock. But I knew he loved me. And I knew you loved me, too. It was a mistake. An innocent accident. Nothing came of it, so I moved on."

Kelly wiped her tears away.

Nina continued. "After he proposed, I went home to write, and he went out to *Mermaids & Minotaurs*. I told him that if I finished early, I'd stop back by his apartment. Well, I missed my fiancé, so I finished early and -"

"And you came back to his apartment. Oh my god, Nina. I can't believe this. I am so sorry." She paused. "But - I don't understand. If you've known all this time - "

"I knew you'd tell me eventually. Either you or Jack. You are both decent, wonderful people who love me dearly and yes, while what you did was a mistake and never happened again - "

Kelly swallowed a lump in her throat.

"- I knew one of you would break down and tell me." She crossed her legs and sat back in her chair. "My mother owes me fifty bucks."

"Wait, Willa knows?"

"Of course. I had to tell someone! But she bet me Jack would cave and tell me before you. I can't wait to tell her dinner is on her."

"So...you and me? We're... we're good?"

"Honey, we're better than good. We're perfect. You're my sister and I know the circumstances were less than ideal, but we've been through a lot and I've had a long time to digest my feelings and what happened but my love for the two of you eclipses all of that. So yes, we're good. Besides, remember in *A Dutiful Wife* where Catherine drives over and kills her husband because he was cheating on her...?"

Kelly's eyes popped open. "That was based on this?" she asked in amazement. "That was brilliant!"

"That was therapy."

Nina and Kelly burst into laughter. Once it subsided, Kelly spoke first.

"God. I'm exhausted. That was a relief to get off my chest - you sure we're okay?"

"Yes. Now shut up," Nina saw how drained Kelly was. "Bet you wish you could have some tequila right about now, huh?"

"Wow. Now you're just being mean."

"And you slept with my fiancé. Guess we're even."

They laughed and hugged.

As they hugged, Kelly's eyes stared over Nina's shoulders. *Not quite. But what she doesn't know won't hurt her.*

CHAPTER FORTY-EIGHT

June

I was not ready for this next one. Prepared, yes. Ready? No.

It's true I've been planning this for at least 6 months but the idea of 'how' didn't strike me until her book launch party in January, of all places. It was as if God himself had illuminated my path to the end result. Or maybe it was just me being in the right place at the right time. Yeah. I'll go with that.

My heart has been hurting a little bit lately, so I made sure I took my medicine. I don't talk about my heart condition to anyone. I take care of myself, so they leave me alone about it. I take my Propafenone on the regular and no one needs to remind me. And that's that. But today, it's beating harder than normal. And I fear it's not because of my arrhythmia but because of what I'm about to do. However, I cannot let emotion get the best of me. I need to keep my eye on the prize.

I've been through a lot lately. My emotions and mental state have been up and down like an elevator in a short building. I need to focus because I have more to do than sit and wallow in self-pity.

As I walk the street to my destination, I marvel at my surroundings. I am shocked people live like this, in these huge houses with staff and water views. The irony is not lost on me. I know these houses. I know the owners. And I know this estate.

Scribbler's Cove. The home of bestselling author, Willa Greyson.

It really is a nice place.

For now.

Soon it will be crawling with news crews and paramedics and family members and friends and nosy neighbors. That is, if all goes according to my plan.

And if my history is any indication, my plan will be executed perfectly.

Execute. It's a funny word. It has two distinct definitions.

First, it means to carry out or put into effect, like a plan. Like today, I'll be executing a plan. A very careful and well-thought-out plan.

Secondly, it means to carry out a sentence of death on a person. And that's exactly what I'm going to be doing. Executing someone. Bringing death to a person.

Goodbye, Willa Greyson.

It is with great sadness we announce
the passing of
WILLA
GREYSON
on June 10, 2022
SERVICES WILL BE HELD AT
ST. JOHN'S CEMETERY, DARIEN, CT
ON JUNE 14, 2022

CHAPTER FORTY-NINE

June

The author Mitch Albom wrote "when your parents die, you feel like instead of going into every fight with backup, you are going into every fight alone."

And even with family and friends close, Nina felt so utterly alone.

Her dad, Roy, was seated beside her in a hard chair covered with some sort of green fabric that had seen better days. And in front of her, resting on belt straps that would soon loosen to lower their weighted cargo down, laid the coffin containing her mother, Willa.

Someone around her sniffled. She could physically feel her children shaking as they held on to her from either side. Her father looked weary, pale, lost. A ship without its rudder. Drifting further and further away. Roy Greyson wasn't a big man but to Nina he was always larger than life. He was, to Nina, the strongest man she had ever met. And you would have to be, wouldn't you, to be married to the bulwark that was Willa Greyson. He was the Prince Philip to her Queen Elizabeth. Letting her star shine while allowing his to dim. He knew his place and couldn't be happier for it. He was a professor at Fairfield University and was used to projecting his voice in large auditoriums. A deep voice, it resonated from walls and every person in the room could hear and understand every word Roy Greyson was saying.

But today, today was different. Today he looked shrunken, a bent over body with no bones. Today, he wept softly. His voice lost in a mist. He had no words. No resonation. Just tears amidst defeat. Nina felt sorry for her father. He loved Willa with every cell in his body.

Her parents' story was one of love and triumph. Willa Masterson came to Westport when the creative types ventured from the city, yearning for quiet suburbs and looming orchards to replace the cold pavements and towering skyscrapers.

She met Roy Greyson when she spoke at a literature symposium at Fairfield University and from that day forward, Roy Greyson's life was dedicated to wooing, courting, and eventually marrying Willa Masterson.

Roy was nineteen and Willa was twenty-one. It took ten long months of Roy happily exhausting every avenue to win Willa over, but she wouldn't budge. He asked her six times to marry him and each time he would give her a single lilac, her favorite flower. And after every proposal she would flatly say "No," turn on her heels and leave him, mouth agape. She provided no explanation, no reasoning, nothing. But Roy was not discouraged. Her feistiness only fueled his determination even more.

When Roy turned twenty, his buddies from the college had thrown him a party at the local pub. In the middle of his third beer, all heads turned as the most beautiful girl walked in, and straight up to Roy.

"Willa?" he said. "What are you - "

But he never finished his sentence.

"Yes," she said. And she started to leave.

"Wait. What? 'Yes' what?" He ran up to her and spun her around.

"Yes, I'll marry you."

Roy's mouth flew open. "Wh-what? Why? I mean, why now?"

She curled her lips. "Because I refuse to marry a teenager," she said, straightening her neck. "Happy twentieth birthday," she said. She kissed him on the lips then turned to leave.

They were married the next week.

That was forty-one years ago. And now, Roy is burying the love of his life. He stood and walked quietly to the coffin. His hands were in front of him, clasped. Slowly, his head fell, and he saw the single lilac he was holding.

"Oh, Willa…my darling. What am I to do without you? I have no more world, no more…life. I cannot imagine living without you." His voice was soft, meaningful. "My heart will never beat right again. For it is with you now and always. You're an angel. And I miss you so much…."

He pulled out a handkerchief and wiped his nose then softly laid the lilac on top of the coffin. He closed his eyes, turned, then started walking back towards the car.

Nina reached out her hand to find his, but he just kept walking. "Oh, daddy," she murmured. Tears flowed down her cheeks as her heart broke all over again for her father.

"Nina…." Jack whispered.

"I'm okay," she sniffled. She stood and walked up to her mother's coffin. She could hear Addy and Noah crying softly behind her. She knew Jack would squeeze them tight and love on them.

As she approached the coffin, she wasn't sure she would be able to do this. She wasn't sure about anything anymore. Her mother was her stalwart her entire life. Willa was there for every single good - and bad – thing Nina had ever been through. After the failed IVF and IUI trials and miscarriages, Willa always encouraged Nina to follow her heart and do what she thought she could handle. And after the adoption of Addy, Willa was the most ecstatic grandmother in history. "I don't care how she got here, I'm just overjoyed that she's here," Willa would say, and Addy would beam.

Standing at the casket, Nina could smell the lilac laying solitary on top. The wind picked up and the delicate perfumery scent penetrated the air. The breeze stung the tears in Nina's eyes.

"Mother…you were my best friend. You made me laugh more than anyone in my life. People didn't give you enough credit for your sense of humor, but I knew. It would get me through the tough times." She paused to wipe her eyes.

"You would make me so angry sometimes and get on my last nerve but then I would feel guilty because I knew despite all that, I would miss it all when you were gone. And now, here we are…." Nina's tears were flowing now.

She cupped her mouth with her hands in a praying motion and slowly shook her head. "What am I going to do without you?" Nina's throat closed. "Don't go," she whimpered. "Please don't leave me," she sobbed. "Please!"

An arm wrapped around her waist. Jack. He pulled her in to him. She laid her head on his shoulder and placed a hand on his chest. "I can't believe she's gone…." Nina wept.

"Shhh. I know, hon." He tugged her gently. "I think it's time we head back. Let's get you home and resting."

She nodded.

"Come on, kids," Jack said, reaching out his hand to them.

They left their seats and joined their broken family, hugging the legs and waists of their parents. As a unit, they walked away, down the hill to the cars.

Halfway down, Nina stopped and looked back. The cemetery staff were lowering the casket into the ground. It was at this very moment Nina knew, if she ever wanted to see or speak to her mother ever again, she couldn't. There would be no more funny conversations or serious talks or hugs or smiles or laughs. Nothing. And it was here, standing on the hillside, Nina's heart was broken forever. She heard a rumble above her. She looked up and saw a darkening cloud lumbering ahead. A storm was coming.

Nina stood on that hill, her family hugging her tight. But to her, she was detached and drifting, wafting through the air like the soft fragrant petal of a lilac.

CHAPTER FIFTY

June

The gathering at Nina's house was intimate after the funeral, just a few friends and family. Roy had decided not to come back to Nina's but instead, retreated to Scribbler's Cove.

"I'm really just mentally weary, honey," he had said to her when she caught up to him at the graveside and told him about the small reception at her house. "I honestly just want to go home and spend time with my thoughts, if that's okay with you."

"Of course, it is, daddy. Whatever you need." She hugged him close.

"Please tell your friends they are all lovely and very dear to me for honoring your mother today. It means the world."

The sky rumbled above them. She looked up. "It's getting dark daddy."

He held her gently by her shoulders. "Oh, my girl. It's because my light is gone." He pecked her on the cheek and got into his car and drove away.

"PENNY FOR YOUR THOUGHTS." KELLY CAME UP BEHIND NINA AND WRAPPED HER arm around Nina's waist.

"Oh, I was just thinking about dad and how he's going home to an empty house for the first time in his life." She turned to face Kelly. "Did you know in all their forty-one years of being married, they only spent one night apart from each other for some book thing mom had in Boston once? Daddy was beside himself and vowed after that night, he would never leave her side again. So, any time she had to leave for an overnight trip, he was there. He'd stay in the hotel room or go see a movie while she was doing her thing but yeah, he was with her every single night after that."

"You're kidding," Kelly said amazed. "In forty-one years? That's unbelievable. I mean, there are nights I'd give my left tit to someone to take Owen off my hands for 24 hours."

Nina laughed.

"What?" Kelly asked. "I would! He's a pain in the ass sometimes!"

Nina laughed again. And again. And it felt good. "Oh, Kelly. Thank you!"

"For what?"

"For being…you." She smooched Kelly's cheek. "And if you ask me, your left tit is the nicer of the two. I'd keep that one if I were you."

"Ha!" Kelly burst out.

"What's so funny?" Owen asked, approaching the girls.

"Nothing," both girls said at the same time. They linked arms and walked towards the kitchen.

"Owen. You got a sec?" Jack was trying to be cordial, but his impatience was getting the better of him.

"Sure, bud," Owen said. He scanned the room. "Here?"

"No. The office."

Once inside, Jack closed the door behind them.

"So," Owen grinned, "what's got you so antsy?"

Jack went to pour himself a bourbon. *I need all the courage I can get*, he thought. He looked out the window. The waves in the Sound had gotten choppy from the gusty wind, a prelude to a storm.

"Look, I know there are…. *things* between us. Things Nina - and *Kelly*, I might add - are better off not knowing. But a while ago, at dinner, Kelly mentioned she…that she was pregnant before and -"

"Is that what this is about? Kelly and the baby she lost? Why didn't you say anything sooner?"

"Because I've been busy, Owen," Jack said, irritated. "I have a big project at work and Nina's been busy writing and- who cares why I haven't asked sooner? I'm asking now!"

"Whoa there, big boy. I can see you're riled up. But what about I'm not quite sure. Care to elaborate?"

Jack swallowed his bourbon. His left hand was balled into a fist. "Look, I know you know about me and Kelly…in college," Jack said. "She told me she told you…"

"Yeah, I knew," Owen said. "But what does that have to do with -"

"And then she got pregnant."

"Yes…. but she lost the baby, Jack. Look, what are you driving at?"

"Your sister owns a daycare…and, she could have..." Jack grabbed Owen by the shoulders. His next question came out in sharp bullets. "Is. Addy. *Mine*?"

Owen's eyes flew open. He knocked Jack's arms down. Then he laughed. "Are you joking? You think…. you think- God, I don't even know what you think!"

"Owen, Kelly got pregnant right after we…. right around that time in college. And then she dropped out to *travel*", Jack used air quotes. "And I know you said she lost the baby, but I know you! I know just how calculating you can be - oh, believe me! Kelly never even saw her baby before you whisked it off to God knows where. And then I remembered your sister owned the daycare - "

"So, you think," Owen said, raising his hand like a lawyer about to get his point across, "*you* got Kelly pregnant, then I lied to my wife about her baby being stillborn, took the child to be raised by my sister and then sold your biological child *back* to you two years later?"

"That's *exactly* what I think," Jack spat. But Jack had to admit after hearing it out loud it sounded a little bizarre.

Owen shook his head and walked towards the bar. He poured another bourbon and swigged it down. "Jack, buddy, come on. You can't possibly think that." He put his hand on his chest. "I have morals." He walked towards Jack. "Look. Kelly *did* lose the baby. I took my daughter - yes, *my daughter* - from Kelly before she could lay eyes on her, fall in love with her and get her heart broken even more." He paused. "I think you've been reading too many of your wife's books. All those twists and such."

"Don't patronize me, Owen. I know what you're capable of. I'm experiencing your *morals* now," he said sarcastically.

Owen's smile disappeared. "Look. I might not be the most upstanding person on this earth, but let's face it, neither are you. How many secrets are you still keeping from your wife?"

Jack's shoulders stiffened. Owen was right. This was futile. Jack hated surrendering but he's learned never to go up against someone as wily as Owen. "Fine. I believe you. Addy's not mine. *Biologically*," he added quickly.

Owen looked at Jack in the eyes. He smiled broadly and there was something sinister in his voice. "Or legally."

Jack's eyes squinted and his mouth turned in anger. He knew what was coming. It was always the same thing. For years Owen was blackmailing Jack about Addy's adoption. Addy's adoption did not go through any legal system. After all the failed attempts to get pregnant and Nina's fracturing career and her hanging on to her sanity by a thread, Jack was desperate.

Enter Owen. He found a child in need of a home, and his friends Jack and Nina had a home to give a child, Jack thought ironically. The puzzle pieces fit. A million dollars later, Jack was the proud owner of a little baby girl. And he hated every minute since. Not the time with Addy, no, he loved that little girl with everything he had. But he couldn't help feeling like shit every time he looked at Addy because he saw the fraud and deceit. It was a secret he could never tell Nina. It would destroy every bit of her. And every time Owen brought it up, Jack had to pay. But not with money. Never with money.

And where Jack was trapped, Owen was in the clear: his name was nowhere on the adoption paperwork so he wouldn't be culpable should any of this come to light. But for Jack, his entire world could fall apart. Jack had signed the papers assuming Owen would do the same. But he hadn't. He detested Owen. He hated him like a malignant tumor. But Jack's love for his wife was stronger than his hate for Owen. And for the sake of that love and their future, and because he needed to keep the secret that Addy was not their daughter legally, he continued with Owen's little game. Like always, he felt sick to his stomach.

Owen put down his drink and leaned against the desk. "And if you want to keep *that* little secret from your wife, then do what you do best and come over here and fuck me."

CHAPTER FIFTY-ONE

June

Margo quietly shut the door to her office. Seeing Willa being buried had taken its toll. She tore off her coat and flung it on a chair. Stumbling to the desk, she ripped open the drawer and grabbed the Vodka. She sat down on the sofa and took a gulp from the bottle. The tears were still flowing ever since she left the cemetery. She took another gulp. Her mouth cringed at the burn.

"Oh my god," Margo said. "Oh my GOD!" She yelled it this time. Margo hated losing her friend. At this point she wasn't sure if she was more upset she lost a friend or that she lost half of her income. Margo despised herself for even allowing her mind to cross that line.

But if she were truly to admit to herself, Willa and Nina were like family to her. But now she didn't have anyone and with everything she was going through with Harris Markham lately, she could use a friend to talk to.

Especially now that the media had linked the deaths of Rachel Meadows, Gregory Wynn, and Willa Greyson to Margo since she was their agent. She was the common denominator. And now another ex-client, Harris Markham, was a person of interest in the deaths of his family. It was weighing heavily on Margo's mind. Her face flushed with heat, and she held the bottle to her lips for a two-second mouthful of vodka.

Suddenly, Leslie Fontaine flashed through Margo's head. She wasn't sure why. Maybe because ex-clients have died or maybe just because Margo missed Leslie. Margo made a mental note she needed to visit Leslie. And soon because -

What was that? Margo turned her head towards the door. She thought she'd heard a noise. She went to the door and opened it and all she saw was the hallway leading to the stairs to the outside door. She could hear a slight howling outside. Margo shrugged. Maybe the noise was just-

BAM!

Margo's eyes flew open. The noise came from outside her office window.

BAM!!!

Again! She rushed to the window and saw blood dripping down the panes. Long crimson streaks oozing down the glass.

No. Not blood. Paint. *But why?*

BAM!

From her second story office window, she could see someone throwing red paint bombs at her window. She ran to the other window and looked down. She saw a streetlamp and darkness. But then her eyes focused, and she saw someone standing next to the light post. Harris Markham! Harris was throwing paint bombs at her! *Oh my God! He's crazy!* A thought crossed her mind: Harris could have murdered his family in cold blood and had eluded the authorities and was now outside her window! Margo's heart was beating through her chest.

"Harris, stop! Stop it right now!" Margo yelled through the shut window as another paint bomb hurled upward and made contact with the second window. *craaaack* The impact caused the glass to splinter. "I'm calling the police!"

Another *BAM!!* and then a *chinking* noise as a shard of glass hit her office floor by her feet.

Margo's heart was pounding and she ran to her phone and dialed 911. She spit out information as fast as she could, trying to answer their questions and remain calm but it was futile. She was a nervous wreck. Then she noticed the silence. The paint bombs had stopped. She waited another minute before speaking into the phone.

"Umm, I...I think...I'm okay. Yes. No, I'll be fine. It was all a misunderstanding. Just someone kicking the trashcans. I'm...good. Thank you, though. Yes...I'll do that. Good night." She hung up from the police. She knew if the police showed up and arrested Harris, this situation would only escalate to God knows what so better to let Harris know she is on to him and scare him into fleeing. *For now.* But now that he was gone, Margo worried she just helped a fugitive escape.

Her heart felt like it was about to jump out of her chest onto her desk. She swallowed one of her pink pills.

It took a good hour for her heart to regain its normal pace and for her to regain her nerve to head home. She reached into her handbag and pulled out her keys and put them in her pocket. She reached back into the bag and her fingers wrapped around a small cylinder can. Ever since the night Harris Markham barged into her office, Margo carried a small can of Mace with her, her finger on the trigger, always at the ready.

Margo headed down the stairs and out the door onto the sidewalk, a gust of thick wind whipped across Central Park hitting her and taking her by surprise. She pulled the long sleeves of her light coat down further and walked towards her car. Inside her handbag, her finger tightened on the Mace trigger. As she headed to her car, she noticed something on her windshield, held down by the wiper and flapping in the wind. A piece of paper with what looked like red fingerprints smudged on the edges. *Red paint. Harris.*

Margo snatched the paper off her car. It was a note.

And the words chilled the air and rattled Margo's bones.

"The blood of everyone is on your hands!"

Margo bent over and threw up.

CHAPTER FIFTY-TWO

June

"How are you doing, luv?" Robin asked Addy. "I know it's been a very rough couple of weeks for you, losing your grandmother and all. And today, with the burial - "

Addy shrugged. "I'm okay, I 'spose," she said. "I don't know."

"What don't you know, pet?"

"How to feel. How to act. I've never lost someone close to me before so I'm not sure what to do. Do I cry? Do I stop talking? Do I eat a gallon of Rocky Road?" Addy smirked and shrugged again.

"I think that's a splendid idea," Robin smiled softly, opening the freezer. She got two spoons from the drawer. She set the gallon container on the island and handed Addy a spoon.

"Don't we need a bowl?" she asked.

"Not if you do it right," Robin said, as she scooped up an oversized spoonful of the dark ice cream and put it in her mouth. "Delishush," she said, her mouth full.

Addy let out a soft giggle. She emulated Robin's actions with the ice cream.

"Good, yeah?" Robin asked.

"Delishush," Addy replied, then laughed again.

Quiet then surrounded them. Neither spoke for another minute.

"Addy," Robin probed. "Do you want to talk about that day?"

Addy's eyes locked on Robin's for three seconds then quickly darted down to the countertop.

"I mean, you don't have to, but it might help you talk about it to someone. I'm a great listener."

Addy asked, "What do you mean it could help me?"

"Oh, luv, I've just noticed ever since the day your grandmother died, you've been...distant. Not your regular cheery self." She paused. "A little sorrowful, I guess."

It was true. Addy wasn't herself. But not for reasons Robin would ever understand. She loved her grandmother, and they had a special bond, the two of them.

"Addy? Luv? Where did you go?"

"I'm right here."

Robin smiled at her innocence. "No, hon. Up here," Robin tapped her temple. "Where did your thoughts just take you?"

"Just thinking. About that day." She sighed and dug into the gallon for another spoonful. Robin put one elbow on the island and dug into the ice cream right after Addy. She leaned in as if to listen. To urge Addy to continue.

"That was the day we were supposed to gather fruits but I guess she didn't want to wait on me so she started ahead of time. Mother said she kept complaining of being tired lately, but she didn't urge her enough to rest so now she thinks it was her fault grandmother died..." Addy's voice started to crack. "Is it her fault she's dead?" She started sobbing.

"My dear Addy," Robin consoled, "none of this is your mother's fault. Your grandmother just," she waved her hand in the air, "couldn't wait and wanted to get a head start. Her heart just.... gave out."

Addy dropped her spoon and covered her face with her hands.

Robin remembers Jack describing the scene.

"Willa was found lying on the ground. Her hat was next to her and so was an empty basket. There were lots of fruit around her, too. The police think she had tried to carry a heavy weight in her basket and while she was walking her big property, her heart just gave out on her and.... well, it was very sudden. She just fell and..."

"And what?" Robin asked.

"I didn't tell Nina this, but it looked like Willa had crawled just a little bit. There were some drag marks in the ground where her legs ran along the grass and there was also some dirt under her fingernails."

Robin covered her mouth with her palms. "That's horrible!" Robin said. "She didn't die immediately. She...suffered?"

"It appears that way...maybe just a little bit. We're not 100% sure, but yeah. It's pretty horrible."

Jack brought a hand to the back of his neck and massaged it. "Willa had said not too long ago she was tired and not feeling so well. The doctor wanted her to slow things down. But you know Willa, she wasn't going to listen to anyone."

"That's for sure. How's Nina?"

"As expected. She's pretty devastated. The valium seems to be helping. Nina blames herself for not pushing her mother to rest more." He took off his glasses, huffed a breath on them then wiped them clean with his tee shirt. "But she's not at fault. No one is. I'm just trying to keep everyone stable, I guess."

"You're doing a fine job, Jack. And I'm here to help, okay?"

"Thanks, Robin. You're a lifesaver."

"Now where did *you* go," Addy asked Robin.

"Sorry, luv. I was just thinking of putting this ice cream away and maybe going out for a bit of shopping. Care to join me? I'm going to Stella's."

"That's my favorite place! They have a huge unicorn selection of stuff!" Addy wiped her eyes.

"Then let's get ready and go! Go put on some shoes and meet me back down here in ten, deal?"

"Deal!" And Addy jumped off her stool and ran upstairs.

As Addy bounded up the stairs, Robin put the half-melted ice cream back into the freezer. As she closed the door, she remembered.

Jack: "Nina blames herself for not pushing her mother to rest more. But she's not at fault. No one is."

Robin did her best to assure Addy her mother wasn't at fault. *Was the deflection working?* Robin grabbed her handbag and car keys. She felt a chill. The keys started clinking together as Robin's hands shook. *If people knew who was really at fault here, they'd never believe it.*

CHAPTER FIFTY-THREE

July

Julys in Darien are the hottest months but even then, thanks to breezes skimming off the Sound, the temperatures rarely rise above 84°. Jack loved running on these days: the warmer the better. After working up a good sweat, he could just plunge into the cool waters of their pool. Next to running, it was his favorite way to relax.

But today, there would be none of that. No pool. No relaxing. He had asked Owen to meet him at the house since Nina and the kids and Kelly were planning a trip to the farmer's market, taking Imelda's jars of spreads and fresh pies.

So having the house to himself, Jack asked Owen over. Owen, Jack was sure, would think he was being invited over for something else and Jack was counting on that. Jack used Owen's desire to be with Jack to his advantage. And like a fly to honey, Owen agreed to come over.

Jack finished his run then took a cool shower. He dressed in off-white Southern Tide shorts and a blue cotton polo that showed off his eyes behind his dark glasses. He left his hair wet and styled it with his fingers. Looking in the mirror, he smiled. He knew Owen would be putty in his hands. But he knew Owen was no dummy. He was a very intelligent lawyer who didn't let much get past him. Jack would have to play his cards carefully.

The sound of the doorbell snapped Jack out of his thoughts. He hopped down the stairs and opened the front door. Owen smiled when he saw Jack. "Looking good, brother," Owen said.

"Thanks. Come on in."

They retreated to the den. "Beer or something else?" Jack asked.

"Beer now. Something else later," Owen grinned.

Normally, Jack would cringe. But today, he needed to ensure Owen they were on the same page, so he just raised the corner of his mouth in a knowing grin. He got them both a beer and motioned for Owen to sit down.

"Sitting down? This must be serious," Owen said, half smiling.

"Kinda," Jack said. He took a deep breath. "Look, I know we've been.... involved, in a way...but...Owen, it has to stop. I care for you, I do." *Careful, Jack. Don't reel him in too much.* "I mean, you're the best friend I have, and I don't want to lose you, but..." *Better. Make it sound like it's you two against the world.* "...I'm not...I'm not gay and I can't do this anymore. You and me. It has to stop."

Owen took a sip of his beer. "Jack, Jack, Jack. Do you really think I'm gay? I'm not!" He laughed. "I have a wife. And a kid on the way! I'm not gay, I just like...I just like your company. We help each other, right? I mean, I don't tell Nina about the adoption not being legal and you...you provide me your.... company." Owen flayed out his arm and hand as if the description just came to him.

Jack stood up. "No, Owen. That's not 'company'. That's blackmail. And it's over! No more blackmail. No more...'helping each other'. If you really want to know, I could go to Kelly about all of this and see just how quick she'd divorce your ass!" *So much for being on the same page.*

Owen threw back his head and laughed. "Are you serious? Kelly? She doesn't give a shit about me. And she knows. Of course, she knows! How? I told her. She didn't want to hear anything about it, of course, but I told her anyway. She's so spoiled I couldn't wait to tell her her husband was getting screwed by her best friend's man."

Jack stood with his mouth open. "But how..."

"We have a marriage of convenience, my friend. I married her so she could get her trust. I played the clean-cut young man on a mission to be the best lawyer I could be so good ol' Charles and Evelyn would be impressed with Kelly and forget about her wild days. They fell for it and the trust was hers in no time. But then there was that damn codicil. So, we had to wait on children. *Prove* to them we were a happily married couple." He rolled his eyes in annoyance. "And the only way to do that was for her to have her fun and me to have mine." He paused and drank more from his bottle. "I'm not even sure that baby she's carrying is mine, but I don't care. The money is mine and once we get divorced, I'll have a solid half of her estate. It was an easy payday. And you! You played right into my hands. It was perfect."

"But once the illegality of the adoption comes out, you'll be ruined!"

"Ahhh, that," he smirked. "As you know, there is no paperwork with *my* name on it. No one can prove I had anything to do with it. I never met Addy until you got her, and no one can prove otherwise. I'm clean as a whistle." He walked over and stood in front of Jack. "You, however, have everything to lose. Nina. The kids. Your reputation. Do you really want to risk all that? Come on, Jack," he cocked his head and curled up his lips to the left. "What's a little fun between friends if you can guarantee security?"

Jack knew he had lost. He was at Owen's mercy. He had nothing to hold over Owen's head. It *was* over, just not the way Jack intended.

"And" Owen continued, "don't get all high and mighty on me about blackmail. It was you, after all, who came to me to find something on that Rachel Meadows girl so you could use it against her. I don't know, to throw her off her writing game? To leave Nina alone? Who knows? Smart idea, bad execution. I thought you were smarter than that, Jack." Owen looked at Jack in the eyes. "We are far from over." Then he left the office.

Jack was defeated. Without anyone or anything to prove Owen was involved in the illegal adoption, Jack knew he was completely alone and would never be rid of Owen Ford.

CHAPTER FIFTY-FOUR

July

Okay. So, I know a lot of people are sad over Willa Greyson's death, but I couldn't help it. It had to get done. There are so many people in my way, but I had to start with the biggies: Rachel, Gregory, Willa.

And my next one. Wow. I can't believe I have to do this one. She's already a big mess but I can use that to my advantage. I've been planning this one over the whole summer and it's just about time. Another couple of days and, well, as Queen once sang, another one bites the dust. Only, if things go according to my plan, it won't be dust. It'll be soggy and wet.

I must move quickly because I feel like they're after me. I might just be feeling paranoid, but I truly think someone is on to me, so I have to be extra careful. But I've planned this one down to the T - or should I say lemonade? Ha!

Okay, I need to focus. Why do I think someone is after me, you may ask? Because I notice things. I notice everything. Nothing gets past me and yet, something was out of place. Something I know I've been super careful with and yet…there it was. Moved. Shifted. Ever so slightly. But shifted, nonetheless. So, I know someone has seen it, but who? It's my most treasured possession so you don't think I wouldn't notice if it was moved?? I'm no dummy! But who?? Who has seen my treasure? This pisses me off!

I'm taking a deep breath here because it's time to go. I have a couple more things to wrap up and then I'll be on my way. Time for another visit.

And this visit should mark Leslie Fontaine's last time that she'll ever see me.

Wish me luck!

CHAPTER FIFTY-FIVE

July

It's been over a month since Margo last saw Harris Markham. So having him stand in front of her right now at her office door shook Margo to the core.

"Harris…what…what are you doing here?"

"I had to see you, Margo. Please. I have nowhere else to go."

Margo glanced at Harris head to toe. He was unrecognizable. His once crew cut hair was now long and shaggy and thinning, gray from dust and dirt; he sported a beard at least 3 inches long that had something moving in it. Margo shivered. He had definitely lost weight, probably twenty-five pounds or more and his out-of-season overcoat just hung on his skeletal body. But it was his eyes that had changed the most. Once upon a time, they were a kind, soft green. But today, they were dark and brooding, hollow. Surrounded by drooping eyelids, they showed a lot of pain. If Margo didn't know this was Harris, she wouldn't have known him from Adam.

"I was just…. on my way out…" Margo stuttered.

"Leslie Fontaine is dead," Harris said softly.

Margo stepped back. *What? Oh my god. Leslie. How does he….* "How do you know this…. Harris?" Margo asked, her voice shaking.

"I just do. It's a big deal because it's the fourth client of yours to have died in 7 months. What do you make of that?" His putrid breath was heavy on her face. It smelled of rotted meat.

Margo's knees felt very wobbly, and she knew she might faint at any moment. She turned and walked to the sofa to sit. She didn't care that Harris let himself in and closed the door and walked over and sat next to her. He placed his hand on her knee.

She didn't move. She was numb. Margo really wanted to get the vodka from her desk, but she dared not get up for fear of collapsing.

"How - "

"Drowned. In her pool. I think her gardener found her. Her poor dog was standing at the edge of the pool just barking its head off."

"Bella..." Margo sighed.

"She had been drinking and was found at the bottom of her pool with her wheelchair on top of her. She was pinned to the bottom of the pool and she just.... couldn't move. They ruled it an accident. Like all the others."

Margo whipped her head towards Harris. *Like all the others*. Margo bent over and put her head in her hands.

"Margo, look, I know now might not be the best time, but I wanted you to know I almost killed myself but you...you saved me, in a way."

Margo lifted her head and she turned to look at Harris. His dark eyes seemed...lighter. "What? What are you talking about, Harris?"

"I was sitting on a bench in a bus shelter downtown. I had a gun, see, in a brown bag. And I was sitting there, my wife left me and took the kids and remarried - I was all alone. I had nothing to live for, so I figured, why not? I could just end it here in this shelter and that would be the end of that."

"Oh, Harris. I...I...". For a moment she wondered if he was carrying the gun on him now.

"But then I saw you on the sidewalk. You were in a hurry to go somewhere, and I had this thought that I could give it one more shot - *just one more shot,*" he emphasized, pinching his eyes shut, "to beg you to let me come back."

She looked at him.

"I finally caught up with you. You were there. With *Gregory Wynn*." He said Gregory's name like it was acid on his tongue.

Margo remembered that day. She wasn't sure Nina would come through with her new book so she had gone to Gregory to ask him to let her be his agent again, but he had laughed in her face and basically told her to 'go to hell'. Margo closed her eyes and shook her head. It was a backup plan that didn't pan out. But Harris was there? Harris had seen her and Gregory together? And this made him angry because - and then Margo understood. She finally understood why Harris was so enraged with her: he wanted to come back as a client and here Margo was asking someone *else* to come back instead. Harris was crushed. And now he wanted to take his revenge.

"I was hurt," Harris continued. "But then.... then I heard Gregory laugh at you. Not with you, but *at* you. He called you pathetic or something like that. And I realized you were just as desperate as I was. Just as sad and...alone."

Margo looked at Harris. She looked at this man who she had dropped and then actually judged his reaction. Didn't she realize what she did was crushing? Harris Markham was proof. Here he was, sitting beside her and -

Suddenly her eyes flew open at a realization: he was wanted for the murder of his entire family and he was sitting right next to her! Margo couldn't believe she had let her guard down so easily. She had to do something.

"You then gave me the inspiration to do what I needed to do. To write the book of my career." Even while telling me about the deaths of his loved ones, he sounded almost...*proud*, of what he had written. "So yes, you saved me. Thank you."

"Harris, can I get you some water or something?" Margo grabbed her handbag, stood, and started to walk towards her desk. Her cell phone was just inside her bag.

"Sit back down, Margo," Harris's voice was firm. "I'm not finished yet."

She spun around and he had the gun aimed right at her.

"Dear god, Harris. Put that down...please...I - " she started.

He continued his conversation as if she hadn't spoken. "You told me to write something *unique*, something *no one's ever read before*. And so, I did. I wrote a book. A good one. And I gave you the manuscript, but I haven't heard anything from you since!"

"Harris, I read it...and the police..."

"*Fuck the police*! I killed my family for you! For my career! The blood of my family is on your hands!"

Margo remembered the note on her car: *the blood of everyone is on your hands.*

He started sobbing, the gun was rattling in his hand. Margo feared a shaky finger would pull the trigger and she'd be dead. "My family…." he sobbed. "…my children. I did it for you!" His sadness turned to an angry disbelief. "Are you even going to have it published?!"

Margo had her hands in front of her as if that would stop a bullet. "Harris, I…I can't…you *killed* your family and now the authorities are looking for you. What do you want me to do?" she pleaded.

"I want you to do what you promised! You said you'd have it published if it was unique enough, and believe me," he scoffed, "it's unique."

"I said I would *consider* getting it published, I never promised."

He raised the gun higher. "Then consider it and get it done! You owe me!"

"I owe - " but saying the sentence was futile. Margo knew Harris held her responsible for all the loss in his life and now, in his eyes, she owed him a new book on the market. She didn't want to argue anymore because Harris held the gun, and he was in no condition to reason.

"Fine," she said. "I will *consider* your manuscript for publication," she placated. "Now, will you please put the gun down?"

"Not until you make the call."

"The…call?"

"To your publisher."

"Harris. Please. I need to read it over again and make sure I give it to the right person, isn't that the best way to do this?" She was stalling for time. *But time for what,* she had no idea. But then she *did* have an idea. If she could get her phone and pretend to call the publisher, she would really be calling the police. *It had to work. It just had to!*

"Okay, you win," Margo said. "Let me get my phone and -"

"NO!" Harris bellowed. "NO!! I know what you're doing! Stop it right now! Use your desk phone so I can see you dialing." He was waving the gun frantically, maniacally.

"Harris…I'm sorry…I…"

"NOW!" He raged. "GOD! Don't make me do this, Margo!"

"Harris, please! I was just - " but she never got to finish her sentence. Margo heard the loudest *boom* she had ever heard in her life and then a muted silence, like her ears were filled with cotton. The air in her had been punched out of her and she put her hands on her stomach. She looked down and blood oozed between her fingers. She looked back up to Harris, his mouth wide and his eyes were back to dark.

"Harris.... help..." she moaned before falling to her knees.

"I'm sorry...Margo...I'm really....so sorry..." Harris wept. He turned and left the office. Margo was now alone, on her knees, blood covered her shirt and the top of her pants, a puddle of blood on the floor around her knees. There was no pain, just quiet. Just the occasional drip, drip, drip of the blood to the floor.

And it all went black.

CHAPTER FIFTY-SIX

July

It was the incessant beeping noise that woke her up.

So annoying, she thought. *I must get that fixed, whatever it is.* She opened her eyes, slowly and they fluttered, but eventually, they were open. So bright! She squinted and for a moment, considered closing her eyes again. She focused. She was in a bed, staring at a solid white ceiling she didn't recognize.

She strained to turn her head towards the noise. It was a monitor of some sort with wires and tubes coming out of it and they all led to her. *What? What is this? Where am I? Am I in the hospital?*

"Well, look who's decided to join us," a soft female voice said from the other side of her bed.

She recognized it, vaguely. She winced as she turned into the direction of the voice. *I know her. That's Nina Travers. She's my friend. But what is she doing here? If she's there, and I'm in the hospital - have I been hurt?* She closed her eyes, and it all came back to her. Harris Markham was in her office. He told her Leslie Fontaine had drowned. He was angry and waving a gun at her and - *oh my god, Harris shot me!*

"Margo, we thought you had left us. We thought…well, it doesn't matter what we thought." Nina rested her hand on Margo's arm. "You're back and you're alive and all is good." She squeezed her arm.

Margo tried to talk but nothing came out.

"Oh. Water? Here," Nina said, holding a cup with a bent straw in it for Margo to drink from. Margo gulped down the cool liquid. It tasted wonderful.

"Nina..." Margo said hoarsely. "What...where..."

Nina pulled up the chair she had been sitting in and sat back down. "The police found you. Another business in your building heard the gunshot and called 9-1-1. They came in and found you. They weren't sure if you were going to make it," Nina said softly.

Margo scrunched her eyebrows. "And Harris?"

A nurse came in and fiddled with the I.V. "Good to see your eyes are open, Ms. Flagg. Feeling okay?"

Margo nodded.

"Good. I'll be back in to check on you again in an hour. Oh. There are some officers here to see you. Are you up for it?"

Officers? Why? Do I have a choice? She nodded 'yes'.

The nurse stepped out into the hallway.

"Ms. Flagg?" A deep voice said near the doorway.

Margo looked and there were two police officers standing in the doorframe. "Ms. Flagg, do you have a minute to speak with us?" The taller of the two officers was speaking.

Nina looked down at Margo. Margo shut her eyes and nodded. "It's fine..." she assured Nina. "Thank you."

Nina bent down and kissed Margo on the forehead. "I'll be just outside if you need me." She headed towards the door. "Be nice!" Nina ordered the police, pointing her finger at them before walking out, closing the door behind her.

The officers approached the bed. Margo felt a sense of dread coming over her. She knew why they were here. Leslie Fontaine. She was the fourth client of Margo's who had died since December and now she was probably a suspect in their deaths, even though they had been ruled accidents. But somehow, she felt she would be held liable in all of this. Her heart started racing. The monitor beeped rapidly.

She took several deep breaths until her heart rate returned to normal.

"Ms. Flagg are you alright?" one of the officers asked. The tall one again.

"Yes...yes, I'm fine. I'm just...my head hurts a little, that's all."

"That's understandable, ma'am," the shorter officer said nodding towards all the equipment in the room.

"How may I help you," Margo asked, not really looking forward to their answer.

"Well, I'm Officer Chase (*the tall one*) and this is Officer Beckett (*the short one*). We wanted to talk with you about Harris Markham."

"Oh," Margo said, a bit caught off guard. It wasn't what she was expecting. She assumed Harris was still on the run and they were at a standstill. "What about Harris?"

"He's dead, ma'am," Officer Beckett said. Officer Chase looked down at his partner.

"Yes, ma'am," Officer Chase continued. "Can you tell us when you last saw Mr. Markham?"

Margo was stunned. *Dead? Harris was dead?*

"Ma'am?"

"Oh, sorry. Um, what's the date today?"

"July 23rd. Saturday." said Officer Chase.

I've been in here for two days, Margo thought. She shook her head and then saw the officers looking at her.

"Um, the 21st. Thursday. That was the day he came to my office and -" She stopped talking. Everything was just so surreal.

'So ma'am, you last saw him on the 21st? And you've been in here ever since?"

Margo didn't like this sort of accusatory tone, but she knew they were just doing their jobs. "Yes. The whole time. I'm sure there are nurses and doctors that could vouch for me. And stop calling me ma'am."

"There's no need for validation, ma'am – Ms. Flagg. We're just following protocol."

"I understand," she said. "So...what happened?"

Officer Chase spoke. "Ms. Flagg, we understand before Harris Markham died, he had given you a manuscript. A book he wanted you to publish. Is that correct?"

She thought of the harrowing story where the main character slaughters his entire family and then goes on the run, just like Harris did. After weeks of evading the authorities, he finally gives in to the pressure and kills himself. One shot to the head and then his body is found -

"Oh my god!" Margo said, understanding it all. "Harris Markham killed himself and was found in the Hudson River, wasn't he?"

The two officers glanced at each other. "Yes." Officer Beckett replied. "It seems he took his own life with a self-inflicted gunshot to the temple, but the M.E. will know more after the autopsy. But yes, it does seem this is the most logical conclusion."

Margo just shook her head. "So…why are you here?"

Officer Chase said, "We wanted you to know. Plus, there's one more thing."

Margo's stomach tightened.

"Before he died, Markham left a confession on his computer. To the killings of his wife and two children, to shooting you and to other things, but we just wanted to inform you of that news. The computer has been turned over to the D.A.'s office for the investigation."

Margo let out a breath. Was it over? Really over? All the torture and harassment from Harris? The constant living in fear, always gripping the can of mace in her handbag ready for him to jump out at her at any moment. All of that is over? She couldn't believe it. She found herself smiling as a tear fell down her cheek.

"Ms. Flagg, are you okay?" Officer Chase asked her for the second time that morning.

Was she okay? Oh, yes. She was okay. She was *better t*han okay. A huge weight was just lifted off her shoulders and no one in this room could understand that. They didn't live through what she has lived through. But she *did* live through it. And for some reason, she thought of poor Leslie. Her dear friend, no matter if she did drop her as a client, they had remained close. The past couple of years have been heavy on Margo's heart and now that her friends Leslie and Willa were both gone, Margo would have to focus on Nina. And now that Harris and his troubled soul were no longer a threat, she knew that focus would come more easily.

Margo looked up at the officers. She smiled. "I am. Thank you."

With that, the officers nodded and left the room.

On their way out, Nina came in. She had her phone in her hand.

"Margo! I just heard about Harris Markham. It's on my phone. Oh my gosh, that's horrible. And how sad, really. I mean, you told me he was disturbed and really upset after you let him go but I didn't know it had gotten this bad. Can you believe it? Margo? Are you listening?"

Margo cocked her head. Yes, she was listening. Harris had told her this manuscript saved him. He said she had saved him by inspiring him. He had said that. And now, here she was. In a real-life crime story. And Margo was at the heart of it. She lived it. And now, she would publish it.

"Margo. Are you listening to me? Have you heard anything?"

Margo looked at Nina. She had clarity for the first time in months. She grinned. Harris's voice resonated again. "Yes. I've heard every word."

CHAPTER FIFTY-SEVEN

August

"Have you seen Jack?" Owen asked.

"I haven't," Robin replied, standing at the front door. Owen was on the front porch. "I think he's back in Philadelphia this weekend."

Crap. Why didn't he tell me? Owen thought. *Well, he can't avoid me forever.* Owen didn't bother waiting for an invite in, so he walked past Robin into the house.

"Is there something else I can do for you, Mr. Ford?" Robin asked, agitated.

"Oh, no. I'm just gonna grab myself some water and sit outside for a bit. The girls should be back from shopping soon so if you don't mind," he made his way into the kitchen.

Robin closed the front door and followed him. When she got into the kitchen, Owen was leaning against the counter, bottled water in hand and a smirk on his face.

"Gosh darn it, you look so damn familiar. But I just can't put my finger on it," he said, pointing his index finger at Robin.

"I must have one of those faces," Robin said, scurrying over to the sink to rinse off some dishes.

"Yeah, maybe," Owen said. "But I think there's something more. Where did you say you were from?"

"I didn't. But if you really must know, a small town in the U.K. called Grimsby."

Owen shook his head. "Doesn't ring any bells with me." He cocked his head. "And then? How did you come to the states?"

Robin had to tread carefully. "I was working for a family in London who moved to Portugal." She left out her time in Miami. "I didn't want to move there so I moved here, instead. A friend suggested New York and, well, the rest is history." She smiled. Too fake?

"What about family? Parents? Siblings? Children?"

Robin's palms started to sweat. "Mr. Ford, I've already passed the interview," she laughed nervously. "Newsflash: I was hired!"

"I'm sorry, Robin, I didn't mean to make you uncomfortable, it's just that you're watching the children of my best friends and I can't place your face, but I feel like we've met somewhere. I just want to make sure everything is copacetic. Plus, it's the lawyer in me that's the curious one," he said as he took a sip of his water behind a grin.

"I can appreciate the concern, really, but trust me, I'm the most boring, clean-cut person you'll ever meet," Robin said.

"Oh, I wouldn't say that. Everyone has their not-so clean-cut side, know what I mean?"

Robin knew *exactly* what he meant. She had accidentally found out all about Owen and his little side hobbies. She knew she wasn't his type and she probably disgusted him with her appearance. She suddenly knew how to end this meeting.

Robin looked at Owen and tilted her head. "Most definitely, Mr. Ford," she said softly. "Tell me, what does that side in you look like?" She leaned in, her deep cleavage on display.

Owen looked at Robin. She was flirting with him. But she wasn't his type. She was obese and fleshy. Her breasts were heavy and pendulous. He was sure under all that blotchy skin on her face she was once pretty before getting so portly. Her eyes were kind, and her dimples were deep and friendly. If she were thinner, maybe, he thought, looking off.

He looked up and she was standing right in front of him. He was startled. He pushed himself off the counter and moved to the island. "Oh. Well, I never kiss and tell," he said.

"That's too bad. I'm sure you have great stories to tell. I mean, being a lawyer for people who are living on the edge and in need of some sort of... restitution," she purred.

"Uhh, I do, actually, but you know, lawyer - client confidentiality," he raised his hands as if to say "nothing I can do about that".

She pouted. "Aww, phooey. I really wanted to hear a *juicy* story." The emphasis did not go unnoticed.

Owen was losing his patience. Not to mention his breakfast. He was done here. Her flirting was making him ill. He looked at his watch. "Well, I guess the girls are gonna take longer than usual. I'll just see them later." He set his water down and started heading towards the front door.

"Leaving so soon?" She said, rushing up to his side, her arm brushing up against his.

"Yep. Gotta get. Talk with you soon." And with that, he was out the door.

Robin leaned against the shut door smiling to herself. "That was close," she said. She turned and looked into the foyer mirror. It wasn't the same reflection she had known all those years ago and it certainly wasn't the same face looking back when she lived in Miami and Owen Ford was her lawyer after her car accident.

"If he didn't recognize me by now, he's an idiot." She was proud her plan had worked, and he hadn't figured out who she was. Robin knew it was a huge risk coming here and working for the Travers, but she had been so careful with everything.

In Grimsby, she was the most beautiful little girl and her beauty only intensified when she came to the states and worked in Miami. Like Jack and Owen, she, too, was a runner and her body was toned and limber. Her skin was kissed by the southern sun, tanned with a hint of bronze. Her honey-blonde hair, thick and healthy, if it wasn't in a tight ponytail, would usually cascade over her shoulders. She was a knockout, for sure. The typical South Beach beauty.

But her plan did not include her looking beautiful. In fact, she needed to look the opposite and so she went to work. She stopped running and only ate high-caloric meals, full of sugar and salt and preservatives. Gaining all that weight and letting her body and complexion become what it was today was not ideal, but it did the trick. She would only shower and wash her hair once every two weeks. In the end, she looked the part of an out-of-shape, shabby, non-threatening nanny.

Working for Jack and Nina had been a stroke of pure luck. Robin had goaled to come to New York and get close to the family somehow and take it from there. The advertisement for a nanny was pure fate, and Robin truly believed in fate. Fate had brought Owen Ford into her life. Fate had brought her to New York. And it was fate that Margo Flagg had placed the nanny advertisement.

Robin knew she couldn't have just done what she needed to do; she needed the job to get closer to the family. And so she did.

She loved working for the Travers. Nina was sweet and trusting with a hint of gullible. Jack, as nerdy as he looked, was as sexy as they come, with a heart to match. He obviously loved Nina and the kids and would do anything to keep them happy. That much was evident. And Robin admired Jack for sticking with his family through all the hard patches. She hated what Owen was doing to Jack's soul. "Don't you worry, Jack," Robin murmured. "I've got exactly what you need to get Owen to back off forever."

But she still had another job to do. She didn't come all this way to watch over two kids. She had a mission and she had wasted too much time already. There was no use crying over Rachel Meadows and Gregory Wynn. But with Willa, that was a toughie. Robin felt like she had missed something and for that, she would be eternally regretful. But now that Leslie Fontaine was dead, Robin felt things were only getting started. She had to act now.

Robin walked up the stairs and tip-toed down the hallway because the kids were still in their rooms. It was too early for them to be up and about, but Robin couldn't risk waking them up. But she would need them up shortly for her plan to work. She was just outside Nina and Jack's bedroom and opened the door. She looked quickly down the hall for any young eyes peering at her and once the coast was clear, she entered the room. She made her way to the bathroom and opened the mirrored cabinet. When she spotted what she was looking for, she grabbed it and put it in her pocket.

Robin was careful closing the cabinet as not to have it bang and wake up the kids. Once it was closed, Robin saw a face in the mirror. The reflection was staring back at her with a knowing smile. Robin licked her lips, a bit nervous. Finally, the reflection spoke.

"You know what you have to do." Robin nodded her affirmation and left the room.

She pulled her phone from her pocket and opened an app. As she headed down the hallway she typed in a few words. She paused outside one of the bedroom doors. She took a breath and hit "send". Behind the door, Robin heard a muffled "ding".

She still had one more stop to make. One she was looking forward to. So, she called the one man who she needed to accomplish her goal.

She smiled, headed down the stairs and walked out of the house.

CHAPTER FIFTY-EIGHT

August

"I'm exhausted!" Kelly said, surrendering all her shopping bags to a sofa and her body to a chair. "My feet are killing me!"

Nina laughed. "Well, just look at them. They're swollen twice the size of normal."

Kelly lifted a leg so she could see her foot. "I can't see it. My stomach is blocking my view."

"Welcome to your ninth month, my dear," Nina chuckled. She put her bags down on the other sofa. "I'm glad we got an early start this morning. Now you have all day to rest. I'll get us some sparkling water." She retreated to the kitchen.

"I can help," Kelly said, pushing herself off the sofa. "Ohhh!"

"Kelly?" Nina called from the kitchen. "You okay? Finally saw your foot?"

"Oh…my…. GODDDD!" Kelly hollered.

Nina quickly appeared in the den. Kelly was standing there with her legs slightly apart. She was standing in a puddle.

"Kelly?"

"Oh, Nina. I'm so sorry. I've ruined your rug."

Nina stared at Kelly. "Your water broke?! Oh my god, we've got to get you to the hospital!" She grabbed her handbag off the sofa. "Can you make it to the car?"

"Yes…I think sooooOOOOHHH!" She doubled over in a contraction.

"That baby is coming, and we've got to get you out of here. We'll be quicker than an ambulance," Nina said. "Now buck up and let's go, sis!"

Kelly stood up straight and held on to Nina's arm. "You really are…. OHHH…. a bossy bitch…OHHHH!"

They got into the car and sped off.

CHAPTER FIFTY-NINE

August

Robin called Owen earlier to meet her at the Springdale Diner. He was hesitant at first. *Probably thinks I just want to continue my casual flirtation with him.* But Robin knew that was not even on the agenda.

Robin felt it was time she exposed herself to him in a completely different way. He thought he recognized her from somewhere and so she was going to tell him exactly where he knew her from.

She had arrived ten minutes before their appointment time; she needed to ensure the setting was perfect. She picked the table smack in the middle of the restaurant during the busiest time of the morning. If this was any other meeting, she would've chosen a table in a more quiet, out-of-the-way location. But her positioning was part of her plan.

Owen Ford was about to get a taste of his own medicine.

She heard a bell ding as the diner's door opened. She looked up and saw Owen. He looked bothered and out of place.

Good. It's only going to get worse for him.

His eyes scanned the restaurant until they finally landed on her. She smiled brightly and waved; he barely acknowledged her existence as he walked over to the center table. He kept looking around. *Ensuring no one he knows sees him with me, no doubt.* He was still standing, obviously wanting this meeting to already be over.

"Sit down, Owen," she told him.

"What's the point, Robin? I really don't - "

"Sit. Down." She said, still smiling. He huffed but obliged.

"What is this all about?" he asked. "You have to know I'm not interested in you, right?"

Perfect.

"Oh, but darling!" Robin exclaimed, loud enough to gain the attention of the neighboring tables. She clasped his hands in hers. She smiled broadly.

He jerked his hands back. "What's going on here?" he asked.

In due time, pal.

"I just wanted to chat, that's all."

He leaned back in his chair, feeling a little more at ease. He wiped his hands on his napkin. "About?"

"About Miami."

"Miami?" he asked. "What about it? It's a great city."

"I know. I lived there."

Owen's eyes squinted, as if he remembered something. "I thought you said you lived in Granby."

"Grimsby. Yes, but then I moved to Miami. Before coming to New York."

"Wait. When we talked before, you didn't say anything about living in Miami. Why not?" Owen leaned forward on the table, ready to hear more to this story.

For the next hour, Robin told Owen everything and how they knew each other. She started with how he was her lawyer when she was in her car accident, and he got her the settlement that helped her get to New York. The look of doubt on his face was priceless. He was trying to figure out how this woman sitting across from him fit into his life. The cogs were not fitting.

But when she hit him with the more serious connection between them, his entire demeanor changed: his brows furrowed, he squirmed in his seat, his mouth opened ready to debate. But he was silent. He started to sweat. Then Robin went for the jugular.

She slid a photograph across the table. He picked it up and looked at it in disbelief.

Something in him shifted. His face turned crimson. He became angry and tore the picture to shreds. She told him it didn't matter, she had the original on a computer. His anger turned to fear.

"What do you want from me?" Owen asked her.

She told him. He shook his head in refusal. She pointed to the shredded picture on the table.

She could see his mind ping-ponging between his limited options. After a couple of minutes, she saw the defeat in his face. He closed his eyes and took a deep breath. "Fine! We're done here!"

"Not quite," Robin said. "Kiss me."

"Excuse me?" Owen asked incredulously.

"I said, kiss me." She smiled.

Owen looked like he was about to get sick. "You're crazy," he hissed.

Robin looked around at the crowded tables, then said loudly, "Oh, honey! I'm going to miss you so much! What am I going to do without you? I love you so much! I can't raise our baby alone!"

The lady at the next table smiled sympathetically at Robin then glowered at Owen.

Robin puckered her lips.

Owen groused. He leaned in towards Robin. This went beyond anything he was willing to do but he had no choice. He barely brushed his lips against hers then fell back into his seat. He felt ill.

"That was the worst thing I've ever been forced to do," Owen spat.

Robin smiled. "And now you know how Jack feels."

And with that, she got up and left the restaurant.

CHAPTER SIXTY

August

"Owen, I'm at the hospital with Kelly. The baby is coming so please hurry and get here as soon as you can! Love you!" Nina left the message in Owen's voicemail.

Next, she called Jack. She had to leave another voicemail.

"Hey honey. I know you're probably in a meeting, but I just wanted to let you know I'm at the hospital with Kelly. Looks like little Willow is on her way into the world. We're all good right now but just wanted to let you know. I miss you and love you and hope you knock 'em dead in your meetings! Bye honey! Mwah!"

Nina sat in the cold hospital. As hot as it was outside, the waiting room was just as cold. She wondered why doctors insisted on lowering the temperatures of their waiting rooms to arctic level. She shivered and wished she had brought a jacket.

She was so excited for Kelly and Owen and this new addition to their lives. A baby changes everything. It did for her and Jack. Nina shivered again. The memories of being in this very hospital when she suffered her three miscarriages brought back a flood of emotions. None of them good. She stood up to walk off the thick feeling that now enveloped her. She needed to focus on the good happening here now. She looked up and down the hallways at all the comings and goings of the doctors and nurses and patients and wondered which room Kelly was in.

She thought of Margo in this very hospital last month and how close they had come to losing her. Despite all the rants and raves and pressure, Margo was a dear friend and ally. She gave up all her clients for her and Willa! Who does that? Nina caught herself smiling.

And Willa. She never made it to the hospital to get better. She died on the grounds of Scribbler's Cove. It was, for the sake of being melancholy, the best place for Willa to have died. Nina sighed and felt the soft sting of tears in the back of her eyes. *I still miss you so much, mother. So very much.*

Nina found it touching Kelly was going to name her daughter Willow, in honor of Willa. The thought brought a brief smile to her lips.

But then Nina started thinking of the other authors that had died, the other ex-clients of Margo: Rachel Meadows, Gregory Wynn, and Leslie Fontaine. What was going on? Could they really have been just accidents, as the police have said? *It's all too coincidental, if you ask me,* Nina thought.

When Rachel died, it was a surprise but not a shock. It was gruesome, yes, but things like that do happen, especially in a city as crammed and aggressive as New York. Nina couldn't help but think of the last contact she had with Rachel. And as far as she was concerned, that was the day Rachel Meadows became dead to her. Then tragedy struck, and Rachel had been killed. Nina felt bad, but only a little. She didn't believe in karma. *Well, not all the time.*

She sat back down in her chair and put her phone in her lap. She picked up a couple magazines and started reading about Brad and Angelina's latest troubles.

She must've dozed off because she was awakened by her phone's loud vibration in her lap. Nina looked at the screen. She had been asleep for nearly three hours! She started to panic that maybe she missed the doctor but then she realized they would've woken her if anything had happened. She touched her phone's screen.

"Jack! Hey!"

"Hey honey. So, Kelly is about to be a momma, huh?"

"She is, she is! This is very exciting. We had just gotten back from shopping and she went into labor - oh, we need a new rug, by the way - don't ask!

Anyway, I got her here in time and they whisked her off to some room. She's been in labor for about three hours now."

"Is Owen there?"

"No. Not yet. I left a message. Not sure where he is"

"Hmmm, me either," Jack replied. "Look, I'm just on a 5-minute break and about to get back in there. I'm putting my phone on mute so text me with any news. I'll get my messages when I get out of the meeting, ok?"

"Sure thing, hon."

"I'll swing by the hospital when I'm done here."

"Okay. I'll see you when you get here. Love you!"

"Love you, more." And he hung up.

Nina smiled. She and Jack were finally in a good place. It took months – hell, years! – but for the first time in what seemed like an eternity, she and Jack were happy. Happier than they'd been in a long, long time.

Nina walked to the coffee machine and let the machine pour her a cup of, what she assumed, was coffee. She sipped the dark sludge then made her way back to the waiting room and sat down.

She remembered Jack finding her in their bedroom. They sat on the edge of the bed, and he started the conversation that began the mending of their marriage. It was the day after Willa's funeral, and it was short and sweet and welcomed.

"NINA.... I'M SORRY. I KNOW I HAVEN'T ALWAYS BEEN THERE FOR YOU....AND, well, there's really no excuse. I have loved you from the moment I laid eyes on you back in high school."

He looked into her eyes. "You've always been the love of my life. I know I've screwed up and I'll probably continue to screw up but all I've ever wanted was to protect this family. I just...I just want things to go back to the way they were before..."

"Before I stopped writing and messed things up..."

"No. That's not what I was going to say. I was going to say...before things got too complicated and I...we...stopped focusing on us. We lost the balance. We lost the confidence we had as a couple. We lost...us."

"But the kids..."

"The kids are wonderful. They are an extension of us. And honestly, what good are we to them if we're not a solid team ourselves?"

Jack had a point and Nina was happy to finally see the light at the end of the tunnel. She loved Jack with all her soul and would do anything to repair what they once had.

"Do you think we can.... fix this?" Jack asked, taking a deep breath.

Nina looked at Jack. His eyes looked hopeful and full of love. They've made love a couple of times in the past few months but that seemed more of a fling than a marriage. She missed Jack and she desperately wanted him back in her life full time.

Nina looked at her husband. "I do," she replied.

SINCE THAT DAY, EVERYTHING HAD BEEN PERFECT. AND NINA VOWED TO NEVER let anything – or anyone – come between her and Jack ever again.

CHAPTER SIXTY-ONE

August

"Are you ready to hold your precious little girl?" the nurse asked Kelly. She walked over to the bed and placed the little bundle in Kelly's arms.

"Oh my god, she's so tiny!" Kelly exclaimed. Willow's little head was just about the size of a grapefruit. She was 20 inches long and weighed 7 pounds 8 ounces. Her skin was pink and wrinkled and she looked like a little old woman. "She's beautiful," Kelly sighed.

"Just like her mother," the nurse replied.

Kelly couldn't stop smiling. The excruciating pain she just went through was all worth it, worth every minute, just to have this amazing, precious, little girl right here, right now, in her arms. Willow was the first child of hers she had gotten to hold. This meant everything to Kelly.

"And I don't think I've ever seen a baby with such a head of hair on her. So dark and thick." She looked at Kelly's thin, auburn tresses. "Must have gotten it from her father."

Kelly's heart stopped. *What did she just say?*

"Well, I'll leave you two to bond. Call me if you need me," the nurse said as she left the room.

But Kelly was no longer listening. She looked down at the baby in her arms. The nurse was right: Willow had a full head of hair, for sure. Thick and black.

"No," Kelly whispered. "This can't be." But the realization washed over her quickly as she thought back nine months.

December? Had she and Owen made love? They did but that was at the beginning of the month. Nine months. That would be the end of November. Thanksgiving –

"Oh my god," Kelly said, raising a hand to her mouth. She had been hoping she was wrong. The night came back clearly to her. She was in the kitchen with –

She looked back down at baby Willow and held her up to look at her face to face. She cooed and gurgled, the lips on her perfect heart-shaped mouth pursed.

Then Kelly looked at Willow's brown eyes. And there they were. The unmistakable similarity. Like dark feathers extending from the eyelids: eyelashes, long and fluttery, identical to -

"You're Jack's," she said aloud.

"What?" Jack said, standing in the doorway to her hospital room.

Kelly gasped. She hadn't heard the door open. She whipped her head towards Jack. There he stood, his eyes were wide as they darted back and forth between Kelly and the baby.

But Kelly couldn't say anything. She had no words.

CHAPTER SIXTY-TWO

August

Nina looked at her phone for a message from Owen but there was none. But there was something else there. It was an email that must've come through while she was talking with Jack. She clicked on her email app. It was an email from Robin. Usually, an email from Robin was just an update on what she and the kids were up to, just to keep Nina in the loop and lately it was the same ol' thing so she didn't bother doing much more than skim through them. She loved that about Robin. She was always communicating about everything and there were no surprises.

But then something caught her eye. It was one word in lowercase in the subject line: *urgent*. For a millisecond, Nina's breath caught, and she hoped it had nothing to do with Addy's heart condition. Addy never liked to be reminded to take her medicine for her arrhythmia and so Nina and Jack had kept the admonitions to a minimum. With the adoption and Addy being self-conscious about her birthmark, the last thing Nina and Jack wanted to do was to keep bringing attention to something else Addy was uncomfortable with. Addy had promised to take her meds and so far, she had kept that promise. But still. There was this "urgent" email from Robin. Nina inhaled a deep breath and closed her eyes in a prolonged blink.

She looked up and down the hallways again. No doctor or nurse was heading her way.

Nina decided she had nothing to do but wait so she clicked on the email to open it. She expected an urgent update on the kids' day and maybe, worst case scenario, one had scraped their knee or something else trivial to her, yet urgent to Robin.

What she didn't expect, was that her life would never be the same.

My dearest Nina,

This is the hardest email I have ever had to write, and by far, the hardest thing you'll ever read in your life. But unlike your fictional books, this tale is one hundred percent truth.

I don't have much time left so I will get to the point swiftly. And please forgive me for the abrupt dread I am about to put you through.

There's no easy way to say it. Nina – Addy has killed four people. And had plans to kill more.

I came to this hotel to...

But Nina could read no further. Her heart stopped and her phone dropped from her hands. Her world was stopping. She did the only thing she knew what to do. She took a deep breath and let forth a chilling cry for her daughter.

"ADDY!!!!!"

BOOK TWO

CHAPTER SIXTY-THREE

ADDY

August

They weren't before, but for now, things in my life were going marvelously.

But just two days ago someone revealed something to me that turned my world upside down. I mean, seriously? This was big news! It was only going to make things better for all of us in the long run. I could feel it in my bones!

But life wasn't always so smooth. I nearly chickened out moments before I killed Gregory Wynn, but the fact is, I didn't, so I was free to continue my hard thought-out plan and he, like all the others, paid for what he had done to my family. He wasn't my hardest kill, no, that would be my grandmother. But I digress. I'm always needing to think things out from the beginning. Did I miss anything? Is there someone who should be next? There's *always* someone who should be next but not everyone is convenient to me. I did the best I could with what I had to work with and dammit! I'm proud of my accomplishments. Not bad for a thirteen-year-old with acne, a creepy birthmark under her chin and a heart condition.

Now, I'm on this train from Darien to downtown NYC wondering why Owen texted me so early this morning and said he needed to see me. Why him and why me? He said he desperately needed to discuss something with me. I'm at a loss for words. What could he possibly want from me? Does he know what I've done? Is he going to turn me in? Is this some sort of set up? For the first time since all this started, my stomach turns at the thought that I'm a mouse on my way to a trap.

No. I've been careful. Very careful. I covered my tracks, and it was ruled an accident. Like all of them. But Owen is a cunning lawyer. He could be on to something. I'm just a bit confused right now.

Of course, all my fears about Owen could've been avoided had Noah done what I had set him up to do in the first place. Noah is prone to sleep-walking if he's up way past his bedtime. It's why I begged to stay up late to watch the horror movie, because I knew it could trigger his sleepwalking, and I was right! I had hidden the knife in my costume and when we went upstairs to watch "Halloween", I put the knife in his bed after he fell asleep. When we were trick 'r treating, I saw Owen and daddy behind the bushes and heard Owen forcing daddy to do that to him, and I was mad at Owen for it. Later, I whispered in Noah's ear how Owen wasn't that nice of a man. So, all Noah had to do was sleepwalk into Owen and Kelly's room and scare Owen into leaving our house. Everything was going perfectly - except I didn't count on Kelly being awake. Phooey!

I look out the window of the train and see the blue waters of the Long Island Sound. Besides the metronomic clacking of the train's wheels on the track, I'm surrounded by quiet. That is, until my watch alarm beeps, reminding me it's time to take my Propafenone. I take it for my arrhythmia, the heart condition I have had since birth that could cause heart failure. I take the water bottle out of my trusty backpack take a pill and chase it with water. It's bitter but that ends quickly.

My mother pops into my head, and how everything I'm doing – have done – has been for the sake of her. And my father. Getting them back to the happiness they deserve. That is my motivation. Plain and simple. And there were too many "obstacles" out there smothering that happiness.

My first obstacle was Rachel Meadows. She had churned out eight books in two and a half years so you can just imagine their quality. Unless she had sold her soul to the literary devil, her books were just crocks of poop. She seemed incessant in her ability to pump out a ton of books.

And I needed that to stop.

CHAPTER SIXTY-FOUR

August

It was easy to spend time downtown. Sometimes, when my parents thought I'd be at Valentina's, I would jump on the train from Darien. Other times, I would go into the city with daddy, and he'd drop me off at my language lesson, but I could whip through those lessons lickity split and still have lots of time to spare. I would use that time to prepare my plans.

It hadn't been hard to find Rachel Meadows, I'm always looking up things on my iPad, but it did take some time to set in motion. On one of the days I was doing a trial run, I found her.

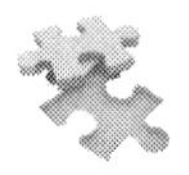

[FROM ADDY'S DIARY]

She smiled like a hyena and raised her phone in selfie-position. "Hey there, Meadowfiles!" (really?) "Going to be at Tailor's Books on Grand this month on Saturday the 15th! I'll be reading a little bit from my new book "Death Chance" and signing all bought copies of my book! I'll be there from 2-4! Can't wait to see you all! mwaaah!"

Her sign-off signature was always blowing a kiss to the viewers. Gag me. Well, this was one appointment she wouldn't be keeping.

So it was through her self-exposure I knew where she was going to be and at what precise time she'd be there. For two weeks I had done test runs from our home in Darien to NYC and knew it would take me a little over an hour and a half for the journey, catching the train from Darien to Grand Central Station, walking ten minutes to the subway at 42nd Street - Bryant Park and taking the subway to Grand Street then walking the 9 minutes, finally arriving at my destination of Tailor's Books on Grand Street. That part I had down pat. The next part would be trickier. So, I'd go across the street to the Bagel Barn, sit and think through the plan. I was confident in the plan. But all the moving parts needed to work perfectly. Fingers crossed!

When the day finally arrived, I wasn't that nervous, but I could feel a bit of a tingle in the back of my neck, like on Christmas morning, all those beautifully wrapped secrets under the tree waiting to be opened. The anticipation was remarkable. Rachel Meadows was going to be my first. But with all my planning, it seemed like I had done this before. I'd planned it, I just needed to execute it. And if it went well, then the others should be a breeze. If it went wrong.... well, that wasn't an option.

I was on the sidewalk and saw her ahead of me as plain as day. Her red hair swayed, her cognac boots clacked down the sidewalk. I made my way through the crowd, and as planned, I blended. I was a kid in a grey hoodie listening to music on a crowded New York City sidewalk. For all intents and purposes, I was invisible. Unseen. And for the first time in my life, I appreciated that characteristic amidst the crowded sidewalk.

Suddenly, I found myself at Rachel's back. I reached out, hesitated slightly then ever so slightly brushed my hand against her mustard color jacket. It felt soft and pricey. At my mother's expense, no doubt.

The scene was set. The countdown had begun. The lights were flashing. And right on schedule, I saw the bus barreling towards the intersection, just inches from the curb.

This was it.

This was for my mom.

I smiled, raised my head and my hoodie fell. I was bathed in light - and I pushed.

The rest was history.

I left the screaming, blood-spattered crowd feeling a little heroic.

I had begun the campaign to save my mom's happiness.

Marvelous!

I WAS JARRED OUT OF MY FLASHBACKS AS THE TRAIN SLOWED THEN JERKED BACK to life. The Long Island Sound still stretched lazily to my left. As it turned out, there wasn't much in the news about Rachel Meadows' death other than it had been ruled a "gruesome accident" and was yet "another casualty of the busyness of the city". I remember my mother saying what a shame it was a bright, young author's life and future was cut short. The end.

I wasn't sure how I felt about that. After all, Rachel died so my mom could live. I guess I expected my mother to be a little more satisfied and, in a way, relieved, that she needn't worry anymore about Rachel Meadows and her popularity-hogging ways. But obviously my mother had yet to feel the same as I did.

Yet.

I would just have to up my game.

And that's how Gregory Wynn came into my life.

CHAPTER SIXTY-FIVE

August

Gregory died in March, but it took me nearly 2 months to get to that point. I didn't see him on social media (like Rachel) and I wasn't with him a lot (like grandmother and Leslie Fontaine) so I had a lot of planning to do with this one.

It was mid-January at grandmother's book launching party. I remember as mom's guests mingled downstairs, I was atop the stairs peering through the banister rails trying to locate my marks. Mommy blew me a kiss.

I saw a group of distinguished-looking gentleman in tweed vests and pocket watches near the fireplace, glasses of bourbon in hands. The tableau was straight out of an Agatha Christie book. And there was Leslie Fontaine, drink in hand, sitting in her wheelchair close to the open bar, a handsome young man attentively holding onto the chair's handles. She was leaning a little to the left because she was already tipsy, I'm sure. But there was one author I couldn't find: Rebecca Sanchez.

Our maids, Norma and Vivian, walked past and stopped just beyond me and asked me what I was doing. "Wishing I was one of the beautiful selected few," I lied, rubbing the red thistle-shaped birthmark under my chin.

"Now Addy," Norma said, "you don't want any of that! Those people may look comfortable and elegant and at rest but don't let the facade fool you. Trust me. I know!"

I smiled up at her. She knew nothing.

"Look!" Norma said, pointing. We turned and followed her eyes to a tall, larger built man standing alone by the French doors.

"Who is that?" asked Vivian.

"That," she said excitedly, "is Gregory Wynn, the brilliant writer of children's books. My little Maria adores his books, but he's better known in the Thriller and Suspense world as Rebecca Sanchez."

I jerked my head towards Norma. She had my attention. As did Gregory Wynn. I turned towards the railing. My eyes squinted as I looked at his name badge. It said "Rebecca Sanchez / Gregory Wynn". *What?? How did I miss that?* So, this plain man wrote adult fiction under a female pseudonym AND was the author of one of my favorite children's series ever? "*The Many Misadventures of Magnolia Muckitymuck*" was sheer genius and there wasn't one kid in this world who didn't know who Magnolia Muckitymuck was. Gregory Wynn was a gift to the children's world of writing. I heard Norma speaking.

"I shouldn't be saying this, but...." she lowered her voice to a whisper, just loud enough for Vivian to hear and for me to overhear, ".....my sister Gloria works for his neighbor in the building. And Gloria said there are a lot of young girls coming in and out of his apartment." Norma wrinkles her nose. "I mean, maybe he's doing research for his kid's books. But it's probably because he's a sicko. I'm not sure, but I can't say anything because he'll find out the information came from Glo, and she could lose her job!" She actually sounded sad that she was protecting a potential pedophile.

My plan started to form.

But I was interrupted by the near-death of my grandmother, at her very own launch party. Apparently, someone had inadvertently put Mortadella ham on the charcuterie table and the traditional pistachios that were cooked into the ham were enough to flareup Willa's nut allergy. She thought the green pieces were olives. That's when Margo saved her life with Willa's EpiPen. It was so exciting! But Willa survived that episode. And I had already put that bit of information into the back of my mind.

I got Gregory Wynn's address from mother's party mailing list and discovered he lived in a modern low-rise apartment building in the Garment District, conveniently across the street from a middle school and playground. I found a picture of him online and he really didn't look like a pervert but then what exactly does a pervert look like? He looked like anyone's next door neighbor. And it was then I understood his appeal. It was time I put my plan in motion.

I recognized him immediately when I arrived at the park.

[FROM ADDY'S DIARY]

I was taking Portuguese lessons downtown close to his building so after my morning class, I could easily go to the park. I blended in with the neighborhood because the school was for my age group, and I could just be another child in the park waiting for their parents to pick them up. The playground was always populated with nannies and their charges, the latter usually playing together while the formers would convene in a circle and gossip about their employers, oblivious to the trash lurking at the other end of the grounds.

I would watch Gregory closely, but unseen: how he'd come to the playground and sit on one of the benches at the west end, hidden from the nannies. I'd watch how he would interact with the kids, especially the girls. I noticed how they dressed and what he was drawn to. It was so obvious to me what he was doing but the nannies probably just thought he was a devoted, single father of one of the lone children. But thanks to Norma, I knew better.

On the day I decided to let myself be seen, I wore a white turtleneck with a colorful unicorn on it, pink jeans, and white tennis shoes. My pink coat and pink scarf and pink pom-pom topped beanie exuded 'little girl'. I even had a backpack adorned with unicorn stickers filled with schoolbooks to complete the schoolgirl appearance. I looked as innocent as I wanted him to think I was. But I also knew there was a possibility he would recognize me as Nina Travers' daughter, as I have been photographed plenty of times, so I drew a little mole on my upper lip, styled my hair now with bangs (yuck!) and covered my birthmark with a little concealer I got from my mom's vanity. I saw him sitting in the middle of his bench, his arms to his sides. He was sitting on his hands. He was wearing dark denim jeans and a brown long- sleeve button down. He blended into the brown bench. Smart. But I was smarter.

Comfortable with my new look, I went out to the slide directly in front of him and climbed the ladder, making sure my backside was on clear view. I had watched enough Law and Order to know how to play this game.

It was a game I was determined to win.

CHAPTER SIXTY-SIX

AUGUST

[from Addy's diary]

I got to the top of the slide and slid down, squealing with delight all the way down. I looked over and he was not paying attention to me. I climbed the ladder again and repeated the whole act. Nothing. Then again. But this time, as I landed on the ground, I yelped. I stood up and rubbed my behind like it was sore from the landing. I glanced towards the bench, and he was looking. I kept rubbing and went to the bench to sit down.

"Hard fall?"

I looked up at him with a hurt look. "Yeah. A little."

"It's all in the planning," he said. "Always look ahead and anticipate what's coming. That way you're always prepared, ok?"

I smiled. "Ok."

"My name's Gregory. What's yours?"

He was fast, I'd give him that.

"Addy."

"Nice to meet you Addy," he grinned. "That's a pretty name. Is it short for something?"

I debated on telling him my full name. What the hell.

"Aderyn."

"Aderyn," he repeated, as if trying it on for size. "That's beautiful. It means 'bird' if I'm not mistaken. It's Welsh."

"How do you know that?" I only knew because Robin had told me once.

He laughed. "I'm a writer, dear Addy. I've done a ton of research on a lot of topics. Plus, my family is from Wales. 'Wynn' is Welsh. I know a little on the subject."

From that day on, I felt a connection to Gregory Wynn and knew because of that, this project would come more naturally to me. And he would fall for it easier than expected.

Whenever I would visit the park and see Gregory on the bench, I'd catch him watching me and then he'd wave. I'd wave back, bounce over and say "hi" then go back to playing. The nannies were wrapped up in their own dramas, still oblivious to our presence. It was a wonder the kids they were watching weren't dead.

I would tell Gregory I was waiting for my mother to pick me up after her work so I could play until she got here. Just when I could feel him getting more attached to me, I'd wave to the street at my nonexistent mother pulling up in her car and I'd tell Gregory "Bye! See you tomorrow!" and I'd grab my backpack and leave him. I could see him deflate as I'd walk away, and I knew I had him hooked.

After another week, I wouldn't play on the slide or swings anymore but instead would just sit next to Gregory, as he would regale me with stories of Magnolia and other little fictional girls he had created that would have wild adventures and lessons learned. It was on the 14th day after we'd met things started moving at a breakneck pace. At the end of one particularly silly story, I laughed a lot and Gregory was laughing and suddenly I felt his hand on my knee. It was as casual as that. Anyone that wasn't aware of him wouldn't have even noticed the subtlety. But I saw it plain as day.

One day, I rubbed my tummy and he asked what was wrong. I told him I had left my lunch on the kitchen table and hadn't eaten all day. I was starving!

He smiled and said, "I live right there," and pointed to a 4-story building. I was well aware that was his building. "I could make you a sandwich. Or whatever you'd like. I have a big kitchen stocked with everything you could want."

No doubt. Obviously, his way to get kids to his apartment is to lure them with never-ending sweets and junk food parents would never let their children eat. It was his version of "can you help me find my missing puppy?" that kidnappers use. If I were stupid, I'd fall for it. But I'm not stupid. So, I grin, and act unsure. "Are you positive? I mean, I'm hungry but I don't want to be any bother." Good.

Make it sound like you're comfortable but not too smart to detect his ulterior motives.

"It's no trouble at all, Addy." He stood and held his hand out to me as if waiting for my cue. Acting the part, I stood up, grabbed my backpack, and took his hand. He raised his perfectly plucked eyebrows and smiled a toothy grin. "Let's go eat."

Once inside his building, we approached the elevator and I noticed he was still holding my hand. He pushed the up button and the doors slid open. Once inside, he pushed the 4th floor button and we started to ascend. I looked up at him, like a child would a father. He looked down and grinned. I felt a little uneasy. Could I go through with this? Would I chicken out? What if he overpowered me? Am I in over my head? What if....

I pushed all those thoughts out of my head once we exited the elevator.

We walked down the marbled-floor hallway to the last door on the right. "Here we are," Gregory said, unlocking the door and letting the door swing in. "After you." We entered and the door closed behind us. I heard the lock click.

Inside, I was immediately drawn to four huge floor-to-ceiling windows ahead of me. I approached them and took in the view. I'm not surprised to see we were overlooking the very park we just left. He actually had a bird's eye view of his prey, like a vulture ready to swoop down and snatch up his next victim.

I continued the visual tour and saw two plush sofas facing each other in front of a beautiful quartz gas fireplace. I heard a noise behind me and noticed Gregory in the kitchen, pulling out all sorts of things from the fridge.

"Turkey ok?" he asked. I nodded my approval. He proceeded to make me a yummy-looking turkey and tomato sandwich with a side of chips and a soda. I sat at the island, and I took a bite and suddenly felt the need to hurry this charade along.

I put my sandwich down. "I...I really should go. My mom will be worried." I raised my eyebrows with mock concern and made my voice quiver. I headed to the door, picking up my backpack before reaching for the door handle.

It was locked.

"Addy," he called, almost sternly.

I stopped, aware of his eyes on my back. I started to feel uneasy. I turned expecting him to be right up on me, hands outstretched towards my neck ready to throttle me into unconsciousness. But he was still in the kitchen. I released a breath.

"Addy, don't go. I thought you were hungry."

"I...am. I.... was. Yes, but my mom will be waiting. I didn't realize how late it was."

Would he believe me? Would he call my bluff and move towards me like a snarling panther ready to bite into my neck? He grinned and I sighed in relief.

"Of course. I understand." He came out of the kitchen towards me, smiling. I instinctively clutched my backpack to my chest as some sort of shield of protection. He stopped in front of me then reached for the lock on the door, released the knob and opened the door for me.

"Can I walk you to the park?" he asked, all gentlemanly.

"No.... thank you. I'm good." I started walking towards the elevator. I turned. "Thanks for the sandwich."

He smiled a toothy grin. "You are welcome, young lady. I hope to see you again soon."

I walked towards the elevator, feeling his eyes burning into my back. Part of me should feel uncomfortable. But the real side of me knew I was on a mission, and I was satisfied with how the day went. I saw what I needed to see. A few more days like today and my job will be complete. I could not afford to mess this one up.

I pressed the down button on the elevator, and it opened immediately. I turned back to Gregory and waved a little girl wave accompanied with an innocent-as-pie smile before taking the elevator down to the ground level. I exited, knowing full well he was looking out of his massive windows as I decided to act the part and skip across the street, turned left out of eyeshot, and walked away to pretend to meet my mother.

CHAPTER SIXTY-SEVEN

August

The train slows as it approaches Central Station. I gather my bag and get up and walk to the door, ready to disembark the moment we stop.

I've made it this far and I'm still at a loss for why I was invited to this meeting. And a little nervous I must admit. What does he want? I know I've been careful but I'm not an expert at anything, so mistakes could've been made.

No! I shake my head. No mistakes were made. Not even with Gregory. What was it he once said: *"Always look ahead and anticipate what's coming. That way you're always prepared."* Well, I've always been one step ahead of everyone else. One thought in front of where everyone else was. Always prepared.

If only Gregory had taken his own advice, he'd be alive today.

The train stops and I get off, walking across the platform towards the exit. The station is crowded and crammed with people in a rush going somewhere. But I'm in no hurry. I will arrive with plenty of time to think things through, get my thoughts together, to have answers to Owen's questions before he even gets to ask them. Stepping out of the station I am greeted by a gush of hot air. It's night and day from the air-conditioned station. I turn left and begin my walk. I have about 15 minutes until I reach the Bryant Park subway entrance. The scorching heat is absolutely unbearable.

The thought of fire brings me back to Gregory.

[FROM ADDY'S DIARY]

On the last day we were to meet, I had worn black tights, Ugg boots, a fluffy cream-colored sweater, and my pink coat. My trusty backpack with a unicorn sticker on it was slung over my left shoulder. I wanted to look like a normal kid even though I knew what I was doing wasn't all that normal.

We met at the park. I saw him before he saw me, sitting on his bench. He looked forlorn. It'd only been a few days since we'd seen each other but I could tell he was going through withdrawals of not seeing me. I was his drug. He looked even more lonely than usual. But when he saw me coming towards him a grin lit up his face like the Cheshire Cat. It wouldn't be so creepy if I hadn't known better.

"Addy!" he smiled, and his dimples were deep, his eyes showed how relieved he was to see me.

"Hi, Gregory." I walked a little faster and plopped down on the bench next to him. I set my backpack beside me.

"It's good to see you. How're things?"

"S'ok," I said. "Noah caught a frog last night and it got loose in the house. We still haven't found it. I think he's in trouble."

Gregory chuckled. "Boys will be boys," he said matter of factly.

"I guess." I decided to go for broke. "But daddy won't let Noah stay in trouble for long. He likes him better," I started to whimper a little bit. "It's because I'm adopted and Noah is his real child so…so I don't mean as much." My voice was filled with certainty and my whimpers turned into sobs.

It worked. Gregory put his arm around my shoulders and gently pulled me towards him in a side hug. I turned my face closer into his chest and really started crying. He began to stroke my hair in a fatherly way.

"Shhhhh. It'll be okay. I'm sure your father loves you just as much as your brother."

"NO! He doesn't!" I raised my head from his chest. "I'm not even related! Why should he care about me? Why should anyone care about me?!"

"Listen. Your father is a good man. It's just that.... well, he probably doesn't know how to deal with pretty little girls as well as he does with rough, ugly boys." He looked down at me and smiled. That was cute. And funny. And probably a bit true, to be honest. Despite myself, I smiled.

"See? It's not so bad. You'll be fine." He put his hand under my chin and raised my eyes to look at him. "Let's go get you some ice cream. I know it's cold, but ice cream always makes me feel better. You?"

I sniffled. "I like ice cream."

"Then it's settled," he reached for my backpack, but I grabbed it from him.

"I can carry that. I'm not a baby!" I did not need him to accidentally see inside.

He raised both his hands in mock defense. "Yes ma'am!" He smiled again and we made the short walk to his apartment building.

Once we're in his apartment, I carefully placed my book bag on one of the sofas near the fireplace and sat down next to it. I removed my coat and draped it over the back of the sofa. Gregory was in the kitchen rummaging for an ice cream scooper and a couple of bowls. I stared at the fireplace. The logs were stacked in an "A" formation on a beautiful iron base. The pilot light was mesmerizing and glowed a purplish blue beneath the stack of logs, beckoning to be turned on.

I'm startled back to reality as Gregory said "Here ya go," and handed me a bowl of vanilla ice cream topped with caramel sauce. "Eat up. Feel better." Gregory sat on the sofa opposite me.

"I already do," I said, spooning up a bite. It's cold, creamy, and delicious. I said as much, and Gregory released a little smile and his head tilted at the use of "creamy" and "delicious". As a kid, I'm too young to flirt, but as an adult, he can misconstrue anything at any time. And he did.

I kept eating the ice cream, making little "mmmm" noises that were sure to stir him up.

"Now I'm getting cold," I said, my voice shaking a bit.

"Here," Gregory said as he stood and grabbed a remote on the coffee table and pressed a button. The fire came to life instantly. The flames danced around the logs and the heat started to fill the space of the den. As he began to sit, he moved to the sofa I was on and sat next to me, closer than we usually sat on the park bench.

"Better?" he asked.

"Much. Thank you."

He set his bowl down on the coffee table. He wrapped his arms around my shoulders and pulled me closer to him like he did when we were at the park.

"A little body heat will warm you up," he said as he quickly rubbed his hand up and down my arm like he was trying to light a flint.

I looked up at him, a little uncomfortable - okay, a lot uncomfortable - but I let him continue his power play, falling into my trap further and further.

"I'm sorry I was upset earlier in the park," I said. "It's just that Noah gets away with everything!"

"I know. But you're a beautiful young lady with so much more to offer than Noah," he says. And with that, he bent down and kissed the top of my head. I shivered. From the cold? From him? I wasn't sure.

"You really think so?" I asked.

"Of course! Just look at you! Pretty as a picture, smart as a whip and if I do say so myself, a much-improved slide rider!" He paused. "Actually, you're prettier in person than you are in your pictures."

Busted. I had nowhere to go with this. He knew who I was. But if he's known, he still wanted to be close to me. Interesting.

"You know who I am?" I asked, looking into his eyes.

"I've always known, Addy. The literary world, especially our genre, is a small world. Same circles, that sort of thing. I've seen your family's pictures in the magazines and online. You're famous," he said with a flare.

"Famous? Hardly," I laugh. I wiped the smile off my face, looking serious. "And you're not mad I'm here?"

"Are you kidding? I'm thrilled! I love your mother's work. I've been a big fan of hers for years. I've gotten the chance to meet her on occasion and was even at the book launch of her mother's book. Her writing was amazing," he said. "She really was the best of the best. Getting to know her daughter is just icing on the cake."

Was *amazing.* Was *the best. Past tense. That's not good.*

"You're funny!" I giggle. "And super-duper nice."

"Well, Addy, I can be even nicer to you if you'd let me," his voice got smoother. He took my bowl of ice cream and set it down next to his. Then he took my free hand and placed it in his lap. I felt something hard. My eyes grew big. He tightened his arm around my shoulders. "Would you like that?"

Now, this is the part where someone in this position would say "Hell no!" and run for the hills, but I just needed him to do one more thing so I could complete my mission. But I really needed to sell it. I pulled out all the stops.

"Yes, I think.... I think so...." I stammer, trying to sound sure of myself but also a little timid. Can't be too overzealous, he'd never believe it.

"Are you sure? Are you super-duper sure?" he asked. "Because we don't have to do anything you don't want to do but I've gotta say, you are one sweet, pretty young lady and I'd love to make you happy."

A normal me would be vomiting right now but I've only had a couple scoops of ice cream so there's not enough to throw up.

"I'm...sure...I think...yes. I'm sure. But I don't want to get sick."

"Oh, never. I'll use something that will protect you, don't you worry." He smiled. "This is great. This makes me very happy, Addy." He stood up. "Let me go to the bathroom and bedroom and clean up a little bit and, uh, get something and I'll be right back.

"Okay," I responded meekly.

Gregory bent down and kissed the top of my head again and with a smile plastered on his creepy face, he left the room.

As soon as the coast was clear, I bolted up from the sofa, grabbed my backpack and undid the zipper. I removed my Barbie lunch box and opened it up. Inside was a small ladle and Tupperware container filled with crushed up charcoal. I was thrilled I caught the rerun of the episode of my favorite show, C.S.I., where the killer used this method to off his victim. I had no idea how I was going to carry this one through, but I sure hoped it was gonna work!

I used the remote control and turned off the fire. Then using the ladle, I carefully scooped up the charcoal and placed it onto the logs. I was gentle because I didn't want any charcoal dust to be floating in the air when....

"Addy, you okay? Give me 3 more minutes," he called from the back. He had a sing-song lilt in his voice. I could hear water running.

"Yessir.... I'm good...just waiting...." I called back.

I had to hurry!! I finished ladling all the crushed-up charcoal onto the logs and sprinkled the rest of the remnants in the container onto the top. I closed the Tupperware and repacked my backpack. I threw my coat on, slung the backpack over my shoulder and turned the fire back on.

I hurried to the front door and let myself out. My Uggs made no noise as I ran down the hallway and into the elevator. It seemed like forever to get to the first floor. Surely Gregory had come out and discovered I'm not there by now! He's going to be pissed and looking for me. Finally, the elevator doors opened on the first floor, and I ran out, down the hall and out the door.

From the first day I was in Gregory's apartment and looked out those floor-to-ceiling windows, I found two routes: one where he could see me and one where he couldn't. The day I skipped away, I wanted to make sure he saw me. But today was a different story. I needed to flee unseen, so I took the invisible route. I ran like the wind.

Away from the building.

Away from the park.

Away from Gregory.

Towards making my mother that much happier.

Almost a week had passed since that day at Gregory's, and I was getting nervous, and I was agonizing over whether I had succeeded or not. But then on the eighth day, as we all sat around the table eating pancakes, my mother read the news from her tablet and informed us Gregory Wynn had succumbed to carbon monoxide poisoning in his apartment building. We were rushed out of the kitchen (darn it), but I just looked it up later on my iPad. Apparently, he was found on the floor in front of his apartment window. Had he been looking for me? When the coast was clear, we went back to the kitchen to finish our breakfast. Noah paid no attention to the new dynamic around us as he played and let his little dinosaur figurines destroy his pancakes. I never looked up from my breakfast, but my ears were all at attention.

I couldn't believe it! Oh my God, had it really worked?? I kept my head down because I didn't want to give away my glee.

I smiled broadly and content, but only inwardly. I had done good. I had rid the world of a pedophile. I should get a medal. I didn't want to spoil this moment, but my stomach grumbled. I spoke for the first time that morning.

"Can you please pass the syrup?"

CHAPTER SIXTY-EIGHT

August

I had finally made it to the Bryant Park subway stop. Through the August heat, I had forged, and I felt I had walked for hours although in reality, it had only been 15 minutes. Ugh. I was melting. My hair was sticking to my forehead. I needed to be in Leslie Fontaine's pool. I had only sweet memories of Leslie Fontaine's pool. And just the thought of the cool water surrounding my body oddly cooled me off a bit.

At the entrance of the subway stop, hundreds of people were coming up the stairs signaling a train had just left the station. I head underground and make my way through the turnstile. The low-ceilinged subway area smells of hot dogs and sweat. I look overhead at the LED screen and see that my train is due to arrive in 4 minutes. I find an available concrete bench and plop myself down. Its stone is cool, and the relief is welcomed. I'm not scared of being here alone. After what I've done, I feel pretty invincible.

But still, as I sit, I clutch my backpack to my chest like protective armor. I stare at the innocent unicorn sticker, the horse's mane multicolored like a hideous rainbow. Its teeth dragged into a gigantic smile. And I, too, smile, as I remember just how important a part this bag played in all of my plans.

It would play a big part in my next act, too: the death of my grandmother, Willa Greyson.

[FROM ADDY'S DIARY]

I slung my backpack over my shoulder as I made my way to Scribbler's Cove. In a half hour, I arrived and was greeted by a huge wall of massive 25-foot Leyland Cypress trees that stretched at least the length of a football field along the front of the estate. At the far end of the tree wall was a ginormous iron gate that, when I inserted my special key, opened wide to a gravel entrance. I entered the gate and was immediately transported to a world of color: green, purples, pinks, yellows – it was like stepping onto the yellow brick road and seeing the long way towards Emerald City.

Throughout the massive lawn were lilac trees and peony bushes, wild jonquils, and tulips. It's absolutely magical. I bet if I looked hard enough, I'd find a white rabbit with a pocket watch shrilling about how late he was for an important date.

It took me a full 5 minutes to reach the enormous white New England colonial. I walked around one side and I saw grandmother on the lanai. She was sitting with her laptop and a glass of water with lemon. Her purse was by her side in another chair. I remembered what was in the purse and I needed to make sure it stayed right there in that chair.

When she heard me approach, she lifted her head and her eyes smiled.

"Hello, my darling. Come. Come give me a hug."

I kept my backpack on my shoulder and walked over to her. We kissed on the lips. Another tradition that means a lot today. "Hi, grandmother. You look lovely this morning."

"Thank you, sweetheart," she replied to my genuine compliment. "And so, might I add, do you," she said. "Let me look at you."

And with that, she held onto my hands and pushed me arms-length to look at my entire jeans and tee shirt ensemble head-to-toe. Grandmother always did know how to make me feel like I was the best thing in the world. It was the main reason today was going to be so difficult. But I kept reminding myself that my parents' happiness was the most important thing in life. So, what I had to do today was a necessity. Sad, but necessary. I closed my eyes and shook off the guilt that crept up my spine and onto the back of my neck. Still holding my grandmother's hands, I opened my eyes and smiled. It was going to be a good day, death be damned.

"Are you ready for our traditional picking?" Willa asked.

"I am," I smiled.

And I was. More than ever before.

"Good! I gave the crew off for the day and it's just you and me! Just us girls!" Her elbow nudged me in the side. "Then let's go!" Willa announced. "Oh. Did you bring...."

I patted my backpack. "Yes, ma'am. I brought our lunch. Like always. Cucumber sandwiches, apple slices, carrot sticks and two bottles of Perrier." I also had a little surprise packed away.

"That's a good girl. Addy, you are just such a pleasure to be around. We are so lucky to have you in our lives!" She hugged me tight. A bit unusual per our summer routine but not totally unwelcomed.

I hoped the surprise I brought this trip in my backpack would do what I needed it to do. I said a silent prayer and squeezed her hug a little tighter.

Willa grabbed a large-brimmed hat with a yellow and white striped ribbon around the band of the hat. The ribbon flowed about 12 inches down her back, and she suddenly looked like she was ready for a photo shoot with Vanity Fair. We each grabbed a medium sized basket for our hauls.

We started walking her lawn and I couldn't help but marvel at our surroundings. The property was easily 20 acres big – I think the total property took up five actual lots. The grass was a beautiful shamrock green and looked like a perfect, feathery carpet softly placed on low hills.

But it was the 5 acres of the property to the east end of the property, just before the Sound, that was our destination year after year. This part of her land was home to amazing, thriving fruit trees like pear, plum, fig and cherry. Picking fruits off these trees was our tradition. And today we were after the multitude of pears and plums. As we approached the trees, I could tell the branches were laden with the weight of our treasure.

A SUDDEN RUMBLING FOLLOWED BY A RUSH OF TEPID AIR BREAKS MY THOUGHTS and I stand up from the concrete bench in the subway station as the loud *whoosh* of the train zooms past me at an impossible speed, finally slowing down and coming to a complete stop. A hollow 'ding' announces the opening of the doors and people flood out like rats on a sinking ship. Once the coast is clear, I move with the crowd and walk onto the train.

I quickly find a seat next to an elderly lady who looks at me and smiles. Her bright grey hair is pulled behind her ears and her watery eyes make her look like she is seeing right through me. God, I hope she doesn't strike up a conversation. I smile back as I reach into my backpack and pull out my AirPods and put them in my ears. The noise cancellation starts, and I sit in blissful silence. I have nine minutes to ride. I settle in, backpack in my lap, silence surrounds me, and the old lady has dozed off. I look at her and think how peaceful she looks. Almost dead.

And she reminds me of my grandmother on that fateful day.

CHAPTER SIXTY-NINE

August

[from Addy's diary]

As we headed towards the property's east end, the design of the orchard had the pear trees right in front of us and the plums were further down the lawn, hidden behind the awaiting cherry trees. Willa called it "Fruit Tree Feng Shui". She didn't believe in having all the blooming trees together and all the leafy trees together. "This way, the orchards look appealing and beautiful all year round, left to right. Comforting."

Whatever you say, Gran. I'm just thankful she believed in this stuff. Her little obsession with Chinese harmony and balance was going to help me out.

"Wow!" we both exclaimed as we got closer to the pear trees. Willa put her hand on top of her hat and leaned her head back, peering high up into the tops of the trees. She let out another one of her whistles. "There certainly are a lot here today. We'll have an easy time filling our baskets quickly. And what we can't get, the birds will be able to fill their bellies with."

With the plethora of fruit, it appeared our time might be cut short today in the orchards, so I needed to step up my plan.

"We could really get a lot done if you do one fruit and I do another," I suggested, shrugging for emphasis.

Willa eyed me suspiciously. This was definitely a break from our tradition. I had to sell it. "That way," I said, "we'll be finished earlier than normal, and I can show you my surprise." I patted my backpack again for reiteration.

"Hmm," she said, cocking her head. Would she go for it? "Fine. Rock, paper, scissors! Winner gets the closest orchard, and the loser has to take the furthest!"

I smiled.

"Ready?" she asked. We put our right fists in our left hands, and she started counting as we pumped our hands up and down.

"One.... two.... three..."

We showed our hands. She was scissors to my paper.

"Ha! Take a hike, my darling." She hitched her thumb towards the plums.

"I'm going," I said, head down, fake sulking.

"And don't come back until your basket is full!" Willa booted me with her foot. "Shoo!"

As I reached the plum trees, I set my backpack down on the shaded grass. I grabbed my basket and started picking the fruit. I took one particularly plump one and wiped my tee shirt around it to lightly clean the stone fruit. I bit into it and enjoyed the sweet taste. Juice dribbled down my chin but the flavor of these organically grown plums was just incredible. I felt a bittersweet prick on my neck as I realized that after grandmother was gone, this was probably the last time I'd get to enjoy these fruits and our special day. And in reality, I did enjoy it. Despite the urgency of my task, I was going to miss her tremendously. I fought back tears. But now was not the time to show emotion.

Sad but necessary, I kept telling myself.

Within a half hour, my basket was overflowing with the purplish, meaty fruits. As if on cue, from somewhere in the orchard, my grandmother called out to me.

"My basket is full, sweetheart. Where are you? Ready to head to the oaks?"

"Yes, ma'am," I hollered back. "I'll meet you there!" Last thing I needed was for her to come to me right now! She couldn't see me from where I stood, and I realized my trip down memory lane cost me valuable time. I needed to hurry up and continue my plan. I ran back to where my backpack sat. I reached down into the side pocket and rummaged around until my fingers found what they were looking for. Crossing my fingers, I proceeded as planned.

A few minutes later, I met up with grandmother under a large oak tree. She was perched on the iron bench in the shade looking like a perfect glass of summertime lemonade. I proudly showed her my full basket of the purple-red stone fruit and in turn, she pointed to her basket on the ground by her feet. It was filled with gold pears that had a bit of red on them, as if they were kissed by the sun itself. I took a seat next to her on the bench. It was cool to the touch.

"Looks like we both made out, my darling."

"Yes ma'am," I said. "I can't wait to taste them!"

Willa reached for a pear. "By all means, my dear, have one," she said, thrusting the fruit my way. "There are plenty where that came from."

My eyes widened. I couldn't eat the pear. It would ruin everything. But I took it from her as to not arouse suspicion. "I'll save this for dessert," I said setting it down on the bench between the two of us.

"How about some lunch then?" Willa asked. "And I can't wait to see what your surprise is!" She pulled her sunglasses off and held them in her lap. Her bright, grey eyes looked as though they were dancing with excitement.

I smiled. "Ok..." I said slowly. But then I paused.

"What is it, dear?" my grandmother asked, sensing my hesitation. Gran always knew when something was on my mind. She reached over and clasped my hand in hers.

It was now or never! With everything I could muster, I said what I needed to say with as much emotion as I could conjure up.

"I just.... I just love our time together, grandmother. And...well, these days here at your house where it's just you and me...it's special. And I'll never forget it. I love you!" My eyes watered as a legitimate emotional response. I knew I would never forget our times together. But I also knew these times had to come to an end. I went in to seal the deal.

I leaned into her, wrapped my arms around her neck and kissed her gently on the lips. I loved my grandmother and I wanted her to know it. I was her little granddaughter, her treasure. I kissed her again and then burrowed my head against her neck. I was sobbing now, and she held me tighter.

"Oh, my sweet angel. I love you, too! So much! And there will be many more special times for us. Always! Don't forget, the cherries and figs will be next for us." She pulled my head up and looked me in the eyes and then kissed me on her own that time. She wiped away the tears from my eyes.

Gran's grey eyes grew wet. She mustered a smile and said, "Addy, when your parents seemed to be at their lowest, the universe decided to change the course of their fate and brought you into their lives. It was because of you that your mother and father survived that terrible time."

Willa paused for effect, then chose her words carefully.

"I'm sure both of them were at some sort of fault for their marriage weakening during this time. But then you, my sweet, Addy! You came along and all was right with the world. Your mother and father were elated and nothing else mattered but to ensure your happiness. And they did everything they could to make sure you were the happiest little girl in the world. Do you feel that, my dear?"

"What?" I asked.

"That you are the happiest little girl in the world?"

I had to only think for a nanosecond because I was *happy. I planned on being happy forever with my family. As long as they were happy, then everything would be alright.*

"Oh, yes! I do! And I want my parents to be happiest of all. I'll do whatever I can to make that happen," I beamed. Because it was true. "Cross my heart."

"Oh, my dearest, Addy, I know you will. They – we – are so lucky to have you in our lives. You are j.... ust about the swww.... sweee..." Willa stuttered. She stopped talking and stared at me.

I looked at her quizzically.

She took a breath. Then exhaled. She gave a small scoff. "Well, I think maybe the heat has gotten to me a bit, darling." She stood from the bench and reached down and picked up her basket of pears. "Let's head back to...to...the..." She stopped. She didn't move. Her lips vibrated but nothing came out.

I kept staring at her. "Grandmother? Are you....ok?" I sounded scared. And to be honest, I was a bit. What exactly was happening? What was going through her mind? Did she suspect anything?

Willa shook her head as if she could shake this odd, weightless feeling away. Her eyes were glassy, hollow. Suddenly, Willa dropped her basket, pears scattered about on the lawn. Her hands rushed to her throat. "Can't...can't...brea..." Her breaths came in huge gasps and bursts, each one more dramatic than the last, each one sounded like she was sucking in what little air there was in a bubble.

She fell to the ground on her side, her hat landed next to her, the ribbon was blowing beautifully in the wind while the hideous scene played out. One hand was still around her throat, the other stretched out above her head. Clumsily, she rolled over onto her stomach like a zombie from one of those movies. Her outstretched hand clawed the ground ahead of her, dragging her.... somewhere. Her legs were numb and her left one bent at the knee as to help her with gaining traction on the grass. Her well-manicured fingernails clawed and snapped off in the hard dirt. She moaned from the sharp pain.

But her efforts were futile. She had only moved an inch. I saw her eyes were wide as saucers, her black pupils huge and bulging. She still gasped and made grunting noises, but I could hear her weakened breaths getting more and more labored. Shallow. Anguished.

Grandmother was now in full anaphylactic shock. From what I'd read, at this point she could feel her lungs seizing up, her breathing practically stopping yet coming in short pops of air. I watched every bit of color drain from her face – her blood pressure obviously plummeting rapidly. Her white hair and nearly translucent skin made her look devoid of all blood.

Her body was at a weird angle on the grass, her arms flayed out and her legs bent, feet digging into the ground for traction. But it was no use. Her face was strained, and her eyes bulged, looking straight towards the house. Where her purse sat on a chair. Her EpiPen inside.

I backed up, the house fifty yards behind me. I knew what I should do, and I knew what I needed to do. The need took over. I looked down at a dying Willa, her face ashen and stretched like a skeleton, her lips parted for one more breath of air that would never come. Her ragged breathing had ceased.

And with that, she was dead.

I paused for just a moment before I stepped towards her. "Grandmother?" I asked. Her now-unkempt hair covered her face. I gently pulled some strands back exposing her gaping mouth and widened eyes. The sight made me gasp. But I was still unsure of what had happened. I put my fingers on her neck and felt for a pulse. There was none. A lone tear fell from my face and landed on her cheek.

"I'm so sorry, Gran. I really am. But I had to."

And I did. I had zero choice. I've never known happiness like I had with my family. My grandmother's success overshadowed my mother's, and mother would die a little every day knowing she'd never be as good as Willa. And I couldn't let that be a factor anymore.

I reached into my backpack and pulled out a sanitized wipe. First, I wiped my tear off her cheek. And then I wiped her lips. Carefully. Lovingly. I needed to get all the peanut brittle residue off.

The peanut brittle was my idea. When I saw her reaction after eating the Mortadella ham with the pistachios baked in, I knew how things had to happen. This was the surprise I had brought to Scribbler's Cove that I had kept hidden in my backpack.

My plan had worked where we had each gone to different parts of the orchard. She had hollered that her basket was full and was ready to head back to the oaks. That's when I hurried back to my backpack, took out the peanut brittle and lightly rubbed every bit of my lips with the sweet candy. Then I met up with grandmother under the large oak tree.

And then, I kissed her on the lips.

Now, my grandmother was dead. And I killed her. From love's kiss. The peanut brittle had done its job.

I should feel horrible for this. My mother will be devastated. Absolutely devastated. But I think she will also see this as a righteous way to regain her crown once again at the top of the leaderboard. She must. Everything depended on it.

I looked down once more at my grandmother. I took the two baskets of fruits and dumped their contents all around her body. I dropped the empty baskets and looked at the scene. For anyone that looks, it will appear she overexerted herself picking two baskets of fruit and then simply had a heart attack as she was walking her vast property. After all, no one knew we did this together. I never told anyone.

Cross my heart.

CHAPTER SEVENTY

August

The old lady next to me must have been dreaming because her arm jerks and jabs into mine. I feel the train slowing down. We must be entering the Grand Street station already. I hug my backpack to my chest.

I feel my face and it's wet. Had I been crying? I'm not surprised, really. Memories of my grandmother will always bring tears of happiness – and now sadness – to me.

The train continues its slowing arrival into the Grand Street station.

My heart flutters.

Less than 10 minutes. That's all the time I have until our meeting. He texted yesterday it was urgent for us to meet. That he had something very "dire" to discuss.

This man, who is in my life now wants to meet me to discuss something. But why not at the house? Are there too many ears? Does he not want to cause a scene with Noah around? Our house is always filled with people so maybe this is his way of getting us alone. And I do love the Bagel Barn. So, meeting him there shouldn't be as alarming as I'm making it out to be. After all, I owe him my life. But should things go wonky, and he starts accusing me of the things I've done, I will feign innocence and pour on the tears and act betrayed and brokenhearted if that's what it takes for him to believe me.

But as well as I know him, I can't help but be a bit nervous. I've done so much in the past few months and though I've been careful, I can never be too sure I haven't been found out. In fact, I *know* someone knows. My diary was slightly off kilter in its hiding place. Always under my bed, above my sweater box. I always line it up perfectly with the wooden crossbeams and then move it 30° to the right. But one day, it was not off 30°. It wasn't off anything. It was perfectly in line with the crossbeams. Someone had gotten to it and then aligned it back. Only it was wrong. And now that I'm thinking about it, I'm getting more and more nervous about this meeting. Owen has stayed at our house enough to go snooping. He's a lawyer after evidence every day of his life. What if…. I can't think about it.

I will meet him but still hold my cards close to the vest. I should be fine. I will give him the benefit of the doubt.

But still, there's a nagging in the back of my mind I cannot shake. I can't quite put my finger on it but maybe our conversation will lend itself for me to ask my own questions. I still need to keep the upper hand.

I stand on the train as it comes to a complete stop. The doors open and I walk out onto the platform, up the stairs and I'm out onto the sidewalk. The heat is instant. August in New York City is like Calcutta. Sweat comes out of pores you never knew existed, to the point you feel like you are literally melting.

As I'm walking the final nine minutes to my destination, I'm already sticky with sweat and I immediately think of how to stay cool. My mind wanders back to another threat to our family and how I went from being a sweet kid doing her chores to a concerned daughter, once again doing what I needed to do.

Poor Leslie. She never saw it coming.

CHAPTER SEVENTY-ONE

August

After Gregory died in March, I decided I needed to start planning how to deal with grandmother and Leslie. In January at the book launch, I got my answer to Gran's predicament. Leslie, however, I had no idea what to do. So, I thought I'd start by seeing what she was all about. What kind of author was she that she was taking my mother's spot at the top? I went to the bookstore and bought her latest book: *My Husband's Boyfriend*. It was, as expected, not very thought-provoking and only took me four hours to read. I had just finished reading the book when I saw Leslie's bio on the inside back jacket.

Suddenly, I knew how I would do it. I knew how I would kill Leslie Fontaine.

"Leslie Fontaine is the New York Times bestselling author of seven psychological thrillers including "Killing with Kindness", "The Eighth Deadly Sin", and *My Husband's Boyfriend*. When she was 29, Leslie became one of the top equestrians in the country but her Olympic dreams were dashed when she had a serious fall after her horse refused to jump the 10th set of hurdles. Paralyzed from the waist down, Leslie became

confined to a wheelchair and suddenly with time on her hands, turned to writing.

Leslie's only daughter, Charlotte, lives in London and is a photojournalist for The Guardian. Charlotte has designed all the book covers for her mother.

Having been born and raised in Connecticut, Leslie continues to live in her beloved state and makes her home in Norwalk with her cherished Maltese, Bella."

The picture that accompanied the bio was of Leslie Fontaine sitting in her state-of-the-art wheelchair, smiling for the camera as she sat at her computer. Bella sat in her lap, tongue hanging out. Leslie's shoulder length salt and pepper hair was wavy and pulled back tight into a small ponytail, held together neatly by a blood-red bow. She was a beautiful lady that belied her 70 years of age.

I felt I was armed with enough information to do what I needed to do.

[FROM ADDY'S DIARY]

It was the third week of June, and I was out of school for the summer. I told mommy I wanted a summer job to earn my own money for books and ice cream (whatever she would believe). She told me I didn't have to work, that she would pay for whatever I needed, but I had other plans. I finally convinced her it was good for me to get out and possibly meet other people and she seemed to warm to the idea because she knew I preferred just the opposite, and she secretly loved the idea I would be out in the sunshine mingling with the common folk. Ok, those are my words, but I knew she felt that way.

Mommy was still walking in slow motion after grandmother's death last week so I'm not sure she really knew what I was asking before she agreed with me. So, with her blessing, I headed out into the community of Darien, CT and began my mission. I jumped on my bicycle and headed east on Long Neck Point Road. There are plenty of houses I could stop at and inquire about a summer job, but I had a specific home I was looking for. It was in Norwalk, only 10 minutes by car from Darien but more like 23 minutes by bike.

I headed up Post Road and passed all the cute little stores and restaurants that made Darien a classic eastern shore community. I turned right at Trader Joe's onto Old King's Highway and rode until I could turn right onto Tokeneke Road, where I eventually crossed the Long Island Sound. I found myself on Rowayton Avenue, and I couldn't help but take in all the old, beautiful homes in this area. At Pinkney Park, I turned left onto Pennoyer Street and found the home, a large white Colonial with a small driveway. I saw the wheelchair ramp leading from the driveway to the wrap-around front porch and knew I had finally arrived at Leslie Fontaine's home.

I stopped on the street in front of the house and admired the home for a minute before hopping off my bike and walking it up the driveway. I found a large blooming hydrangea bush and hid my bike behind it, leaning it carefully against the white brick wall of the home. I walked around to the front of the house, up the steps to the right of the ramp and found myself at the front door. I took a deep breath and pressed the doorbell. A melodic 'bing bong' echoed through the home.

I heard a couple of short yaps. Bella.

After a couple of minutes, I could see movement behind the thick beveled glass window on the front door. A wheelchair was rolling my way. This was it. Time to sell it. "Hush, Bella. Coming," I heard a female voice. Was it slurred? I looked at my watch. It was 10:23 in the morning. If she's drinking already this could be easier than expected. Time to go fishing.

With some effort, the front door opened and there sat Leslie Fontaine. Bella was sitting on her lap, tongue hanging out. I swear it looked just like the picture in her book bio, blood-red bow and all. Except now, in her hand she had a short glass filled with a light pink drink. Vodka and cranberry would be my guess.

She eyed me up and down. "Yes? How may I help you, dear?" Perfect. No recognition at all. I knew I was taking a risk because Leslie had seen me before. Not a lot, mind you, but at a party here and there and probably in magazines. But Leslie Fontaine was usually marinated in alcohol, and I was counting on the fact that her recollection brain cells weren't like they used to be. I was right. She had no idea I was Nina Travers' daughter.

"Hi!" I said with heightened enthusiasm. It sickened me I had to pretend to be so desperate and childlike. I rattled off my speech, sounding as rehearsed as a normal child would sound. "My name is Charlotte Hanover, and I am in 8th grade at Andrews Preparatory Academy, and I am here to help you for the summer!" Good lord. I sounded like I was on Shark Tank.

I noticed Leslie's eyes squinted a little at the mention of my first name being

Charlotte, the same as her estranged daughter in London. She took a sip of her drink. I heard the ice cubes clink.

Hook.

I continued. "For the summer, I am trying to earn some extra money to help my baby brother get a puppy for his birthday. He loves dogs. My whole family does!"

"Awww. That's so sweet," she said. The ends of Leslie's mouth curled into a knowing smile. Bella laid down on her lap. Leslie looked down at Bella and she scratched the little dog on her head.

Line.

"My mommy and daddy say the only way he can get a puppy is if he pays for it himself. But he's too young to really do things to earn a lot of money so I decided I would help him." Leslie's hand lifted from Bella's head and went to the doorknob. Had she already made up her mind against me? I spoke quickly.

"See, he has a disease, Lupus, and it makes him really sad. He's so young that something like this makes his friends stay away from him. He gets so lonely." I conjured tears and let two of them fall down my cheeks. "I think a puppy would really help him. To be his real friend. A friend that will never leave him." I sniffled.

Leslie's hand was still on the door knob. I noticed that her eyes glistened. Leslie connected the dots and realized her wheelchair had the same lonely consequence my brother's "disease" had on him. As hoped, Leslie felt a twinge of sadness towards herself and my brother and as I stared at her face, I could see the exact moment she resigned herself to being completely on my side.

Her hand tightened around the doorknob, and she pulled the door open fully. Bella rose to sit on Leslie's lap, ready for a ride in the wheelchair. The dog seemed to be smiling at me.

Finally, Leslie spoke. "Come in, dear. Let's see what we can do to help your little brother."

I stepped past Leslie as I set foot into her huge foyer. I felt the door close behind me. I looked around and smiled.

Sinker.

Thirty minutes later I left Leslie's house with the job. I bound down the front steps. As I reached the walkway, I turned and waved to her as she sat bound in her chair. "See you next Tuesday," I said to her. Because she was slightly blotto, she said nothing but raised her hand to wave back and nodded her confirmation. A refreshed drink was in her other hand.

I heard the front door shut just as I retrieved my bike from behind the hydrangea bush, walked it to the street and hopped on. As I pedaled home, I smiled as I remembered just how eager Leslie was to hire someone who was able to do some odd jobs around the house: organize the garage, pick fresh flowers from the gardens for the tabletops, water the plants, walk Bella three times a day for her to do her business, collect the mail – things like that. Things that normally took Leslie hours to accomplish. Things Leslie found arduous and exhausting. Things that, when done by someone else, would free up more time to write her next blockbuster.

It would be her last, I thought to myself.

I started my new job at Leslie's the following week. We decided I would go to Leslie's on Tuesdays and Fridays from 10am-4pm for $10.00 a day. She initially offered $8.00 but I told her the puppy my brother wanted was a costlier smaller breed – "Like Bella!" – and well, that was all she needed to hear. The $10.00 a day was mine. I told her I had to accompany my brother to a doctor's appointment (sad face) on Monday but would be there on Tuesday.

In reality, I needed Monday to plan out my daily chores and tasks I would need to do to complete my plan.

But that was next week. Today was Friday and I had plans with a Disney movie this weekend. I might be overly smart for my age but hey, I'm still a girl who loves princesses and happy ever afters.

Monday arrived and I was up in my room with a large desk calendar jotting down little ideas and suggestions on how to be successful at this latest strategy. Mom was downstairs with Margo creating their own success plan. Mother has taken a lot of Margo's advice and Margo couldn't be happier.

Neither could I. And I smiled. I did this! I caused this resurgence! She will be back on top in no time! I sighed with relief.

I looked at my calendar and all the things I'd written down that I could do to help Leslie out. And in the midst of all my tasks, there was the most important one. Right there.

Friday - 1:00pm - take Leslie outside to sit poolside and enjoy the weather. Prepare lemonade. Pack cups. And bowl.

The timing was important. I would arrive by 10:00am. I needed the three hours to accomplish my goal.

I held up the big calendar and looked at it. I tilted my head and smiled. Satisfied, I put the calendar back in its hiding place under my mattress and headed downstairs to say hi to Margo.

This was going to be my easiest one yet.

CHAPTER SEVENTY-TWO

August

[from Addy's diary]

Tuesday came and I got out of bed at 7:00am. I was excited for my new mission. I put on my pink robe and headed downstairs. The house was quiet, but mom and dad should be up soon. I heard Robin clinking around in the kitchen, so I joined her.

"Morning, Robin," I said, jumping on a barstool at the kitchen island.

"Good morning, luv," she said. "You're up early this bright morning? You must be excited to start your new job with the Hanovers!"

Yeah, okay. So, of course I wasn't going to tell everyone I got a job with freaking Leslie Fontaine. I didn't want a paper trail. So instead, I lied and told everyone I would be working for the Hanovers. They lived more than far enough away, several houses actually, that my absences would easily be explained. Plus, I went to school with Charlotte Hanover, so it was easy to come up with an alias I could give to Leslie.

I noticed Robin staring at me waiting for a response.

I snapped to attention. "Oh yes! So excited! I can't wait to help them out. I think they are going to let Charlotte work with me so that way it'll be super-duper fun!"

Robin smiled. "Super-duper indeed."

After breakfast, I headed back upstairs. I brushed my teeth and dressed in khaki shorts, a navy tee shirt, and my favorite sneakers. I pulled my hair back into a ponytail, slung my trusty backpack onto my back and headed back down.

Mommy and daddy were both there telling me to "be careful" and "have a fun day!" Mommy pulled me into a hug, and I could hear her sniffle. I knew she was a ball of emotions having just lost her mom and I knew the sadness was not for me leaving, but still, I felt a little pride. And a little guilt. It's an odd combo but there you have it.

As we pulled back, she smiled at me. "I'm very proud of you, Addy."

"Thank you, mommy. But I really need to get going. I have a long way to go."

"Yes, yes. Now you be safe out there! You have your phone?"

"Yesssssss, mommmmmm!" I whine, like a thirteen-year-old is supposed to whine.

"Good. You call me or daddy if you need us for anything. Are you sure you don't want us to drive you to the Hanover's and drop you off?"

No way! Not happening.

"I appreciate that, mommy, but I've got this. I'm a big girl, remember? I'll be back before you know it. I'll text you when I get there and when I'm leaving to come home, ok?"

"Perfect!"

I knew she'd like that.

"Ok, I'm off," I told her. She pulled me in for another hug.

"You be good! Text me?"

"Mommmmm! I willllll!" I pulled away and opened the garage door.

Here I go.

I SUDDENLY FEEL A GUSH OF COLD AIR ACCOMPANIED BY LOUD STREET MUSIC. Jolted out of my thoughts, I see a tacky souvenir shop door open and the music from the inside escapes onto the busy sidewalk.

I'm instantly aware of the crowds around me on the sidewalk and the hustle and bustle forcing me in one direction. I stop to get my bearings. I look up and see the sign for Mulberry Street and know I still have a few more blocks to go. The shop door closes, and the cold air evaporates, and I am once again enveloped in the steamy day. I pull out my bottled water from my backpack and take a long refreshing sip. I decide to carry it with me. As hot and as tired as I am, I readjust my backpack to a more comfortable position on my back and I make my feet move and press on.

[FROM ADDY'S DIARY]

The next couple of weeks flew by. I have become Leslie Fontaine's most trusted confidant. And dare I say, an honorary replacement of her daughter, Charlotte. Suits me fine. The trust factor was solid. Plus, I've learned how to make a mean French Martini.

The days would start with me walking Bella, tending to some plants, light dusting, or vacuuming, making lunch, organizing a corner of the garage, making her a drink – whatever I could to look busy. But I was getting bored. Regardless, I needed Leslie to trust me and to agree to my suggestions. And so, I continued to show up, work and get paid. Like a duteous little girl helping an invalid.

Many times, I suggested we go down by the pool and get some sun. "I'll even make us some lemonade," I told her. She was not one for going outside because as she once said, "this contraption was not meant for my bumpy walkways. I might fall out and break a hip and never know it!" Then she'd laugh at her joke about her paralysis. So, we would sit on her back patio, the beautiful backyard and pool teasing us, just beyond our reach. But then I got an idea. One that would cement her trust in me.

I was three weeks into the job, and I once again suggested to Leslie we go down to the pool. The weather was only going to get hotter, and it was a good time for her to enjoy it while she could. And once again, she joked about her breaking a hip should she fall.

"But I have a surprise for you," I told her. "Come on. Let me show you." Her wheelchair was an Eagle, and it was state of the art. And heavy. It was a powered wheelchair that even had a seatbelt in it that Leslie loved because, well, she knew between the drinking and rambunctious Bella jumping up and down from her lap, she didn't want to fall out. I liked the chair because I never had to push it.

I stood by the large, curtained windows in the sunroom and she whirrrred her chair closer to me.

"A surprise? For me? Whatever could it be?" Bella sensed her excitement and leapt from the floor and took her rightful spot on her lap.

"Ready?" I asked with anticipation.

"One.... two...three!" and with that, I pulled the curtains back. From where she sat, Leslie could see her beautiful, immaculately landscaped backyard (by Roberto, her gardener. He came once a month at the beginning on a Monday. He never knew I existed). The lush green lawn splayed out as far as she could see. On the left, there was a beautiful shed, covered with wisteria. Flowering bushes in every shade of pinks, purples, whites, and yellows were everywhere, adorning every square inch of the base of a newly constructed 8-foot-tall white brick fence that sprawled on either side of the yard to the back of the property. A pool house, which was an exact replica of Leslie's main house, sat in the middle of the back of the in-ground pool, between the shallow and deep ends. Thickly padded lawn chairs on the surrounding concrete beckoned us to lay out and enjoy the sun.

Through the windowpanes, it looked like a scene from a magazine. I heard Leslie gasp. One hand flew to her mouth and the other shook and caused the ice cubes in her drink to rattle against the glass. It was then I knew she saw the surprise.

"Oh, Charlotte. I.... I'm just.... but how? When?!"

I followed her eyes and saw my creation: on top of the rugged walkway that led out to the pool, I had placed three rows of 6-foot wooden planks, wide enough to accommodate the width of the Eagle's wheelbase. Now she could get to the pool with ease.

"Oh, I was in the shed one day and saw you still had the thin planks from your old fence stored in there, so I decided to use them like this. So, you like it?"

I heard her take in a breath. "Like it? Oh, my dear, this is the sweetest thing anyone has ever done for me." She shook her head slightly, smiling. Her eyes welled with tears. If I were to guess, those tears were 95% vodka. "Is it...safe? I mean..."

"Oh, yes ma'am. I've ridden my bike up and down them now for a couple of days and you feel absolutely no bumps whatsoever."

That seemed to satiate her. Bella was sitting up taking notice. She yapped her approval and let her tongue hang out wagging.

"So, shall we....?" I asked.

With only a second of hesitation in her voice, she replied, "Yes, let's!"

And so, per my calendar under my mattress, we began our 1:00pm trip to the poolside. I brought lemonade, cups, and a bowl to put fresh water in for Bella. It was during the heat of the day but by the pool in New England, well, it really wasn't terribly unbearable.

It was during our times on the back patio Leslie would talk about her writing career and how lucky she was people enjoyed her books. But I knew her success came at a cost. A cost my mother paid. But Leslie didn't seem to care. We were getting closer, Leslie and I, but I did not for one minute lose sight of the endgame. And that time was quickly approaching.

CHAPTER SEVENTY-THREE

August

[from Addy's diary]

I had been with Leslie Fontaine for a little over a month now and the time had come.

It was Friday and I was getting ready to leave my house and head to Leslie's. Mommy and daddy were downstairs with Robin eating breakfast. I grabbed my backpack and headed out of my bedroom. I made a quick stop at my parent's room. Nope. No one was there. I was safe. Two minutes later I was downstairs, and we were all saying our 'goodbyes' and 'have a good days'. I grabbed a bottled water from the fridge and put it in my backpack, slung it over my shoulder, jumped on my bike and headed out for Leslie's.

For the past couple of weeks, we had been going down to the pool with our lemonade and just enjoying the sun and solitude. I had left the planks on the walkway for a couple of days now and it was getting close to Roberto's monthly landscaping appointment. I had to do this now or else he'd see the planks and might question Leslie about them. I couldn't risk it.

I had just finished watering the plants by the house and my watched beeped, alerting me it was 12:50pm. I turned off the hose, rolled it back up and went inside. I filled a pitcher halfway of lemonade and set it on the counter. Normally, the lemonade is pure lemonade. Today's, though, would be different. I grabbed two cups then went to the liquor cabinet, grabbed a bottle of vodka, and dumped the contents into the pitcher and gave it a stir. I got my backpack and went into the hall bathroom. I heard a slight whirrrrr in the hallway and knew Leslie was ready to go outside. I flushed the toilet for good measure and stepped out into the hall.

"Are we ready?" I asked her. Bella, sitting in Leslie's lap, perked up her ears. Leslie had a vodka tonic in her hand and by the looks of her glassy eyes, it was at least her third. Today should be easy breezy.

"That we are," she said. I grabbed the lemonade and gave Leslie two cups. She buckled her seat belt and we set off. Leslie liked the lemonade because it was a sobering factor to her daily drinks. She didn't want to drink in the heat, she said.

The planks did a great job of getting Leslie down to the pool, but I knew she'd never use them again. With each step I took next to her, I silently thanked them for their purpose.

We reached the pool deck and Leslie whirrrred over to sit under the umbrella shade. She turned the toggle switch to "off" then set the brakes on her chair. I set the pitcher down on the patio table and then put Bella's bowl by Leslie's wheels. I also put Roberto's gardening gloves I had gotten from the shed, on the table. I'd use those later. I got the bottled water from my backpack, gave it a swirl, and poured it into the bowl. Bella jumped down and took several laps.

"It's a little warmer today," I said, and poured us each a glass of lemonade.

"Ugh. It is," she said, fanning herself with the pop-open fan she brought. She took a sip of the lemonade and made a face.

Uh oh.

"This tastes different," she said, brows furrowed.

Yikes. Could she taste the vodka? My heart seemed to beat out of its chest. Did I need to take my heart medicine? I felt sick.

"I, uh, you were out of sugar, and I had to use sweetener instead," I said quickly. "That's probably what you taste."

"Hmmm," she said. But instead of accusing me of lacing her lemonade, she gulped it down in one swig.

My eyes grew big.

Bella followed suit and emptied her bowl of water.

"Mmmmm!" she said. "Thass tasty! Sweener from now onnn…" She held up her empty glass for a refill.

"Oh, sure. Yes!" I said, obliging and refilling her cup, which she emptied just as quickly as the first. I saw her sitting there. Paralyzed. Alone and estranged from her daughter. She looked so helpless. And almost sad.

"Thasss refreshening," she slurred, but she didn't seem to notice.

"It certainly is," I said, dumping my contents out into the grass behind her. "Mmmm." I wiped my mouth as if I couldn't contain the goodness.

"You know, Charlotte, you're a good frin. I'm so glad you work with me. Bella likes you, too. Dontya Bella?" We looked for Bella, who was zonked out on top of a lawn chair.

"Awww, she's sleep."

One down. One to go.

I had grown a tad fond of Leslie. Rachel and Gregory were easy: one was a leech and the other a pervert. But I had spent time with Leslie and every day I spent with her, I grew more and more attached. But not so much that I lost sight of my mission. I'm still human, after all.

Leslie seemed to be looking around her property. Her eyes got watery. I handed her a refilled cup.

"I'm so lucky. I'm famous!" she said. "I write good books that people love…I make tons of money…" She gulped her lemonade. "I have all this because of ME!" she said, swinging her arms for dramatic effect, her drink sloshed out of her cup.

"Yes," I said, slowly moving towards the back of her chair. "You certainly have it all."

"My ungrateful bitch of a daughter won' call, won' write…. nothin'. So….so…. she's out! Where'd you go?" she asked, tilting her head back. "Look at all this. Isn't this b'ufull?" Leslie was so fermented, the vodka must now taste like water.

"Uh huh," I murmured then reached down to the toggle switch on her chair.

She was aimed right at the deep end of the pool. Only feet away.

"And no one helped. I got it all by m'self."

I turned rigid. My hand, only inches from the toggle, jerked away. I was taken aback by those words. For that statement was exactly why I was here. But to hear it so blatantly and without any sort of remorse – well, I was suddenly transformed. If I had any bit of sadness for what I had done to Rachel and Gregory and even my grandmother, it all went out the window with that one statement. At that moment, I realized I had done what was absolutely necessary. And they each deserved what they got. And now, Leslie would pay. And then others would follow. I would do what it took. I put on Roberto's gardening gloves.

I reached down and switched the toggle to "on". The chair started to whirrrr.

"Whaaat're you doing?" Leslie asked, confused.

I put my hand on the break release.

"Helping my family." And with that I pulled the release and let go, and I watched the chair roll straight towards the pool. This was it! Leslie's arms gripped the arms of the chair, her knuckles turned instantly white. But thankfully she was too distracted to turn on the break or turn off the chair.

"Wha....? Wha...aaaahhh!" She frantically kept shaking her head left and right. "Hellllpp!" she cried as she headed towards the pool's edge.

But the chair suddenly came to an abrupt stop. I...what was happening? I looked and saw that the front wheels had stopped on the raised lip of the pool. The chair was whirring loudly at its inability to move forward.

She wasn't going over! I could hear Leslie breathing loudly. Leslie's arms suddenly dropped to her sides. She had figured it out. Her hands had found the break release and power button. Panic seized me.

If she switched either one of those, it would be over. Leslie's hands were gripped around the power toggle but she was too drunk to know what to do. She kept grunting and I could feel her willing something to happen, someone to help her. I had to think quickly.

I ran up to the back of the chair and pushed with all my might. It didn't budge. I couldn't give up. I just couldn't. I pushed some more and felt the chair give. It rolled back and then whirred up, getting stuck on the lip of the pool once again. And then I got an idea. But it required split second timing.

I turned the toggle off. Leslie turned slightly and looked me in the eye. She opened her mouth to either thank me or yell at me. I didn't know which.

With the chair now turned off, it rolled back about a foot. I reached up and turned the chair back on. It whirred forward and then I pushed with all my might. And that did it. Like in slow motion, the chair went up on the lip and its momentum caused it to sail over the lip and fall into the pool, causing a giant splash.

I watched as the chair sunk into the deep end of the pool, the weight of it pinning Leslie's seat-belted body, submerging her until it finally came to rest on the bottom. The chair on top, Leslie trapped underneath. I looked down into the churning water and saw her arms moving frantically on either side of the chair. Bubbles from her mouth rose to the surface. But within minutes, all movement stopped. There were no more flailing arms. There were no more air bubbles. There was no more Leslie.

I stood back and felt my heart racing from the last few minutes of activity. I looked over at Bella. Still zonked out thanks to the valium I got from my mom's bathroom this morning. I had gone into Leslie's bathroom earlier and crushed it into the bottled water and then I filled Bella's bowl. She'll sleep for a little while longer. The last thing I needed was a yapping dog to alert any neighbors.

I left the lemonade on the patio table as I made my way up the walkway. It would be more proof of Leslie's intoxication. I collected every wooden plank and put them back in the shed just as I found them. I put Roberto's gloves back on the shelf in the shed and closed the door using my shirt tail. On Monday, Roberto will find Leslie dead in the bottom of the pool. The autopsy will show a large alcohol intake. The death will be ruled a tragic accident.

I made a final tour of the house to make sure nothing of mine was left behind, grabbed my backpack, got my bike from the hidden space behind the hydrangea bush and rode home. My watch beeped. It was 4:00pm. Perfect timing. As always, I texted mom to let her know I was just now leaving the Hanover's.

Be safe on the roads, mom texted back. I gave her the thumbs up emoji.

I felt as though I ruled the world. I mean, I knew I didn't, that would be silly. But what I have done for the sake of my mother and my entire family was nothing short of sovereignty. It felt good. Sure, there was a little bit of sadness and bitterness left in the wake of it all, but I could not focus on the past. I needed to only look towards the future.

And the future had names:

- *Carly Kaufman*
- *Bridget Fraley*
- *Henry Corbyn*

I was just beginning.

CHAPTER SEVENTY-FOUR

August

I don't have many friends and that was fine by me. No one understands me. No one was as smart as me. And although my heart wasn't in the best shape, I did have one, and on occasion, I allowed it to get hurt. Like when some of the girls in school had sleepovers I wasn't invited to. Or after a football game, some kids would go to Kyle Barker's basement and play video games on his massive TV. I was an outsider and would find myself literally on the outside looking in. Peering through their windows, sometimes wishing I was one of the popular crowd. But I would eventually realize those kids were silly. Trying on fancy clothes and playing expensive games. None of that mattered in the real world. My brain would carry me much further than their materialistic lives.

Even though my family was wealthy, I only had a very few things that were of any real value to me. Like my iPad and AirPods where I could watch my favorite shows (like C.S.I. with the dreamy William Petersen!) in silence. My books and puzzles should be challenges to me but aren't at all, really. And my diary. Every day I make an entry then hide it under my bed. I've documented everything in here. Very cathartic. Some of my notes on these people are simple:

Rachel Meadows: her Instagram, the bus schedule, the timing of it all
Gregory Wynn: his "interests", his address, his routine, the C.S.I. show
Willa Greyson: her allergy, the EpiPen location, the peanut brittle, the kiss, the dumping of the baskets of fruit
Leslie Fontaine: the paralysis, the isolation, the alcoholism, the planks, the dog, the valium

And as I got closer to the time to rid the world of the others, I'd jot down notes on them, too.

It all had to work. Every one had to look like an accident. And they all had. I couldn't believe it. But then there was Harris Markham. I overheard Margo telling mommy she is thinking about publishing Harris's book. Even though he's dead, I'm not worried about his book climbing the ranks if it's published. It'll sit in the "True Crime" section and not be an obstacle for my mother's Psychological Thrillers. And anywho, it'll be his last book ever. I know, I know. Silly way of thinking. But whatever.

Speaking of Margo, I really have to thank her for a couple of things. She saved my grandmother at the launch party which allowed me to do what I needed to do. She was *my* grandmother, after all! Killing her was an honor that belonged to me. And with Harris, if Margo hadn't fired him, he never would've killed himself. Margo really is my unsung hero! At the end of the day, by Harris doing himself in, he saved me the time and energy. So, thank you, Margo! You were instrumental in getting me to accomplish my mission.

I look down at the sidewalk I was walking on and smile, knowing I had gotten away with all of it. I wasn't paying attention to where I was going. My shoulder was bumped by a passerby.

"Watch where you're going, jerk!" the man said to me.

I roll my eyes. This city. This metropolis. Full of inconsiderate people. I was an innocent walking the sidewalk and I'm pretty sure he bumped into me. I look back and yell, "Jerk this!" He didn't care. Or, like most people in my life, he didn't hear me. I was still a zero. A nothing. In a sea of millions, I simply did not exist.

Well, to Owen, I *did* exist. And I realize I am almost at my destination to meet him. I can see The Bagel Barn across the intersection. I am only a few yards from the crosswalk and it's teeming with people. There must be fifty people just waiting to cross the street. And on the other side, just as many. This intersection at 42nd Street is always so busy and….

Wait…. *why do I know that?* How is it possible I know this intersection is always busy? I mean, I've been to The Bagel Barn a few times, but I've never really paid attention to my surroundings. But somehow, I know that this specific intersection is always super-duper busy.

And then it hits me.

This is where I killed Rachel Meadows.

This is the exact intersection I visited for over a month to ensure the timing of the bus and lights and crowds were always consistent. This is the exact intersection where I blended into the crowd and counted on the fact I was invisible to the world.

This was the intersection where it all began.

My heart beat faster. This can't be a coincidence, could it? I take a swig of water. I take another Propafenone for the heck of it. If it was possible, I started to sweat even more. Cautiously, I entered the throng of people waiting for the light to change.

Why was I so apprehensive? This is purely a coincidence. He just knows I like The Bagel Barn and that's it. There's nothing sinister about it. I look around to see if I see his familiar face. But I am too short and only see the chests of everyone around me. I push the feeling of claustrophobia out of my head. I take long, even breaths. My heart starts to slow and steady itself. Everything is going to be fine.

The cars are whizzing by. I look up and see the red hand on the crossing sign is blinking for us to stay put. And there is a countdown already in progress. I tighten my grip on my backpack strap and pull it closer to me. It's been my trusty companion for many adventures. I need to hold on to it. I trust no one in this crowd. This town is full of pickpockets. The hand flashes…

25 seconds….

I am smack in the middle of this crowd. They are itching to cross the street. The sounds are deafening: taxis honking, cars zooming by, people yelling above everyone else just to be heard, the *shoooosh* of the underground subway coming through the grates beneath our feet….

20 seconds....

Suddenly I can't breathe. The crowd's anticipation to cross has caused them to press so much into me that I feel my lungs starting to constrict. Is this how Rachel felt just before? Did she have any idea what was coming? I need to get out of here. Being shorter and beneath the flow of air, it is stuffy, and the lack of oxygen is making me panic....

15 seconds....

I try to block out all the sound and suffocation and suddenly, the image of Rachel Meadows is before me. Her long red hair and porcelain skin make her look like a Greek goddess. She is glowing and smiling. Is this her ghost? Is she haunting me? *Snap out of it, Addy,* I tell myself. But then she floats away. And in her place, I see Gregory Wynn. And grandmother. And Leslie Fontaine. They all look so beautiful and at peace. But what are they doing here in this crowd?

10 seconds....

And just like that, they are gone. Grandmother seems to linger a bit longer. Beautiful and ethereal. Then gone. I'm not sure what I have just witnessed but I silently thank them for not taking me with them and I thank them for sacrificing what they did for mother to get back on top, and for our family to be a happy unit once again. Not that they had a choice.

5 seconds....

The crowd surges forward towards the curb. I look to my left and just like clockwork, I see the huge bus coming our way. But I am safe. I am back far enough from the curb that I feel secure.

Then suddenly a female yells: "Oh my God! It's Taylor Swift!!!" And the mass of people shifts so quickly towards the edge of the sidewalk that I have no choice but to move with them. I have no control. The teeming throng has become a turbulent ball of chaos: there's screaming and laughing and people pushing to get across the street.

3 seconds….

And then I feel a gentle hand on my back. Is it Owen? I turn around - but it's not Owen. I'm face to face with…*her*. And she is smiling. It's a gentle smile. A sorrowful smile. One I know well. But there is a tear from her eye. *Why are you crying? What are you saying?* Jesus…something. Forgive me? Jesus, forgive me?

I look around for Owen. But I can't find him anywhere in the crowd. He's got to be here. Afterall, he texted me to meet him and…. I look back at her face. The smile is knowing.

Then I realize, I wasn't here to meet him at all. It was her. This whole time. But why? Does she have a surprise for me? Her revelation to me two days ago was already life changing. What more could she possibly want to give me? I let a smile creep on my face but only for a second. I see her face and she is not smiling anymore. It's as if she's looking *through* me and not at me. She looks…haunted, almost. I'm getting scared. For the first time in my life, I'm scared. But then something happens. Her lips curl up into a familial, loving smile. And I begin to relax.

She extends both of her arms now. I take a step to give her a familial hug, but instead, her palms turn up, and I feel a push. A hard, sturdy push. And I begin to fall backwards. Somehow while the crowd rushed to find Taylor Swift, I ended up on the curb.

My feet dangle on the edge of the curb, my toes curling in my shoes, willing them to grip the concrete and hold me up. But it is of no use. I stagger back and fall to the street. I feel the hot asphalt scrape my palms, my tailbone cracks. I have but a split second to look up and see the monolithic bus barreling towards me. I knew this was the end. I heard the beginning of a crunch.

And in that last millisecond of my life, I look back at the woman who had done this to me, and my very last word is her name to me now:

"Mama."

THE EMAIL

My dearest Nina,

This is the hardest email I have ever had to write, and by far, the hardest thing you'll ever read in your life. But unlike your fictional books, this tale is one hundred percent truth.

I don't have much time left so I will get to the point swiftly. And please forgive me for the abrupt dread I am about to put you through.

There's no easy way to say it. Nina – Addy has killed four people. And plans to kill more.

I came to this hotel to send this email because I simply could not risk going back to your house. My personal story will not end pleasantly but it will end necessarily. I have your bottle of valium and a bottle of vodka. Today will be a good day: an ending any one of your books would covet.

The story I told you about my time in Grimsby was true. All of it. I did, however, leave out a part that I will now tell you about.

When I was raped that night in my own home, I was only twelve years old. I felt God had left my side, abandoned me to the sludge and sick that inhabited my mum's whorish lifestyle. She had different men in and out of her bedroom night after night, sometimes two at a time. She had money saved in jars. "Hush money, that is", she would call it. Men would pay my mum for sleeping with her and she kept the money in plain sight of them. "Keep the jars filled and my mouth won't tell your wives you've been here," she would tell them. "*Byddaf yn cadw'n dawel.* I will keep quiet," she would purr, her Welsh tongue spewing.

As much as the faces of the men would change nightly, there was one constant: Herman Epps. He was a brutish man, a hulking bull who might've made love to my mum, but he fucked her daughter. The bed would quake from beneath his merciless poundings, rattling my porcelain bird figurines on the sideboard, like bones clacking in the slicing winter wind. For months, I was nothing more than holes to be filled by Herman Epps. Every time he would yell "Oh God!" before he'd finish, I knew God was nowhere near me. I was alone. No God in sight. Herman Epps was a destroyer. My mum knew it and did nothing to save me. I had to save myself and so I fled.

I emptied her jars and never looked back. *Jesus, forgive me.*

You, Nina, were my saving grace, and never even knew it. I loved your books. I would read them voraciously to flee my hellish life. Like Catherine in *A Dutiful Wife*, I longed for the beauty of another world, the tranquility that came from escaping her abusive past. And like Sonya in *Truth Be Told*, I needed to be a protector, yet secret, vigilante for those I loved.

I was Cat and Sonya.

I had *become* Cat and Sonya.

While they lived one way, they pretended another. Hiding behind one life and resurfacing completely different. With no one the wiser. I learned from them.

So, I resurfaced, in Miami, with the good intention of living a new and tranquil life of going to the beach during the day and reading by the fire at night. But then fate intervened, and I had to change direction. I hadn't meant to come into your life the way I did, but I had no choice. I was at fate's mercy.

Throughout your life, pictures of you and your family would show up in magazines or on social media sites. One day, I recognized something, and it took my breath away. In an instant, my future was decided for me, and the course of my life changed forever. I kept thinking: "What would Catherine do?" "How would Sonya make things right?" And when I put myself in their shoes, in their minds, the answer came to me. It wouldn't be easy, but I knew I had to do something because if I failed, if my plan didn't work, then you and your entire family would be dead.

For the next five months, I transformed myself. If you had known me prior to this, you wouldn't have recognized me. Like Brinley in *Shaken* (your best, in my opinion!), I needed to blend in and become indistinguishable from the rest; camouflaged and commonplace. But unlike Brinley, who transformed from an ugly duckling into the proverbial swan, I had the opposite need.

I was already quite the beauty. And so, I stopped my daily jogs and workouts and began lazing about and eating nothing but carbs and sweets and drinking sodas laden with sugar and calories. I only bathed once a week and found my once beautiful hair start to become dull and thinning out. It was ironic how my hair got thinner as my body got fatter. I gained 175 pounds and my skin became red and blotchy. I was no longer the lithe, tan, flaxen-hair beauty you would write about in your novels, but instead, I became the perfect, plain, chubby-but-nurturing-looking nanny that won Margo over.

But more importantly, I would be unrecognizable to Owen Ford. Yes, Owen and I know each other. He was my lawyer from when I was in a car wreck many years ago in Miami but now, he has never once recognized me from the Robin he knew eleven years ago, although he came close that day in the kitchen. I was glad I had a large bandage on my forehead covering some of my face. We share a secret that, I thought, only he and I knew about. Unfortunately, and as things developed, I realized someone else knew our secret: Jack. I'll get to that later.

But don't be too harsh on Jack. He truly loves you and only wants the best for you. He kept this secret from you so you wouldn't be devastated. And Owen. Well, Owen wanted something from Jack and was blackmailing him so Owen wouldn't spill the beans. Nina, Jack would do anything for you – and I'm sorry to say, that included screwing Owen to keep him quiet. It's been going on for years. I'm sorry for being crass, but I know of no other way to get you to understand how rotten Owen really is. Jack was forced to do what he did and managing Owen's silence of what he knew was more important than anything. And if Owen divulged what he knew, life as you knew it would be over. And Jack did everything he could to keep these secrets from you and if that meant screwing a blackmailing Owen to keep him quiet, then that's what he did. If Jack ever seemed withdrawn or quiet, now you know why. It wasn't you. It was never you.

I only found out about them because of Addy's diary. One day I was trying to get her box of sweaters from under her bed but there was a sweater on top with a 3D unicorn which had forced the lid to get stuck under the bed boards. As I tugged on the box, a book fell from under the bed: her diary. I read it and my life changed.

Apparently, at that point, only half of her evildoings had been done. I put the diary back exactly where it had been hidden and periodically, I would return to read more and discover more and more horrors. It's quite the memoir, by the way, and so you know, I left it for you in the empty space on your shelf in the library. Evidently, Addy witnessed Jack and Owen behind the shrubs when they all went trick 'r treating last Halloween. She wrote she never mentioned it because it seemed whatever they were doing concerned her (she heard her name mentioned) and she was afraid if she brought it up, her family would be unhappy and that was something she simply could not have.

So why was Owen blackmailing Jack? It was sex for silence. If Owen got what he wanted from Jack, he would never expose that Addy's adoption was illegal. I'm sure you wondered how the adoption came to be so quickly. Now you know. Addy came to be with you but does not belong to you. In the eyes of the law, anyway.

Let me explain. Owen is an opportunist and in his early days, the gleam of money was a relentless temptation. He knew you and Jack were having trouble conceiving and knew Jack would do anything to make you happy. This was music to Owen's ears. Owen pulled strings, bypassed court proceedings, ignored the law and the whole process took less than two days. Jack couldn't have you find out Addy's adoption was illegal because it would devastate you especially after all you'd been through with the miscarriages. Owen used this to his advantage. So, keeping this secret from you was worth the times Jack was forced to spend satisfying Owen. It cost Jack a million dollars to adopt Addy. But in the end, it cost a lot more.

Unfortunately for Jack, there were no legal papers or signatures implementing Owen in this conspiracy. Jack just wanted to make you happy so if you can forgive Jack for his involvement and his proof of his love for you, then so be it.

However, as for Owen, and for what it's worth, I took a picture of him leading two-year old Addy by the hand to his car the day he picked her up. She's looking back up at me, and you can clearly see her birthmark. The picture proves he knew Addy before she came into your lives. I already showed this photo to Owen, and he knows his days are numbered. His lips about Jack's involvement are sealed and he is definitely done blackmailing Jack. I'm attaching the photo to this email so you can have a copy. It proves Owen's culpability in the situation.

Now, about Addy. For the next few years, Addy was safe in your arms.

Oh, Addy. She truly is not the sweet child you think she is and once you read her diary – and I warn you to brace yourself – you will understand why I did what I did. I don't mean to sound confusing, but your eyes will soon be opened.

Have you figured it out yet? Addy, out of darkness, is a child of rape. *My* rape. From the evilest of men - a brutish, bull of a man that tore apart and impregnated a twelve-year-old innocent child within earshot of her own mum. I remember how my porcelain bird figurines clattered like broken teeth. I fled to the states. And then I, a God-forsaken girl, gave birth to the spawn of such hate and malevolence. And the baby, marked by a thistle-shaped talisman, would grow to be, from no fault of her own, a misguided, rotten butcher. It was her destiny to be evil.

Evil begat evil.

While in Miami, I had recognized her from a Travers family photo at an event. You were holding a smiling Noah, big grins all around and there was Addy, looking up dotingly at Jack. And that's when I saw the birthmark under her chin. The unmistakable thistle-shaped birthmark that spread on her chin like a fire spreading and destroying everything in its path. Fate had changed the direction of my life. No more days at the beach and nights by the fire. I needed to get to my daughter.

Yes, she was your daughter. But she was my daughter first.

I named her Aderyn, meaning "bird" in my Welsh heritage. A bird, like her mother, Robin. We were two birds, from the same nest. I had hoped she'd be graceful and sweet like a chirpy feathered friend who would light gracefully on a branch of a Rowan tree. But my fear and lack of God was strong. I had to find her. I had to see if what I believed was true. I thought I could save her.

I was still relatively new to the city when I was on a bus heading to my interview with Margo for the nanny position. I was sitting by the window in the very front seat because I didn't want to miss any of the sights. I wanted to make sure I saw everything. And I did. Our bus was involved in a tragic accident, and I witnessed a young lady in a hoodie cause the whole thing. When she looked skyward, I could see the birthmark. It was Addy. Her hoodie was down and God was shining a light on her, exposing her to me. I knew in that moment, I was on the right course and my conviction was cemented. Her diary will prove that to you. And I will be vindicated.

Two days ago, I told her who I was. That I was her real mother. I felt she needed to know. Or maybe I just wanted to tell her. It was a shock, of course, but my story of how she was conceived and how she came to live with you came flowing out. I couldn't stop the words from coming. I told her to call me "mama" whenever we were alone, if she felt comfortable doing so. It would be different from her calling you "mommy", so I wanted, at least, to make that distinction, out of respect to you. If it's any consolation, she only called me "mama" once.

It was I who lured Addy to her final steps. It was easy enough to spoof Owen's phone and have Addy believe he was texting her to meet. I overheard Jack telling you about someone's phone being cloned and them receiving a fake text and how that was possible and when he explained it to me, it made total sense. Funny how the brain compartmentalizes information for later use, isn't it? I couldn't risk exposing myself to her too quickly, but I knew she would be intrigued if Owen were texting her, especially since she knew what he was forcing her dad to do.

But Addy is dead now, her blood is on my hands, and I feel bad for the loss your family will experience, although I cannot – I will not – apologize. Fate has made its final decision. I was merely the vessel. Perhaps she's in a better place now.

Nina, my friend, you, and your family are safe now, for I have rid the world of this scourge. I am sorry I did not get to protect Willa. I had no idea Addy would target her own grandmother. I am truly sorry for that. I am also sorry I did not get to stop Addy sooner. More lives could've been saved. I just had not perfected my plan yet.

Your life will go on but mine will not. I sit on this bed in this hotel room, alone and solemn, content in my actions and decisions. I realized I needed to be with my baby, only, she could no longer walk this earth so there was only one solution for us to be together.

The bottles of vodka and valium are now empty, and my head is getting heavy, my eyelids drooping. I will sleep soon. Forever.

Goodbye, my Nina, my saving grace. As I lay down, I shall fly with my daughter. Robin and Aderyn. Two birds killed.

And I am the stone.

Robin

send

EPILOGUE

September

Against all odds and inspired by her talks with her nanny, *Broken Flight* was released by Nina Travers. It was, as predicted, an overnight sensation.

Nina took the acrylic box Kelly had given her to display her new book and instead, sealed Addy's diary inside. Safe and secure from the world's eyes.

She placed it in the empty spot on the shelf next to the rest of her books.

She walked from the bookshelves to the windows overlooking the Sound. Nina couldn't believe her life over the past few months. She and Jack had certainly been put through many trials but for the most part, they came out stronger and closer. She picked up a photograph from the desk. It was of her and Jack at Kelly and Owen's wedding. Jack looked so handsome. His eyes and those impossibly long lashes were looking lovingly at Nina. So much had happened since that photo was taken. Owen was no longer welcome in their home, but Kelly understood and promised to visit soon, without him.

Addy's death was devastating to everyone in the family, but the reality behind how she died and why she died, Nina never revealed. Poor little Noah has had a lot of questions about Addy's whereabouts. He's been through so much loss lately: first Willa, now Addy. He's sad and Nina isn't sure how to fix it. Her heart broke for her son. It also broke for her precious daughter.

Nina refused to believe Robin's accusation of Addy being evil but still, there was the diary. Words written by Addy herself. Wasn't that an admission Nina couldn't deny?

She shook her head. She didn't want to believe her daughter was a cold-blooded killer. Nina's heart was still hurting over the revelation but maybe, like Robin said, Addy is in a better place now. No more bad thoughts swimming through her head. Nina is not sure she'll ever reach the point where she can forgive Robin for killing Addy, but then, if she did, wouldn't she have to forgive Addy for the same thing?

Nina sighed. The loss of her mother, Willa, still impacted Nina every day. Willa had been her inspiration; selfless and encouraging in every aspect of Nina's life. She knew she'd miss her mother forever. Was Addy really responsible for Willa's death? Nina didn't want to believe it.

Still, Nina felt guilty. Addy just wanted everyone to be happy and if Nina hadn't let her marriage to Jack crumble, then maybe Addy would never have –

Nina couldn't finish the thought.

"No," she said aloud. "No one is to blame." *Keep telling yourself that, Nina,* she told herself. She closed her eyes and took a deep breath then let it out.

But as bleak as things had been, there was a bright spot in Nina and Jack's lives. She touched her still-flat belly and let herself feel a little bit of happiness: a baby. A baby she and Jack couldn't wait to welcome into this world.

The struggles they experienced to get pregnant were far in the past, and this baby was the future. What do they say? One must die for one to live? *Something like that,* Nina thought. In the deep reservoirs of her mind, she silently thanked Addy for her part.

Nina was positive nothing in the world could take away the immense joy she felt at this very moment. She could sense, for the first time in a very long time, her life was perfect. And nothing could spoil it. *Nothing.*

This pregnancy would provide a sister or brother for Noah, and she couldn't wait to tell him the good news! This baby would also be close to Willow's age so they will grow up close like she and Kelly did.

And Nina hadn't told Kelly the news yet, but she would in about – Nina looked at her watch – *Shit! She'll be here any minute!* Nina hadn't seen Kelly or the baby since Willow was born because so much had to be dealt with since that time. But Nina was beyond ecstatic Kelly was on her way over and bringing Willow. Nina couldn't wait to lay eyes on Willow for the very first time.

"I wonder if she looks like her mother or her father?"

The End

ACKNOWLEDGMENTS

They say your first book is the hardest. They were right. But not for the reasons you might think.

I've always liked to write and I feel like my mind is always full of some story to tell. Someone once told me after you write the book, the hard work really begins. They weren't kidding. All the steps to get the words and ideas turned into a physical book are quite daunting - especially if it's your first one. Maybe by my eighteenth I'll have it down pat. Probably not.

Now comes the easy part: thanking the folks that helped turn my dream into a reality. If you didn't like the book, it's their fault.

My family is one of a kind and I couldn't do anything without them. Mama, Becky and Bonnie: you are the best women I know and I'm just lucky to be in your universe.

To my beautiful and talented nieces Shirey, Shaley and Jalynn: thank you for making me an uncle. I'll do my best to put you in a future book - either dead or alive. Cross my heart.

To my Aunt Anna Lee: even though you are 800 miles away, you've been by my side throughout this entire process. Thank you!

Thank you to my beta readers, Louise, Matt, Joyce and meine Leseratten family, Elizabeth and Petra. Y'all's input was invaluable and made this a much better manuscript.

Rob Kaufman and Freida McFadden, you guys are my inspirations. Your books are absolutely some of my favorites I've read over the past few years and your help and input and guidance through this process from beginning to end was absolutely mind-blowing and extremely generous. Thank you, thank you, thank you! I will continue to garner motivation and encouragement from you two.

And finally, to you, the one who paid to hold a copy of my book in your hands: I treasure you the most because you believed in me enough to muddle through my work. And for that, I will always be grateful.

I hope you loved *With One Stone* and if you did, I would be very grateful if you could write a review. I'd love to hear what you think! You can also email me at markjenkinsauthor@gmail.com

Thank you again! I couldn't do this without you.

They say your first book is the hardest. They were wrong.

Mark

Made in the USA
Columbia, SC
21 May 2023

17094697R00195